Waldwick

Waldwick...And/Or

Kenneth Linde

Waldwick Books
www.WaldwickBooks.com
McHenry, Illinois

Waldwick: And/Or

Waldwick Partners, Inc.
dba Waldwick Books
www.WaldwickBooks.com

January 2025

Printed in Wisconsin, United States of America

First Printing: January 2025
Wisconsin. United States of America

For more information or to order any of the Waldwick Series books, visit: www.WaldwickBooks.com
email: KJL1946@aol.com

ISBN 979-8-9852613-9-4

ISBN: 979-8-9852-6139-4

9 798985 261394

"FOR EVERY ACTION, THERE IS AN OPPOSITE AND EQUAL REACTION"

NEWTON'S THIRD LAW EMPHASIZES THE INTERCONNECTEDNESS OF ANY AND ALL ACTIONS AND THEIR OUTCOMES, WHETHER IMMEDIATE OR LONG-TERM WHERE THE NET SUM OF THE UNIVERSE IS, WAS AND WILL ALWAYS BE ZERO.

Elephants:

It's funny how a thought will jump into your mind, if only for a millisecond before, whoosh, it's gone and your brain moves on to something else. Such was the case when I saw an article about an elephant in Cambodia, used for logging, finally free to live out its life in tranquility.

I know the saying 'elephants never forget' is a bit of an exaggeration but they do have remarkable memories. Like humans, elephants might not remember every single detail but they also have exceptional spatial memory which allows them to recall events and locations for decades crucial for their survival.

What I'm about to share is precisely that... like elephants, things I cannot forget. Some incredibly bad, others profoundly good with people I once loved and trusted who I now perceive as a threat to my existence. Along the way, I came to realize the consequence of action where a decision made can affect one's destiny. While small or insignificant they might seem, it's the interaction of events and circumstances that can have a profound effect on who we are, how we live and the results of our reality.

My name is George, simply George. I founded the Derrick Williams Foundation that helped create a method by which people around the world could get a free medical exam by simply wearing what was called "Mediglove" supported by the first-ever, self- learning, quantum computer that took artificial intelligence to a level beyond the scope of virtually anyone's imagination that we named 'Simon" for **S**uper **I**ntelligent **M**onitor **O**f the **N**et. For our efforts, we were awarded a Nobel Peace prize.

As things became somewhat 'routine' at the foundation, I elected to start a business called Terrill B&B with my brother Tommie that produced, marketed and sold Wagyu beef, premium bourbon and some of the finest Pino Noir marketed around the world.

With homes in Wisconsin, France, and Saint Martin and a private jet to take us anywhere we wanted to go, Amy, my wife and my outlook on life was one of gratitude for all we'd been able to accomplish.

Having been married for 30 years, Amy and I finally decided to let loose of the reins of our primary company called Wilco, founded by Amy's dad and let our son, Derrick assume leadership. Little did we realize that Derrick's insatiable hunger for money, perks and power would lead him to create a Ponzi Scheme that saw literally billions of dollars flow in and out of Wilco until the day when, like all Ponzi Schemes, and the cash flow to cover the 'earnings' of the previous class of 'investors' no longer was met by the cash inflow from new investors.

Little did we know that, to cover his 'needs', Derrick turned to a group we called the "Bad Guys" consisting of global organized crime members where Derrick sold Simon and his capabilities.

When the Bad Guys realized they couldn't physically take Simon, they demanded the software. Derrick never realized that safeguards had been imbedded in Simon's programming so that Simon's knowledge, expertise and abilities required program modifications that necessitated the simultaneous insertion of identity codes controlled by two-of-three people, the co-founders of the Foundation, Peter, Luke and myself.

Feeling as if they'd let's say, *'not got what they paid for'*, the Bad Guys decided to capture two of us and force us to release the software for their use in controlling everything from medical data on nearly a billion people to the financial, power, water and air traffic control systems of the United States.

As they chased me, I elected to hide in one of the limestone wine fermenting caves on our farm that had been developed with an area used by our sommelier such that he could work blending the wine without needing another place to live. I was accompanied to the cave by CIA Agent Langdon and was told to stay there until the CIA, FBI and all the other good guys said it was safe.

I was provided a computer that only allowed a few minutes each day and was programmed such that I couldn't communicate with the outside world to protect me from the bad guys learning where I was hiding.

Things happened where the electronic locks to the cave were destroyed and, for six months I was trapped alone, totally devoid of any form of neural stimulation where the light was always the same, the temperature always the same and the silence always the same which I could only associate to what it's like to die and be buried and there were many days when it truly represented my last wish as the world simply passed me by.

I was 'saved' or anyway thought I was, and yet remember the day when I literally became a government prisoner at Area 51 the high security base, with my fellow co-founders of the Derrick Williams Foundation, Peter, James and Luke.

Like anyone who's been severely injured, it's taken a long time to recover. The pain within me remains but I've become somewhat free of the nightmares and trauma that dropped me deep within the abyss where my disgust for our son and what he did to Amy and me is the only thing that remains etched in my soul like a circular saw cutting a piece of wood....not deep enough to fully penetrate but profound enough to weaken the board to something so meager it could break at any time.

Area 51

If my infirmities weren't enough, while at Area 51, I was informed our daughter Melia and her family died in a tornado. I remember the joy and relief when we were herded into a conference room and the big screen came to life with Melia assuring me that she, Jack and the kids were safe and away from harm's way. Melia noted the government had provided a new identity to save them from the scorn of those who thought her life was nothing more than a pawn to get what they wanted which was power and domination.

In speaking with Melia, I inquired about her mother.

I remember the very long pause as I watched Melia look down at the floor and then back at the camera and replied. "Dad, mom thought you were dead. We all thought that, simply because Peter reported you were with Agent Langdon the morning of the car accident and fire.

"Mom's still alive?" I inquired. Melia reiterated, "We think so." "What do you mean?" I asked.

Melia looked at the floor again, raised her head, closed her eyes, took another deep breath and then, with tears forming to the point I could sense her the reservation, noted. "Dad, mom went with Derrick."

I was incredulous as I replied, "You mean she... she wasn't going to Carbone for cancer treatment?"

"Dad, she did. They were able to transplant some of my stem cells and she's in remission from her leukemia."

"I... I can't believe this." I offered, simply shaking my head, shrugging my shoulders and raising my hands to my mouth in disbelief.

Melia reiterated. "Dad, she thought you were dead. She was all alone and then...well, you remember Karen, don't you?"

"Yes! I remember," replying, somewhat cryptically.

"Well, because we all thought the same thing, mom started staying with Karen during her recovery. One thing led to the next and... well dad, mom and Karen left the country with Derrick,

Uncle Tommie and Su."

"Where did they go?" I asked.

"Everyone thinks Peru," Melia replied. "Peru?" I asked with a frown on my face.

Melia responded. "It was probably mom's idea simply because of Karen. Peru has recognized same-sex couples since 1924 and the Inter-American Court of Human Rights ruled in 2023 that Peru must guarantee equal rights and protection against their discrimination."

Melia paused and then added. "Derrick probably agreed because of the treaty agreement between Peru and the United States regarding extradition where, as long as Derrick doesn't break any Peruvian laws, he can't be brought back to the States."

"One final question," I offered.

"Why didn't my brother check the Cave?"

I remember that Melia looked at the ground, bit her lip, shook her head and then broke my heart. "Dad, I haven't spoken to him but I really don't think Tommie ever forgave you for his divorce from Heather. I think he knew you were there and it was his way of getting even while, also, acquiring all of Terrill B&B."

"You mean, he left me there to die?"

Melia looked at the floor in an embarrassed way and then added. "I'm not sure. All I know is Tommie told the authorities he checked the North Cave."

I remember Peter glancing at me and offering. "I'll bet Tommie is the one who fried the lens on the security panel. All he needed was a laser pointer aimed at the sensor and the panel would have been frozen in its locked position. That's probably why the bad guys stopped trying to remove the panel when they saw the smoked lens and chip. "

I realized that, by trying to kill me, Tommie probably saved my life, as the bad guys didn't come back and try to open the cave door again.

Melia responded. "Uncle Tommie always felt you were looking down at him. He wanted to be important. He wanted to be the success story."

I thought of my conversation with Amy and how she used Fredo, from the 'Godfather', as a reference point. My God, had I been that blind? I simply shook my head in disbelief. I'd spent six months locked in a cave where everyone thought I was dead.

My daughter and her family were reported dead but were alive and hiding from the bad guys. My wife hooked up with her former female assistant and went with our son, who's a fugitive from the Federal Government and probably living off several billion dollars stashed somewhere, which is probably in Peru, because they can't be extradited and same-sex couples are recognized.

"Dad, I'm getting the high sign and need to go. We love you and look forward to seeing you soon."

With that, the screen went black and I sat profoundly shocked as we all took a deep breath, realizing a horrible situation was ending as the monitor presented the logo of the National Intelligence Agency for my eyes and tears to see.

Wilson Street:

After the session, Peter, James, Luke and I were released from Area 51 and came back to Wisconsin. The trio went back to living their lives while I went to hell. For months, I had nightmares and literally could not leave our Madison condo. I was in remote therapy on Zoom and slowly began to recover. The journey was long, yet, there had been enough progress to the point I knew I needed to leave Madison and the only place was back to Waldwick and the family farm.

I wanted to sell the Madison condo but couldn't, simply because it had been transferred to Melia's name. Instead, I was able to rent it. Fortunately, if it hadn't been in Melia's name, Amy and I would have been out in the street when you have no money. How do you get hold of someone who's got a new federally protected identity? I simply shook my head and moved anyway. I had what few personal items from my office shipped to the farm.

Our son 'V' took it upon himself to have my most prized possession - the old trunk, which was my link to the past, delivered before I moved and placed in the downstairs parlor which mom and dad converted into their office. Little did I realize, it would be months before I'd even be able to go into the room as I was in no condition to function in any way.

Moving day came and, as I walked into the farm house, it felt good to be home and great to have the things that mattered most - 'Waldwick', the trunk and my Amelia Earhart Lockheed Electra 10E model airplane I'd made as a boy and given to Amy when we were dating. For the first six months in the farmhouse, my social fears remained. I simply stayed in the house, afraid to even go out to the barn. Sadly, I was afraid to walk in the forest or simply feel what surrounded me. Fear simply overwhelmed me as I'd think about the

Foundation that had been destroyed in the name of retribution and how it could have been me.

My mind would beckon me to examine the few remaining

boulders that outlined the remnants of Skunk Hollow School that had not only been the underpinning of the structure but the groundwork upon which five generations of Terrills had started their lives.

I knew I needed to move on. Yet, I couldn't take that first step towards sanity. I would think of the obelisk as memories of Great Grandfather would flood my mind only to be drowned in guilt. I needed to go, but couldn't. I wanted to go, but couldn't. I knew I should have gone, but didn't. I ached for the majesty of the Springs and my baptism in purity, but I couldn't take that first step as sadness roiled within me while every day, I prayed tomorrow would mean a better day.

For six more months, I remained alone, away from everyone and everything, never going into town as the silence of singularity that once offended me kept me at peace. Perhaps it was the six months in the cave that turned me inside out. Perhaps it was the pain I felt since the love of my life departed that burrowed itself so deep within my soul that it darkened the sunny sky to the point I wondered if I'd ever allow the outside in again. Perhaps after all the glamor and glitz of power and wealth, truth was actually being told.

For that period, it seemed strange sitting in our old house filled with things that were never mine. To keep myself busy, I began sorting and cleaning, organizing and eliminating articles that had no meaning. I found the family Bible that had come with George the First across land and sea, that observed the brutality of mankind and the majesty of love nearly 200 years ago. I would cradle my great, great grandfather's 'Waldwick' epistle that put meaning in my life and simply ask that his greatness transcend to me.

How did I justify my existence? I concluded, I'd gone full circle and the farm house was my final destination, away from anything and everything - solitary - accompanied only by my thoughts and memories. My God, Alice was right! There is no bottom to the rabbit hole. While no longer imprisoned in a cave, I was a captive of my mind. Afraid! Afraid! Afraid! As the dark shroud of fear blocked any sense of sunshine in my life.

With time on my hands, I continued to reflect back on our son, Derrick, and simply asked myself why? Why did he never have enough? Why was his greed so profound that it destroyed not only himself but our family? Was he truly that unhappy or was it an inherited trait that transcended from his grandfather? I finally accepted I'd never be able to find the answer but certainly learned the lesson.

In a world driven by ambition, success, and material wealth, it's easy to get caught up in the insatiable desire for more as it consumes one's thoughts, actions and, ultimately, happiness. Some say greed is simply a bottomless pit which exhausts the person in an endless effort to be satisfied without ever reaching fulfillment, simply because the pursuit of material wealth can never truly fill one's heart and soul.

Periodically, I would glance at our family photo resting upon the top living room shelf of the bookcase next to the fireplace and realize that greed is a dangerous beast that devours the soul, consuming a person's inner self, leading to a loss of moral compass and emotional well-being that turns even the most harmless individual into a ruthless monster.

In the end, the pursuit of 'more' fails even the greedy simply because the search never brings lasting happiness. It's not a financial issue, it's a heart issue that blinds us from recognizing the true value of what we already have, distorting our perception of what truly matters in life. By appreciating the abundance of love, health, and happiness we can break free from the grip of greed and cultivate a mindset of gratitude and contentment.

These thoughts pervaded my actions as I spent virtually all my waking hours cleaning out the house of things that didn't matter. Tommie's things! Su's things! Mom and Dad's things! Every nook and cranny, whatever nooks and crannies are, was checked and inspected. Every box opened and scanned until I'd finally reached the point where the house was mine in terms of emotions equated by something I valued or cherished.

Secrets:

All that was left were the boxes I'd brought from the condo that I didn't have the gumption to open and find whatever was within. Finally, when I got to the point I had nothing else to do, I simply began to go through the condo stuff.

The first box held family photos. A look of sadness infiltrated my soul as 'now' came into play. Melia and her family were hiding with a new identity. 'V' and his Amelia were doing their thing trying to save the world. Derrick had gone somewhere with everyone else's money. Tommie and Su had gone with him. In each instance, I looked at their photos and simply put them in the bottom drawer of the desk hoping someday I'd be able to get them out without the pain of memories.

Finally, there was a photo of Amy and me on our 25th wedding anniversary. I held the photo in my hands for an extended period of time and thought of all the things I loved about her. I guess I understood why she left. First, she thought I was dead. Next, she thought the government was going to put her in prison. Finally, she found someone else. There's an emotion called remorse and finally, after so many months of sadness, I was able to realize that my love for Amy was still profound and our journey through life had been worthwhile. No regrets! No do overs! Nothing I'd change except having her back.

I thought everything was done and it was time to start anew until I realized there was one more box I needed to go through. I opened the box to find our Sentry fireproof safe. Amy and I used it to keep somewhat important, but not too valuable, things that possibly should have been in our safety deposit box we never got around to taking them there.

I opened the Sentry and looked at the hanging folders. Owner's manuals, copies of tax statements and, in many cases, simply 'stuff'. I took each file out and examined its contents. If it was no longer appropriate, I simply ran the contents through the shredder until it was full of shredded memories.

It took all morning to empty the Sentry as the inevitability of what had been in a different time and world became eternal in my mind. As I was about to put the empty folders back and close the cover, I noticed a fragment of black electrical tape attached to the bottom of the box with a small lump beneath it. I carefully pulled off the tape and discovered a thumb drive. I knew it wasn't something I'd put there and surmised it had to be Amy's and wondered why she'd concealed it there.

Going to my laptop, I inserted the thumb drive and had my breath taken away. Included were electronic folders that contained dozens of photographs. I sat, fairly embarrassed, somewhat reticent but totally intrigued by what I saw which was a completely different side of the woman I'd lived with for 30 years.

I opened the first electronic folder and saw a copy of a report from when Amy was in college called the Graffenberg Chart with the name Amelia Marie Williams typed across the top. I should have stopped but couldn't as I read what the report was all about. I guess there is or was, an analysis that measures pupil dilation and pulse variation to determine a person's sexual orientation that can range from totally gay to totally straight with bi-sexual somewhere in between. The report included a section called 'methodology' which I opened and sort of cringed simply because, to take the test, the psychologist equipped people with goggles, noise canceling headphones and a finger clip to measure pulse rate and had them watch a ten-minute graphic video during which time they measured pupil dilatation and pulse rate to determine how they were reacting.

I began to realize this was the point in time when Amy was answering long held questions regarding herself. Based on her score, Amy's pulse must have gone up and pupils narrowed in the different scenarios and returned to normal during the generic or 'relaxation' scenes intended to bring her back to an ambivalent state.

The report provided a linear representation in 0.5 increments ranging from L5 to R5 with zero in between. L5 represented complete homosexuality. R5 reflected being totally straight. Zero represented complete bi-sexuality. There were .5 gradations simply because the pupils and pulse participants to represent anywhere in between 'L' and 'R'.

What was interesting was, on the bottom of the report was an asterisk indicating that most women normally scored about R2.5 indicating some degree of same sex inclination while straight men were R3.5-4.0. According to the highlighted point on the chart, Amy's score was R0.5 or just to the right of total bisexuality which was probably the reason for her guilt complex.

The final statement of the report was a disclaimer that noted the numbers didn't mean the individual was going to do anything about what they learned, just that they had tendencies. It also noted there was nothing wrong with any level of orientation as it is part of a person's nature and nothing could be done about it.

I took a deep breath and concluded Amy must have had questions, took the test, saw the results and realized all she had been fighting and hiding for so many years was, for her, quite natural. She was what she was. As I told her before we were married, there was nothing wrong with that.

I closed the Graffenberg file and opened the next one entitled 'H-O-H' that contained photos I recognized from Amy's bedroom at House-On-The-Hill when she was in her worst stage with Leukemia. Weighing somewhere around seventy pounds, I saw a bald, emaciated skeleton with sunken cheeks, sunken eyes and fallow skin forlornly looking back at me. She was literally a walking silhouette whose expression emanated someone scared, sad and remorseful. My, God, she looked sick as this represented what I believe she thought would be her final photo.

Within that electronic folder was a sub-file entitled 'Sydney'. I knew who Sydney was. I'd actually met her twice. Once when Amy and I were engaged and went to surprise my best friend Rodney and his wife Ann on Saint Martin and then again when we'd gone back and she was a server at one of the restaurants after Hurricane Irma.

I clicked on the file and saw dozens of photos as to witness Amy's recovery. Photo after photo after photo captured Amy regaining her body form, re-growing her hair and resurrecting her life which made me smile.

Inside that file was yet another digital file I clicked on and will always regret I did. There are things in life better left unsaid and unknown. Instead, I perused the contents that contained numerous photos of Amy and Sydney that were certainly meant for their own eyes and not mine. While some appeared to be quite genuine and loving, others represented what I'd expect to find only on an adult website.

When I looked closer, I saw that things were different. This wasn't casual interaction, this was Amy physically presenting herself to Sydney and appearing to enjoy it. In all, there were over fifty photos of the two of them which was more than enough for me. At first, I could only imagine who took the photos until I realized, back then all cameras had timers built in and these two were simply creating their own very personal and very private ensemble.

I opened file after file with of other women, including one with literally hundreds of photos and dozens of videos of women that must have been used to satisfy Amy's cravings. In the personal files I saw the same progression from photos of a social relationship to videos of a physical interaction to a point, in each case, where Amy transcended from a position of equality to a submissive role allowing the other partner to take control. Not only was there physical submission, but emotional as well that expressed vulnerability and surrender to her partner's desires and guidance and finally psychological submission which hurt the most.

I began to realize all the personal photos and videos had Amy as the submissive which was totally contrary to her demeanor in life. Publicly, Amy was dynamic and dominant in terms of her character and leadership capabilities. Privately, in what I saw, I began to realize Amy needed the power exchange she experienced to simply validate her own self-concept, willing to give or exchange power with another person through role play and/or being physically restrained.

I then wondered why Amy had this deep, dark secret and tried to rationalize why she would engage in what I considered humiliating behaviors. I simply asked myself, was it sexual masochism where she wanted to be humiliated or made to suffer in order to achieve gratification?

Was it low self-esteem as a way for her to cope with feelings of inadequacy or worthlessness? If it had been just once, it could have been a case of power dynamics where she felt pressured or coerced into engaging in humiliating acts but not the same thing so many times.

Almost out of self-torture, I went through all the files again. Not for prurient reasons but to see if I could determine the pattern being communicated by the 'set-up' photos where Amy trusted the women to the point she was allowing them to have control over her during their encounter. Based on her expressions, Amy appeared to enter an altered state of consciousness where I finally saw the true Amy... someone with a thick facade who thought so little of herself she wanted... make that needed to be humiliated to verify her own depreciating self-concept. To do so, I concluded Amy simply relinquished control while exploring dissimilar aspects of her own sexuality doing, being, acting as commanded regardless of act, event or circumstance.

I know, or didn't believe, it was cultural or societal expectations. I finally concluded that somewhere, somehow there must have been some past trauma that influenced her experiences and desires. Was it the challenge of being mixed race? Was it her bi-polar condition? Was it her bi-sexuality? Was it the combination of all three? While my opinion of my wife adjusted where I realized the woman in my life had 'issues', I still loved her very much even though she was much more complex and challenged than I'd ever perceived but tragically, Amy simply didn't love herself.

I leaned back in my chair, closed my eyes and simply shook my head, somewhat embarrassed I hadn't realized what had been involved in her peccadillos. Peccadillos I'd approved. Peccadillos, that went way beyond anything I'd imagined.

I wanted to close the file, but couldn't and went through all the images yet again where I began to see a pattern. It was only when I looked closely did I begin to identify something that became a constant in each personal dynamic and that was the appearance of the small rose tattoo on Amy's partners. The same rose, in the same spot, Amy had done, in the name of love, for me and it was the little red rose that began to break my heart.

Finally and most tragically was the transition video from exclusively women to the inclusion of a man. Any time I'd discovered Amy's 'involvement', Amy always assured me that it was only with other women and I was the only man in her life. Something I'd agreed to. Something, I'd actually encouraged. It was this video that simply shattered my emotional status quo and finally, totally, broke my heart.

As I gently closed the laptop case, I wondered why? Why was Amy this way? Was this her ultimate self-inflicted indulgence? Her true inner self? Had the strength of her father and mother been so great they affected her self-confidence and self-concept that led to self-denial? I had no idea. What I did know is that, even with what I saw, even with what I felt, I still loved her and wanted her back. It was then I realized, when you dig deep enough, we all have transgressions. It's just the type. It's just the style. It's just how they affect the ones we love that matters the most.

Amy had always been a great mother and wonderful wife for which I would always be profoundly grateful. As I learned, she thought I'd died and I reflected on what I perceived to be the only right mantra of a departing spouse who wants their life partner to simply be happy and that means continuing on, never forgetting the past but always looking towards the future where one is, one was and one will always be the loneliest number.

It was then I thought of Amy's life and wondered if it was her way to process or heal from past traumas where the controlled environment and clear boundaries provided a sense of safety and support. If so, what were those traumas before realizing I would probably never know, simply because Amy was out of my life.

For three hours, I reviewed the images realizing what I saw had been difficult for me to witness to say the least. Yet, with Amy gone, it was also liberating as I sat in a contemplative mode realizing Amy was much deeper and much darker than I'd ever assumed. To be bi-polar is one thing. To be bi-sexual another. To be a submissive was far beyond any inclination I'd ever imagined.

I felt humiliated to see my wife not only willingly participating but recording it and probably watching it again and again and again to provide the spark she needed in her life. If it stopped there, it would have been one thing. However, to have me conclude that the rose tattoo represented Amy's way of denoting a token of acceptance made me determine that, perhaps I was simply never enough of a man, husband or father for her. Perhaps with her encounters, Amy was able to extricate some form of expression that brought out the inner fear within her as she inverted her normal power dynamics. What hurt the most were not the acts, but the fact they were recorded and then not knowing if this was all of them or just those she was able to or wanted to save. All I do know is that she's gone and there's no way for me to ever forget what I saw.

The question became, 'What do I do now'? As an eternal optimist, I simply put the thumb drive back beneath the black tape in the Sentry safe and added the now-empty hanging folders because I still wasn't able to accept that Amy was gone forever. Deep in my heart, I wanted Amy back. If she did return, I wanted her to think her secret was still hers, never to be mentioned and certainly never discussed. It was to be her and my secret that I vowed to carry to my grave.

Sitting solitary in the house I grew up in, having not spoken to another human being in nearly a year was enough. Then to discover what I'd just witnessed took me further down the rabbit hole to a point where, in retrospect, I believe it represented the bottom of the bottom of the bottom as well as my turning point simply because the combination of frustration, sadness and embarrassment turned something on in my brain such that I was no longer feeling sorry for myself but profoundly sorry for my wife, the woman I loved.

Reflections:

It was our 30th wedding anniversary and, like so many other nights, I couldn't sleep. I tossed and turned as I had so many other times since escaping from the cave, yet this night was different as I vowed to break the chains of anxiety that had literally frozen me in fear. Sunrise came. I got up and realized it was a glorious June day and I needed to make a choice, either rebuilding or taking my own life. I chose rebuilding and vowed that, 'Today I'll begin my daily walk into the Forest'.

I made my way to the kitchen and pressed the Keurig button for my wakeup extract. I realized it had been over two years since I'd read any news. I elected to open the laptop and Googled what was simply 'today'. Instead, music came on and it was the Beatles "A Day in the Life". Little did I realize, this would become my anthem as I too *woke up, fell out of bed, dragged a comb across my head, found my way downstairs and had a cup. And, looking up I noticed I was late...but late for what? I had nowhere to go and nothing to do, no one to see and nobody new. I read the news, oh boy, about a lucky man who made the grade. And though the news was rather sad, I just had to laugh when I saw the photograph* vowed to put in my book. My book? What book? The book I wrote while trapped in the cave?

I read what I could until I realized nothing had changed, yet everything had. Instead, I made my way upstairs and thought of a joke then somebody spoke and I went into a dream as the water in the shower covered me in steam. My body was telling my brain it was time to return. Come back, George! Come back to reality! You've been gone long enough!

I got dressed, looked out the window, took a deep breath, opened the door and placed my foot upon the ground and grabbed my first tentative step outside. I shook in fear. I looked around at all that was transpiring. Things I'd learned to take for granted. I heard a car out on the road and it sent shivers up my spine. I watched a rabbit cross the driveway and my fears began to dissolve. I looked at the barn door and thought of dad and said to myself, "Come on George, you can do it!"

It took me until noon to make it to the barn as wave after wave of fear and trepidation cascaded within my soul. By mid-afternoon I'd finally overcome my fears and began the journey. I made my way to where the Foundation facility had been, stopped and looked at the steel cover that represented all that was left of what once helped the world be a better place. I remembered looking at the embossed cover that said 'U.S. Government Property' knowing that below SIMON, our advanced quantum computer, was sleeping and not dead - simply waiting for someone to come and whisper to him, imploring that he come back to life while all the time, he was thinking, adding, comparing, determining more and more and more. Little did others know that he was still alive and simply waiting for us to welcome him back.

After a minute, or perhaps two, I made my way within the trees and stopped at the remaining boulders of what was once Skunk Hollow School where my ancestors dreamed of tomorrow while I only thought of yesterday and continued to ask myself, "What do I do now?"

Slowly I made my way to Great Grandfather's obelisk and bowed my head in respect to the man who taught me so much but left me with so much more that I profoundly regret I've forgotten. I thought of the Medicine Man and relished the thoughts of George the First and how he saved the Indian girl. I thought of my dear friend, Rodney, and how we, in our youthful exuberance, fought to save the sacred land and how wonderful it was to simply win.

I sat on the bench staring at the obelisk and realized I'd become a victim of mental illness that was affecting my mood, thinking, and behavior to the point it impaired my ability to function in many ways. Perhaps the isolation in the cave resulted in the profound depression or perhaps it was the literal dissolution of my family. Unlike Amy and her bipolar disorder, my bout didn't have peaks and valleys. Instead it was simply one dark plane where my only comfort was the silence that had crept into my soul and blocked my ability to feel anything but remorse.

I now believe I'd been at the edge of schizophrenia, disconnected from reality with delusions, hallucinations, and disorganized behavior. My, God, help me!

For more than an hour I sat alone, deep in thought and was then motivated to go to the Springs. I made my way down the cinder path and noted the weeds that had incurred in human absence. I arrived at the small wooden bench besides the emanating water and listened to its melodic murmur escaping from earth's grasp as I accepted that, for far too long, I'd been in an emotional abyss unable to function, simply afraid, unwilling to move beyond yesterday and into tomorrow.

I wanted to capture that moment and store it within my heart for it represented a point of internal peace. I realized then 'now' only exists for an instant and one must rely on the past for guidance and tomorrow for hope. Sadly, it was the past that haunted me. Being trapped in a cave for six months devoid of any tactile changes with no external ways to comprehend time punctuated my condition only to be exacerbated by believing your brother attempted to kill you, your son is a fugitive and your wife has run away with her mistress, creating a vortex that warped the past and made it so dark I felt it was equivalent to a living death!

For the longest time, I sat on the little wooden bench and relived all that had happened. I looked at the spot where Amy and I first made love and nodded in affirmation. My mind went back to Grandma Marie and how her last words to us were at that very spot. I thought of my dearest friend, Rodney, and how we'd grown together and became brothers with different mothers. My realization awakened from its deep sleep as I heard the birds chirp, saw bees fly and leaves rustle as they moved within the wind and realized that life must go on and all I needed do was claw my way back to reality.

I sat there with no idea what day it was, I knew it was June but didn't know the day or date. As for time? My world had been one where my senses had slowly become ambivalent to its existence. Not seconds! Not minutes! Not hours! Not days! Not even months! I was simply existing, floating, as if in space, with no reference to reality.

How sad it is to sit and allow time to wash away 'now' until all you have is yesterday. I knew that time is, was and will always be a subjective sense regarding how long an event or interval lasts.

I realized my concept of time was influenced by my attention, emotion, memory and expectation regarding the context of time melded into one blur, which simply faded to black as nothing more than a dot of reference that had slowly lost its passion. When you lose your wife, your son and your brother, when you fear that you are about to be killed, when all you have is silence and darkness, time becomes insignificant. Unlike a ticking a clock, my existence was not and could not be constant. I'd become nothing more than a blank sheet of paper waiting, waiting, waiting for something, anything to be added so that, once again, my life would have purpose and meaning.

As I sat on the bench and listened to God, life and nature, I closed my eyes, took a deep breath and allowed my senses to become enveloped in all that surrounded me as I said to myself. "Come on George! Give it up! You can do it!" as if to assure myself there could be more to life than the timeless time it had become.

For some reason, I was motivated to return the realm of Great Grandfather and revisit the dominion of his aura. I made my way back to the obelisk, sat again on the bench, stared at the two feathers positioned to tell time and questioned my sanity. I asked myself, "do I understand the nature and consequences of my actions? Can I still distinguish right from wrong?"

To sit in a self-inflicted totality of isolation was not sane, yet the burdens upon me had been such, for the longest time, I simply didn't have the capacity to break down my self-built barriers and re- enter the world from whence I came. I accepted then and continue to accept that mental illness exists on a spectrum with varying degrees of severity and impact while at the same time, sanity is primarily viewed as a binary concept where you're either sane or insane. What happens when you're both or can you be? I knew it wasn't sane to forego social interaction, yet I also knew to immerse myself in a world that had simply passed me by could mean my mental demise.

Ultimately, I was defining my own reality and realizing it was challenging because my perception was limited due to the fact I'd created a filtered view of the world where my brain constructed an idiosyncratic authenticity based on so few events and circumstances. It was then I began to accept that my mind had created fallacious experiences I'd considered to be real simply through a complex interplay of sensory deprivation. When everything remains the same day after day after day, attention selection becomes muted simply because what one can focus on remains stagnant.

As I sat beside Great Grandfather's obelisk, I realized I needed to reassure myself I was no longer there. I asked myself, "Must I rely on past experience when they have been in a living hell or could I simply meld those memories with those that preceded them to create a more balanced existence?" In the end, I began to realize and accept it was my conscious being that created my reality and from that reality, I needed to move forward, cherish the good memories and stop dwelling on the tragic past if I was to survive.

As I sat there in the silence of the trees, I asked myself, what is my reality? Could I really comprehend my being and existence without reference to others? Is reality material, immaterial or both? Could I accept that the universe exists independently of human perception? Were my personal experiences and interpretations of the world, influenced by my senses, beliefs, and cultural background?

I looked at the obelisk and all it meant and delved into a deeper layer beyond my physical world and pondered my soul, spirit, and divine consciousness. I thought back to Doctor Roberts at Area 51 and all we'd discussed and his tacit statement that it was OK to feel how I was feeling.

As I sat there, I began doing the rehabilitation exercises Doctor Roberts implemented that had been simply tossed away like a crumpled candy wrapper during my journey through self-inflicted hell.

First was breaking down my perils into smaller and more manageable segments. I realized fear still lingered within me that the bad guys were after me, even though it had been over two years. Second was the loss of the perks and privileges I'd become accustomed to. I missed Amelia^X, our private jet and my custom shoes, of having "yes sir" and "no sir" bantered about. Finally, and most important, I missed my family. God, I missed them. Not just Amy but Melia, 'V' and even Derrick. They were, are and will always be my definition!

I thought back to Amy and her Mindfulness exercise and slowly, gently began breathing through my nose...count to four going in, hold to the count of four, exhale through my mouth to the count of four. Again, and again and again. Relax! Relax! Relax!

As I sat there, the motivation to take off my shoes took place. Slowly, I slipped off my Sketchers and allowed my bare feet to press against Mother Earth. As I sat there, I closed my eyes and began to feel Mother Earth's warmth begin its journey from the soles of my feet to the soul of my spirit as tranquility began to pervade my existence.

It wasn't long until the sounds and sensations around me began to be accentuated. I heard the birds calling to each other. I listened to the sound of a bee making it's rounds, collecting pollen, I began to feel the soft summer breeze caress my arms and face. I envisioned Amy on Orient Beach and how she immersed herself in the majesty of nature as a contented smile spread across my face. I was at peace. For the first time since I could remember, my mind slowed and my body became immersed in tranquility.

My spell of introspection broke and, once again, I made my way back to the cold Springs as I wondered how there could be something so pure in a world so wrought with pain where the pollution of avarice and greed can desanctify everything in the name of commerce. As I had so many times before, I took the tin cup and filled it with earth's nectar and took a slow sip of the frigid water and waited to see if the feelings I once had would return.

I waited for joy to enter my body as the remnants of my self-analysis slowly dissipated. I'd thought, no make that believed, that today things would be different. Sadly, those special feelings of peace and purity simply were not there.

I took a deep breath of self-admitted disappointment, paused and toasted Agent Langdon who saved my life while giving his own. Even after two years, I shed a tear in his memory hoping, praying, wondering if he was with his wife and found the peace he'd searched for but could never really find.

My eyes traversed all that was around me as I resolved it was simply another day, when I hoped and prayed I'd see 'Him', the mighty Buck who'd been my token of tranquility and wondered again why he was never there. My God, I needed to see him. Perhaps, then my wounds would begin to heal.

I'd been in the Forest the entire afternoon, unaware of the passing of time and was surprised to see the sun had begun to set. Slowly, I made my solitary way back towards the house, across fields once plowed, now nothing more than ruts of indifference, slowly being capitulated into masses of weeds. I was in no hurry, for there was nothing waiting for me except the memories I kept locked inside. I remember I paused at the stone wall that separates today from yesterday and glanced at the markers within, all etched with names and dates, worn smooth by time until they too were fading into yesterday. As I had so many times before I reflected on those who came before me and wondered what it felt like when the one next to them beat them to their final resting place.

The outside light on the barn clicked on as it had for mom and dad and even grandpa. I considered it my beacon and remains so today. It was time to go home. Silence. Silence, Silence. I remember, stopping and turning, looking back at my friend, the Forest. My lips emanated a gentle smile with the realization it was dusk and the perfect time of day when that subtle creep of darkness changes the mood of the day. I focused on the land and the trees in the distance and could see everything clearly, yet the shadows were deepening... inviting... beckoning me to the time when they would gather together in the majesty called night.

I stood looking, looking, looking and then turned back towards the house where, suddenly, I was a kid again, with only tomorrow in front of me. My brother, Tommie, and I were on the rope swing, taking turns being twisted and twisted and twisted in the old wooden seat and then let go as we spun wildly around and around and around only interrupted by our screams of joy and laughter.

I gazed at the barn and looked at its darkened windows. I thought, "Come on, dad, turn on the lights. It's time to milk the cows."

I glanced at the old tractor tire, once filled with sand, now filled with weeds, that allowed Tommie and me to build castles and forts and drive our toy John Deere's up the hills and dales we'd created reflecting a microcosm of life with its highs and lows of which we knew so little back then.

I looked beyond and observed the distant edges of the cemetery and its stillness as if the limestone fence which had once been my ancestors house, erased the clamor of now and shielded those within in a kinder, simpler time called yesterday.

On that day, my mind stood still, if just for a moment, as if to relish all that had been and then a slight glow caught my eye. It was a blinking light so near and yet so far away. It was then I realized it was simply a lightening bug and one more reason given by Tommie and me regarding why not to go to bed. I wondered if the old glass Skippy Peanut Butter jar with the holes in the top was still on the shelf in dad's workshop. I remembered how we'd catch the bugs in that jar, fill it with grass and bring them into our bedroom simply to watch their lights glow on-and-off, on-and-off as we fell asleep to dream about being a super hero or doing something grand. Perhaps summer nights belong to the young and yet the shadows belong to everyone simply to remind us that God is present in both the sunshine and darkness that fills our lives.

I made my way back to the house and went out on the screen porch as my mind glided to here-and-now while I sat enveloped in thoughts of all that had been. Only the sounds of the crickets cascaded my ears. My mind opened to the past and my little buddy, Jake, who would lie beside me. He was there, anxiously awaiting nothing more than me to scratch behind his ears and tell him I loved him until he, too, sadly became nothing more than yesterday.

Even with my reflections, I pondered today and feared tomorrow. I thought of all that was good and all that was bad and realized Steven Hawking was right…the net sum of the universe is zero. Good/bad! Happy/sad!

As if a profound sense of exhaustion came over me, my hands fell to my lap as I succumbed to some sort of stupor. I closed my eyes and when I opened them 'He' was there. The mighty Buck had come to me. Never before had he been beyond the realm of the forest. I looked deep into his eyes and his magnificence transcended from his soul to mine and there was peace... wonderful, glorious peace.

I closed my eyes and when I opened them, he was gone. Was he real or simply an aberration? To this day, I don't know. What I do know is that his brief presence represented my turning point... that instant when I realized my yesterday was not my tomorrow, if and only if, I had the strength to simply forget and move on to a destination where once again I would become myself.

For the first time since I entered the cave two-and-a-half years ago, I felt a sense of purpose. I said goodnight to the yellow moon rising over the empty fields, arose and went to the kitchen, pulled the laptop my friend Peter provided from the pantry shelf and carried it to the parlor that had been dad's makeshift office.

I glanced across the room and recognized the old trunk that

hadn't been opened since 'V' and I shared tomorrow and his greatness. I stood and walked the few paces and gently rubbed my hand across the old leather straps. My eyes dropped to the lock that had sequestered the insistence of others and paused to remember the combination... the date Great Grandfather had passed away. I slowly spun the little wheels until digits aligned and a slight 'click' declared I was permitted to open my soul to the sheltered majesty.

Slowly I released the metal hasp and lifted the lid. For an instant there was a pause and then I was engulfed in the throes of magnitude that had been resting, simply anticipating my return. My hand, gently pulled the white bear skin from within as I caressed its softness. With each stoke, my pain was being erased. With each stroke, my fear was whiling away. With each stroke all that had been, all that had filled me with remorse was being dissipated as I was returning to my own reality.

The albino bear skin that had held so many tales of pain and suffering, that had been transferred to my son, now had space for my sorrow and simply absorbed all that roiled within me, setting me free...free from the pain and agony and free from the sadness and sorrow that had curtailed my mind and made me less than what I'd ever been.

'Now' came back into my presence as I pressed the button and the lap top screen came to life as if it had simply been sleeping. I pondered the original version of the story I wrote while living in the cave and wondered if it would ever be anything more than what it was, icons upon a screen, never to be shared with anyone.

I was finally able to admit to myself, I'd been too sad to reach beyond my here and now and was finally free to press the button to see the messages I'd been too fragile and too delicate to encounter. There were those from the attorneys telling me what I already knew, the resolution of Wilco was complete and I'd been awarded the remnants of the once great company where the only thing still mine was money that ostensibly had no value to me, along with claims to what I thought were titles to the farm and 'The Lighthouse' on Saint Martin.

If I could make it through probate, I might be wealthy again. Yet, it no longer made any difference. My mind wandered as I wondered if I should keep the Lighthouse. Time had a way of softening the yearning that once permeated my veins and yet, I just couldn't do it. I just couldn't sell my dream, even though it was now simply a segment of my nightmare.

I remember scanning deeper into the mass of messages and found one that simply broke my heart. It was from Amy, simply telling me she loved me. My God, from what she thought was my grave came her last thoughts filling me with regrets as I whispered, "I love you, too". Even after everything, I couldn't let go. I simply couldn't.

Email:

It was over three hours from the moment I first lifted the lid on reality and I was only a fraction of the way through all the emails and countless spam. I remember shaking my head and wondering how something that was once so great could be turned into an invasive form of commerce that intercepts your thoughts and emotions where, lurking within, are those whose only goal is to take from you...your money, your joy and above all else your senses of decency and security.

I was about to depart from the remnants of now and simply shut off my reality when a new email appeared. It was from $E=MC^2$. I realized then, I'd never thanked my physical therapist, Megan for saving my life and shook my head in remorse, too embarrassed to simply respond.

I remember taking another bottomless breath and whispered to myself, "Be brave! be brave! be brave!" My hands shook as I took my universe of messages and sorted them by name instead of from now-to-yesterday and found twenty-three E=MC's. My God! I'd focused so much on myself, I didn't think of others. For the first time since my heart was broken, I pressed the button and read what's written…

My Dearest George,

I've been writing to you, hoping my words would help heal your broken heart. My life remains as it was, except for the hole in my soul that you once filled. I fear my choice in life is why you haven't replied and this makes me truly forlorn. In you, George there was a light that burned so bright that now pales my passion by its absence. Please, please write to me and simply let me know you're all right.

With love

Megan

I sat pondering. What do I write? How do I express the pain I feel? How do I apologize for my lack of consideration? I took another deep breath and tried to begin. Words weren't there, only memories.

For what seemed like an eternity, my trembling hands could not touch the keys. I looked at the small clock on the desk and watched as its second hand made its never-ending circle towards tomorrow only to have my silent friend, the sounds of silence, interrupted by the hoot of a lonely owl calling to its mate, making sure it too was OK.

"Come on George! Come on! Come on! You can do it! Climb out of the valley of despair and look at the mountain tops." I pressed the 'D' key and with each stroke, the pain and suffering, sadness and remorse that had been within me was being slowly, gingerly released.

Dear Megan:

The darkness that has surrounded me has been so immense I could not grasp the majesty of friendship, nor the splendor of someone helping heal my wounds. I must thank you for saving my life. Without you

I would have died a hideous death, alone and starved, not only of food but the goodness that comes from love and acceptance.

Like the injured man who must learn to walk again, I must re-learn to live. Like that first step, I must take that first breath.

Like the first belief that tomorrow will come, I must turn my head forward and reach out to those whose hands reach out to me.

I must grasp those hands and feel their warmth.

I must feel the pulse of their heart as it pounds against mine and allows me to see, feel and accept that life must go on.

I cannot forget yesterday and all that it brought forth.

What I hope for is to simply garner those thoughts, feelings and lessons learned and start again. Slowly, gently, cautiously until once again, the sun begins to shine.

Simply, George

I took another deep breath, hit 'send' and gently wiped the tears from my eyes as I slowly closed the laptop cover.

The phone rang and the caller ID indicated area code 404...Atlanta

I smiled. It was Megan as my life began again.

Hello Again...Hello:

It had been over a year since I'd spoken a word. At first I was reticent and then reluctant. I'd only communicated with my lawyer, Tank Kennison, via text. Yet, there was the incessant ring of my phone so alien, so intrusive, so...so obtuse to my existence. I really didn't know what to do as my hands trembled when I picked up the receiver and simply said, "hello."

On the other end was the soft gentle sound that was like more like a summer breeze that made its way into my ears and then my heart.

"Hi George." It was Megan.

Tears formed in my eyes that began to slowly make their way down my cheeks. Megan gently inquired, "How are you doing?" taking great care as if I was nothing more than a wounded dove she'd stopped to see who's lack of fight was due to injury.

I opened my mouth to speak but nothing came out. "George, are you OK?" I could hear the growing concern in

Megan's tone.

I looked at the floor and then out the window at the now-darkened sky as I whispered. "I," which was all I could say.

"George. Is this a good time to talk?" "Yes!" I whispered.

"George. How are you doing?"

"I... I'm OK." When you haven't said a word in over a year, to hear your own voice seemed strange.

"I've been trying to contact you."

"I just found out. I haven't had my laptop on since...since I got home."

"It's been over a year."

"I... I know. It's just...it's just been so hard." "What?

"Everything...I mean everything." "Being alone?"

"Everything!" My mind was flush with things to say and yet I maintained a degree of reticence.

"Do you want to talk about it?"

"What's there to say?" I gingerly countered. "I'm worried about you, George."

"Thank you. Thank you very much." I meekly replied. "George, when was the last time you laughed?"

Laugh? Laugh? I couldn't remember and then I did. It was at Megan's house with the spilled wine and she said "Chateau Laffite George! A new and vibrant Cabernet Sauvignon personally soaked in the clothes of the Vigneron to provide a fuller body." which forced the outer edges of my lips upward into a slight smile as I replied. "When we were together and I spilled the wine."

"Oh, George, that was so long ago."

"I know...so long, long ago," I lamented.

"Are you still working at Home Depot?"

"No. I moved out of the condo in Madison and back to the farm.

You mean back to Waldwick?

"Yes."

"And the forest and the pond?"

"Yes." I noted as warm feelings pervaded my soul.

"How about Amy?"

I sat down, looked at the floor as sorrow filled my heard and replied. "When the bad guys were after me, they blew up Agent Langdon's car that had two people in it. Everyone thought I was the other person, including Amy. She thinks I'm dead."

"Oh, George, I'm so sorry."

I continued my train of thought. "She needed money and applied for my life insurance and the government blocked it. She had no money and thought the government was going to indict her for sedition and so she left the country with my brother and son."

" So, you're all alone?" "Yes."

There was a long pause as if Megan was contemplating what to say next as she inquired. "Do you want to talk about it?"

"You're the first person I've talked to in over a year."

Megan was incredulous as she exclaimed, "What?"

My floodgates of emotions opened and the torrent of repression simply inundated my nature. "Megan, you have to understand, I spent six months alone, locked in a cave where everyone thought I was dead. For six months, I had precisely the same environment. No sight! No sound! The complete absence of contact with anyone. It really screwed me up. If you, you my dear, dear friend hadn't responded, I'd have died there, alone...all alone."

"Oh, George."

"It changed me, Megan. It took the light within me and simply snuffed it out and I've been afraid... afraid the bad guys are coming for me... afraid to see people... afraid to laugh or even smile. I'm all alone and afraid Megan... so, so afraid and today, I'm nothing more than a walking shadow."

There was a long pause on the other end and so I continued. "Then, thanks to you, I was freed but not really free. The government abducted me and took me somewhere and interrogated me. It was there I learned Melia and her family had to go into hiding. It was there I learned Amy thought I was dead and skipped the country with Karen, her ex-administrative assistant. It was there I found out that my son had stolen billions of dollars and was on the run and that my brother was the one who tried to kill me!"

"Jesus!"

"When you're in a hole so deep you can't see the sunlight, you know it's going to take a long time to get back on top of the ground. Some days...some days...some days I wish they'd just pour in the dirt and give me peace."

There was a long pause as I caught my breath and then apologized. "I'm so sorry. I shouldn't...I shouldn't be saying these things. I'm so sorry, I should have thanked you. I'm so guilty that all I thought about was me. Can you please forgive me?"

"George! Of course!"

I was spent, literally spent. All my anger, all my fear, all my frustrations were slowly seeping out of my soul as my head titled down in an exclamation of total emotional exhaustion.

"George? George! Are you OK?"

"Tired! Very, very tired!" "Can I call again?" "Please do."

"Do you want me to hang up now?

"Please do but please, please, please call me again." "I will. Please take care of yourself."

Click!

Mmmmmmm! I couldn't hang up. Instead I listened to the sound of no one except the receiver. There was simply no one there. No one to talk to. No one to listen. No one to laugh. No one to cry. Just me until even the phone made its way to goodbye.

It's Me:

A day passed and with it the yearning began. There was a dim light at the end of the tunnel and I dreamed it would shine brighter. Another day passed and I became anxious. Had my own words destroyed my only link to reality?

I had my second walk in the Forest and made my way back to the house. I looked at the phone for about the 100th time and finally realized the little red button meant 'missed call'. My heart skipped a beat. The call had been from yesterday. I'd simply forgotten to comprehend the little red light.

I picked up the phone and pressed the recall button and the phone rang and rang and rang and finally went to the recorded message. "This is Megan. Sorry I missed your call. Leave me a message."

Shit!

I paused and then recorded. "Megan, it's George. I'm so sorry I missed your call. I forgot to check my phone. Please call me."

An hour later the phone rang. It was Megan. I picked up before she could speak. I blurted out. "Sorry, I haven't been paying attention to the phone in so long, I forgot to check it. Yesterday, I was out for my walk. I promise, I'll carry a phone with me from now on."

"It's Ok. It's Ok"

"How are you doing?"

"A little better! A little better! I have something to look forward to.

I could tell by the tone of Megan's voice that she was touched by my comment as she inquired. "What did you do today?" "I went for my walk down by where the Foundation was and the old school, then Great Grandfather's Obelisk and, finally, the Springs for my drink."

"I checked the weather and it's nice up there." "Uh huh! And the birds are singing."

"Are you done planting?"

Reality hit home. In my depression, I'd allowed the land to go fallow and there were weeds everywhere. "Megan, I haven't done anything with the land."

"Have you thought of renting it?"

I replied, "I haven't thought about farming, renting or anything."

"Are you going into Mineral Point?"

"Not yet. I simply haven't felt like it and now I'm afraid of the stares."

"What do you mean, the stares?"

"It's a small town and I'm certain rumors are flying about the hermit out on the Terrill farm."

"George, George you're not a hermit. You're just someone recovering from a bad accident."

I'd never thought of it that way and realized that, just like my car accident with Jeepers Creepers, I was just beginning a recovery phase. However, instead of physical damage, I was suffering from emotional pain.

Megan continued, "Do you want me to keep calling?" "Yes, please. Very much so."

"I will IF you promise me you'll begin to take some small steps to getting closer to who you were before. You know George, the man who made me laugh. The man who made me think. The man who...who I admired so much."

Wow! An ultimatum. For so long, there had been no one and nothing and my world was simply an endless white with no beginning, nor end and nothing to direct me where to go. On the phone was a voice, a wonderful voice filled with concern and compassion... a woman who... who I could see myself with, who wanted the old George and not the recluse I'd become.

"OK," I replied, somewhat warily.

Megan offered. "Why don't we do this? You know my schedule. Why don't we start having phone dates? You know, you call me and we'll just talk?"

"When?" I asked anxiously.

"When's good for you?" Megan inquired.

"Anytime!"

"How about Sunday nights?"

"OK."

"8:00 o'clock my time?" Megan offered.

"OK!" A weak smile crossed my face. I had something to look forward to.

"Today is Thursday and so, call me in three days."

"I'll call you at 8:00 o'clock this Sunday, your time." I offered as my eyes blinked repeatedly as if to etch the day and time into my memory.

"George, I can't wait to hear from you." "Megan! Thank you!"

I hadn't been keeping track of the days and so I had no idea it was even Thursday. I looked at the Mineral Point Premier Co-Op calendar on the wall and realized it was two years old. I stood up and took it down. I knew it was June but didn't know the date. I finally, simply looked at the top on the computer screen that indicated it was Thursday, June 12th, 2025 - three days after Amy and my anniversary.

Small Steps:

I began to realize that, just like when I recovered from my car accident, I needed to take small steps to regaining myself. With my world now so small, I needed to rely on someone who I could trust. Megan was in Atlanta. Amy was...well, somewhere and locally the only one I'd even communicated via e-mail with was Tank Kennison. Tank retired, sold his law practice but kept his license and I guess I was his only client. Perhaps, just perhaps, I could rely on him.

Friday morning, I got up. Vowed to begin and had the phone in my hand as I looked for Tank's number. I had to see if I could call him. With trembling hands, I found Tank's office number and called. I hadn't realized that when he sold his law practice, he'd also sell the phone number as well. When the call was picked up, the lady on the other end announced, "Anderson, Williams and Cooper".

I was shocked. It wasn't Tank and it wasn't his office. I was about to hang up when the lady inquired, "Hello?".

"I'm sorry, I was trying to call Tank Kennison."

"Sir, Attorney Kennison has retired and we've purchased the practice. Is there anything I can do for you?"

"It's...it's a personal matter. I need to speak to Tank. Can I have his phone number please?"

"I'm sorry sir, we're not allowed to give out that number." "But, I need to speak to him personally."

"I'm sorry, there's really nothing I can do for you."

"OK." I offered in a somewhat dejected tone before inquiring. "Do you accept messages for him?"

"We do."

"Could you tell him that George Terrill called and would like to speak with him?"

"George?" as I noted a surprised tone within the voice. "Yes." "Oh, my God, George. It's Ann Mitchell."

"Ann? I thought you were working at the bank?"

"George, like all banks, there was a consolidation and they decided the manager in Dodgeville could handle both branches. When Mike Anderson bought out Tank, he asked me to manage the office here in Mineral Point. How are you doing?"

"I'm...I'm getting better but I need to talk to Tank."

"I'll call him. I'm sorry for all the hassle. The practice has policies and when you're our age, you don't want to rock the boat." "Understood. Here's my number in case Tank doesn't have it."

"Again, George. I apologize."

"Don't worry about it Ann. It was nice talking to you."

A few hours later, the phone rang. I thought for sure it was Megan and was excited and then confused and then afraid by the incessant ring. Finally, I picked up the receiver and carefully said, "Hello."

"George, it's Tank Kennison. I'm, I'm on the Boundary Waters with my fishing buddies. Ann Mitchell sent me a text and said it's important."

"It is Tank, I... I want to, you know...begin again and I, I... I don't know how."

"George, that's good news. Can it wait until I get back from fishing next week?"

"Next week?"

"Yes, George, next week."

"Well, OK. When you get back, can you come out to the farm?"

"Really?"

"Yes. I... I think it's time." "OK, George."

"I didn't mean to bother you, Tank."

"It's OK, George. You're my only client and, after you paid my son's tuition to Madison, I owe you."

I hung up and a wave of fear crashed into my body. I hadn't seen another person in over a year. Oh my God, how... how do I handle it?

Chamber of Commerce Days:

It was a glorious summer Sunday. The kind my dad used to call 'Chamber of Commerce Days' when Wisconsin is the best place on earth to be. When it was mom, dad, Tommie and me, we'd go to church in town and then the Red Rooster for breakfast and then come back to the farm. When it was hot and humid Tommie and I would go down to the pond and swim. I remember the laughter and innocence. I remember trying to catch the frogs and our silly question, "How deep is the frog pond? Knee deep! Knee deep!" as we would giggle at the silly thought. I remember a time when the world was so grand that anger and shame simply didn't seem to exist and how Sunday night meant steak and mom's homemade pies.

All of it were simply memories that flashed before me this Sunday night at 6:30 as I sat alone, watching the clock. Soon it was 6:45 and then 6:50 and then 6:55 and finally 6:59, I dialed all but the last digit of Megan's number. As my clock turned 7:00 I pressed the final button and listened as the phone rang.

On the second ring, there was a pleasant, "Hello". "Hi. how are you?" I inquired.

"I'm fine. How about you?" Megan offered.

"I'm...I'm OK. I called my lawyer but he's on a fishing trip. It was my first phone call in over a year. I was afraid."

"Afraid of what?"

"I...I don't know. Just afraid!" "George, you're going to be fine." "You think so?"

"Yes, George, I think so."

"How was your week?" I asked. "Well, it's only been three days."

"Oh, Yah, I forgot. How was your three days?" "Same old, same old! You know. How about you?" "Same old, same old, too."

"George, I miss you." "I miss you, too."

"I mean, I really want to see you."

"Me, too but not yet."

"What did you do the past three days?"

"Well, I looked in the bathroom mirror for the first time."

"What?"

"I looked in the bathroom mirror."

"And?"

"And I saw this old guy looking back at me who hasn't had a haircut or shaved in over two and a half years."

"Oh, my God!"

"Well, it scared me and one of the things I want Tank to do is hire a barber to come and cut my hair."

"Why not just go to a barber?"

"You don't understand. Mineral Point is a small town and if I go in looking like this, word will spread and right now I know they think I've lost all my marbles when it's only some of them that are loose."

I heard a giggle on the other end and that made me smile as Megan inquired, "Then what?"

"Well, I think I need to see if Tommie's truck will start. It's been sitting all this time."

"Then what?"

"I... I don't know. Perhaps I can drive it to the end of the driveway and back just to get some practice."

"George, it's like making love. Once you know how, you never

forget."

"I know but I want to make sure. If I take it a little at a time, it won't be so overwhelming."

"The love making or driving the truck?" Megan asked before adding, "What else do you have planned?"

"That's about it. Wait! I think I want to go out in the barn. I haven't been there and see what's in there."

"You haven't been in your barn?" "Nope. No need to, I guess."

There was a pause and I thought I'd been talking too much about me and so I asked, "What about you?"

"Well, we have a big staff meeting on Wednesday. Something's up. I'm supposed to know everything, but I think the clinic is being sold."

"Sold? Why?"

"Because there have been some people in and there have been meetings that I wasn't involved in."

"Aren't you managing the clinic?" "Yes and that's what got me worried."

There was a sense of formality to Megan's voice and so I politely asked. "Is there someone there?"

"Yes. A friend."

"Why didn't you say so?" "Because we had a date."

"But you could have not answered or told me and I wouldn't have kept talking. I didn't mean to keep you on the line if you've got company."

"George, we had a date and it was important. My friend understands."

"Can we talk next Sunday?" "Of course! Certainly!"

"OK. Thank you, Megan."

"Thank you...Love yah!" Click.

"A friend? Love yah?" My mind was a whirling dervish.

Should I be jealous? Should I be concerned? Should I feel hurt?

Respites:

I was measuring my days in walks. Seven walks to the week, rain or shine, mud or hard ground. Like an addict, I needed my three-hour respite from reality as I wandered in thought, spirit and mind. I'd spoken with Megan two walks ago and so it had to be Tuesday.

I reached the Springs and 'he' was there, carefully watching me. The mighty Buck nodded and I knew it was his way of telling me to follow him as he turned and walked into the bog. I took a deep breath and stepped across the tiny rivulets of liquid purity and followed his footsteps. I came to a spot where the tall grass was matted and saw that the Buck had stopped. For an instant, I knew not what to do and then the shakes began...literal nervous convulsions that started in my hands and progressed through my entire body as if I were freezing to death instead of fear.

At first, the tremblers were slight and then began to increase in both temerity and frequency. My body began quaking and I began to convulse. My mind began to unravel. My thoughts were like arrows of light shimmering, shattering, pronouncing anger and pain, frustration and terror. All that I endured was there. Exposed! Not hidden! No longer buried within my soul.

I was in the middle of the north valley. Alone! Exposed! Like some sort of alien. Before me stood my son, Derrick, looking down at me and laughing. Then it was Amy and Karen holding hands, staring at me with no expression, no emotion, simply garnering a matter-of-fact look frozen on their faces, in their eyes and in their lives. Then it was my brother, Tommie, with Su, simply shaking their heads in disdain. My God how could it be? How could they be here? Now? Within me? Without me?

My body was shaking and then I saw Agent Langdon and he was crying. My God, why? Why was he crying? Peter, Luke and James appeared and they were looking at me with frowns and then a look of derision. Then it was Bart, but he was standing. His wheelchair tipped on its side as he was shaking his head in anger.

Oh, my God! Oh, my God! What's happening.

There was a black cloud above. Did this mean rain? The cloud formed just beyond my reach as I grabbed for the sky. Slowly the breeze began and through the clouds, I could see the entrance to the cave.

"Oh God no, not the cave!" I exclaimed. "Not the cave! Not the cave! Not the cave! Please!"

I looked around and somehow, I was there... in the cave. "Not again! Not again! Not again!" I pleaded as I shuddered in fear.

I heard the sound of the trickling water as it echoed off the cave walls. I smelled damp! I felt cool air. How could it be?"

I looked and wondered what's that? Sunlight? Sunlight! Not from the hole in the ceiling but from the cave door. Sunlight! My God, the cave door was open and it was bright outside! My tremblers began diminishing. I felt myself walking towards the door as the sound of trickling water began to wane and with it the smell of damp.

I'm there! I'm there! I'm there. I was at the open door looking out at the shining sun. Bright! Bright! I took my hand to block the light from my eyes and felt the sun's warmth as my head leaned back while I smiled and smiled and smiled.

I took a deep, deep breath and looked up at the blue sky. At first I was apprehensive and then placed my left foot further beyond the door as I began to feel the sun's warmth upon my body. It felt so good.

I took my right foot and continued my egress. I'm out! I'm out! I'm out! I paused and felt the breeze... the soft gentle breeze and heard a redwing blackbird calling.

Before me, on the ground, lay my tattered, torn THD apron with the scribbled word 'Gorge' on it. Someone had drawn a line through Gorge and in big, bold letters printed "Little Spirit."

My son 'V' appeared and nodded. He and his wife Amelia were holding hands. Then it was Melia and Jack and the kids, all smiling, all laughing, all nodding as I nodded back.

I had a huge smile upon my face as I peered across the valley and saw Rodney looking at me, waving, beckoning me. I watched as my body walked across the smooth valley floor to where Rodney was standing but he'd disappeared. Great grandfather stood in his place and offered two feathers. I reached out, but they, too, simply vanished. The Medicine man walked to my side and put his hand on my shoulder. I couldn't feel him, yet his goodness transcended and I felt peace.

I turned to look back at the cave door and Megan was standing there. Slowly her hands rose up with her palms facing in and she beckoned me, summoned me, gestured for me to come closer. I was afraid to return to the bonds of hell but began my approach, never taking my eyes off Megan's face. With each step, Megan became more transparent. A little lighter, a little lighter, a little lighter. In her place I began to see the image of Amy. Oh, my God, what's happening? When I was just a few feet away, Megan was gone and Amy stood there. I looked directly in Amy's eyes and saw tears. Amy looked forlornly at the ground, tilted her head to the side, slowly turned, stepped inside the cave and simply disappeared. I stood alone, unwilling to re-enter the cave and, yet, reluctant to leave. My thoughts. My memories. My emotions all swirled around me and then splattered against the cave wall leaving me alone, so all alone, deprived of love and affection.

My energy was drained. What did it mean? The tremblers that had invaded me began to slow as my body calmed and my senses reappeared? I took a deep breath and realized all that had been was no more and yet I was different. I know not how but I could feel it. I looked down at the matted grass and then to where the mighty Buck had been standing and he, too, was gone as reality reappeared.

I turned again to retrace my steps back to the Springs, gingerly stepping across the rivulets and was inclined to take another sip of purity. I bent down and grasped the old tin cup and felt its cold. I immersed the cup in the escaping liquid and raised it to my lips. As the water flowed within me, my body began to convulse again. All the sadness that had been locked within me was being allowed to escape. All the anger. All the pain. All the frustration! All the fear!

I took a deep breath and realized I'd returned. Gone was the fear. Gone was the sadness! Gone were the regrets! My body accepted my mind and agreed that I was back. My mind became clear. I stopped and thanked God for allowing me to simply return to 'me.'

I took another sip and carefully put the cup in its place and began my walk back home. I stopped and looked at the weeds in the field and vowed to get out the tractor and disc the field. Hundred- day corn could still be planted if I'd hurry. I wondered how I could afford new Wagyu cattle and whether the distillery would work. I thought of the wine that needed to be sold and realized it would be four years before Terrill B&B would have more wine to sell.

I walked to the limestone fence and glanced at the names upon the weathered stones, nodded in respect and realized I no longer needed to join them. Instead of yesterday, I looked towards to tomorrow as I glanced at the farmhouse and realized my life could now go on.

Tank:

The following morning, the phone rang and I noted it was Tank Kennison's number. I picked up and offered in a friendly and positive tone that hadn't been evoked by me in years. "Good morning Tank. How are you?"

"I'm good, George."

I noted the somewhat surprised tone in Tank's voice as he offered. "We had a good time fishing. It's always good to get away with old friends, swap lies, drink beer, play cards, smoke cigars and catch fish."

I could tell that the gentle man who'd I'd come to trust had been refreshed as he sincerely asked. "How are you?"

I paused and then replied. "Tank, I'm fine. I think the last of the wounds have finally begun to heal and I realize it's time to get on with life."

"That's good news George. Good news."

I paused and then noted. "Tank, it's been two and a half years since I shaved or had a haircut."

"Oh, my God!"

"I know. I want to begin getting back but am concerned if I come to town looking the way I do, it will stir up even more rumors about the hermit out on the Terrill farm."

"What do you want me to do, George?"

"Could Harvey Walker come out and cut my hair?" "Gonna be pretty tough, George."

"Why? I'll pay him extra." "Harvey died last year."

"Yah, I guess that would make it a little tough, wouldn't it?" I laughed, which felt good.

There was a pause and then Tank offered. "If you wouldn't mind, Marie's been cutting my hair since before we got married and perhaps she could do it."

I thought of Tank and realized he was nearly totally bald before responding. "I don't know if I want my hair quite that short, Tank."

A loud chortle on the other end as Tank replied. "I'm certain she could leave it longer than mine."

"How about a little bit more?"

Another chuckle and then Tank added, "Well, why don't I see if she can do it and I'll call you back."

There was a pregnant pause and then Tank inquired. "Is there anything else, George?"

"Well yes, but I think we should talk about it in person and perhaps at another time when it's just the two of us."

"Understood."

Ten minutes later the phone rang and it was Tank. "How about Wednesday?"

"Sure, what time?"

"What's convenient for you, George?"

"Hmmm, let me check my calendar. Hmmm, it seems it can just about be any time seeing how I haven't had anything to do in over a year and nothing planned for the next year. Perhaps I could squeeze you in."

Another chuckle and then a serious reply. "How about ten o'clock."

"That works."

"Glad to have you back, George."

"Thanks Tank. See you and Marie Wednesday at ten. Does she have any sheep shears or should I go out in the barn and see if dad's are still there?"

"She'll be fine. It will be good to see you."

"Thanks Tank."

Cave Dweller:

It was morning and my habitual pattern so eloquently summarized by "A Day In The Life" had become my routine. After doing virtually nothing, I realized that something had to enter my life. I opened the laptop and went to the story I'd written in the cave only to realize it was an emotional mess. I knew I needed to edit it or, back when Amy was part of my future, redact it, as she liked to call it.

I knew my mind worked in a way that I couldn't rely on images upon a screen and so I simply hit the 'print' button and watched as page after page spewed forth from within my heart and soul.

My mind wandered back to the books on creative writing I'd brought from the condo and I looked to them for guidance. I then realized that not only my story but my daily life needed a better beginning. I'd simply become the tortoise in a world full of hares where my slow stepping into the meat of the story wouldn't matter to anyone including me. What I'd written about life in the cave was repetitious because I wrote about the same routine until it was no longer filled with thought or reason. With coffee in hand, I became my own editor and accepted that the mish, mash of thoughts had no beginning, no 'arc' and no resolution. I asked myself, why would anyone want to read or worse yet, understand what I was trying to communicate?

I thought back to school and accepted I needed a new lede or opening section of a news story, designed to capture the reader's attention and entice them to read the rest of the article such that the opening sentence would grab the reader's attention and entice them to continue reading. I had to clearly state the main point - to be concise and easy to understand while creating a sense of urgency or curiosity. I pondered what type of lede should fill those first few sentences. Would it be a summary lede to directly state the main point of the story? A question lede to engage the reader? An anecdotal lede to share a personal story or example? Or a descriptive lede to paint a vivid picture to capture the reader's attention? Instead of me making the decision, I opted to write four different beginnings then let Megan choose which one would pique her interest. All I need do was convince her to serve as my editor in chief.

Sunday night came and Megan and I talked and talked and then talked some more. She noted that I was beginning to sound like my old self. My inquiry was whether she was talking about my age or my demeanor which got a, "Ha, ha," out of her.

I told her about my big hair appointment and she replied she was disappointed she didn't get to see the 'Charles Manson' me. I offered to have Marie take a photo before and after and I'd send it to her. She agreed.

I detailed what I wanted to do with my memoirs and she agreed. I told her I'd email them to her and let her choose which one she was enticed by the most. It was then I detailed how a successful story is structured, called a story arc.

"You mean like Noah?" Megan joked.

With no laugh on my part, Megan realized I was being serious as I replied. "A story arc is the overall plot structure of a narrative. It's like a journey that the characters take, full of twists, turns, and obstacles."

"You mean there really is a structure?" Megan inquired. "Yes," I replied. First is the exposition or beginning of the

story, where the characters and setting are introduced. Next is the rising action which is the middle part of the story, where conflicts and challenges arise. Next comes the climax which is the highest point of tension and excitement in the story, where the main conflict is resolved."

Megan interjected, "I do like those," inferring a totally different scenario as I continued on.

"Next is the falling action which is the aftermath of the climax, where the loose ends are tied up and finally the resolution, or conclusion of the story, where the characters' journeys come to an end."

There was a pause on the phone as Megan was putting all the pieces together and noted, "George, I never thought of stories that way but it all makes sense."

"My goal is to take all my thoughts from my time in the cave and see if I can't create a story people will want to not only read but be made to think and feel something."

"I don't want to write a good guy, bad guy story. I want to write about what it was like, how I felt and how it has affected me. I know I've changed. I know that what I took for granted is gone. What I don't know is how to explain my catharsis and how today I'm a different person or perhaps someone whose taken underlying tendencies and simply had them come out such that they've replaced those that had been my emotional exterior before."

"Wow!" was all Megan could reply.

I kept going. "I've set in place a routine to make sure each day begins with a purpose. To do that each night, before I go to bed, I'm going to write down the most important task of the next day. Then, when I get up in the morning, I'll have my cup of coffee and lay out the strategy for achieving my goal which can be anything. I mean anything, as long as it's there and something that needs to be done."

"I'm impressed, Mister Terrill."

There was a pause and then I finally asked about her employee meeting and she seemed reluctant to share it with me. Finally, I said. "I've seen a picture of you naked hanging over your bed and you don't want to share the results of your employee meeting?"

Smartass Megan noted that, although she was 'nekked' as she called it, she wasn't hanging over her bed, the picture was. Touché!

Megan's tone got serious and she told me the rumor was true. Atlanta General had put in a bid to buy the clinic with the intent of putting it under their operational umbrella. In the meeting, the doctors noted that the main reasons were costs incurred in dealing with insurance companies and getting paid for services rendered that were not only financial but emotional. You can only do battle so many times for what is right until it too becomes withering. Reasons here, excuses there, delays,

delays, delays all done in typical insurance company methodology - deny, defer, depose with one goal in mind, playing the waiting game to make the claimants either give in or defer paying as long as possible so that there is a greater return on investment.

Megan said she looked at the six people in accounting and knew they'd be out of jobs. The doctors assured the entire staff that everyone would be assimilated into Atlanta General and receive the same, if not more, benefits and pay.

I thought about Megan's contract where she was afforded a voting share in the corporation and, therefore, remuneration and wondered how it would affect her. I was smart enough to know that when there's a takeover you always put the word 'not' in front of whatever is said by the victors as it's usually B.S. simply to keep the workers working until the 'i's' are dotted and the 't's' crossed, then the new owners get selective amnesia.

As for Megan, when there's eight doctors and one manager and the doctor's all know their revenue stream would remain the same while their responsibilities would be narrowed and hours standardized, gone would be any generalized medicine. Instead, the physicians would become a part of the medical money machine, doing their part, while leaving the little personal things that someone less expensive could do.

I wondered what the doctor's PPD would be or if it even came up. Like any business, there needed to be a return on investment and that was measured with Patients Per Day. Would it be fifteen or twenty, where the thought of anything outside the patient's condition would become alien as time wasted that could have been invested in the revenue stream? I imagined the doctor arriving at the examining room door, taking a moment to read the chart, opening the door and immediately 'talking business' measured not only in the number of exams but other revenue generating channels such as lab work and referrals that increased the revenue stream. It didn't take a rocket scientist to realize what was going on and Megan was about to get the big weenie.

Megan seemed positive and I didn't want to burst her bubble and so we switched subjects as she asked what type of haircut I was going to get. I told her I'd talked it over with Big Brother Rodney and, in honor of him, I was going to get a Mohawk which got Megan laughing as I offered. "Seriously, I'm thinking of a mullet."

"A what?"

"A mullet." "What's that?"

"I think I'm going to ask Marie for really short hair on the sides and back of my head, with longer hair on top styled in a wedge shape that extends towards the back."

"You're serious?"

"Sure! Right now, everyone in town thinks I'm some sort of wacko and so why not give them a cheap thrill and let them think I'm really off my rocker."

There was a girlish giggle on the other end as Megan noted. "Glad to have you back, George."

"No Georgie?" I inquired.

"We'll save the Georgie for when I see you." "Yiikes!"

It was nearly ten and time for bed. Monday meant going into the barn and seeing if Tommie's truck would start. Whoopee!

Mow, Mow, Mow the Yard:

I'd been living in the house for over a year and hadn't set foot in the barn or the old training facility where Francis and Aristotle, our research pigs, had been coached. Today was the day. I looked in the mirror at the disheveled old man and said, "Come on George, you can do it."

When we were kids, the barn doors were always open. As times changed and stories told, especially when some idiot sliced the hydraulic lines on the tractor, we began locking the barn at night and whenever we were gone. The keys had always been 'on the hook' by the kitchen door, as dad called it, and they were still there, touched last by my brother before he and Su went with Derrick.

I went into the kitchen and grabbed the keychain with the clear plastic fob that had the Wisconsin motion 'W' inside to give the ring some girth so that you knew they were in your pants pocket. Slowly, I made my way across the yard to the barn door. When grandpa built the barn, he designed it to milk cows. When the herd got too big, Grandpa and Uncle Tom built a milking parlor that we automated a few years ago so the barn became a great big garage for the tractor and pull-behinds as well as the cars and trucks, bikes, snowmobiles, ATV's and stuff mom didn't want staring at her from the front yard.

I looked at the padlock hasp and saw that the staple had lost its sheen as weather had begun to rust its hinges. The old Masterlock lock reminded me of the TV commercials where they'd shoot a bullet into the casing and the lock still worked. Dad never trusted combination locks and said that when they didn't work and you needed to get the Sawzall to cut the lock shank, you'd have to break a barn window to get the Sawzall as all the tools were inside. Mom would tell him, he'd better not lose the padlock key or he'd be out of luck. The 'conversation' went on for years as Tommie and I would smirk about the fact dad hid the second key, but forget where he put it.

I paused to let the memory pass and then inserted the key and heard the 'click' as the shaft opened and I turned the loop from vertical to horizontal so that the hasp would open. It was then the memories came flying out. The sight, the smell, the memories of all we'd done as kids. The first time I ever sat on the tractor. The first- time dad let me drive the tractor out of the barn. I walked in and the sweet smell of innocence wafted into my soul. It was as if time stood still. The tools were all aligned, hoes and rakes and shovels, hanging, waiting for their turn to be used again, realizing that machines had replaced muscle and time replaced innocence such that they were more for decoration than making a living.

I walked down the center and saw dad's tractor sitting idle, waiting for the day when it could come back from its deep sleep and begin to do what it had been designed to do. In the corner was Tommie's Chevy Silverado. General Motors had an incentive program with a special trim and interior that mom won at our dealership in Dodgeville and even the folks in town thought it was pretty snazzy.

I made my way to the truck, looked at all the collected dust from two years of sitting and vowed to give the truck a bath as I opened the door and saw the keys dangling where Tommie always left them.

I got in, and out of habit, put on the seatbelt and turned the key...'click'. I assumed the battery was dead. I got out and went to dad's workbench and got the trickle charger along with fifty feet of extension cord, opened the truck hood and connected the clamps. I knew it would be a couple of hours and so I decided to go to the Su's lab and see how it weathered two years of nothing.

I walked to the lab and opened the door as memories came roaring back. The one-way glass looked into the training facility where I saw Su's lab with an open notebook on the table indicating she and Tommie had left in haste. On the counter was an empty tea cup with stains on the inside indicating it had been evaporation and not humanity that had emptied its contents.

Where there'd been life and laughter, where the majesty of friendship once existed, now there was nothing but silence. I looked in Aristotle and Francis' area and a sad moment wove its way through me. So, kind! So gentle! So much more than what we'd ever perceived a pig could be. I'd never forgotten our walk to the Forest and Francis coming back and sharing what he experienced and the people in heaven who'd touched his soul.

I looked at the sixteen square communication board and how, with the aid of Simon our computer, Francis learned to talk via what we called the Hawking Talking machine. It was then I realized God's majesty. It was then I accepted we were but one element of this thing called life and dignity only came to those willing to recognize that we were here to share God's gift and not take it from all others.

I opened the storeroom door and it was as if time stood still. Sitting on the shelves were the twenty-gallon BBQ tanks filled with helium and nitrogen intended to keep Simon cool that served as a seven-day emergency supply in case the Linde PLC delivery man was delayed.

It had been two hours since I hooked up the charger and so I went back to Tommie's truck and turned the key...'click'. The battery was charged but the truck wouldn't turn over. With more time than anything else, I decided enough was enough, closed up the barn and with it, my memories, and made my journey into the Forest. The truck could wait until another day.

On my way back from my walk, I realized I hadn't mowed the lawn in nearly two years. My God, what would Tank and Marie think if they came to the house and saw the yard the way it was?

I went to the barn, unlocked it again, went in and saw dad's John Deere 3046R which had been his pride and joy forlornly sitting there. Dad had gone all out with the rough terrain rear attachment, mower deck, tiller, grader, load leveler, post hole auger and front digger with stability arms as well as the enclosed, air-conditioned cabin.

Dad loved the 'little guy' as he called it and went all out. Half the attachments were never used as Mom would say, "the only difference between men and boys is just the price they pay for their toys" and this certainly was dad's favorite toy.

I climbed in, turned the key and varoom the 45-horse engine started right up. It had been over two years since I drove anything and, quite honestly, it felt good. Round and round and round the yard I went using the rear-pull rough terrain attachment. As I made my first turn behind the kitchen, I rolled over the famous indentation in the yard. Dad once explained that was where George the First drowned the pervert in the outhouse who raped my great, great Aunt Dora.

When we were young, we were spooked by the thought a skeleton was there. When I was in college I went out to K-Mart on the Beltline in Madison right before Halloween and bought one of those life-sized plastic skeletons. Mom didn't have a clothes dryer simply because she always thought closed smelled better when they were hung outdoors. The night before Halloween, I snuck out under her lines and stuck the skeleton's hands in the ground. She got up the next morning, did 'a load' as she called it, went out to hang the clothes and almost had conniption fit when she saw the hands sticking out of the ground.

Mom never said a word. The next year, I wasn't home and Tommie had the forearm and hand sticking out of the ground. I guess mom wasn't 'amused'. From then on, every October, we'd hang the entire skeleton on mom's clothes lines over the indentation as if the peddler had risen from the dead. I know, a sick joke, but when you live on a farm and never had any trick-o-treaters, you needed to do something. Mowing took me about four laps to get where we thought the son-of-a-bitch drowned as I realized he got what was coming.

When I finally had the grass and weeds cut, I went back to the barn, disconnected the rough terrain attachment and put on the mower deck and went out and mowed again. When I was done, I stopped and admired my handiwork and realized I needed to trim the hedges, around the oak tree and then mom's birdbath with the two concrete robins perched one on each side. Boy, she loved that birdbath and putting food out for all the birds who came to visit.

Tommie and I would play tricks on mom by sneaking out and laying the concrete birds on the ground and tell her the racoons did it. Now city folks think racoons are cute, but not farmers! Boy oh boy! They'd eat our chickens and do all sorts of things and I remember telling Rodney once I'd be more than glad to send him some racoon stew if he wanted it. I thought he was going to gag on the thought.

I got out the Deere 2-cycle string trimmer and hedger and finished the job, got the watering can and filled bird bath. As I was walking back to the house, I stopped and admired my accomplishment. A little thing like mowing the grass had been something I'd forgotten ever since we moved away from Pine Lake. At times, it's the small things that put the largest amount of satisfaction in your life and this was one of them.

Tuesday I spent cleaning the house and dusting the bookshelves just to make sure when Tank and Marie showed up they wouldn't think I was off my rocker. Well anyway, not too far off. Wednesday arrived, and sure enough, Tank and Marie showed up right at 10:00. I had coffee brewing and we sat and chatted on the screen porch as if nothing had ever been wrong.

With shoulder-length hair, over eighteen inches long and a beard just a little shorter that brushed upon my chest, I asked Marie to take my 'hippie' photo while Tank noted I looked more like a homeless person than a hippie. To overcome his response, I held up my hand and made the 'peace' sign as Marie took my photo to send to Megan.

It was a wonderful late June day and I'd gone out to the barn and brought an old wooden chair and set it in the front yard and ran an extension cord outside in case Marie was going to use an electric-clippers on me. We went out into the yard as Marie put one of those snap-on covers barbers use around my neck.

"How do you want it cut?" Marie asked. "Shorter," I replied.

Now shorter to me meant shorter than it was. To Marie it meant a buzz cut. First, she took her scissors and cut the hair on my head and face that reminded me of the rough terrain attachment on the tractor. When the hair was scissors cut, Marie simply took an electric-clippers, added some sort of plastic attachment and ran it around the sides of my head, then she put a different attachment on and ran it over the top of my head.

In less than five minutes, nearly three years-worth of hair was gone. Amazingly, it actually felt different... cooler... and more... uhh... I don't know, alive I guess, as I took my hand and rubbed it across my head and actually felt the resistance of each strand of hair standing.

When she got to my face, Marie, added some Williams Electric Shave and took an electric shaver and did her deed. Then she slathered some cheap aftershave on and was done! Marie unclipped the cloth as I looked at the ground and saw hair everywhere. My hair! Already blowin' in the wind and Bob Dylan wasn't even singing. I was certain the birds would be using it to feather their nests ala George. I had Marie take her 'after' photo I could also send to Megan. Boy was she in for a surprise. I hadn't had a 'butch' haircut since the days when they called them that which was before the term took on a whole new meaning.

From Marie's bag of tricks, she pulled out one of those old-fashioned mirrors that were called 'looking glasses' in fairy tales and held it up so I could see. Gone was the 'weird' look. In its place was me looking like I'd just returned from Marine Corps basic training. I smiled and hoped it wouldn't take too long for some of my hair to grow back, while also knowing that when I went to town, folks would realize I wasn't some wacko, just plain old George Terrill, wanting to get on with life. Now, all I needed were arms only tanned up to my elbows and just the part of my face below my eyebrows to fit right in.

Tank smiled and offered. "Welcome back to Mineral Point." "I've got a problem with that," I offered.

Tank looked at me with a concerned look and inquired, "What?"

"I can't get the truck started. I charged the battery but it still won't start."

Tank pondered my reply and answered, "I'll bet it's mice."
"Mice?"

"Yah, the government required all the car manufacturers to switch to soy-based shielding on their wiring and the mice think it's their own type of spaghetti."

"Mice?" I again inquired.

"Let's go out in the barn and check while Marie cleans up."

Tank and I went out to the barn and opened the double doors to let the light in. I went to dad's workbench and got a flashlight. Tank had me open the hood and sure enough, down below the crank case was a huge mouse nest with exposed wires.

"What do I do now?" I asked.

"Well, I think you're going to have to have the truck towed in. You got homeowner's insurance?"

"I think so, why?"

"After the deductible, it's probably going to be covered."

I blew a large amount of frustrated air out through my mouth as my cheeks ballooned. Just when I was ready to get back into the world, the mice had won the battle and kept old George on the farm. It reminded me of John Steinbeck's "Of Mice and Men" as I wondered if I was George or Lennie at that point in time.

Tank closed the hood as we made our way back towards Marie as I inquired, "When do you think we can get together to talk business?"

"I've got things in the oven this afternoon and tomorrow. How about Friday?"

"OK. I'm not going anywhere. Same time?" "Sounds good."

I offered to pay Marie and she said 'no' as she and Tank got in his truck and departed. Boy, it sure seemed different with the little hair on my head.

GAD, SAD, OCD, PAD and MAD:

Between constantly rubbing my head to make sure there was still some hair there and my walk in the Forest, Wednesday and Thursday which happened to be the Fourth of July, flew by although Thursday night was a rough one.

I had one of my anxiety attacks Doctor Roberts warned me about when I was at Area 51. They just come on. It could happen for any reason and all of sudden, it would prompt me as my worries, fear and unease would come back to remind me I really hadn't won my battle with depression. I'd been through all the stages before. The excessive worry, restlessness, fatigue and difficulty concentrating. When you're all alone, you really don't know if you're having bouts with irritability. You do know about the muscle tension and sleep disturbances. One would think I'd know better. Doctor Roberts had prescribed some pills but they made me woozy. I knew I still had an anxiety disorder and only hoped and prayed that, with time, it would simply go away.

Doctor Roberts took me through all the different types of anxiety disorders. The first was GAD or Generalized Anxiety Disorder where a person has persistent worries about multiple things. Then there's SAD or Social Anxiety Disorder which is a fear of social situations and scrutiny. Then there's OCD or Obsessive- Compulsive Disorder, with intrusive thoughts and compulsive behaviors. GAD! SAD! OCD! I think I had them all until Doctor Roberts finally concluded I had panic disorder called PAD based on my sudden and unexpected attacks of intense fear.

I think that, because I was finally able to break out of my shell, my problem was one of loneliness. Doctor Richards told me that anxiety can exacerbate loneliness in several ways. He said anxiety could lead to avoidance behaviors, such as social situations or activities that might trigger anxiety and isolation, which I obviously had that contributed to feelings of loneliness. Boy, he got that one right!

Doctor Roberts also indicated that anxiety could lead to negative self-beliefs, such as feeling inadequate or unattractive making it difficult to connect with others and feelings of loneliness. When you're sitting on top of the world and then have all that happened to me take place, I'm certain losing my wife, son and brother all at once and in such a horrific way led to a profound drop in my self-concept.

When I was with Doctor Roberts, I had a really difficult time expressing my emotions, leading to feelings of isolation and loneliness. When I moved back to the farm, I now admit I was afraid. Not only of the bad guys, but of getting emotionally hurt again. I didn't know if I could take it.

When I put all three of the components together, I could see that I'd changed. However, it was being chased, fearing for my life and learning all the people I trusted and loved who left me, that made me hypervigilant, where I'm constantly scanning my surroundings for potential threats. This made it difficult to relax and connect with others on a deeper level, contributing to feelings of aloneness. In essence, the past has created a barrier between me and my social connections and has, now that I've begun interacting with Megan and Tank, lead to the feelings of separation and isolation.

I look back at the past two years. I remember my drive. I remember my joy of life. I remember my confidence and then GAD, SAD, OCD, PAD! When you spend six months trapped in a cave, thinking people want to kill you. When you're 'freed' and put in what Peter called, 'our concentration camp." When you learn your son has stolen billions of dollars, your brother tried to kill you and your wife ran away with her mistress, what in hell would you think? Put them all together I think I'm still suffering from getting F--ked!

I know I shouldn't have. It wasn't Sunday but I needed to talk to somebody and so I called Megan. It took four rings and she finally picked up.

"Sorry, I know it's not Sunday but I needed someone to talk to" I blurted out.

"It's OK," Megan offered with a very unusual tone to her voice.

"What's going on?" I asked, realizing my panic attack was being matched by issues on the other end.

"I... I... I've got to move out.""What?"

"Things happened. Things that shouldn't have."

"What?"

"Well, I planned on making it a four-day weekend and was home. It's been hot and I was out by the pool."

"OK."

"Ellie said she had some work to do at the studio and Charlie's schedule had him flying to South Africa."

"OK. And?"

"Charlie's flight got cancelled and he was rescheduled for tomorrow and came home. George, I was sitting out and Charlie came out and...and try to force himself on me."

"Oh, my God! Megan. No!"

"George, it was horrible. I never expected it. Nothing and I mean nothing had ever happened between us and it's always been so...so plutonic."

"And?"

"He really tried to...to rape me. He told me he knew I wanted it. He said he knew about my... my escapades, as he called them, and if I was going to live with he and Ellie, it was my responsibility to...to you know."

"Oh, Megan! Does Ellie know?"

Megan was now crying as she said, "No, it would destroy her."

"Did he...?"

"No! I was able to fight him off and now I'm scared." "Did you call the police?"

"No. It would be his word against mine and nothing happened that I could prove. Besides, I don't want to hurt Ellie. I just need...I don't know. I'm just afraid."

"What do you want me to do?" I asked, now totally concerned.

"I don't know. It looks like the deal with the hospital is going to go through. I know they won't need me. I know I'll be unemployed. I also know if I leave now, I'll be out of my severance and George, it's a lot of money."

"How can I help?" I inquired.

"Pray for me, George. Pray. I never expected this. I never imagined this would ever happen! I guess, it's my fault. No one was home and I knew Ellie would be at the studio and Charlie was supposed to be gone for four days. I... I felt I'd be home alone and so I guess I let my guard down."

"In other words, you were out by the pool naked?"

"Yes, George. Yes! But I thought the three of us were over that. I feel like a fool."

"Megan, you didn't do anything wrong. Your house! Your yard! Your privacy!"

"What do I do, George?"

I wanted to change the subject and asked, "When do you think the clinic purchase is going to take place?"

"The end of the month." "Then you want out, right?" "Yes."

"So, you've got three weeks?" "Yes."

"Do you want to stay in the house?" "Not when Charlie's here."

"Do you have his schedule?" "Yes, it's in his office."

"Figure out when he's going to be home and then stay at a hotel. Notify both of them you're electing to exercise your option and sell your part of the house because of the hospital acquisition. Hang on at work and when the sale goes through, come to Waldwick until you get everything set as to what you want to do next."

"Do you want me to?"

"Of course."

"Really?"

"Yes, silly."

"But what happens if Ellie and Charlie don't want to buy me out?

"Then, if what you told me is correct, you'll put the house on the market and some phantom buyer from Wisconsin will make an offer and buy the place."

"You'd do that?"

"Yes, of course!"

"I'll buy it, then relist it. You'll get your money and they'll get there's."

"Oh, George. How can I ever thank you."

"I haven't done anything yet. Where's Charlie now?"

"I don't know. He left."

Dime against a dollar, he's with Ellie at the studio spinning a tale that you tried to seduce him."

"Oh, my God, do you think so?"

"Think about it. He knows he's in deep shit. He also knows he needs to make an excuse so that Ellie stays with him and that excuse works. Now go pack and get the hell out of there. Call me when you're settled at the hotel."

It seems that my anxiety attack had evaporated and for the first time in a long time, I was worried about someone else besides me.

Buckhead:

Megan called about an hour later and told me she was staying at the Embassy Suites in Buckhead. I didn't sleep all night worrying about her. Happy Fourth of July where the only fireworks happened to be eight hundred miles away.

Friday morning I was up early, spiffed up the house as I knew Tank would be coming inside. Right at ten I heard the crunch of gravel as Tank's Ford pulled into the driveway. Tank got out, came to the door as I was waiting for him.

"How's the new hairdo?" Tank inquired.

"I'm getting used to it. The only problem is the mosquitos. I never had that problem before. I guess they don't like hippies."

We went out on the screen porch and I watched Tank's entire demeanor change. It was then I knew something was wrong as I asked, "Tank, what's going on?"

"We've got problems."

"What?" I asked as my mouth went south.

"When you and Melia signed the pre-nuptial agreement it noted that everything before your marriage remained your property. With the pre-nup, everything after the marriage was placed in common ownership."

I got a concerned feeling this was going to get complicated as Tank continued. "In the pre-nup, the word 'and' is used to indicate common ownership of everything you acquired from your wedding day on."

"OK."

"It means everything." Tank offered is a serious tone. "And?"

"The Lighthouse, the remaining funds from Wilco and George, the farm."

"Huh?" I said in total disbelief.

"If you hadn't given Tommie the money for the farm, it would have been yours simply because it was yours before you got married as stated in your parent's trust. However, by giving Tommie money you earned while married, which actually was both yours and Amy's, she has right to claim your half."

"My half?" I retorted incredulously and then offered, "So in other words, I only own one-quarter of the farm and Terrill B&B?"

Tank cautiously nodded, 'yes.'

"Holy shit! My brother tried to kill me and is somewhere. Amy thinks I'm dead and living with her mistress and I'm the one getting screwed."

Tank waited for the emotional storm to pass and then reiterated. "You and Tommie signed your agreement. Then you and Amy signed the deed on the Lighthouse. However, because the pre-nuptial agreement indicates common ownership where the word 'and' was used instead of 'or' or even 'And/Or' it's a legally binding agreement."

With a concerned look emanating from my face I asked, "Can't we just go to court and tell them what happened?"

Tank shook his head and noted. "George there are legal consequences using 'and' instead of 'or' in a legal document."

"There are?"

"The substitution fundamentally alters the meaning of the documents where 'and' requires both conditions be met while 'or' would have required only one condition or signature be met. Because 'and' was used where "or" should have been, it's created additional obligations for both parties which could result in a breach of contract."

"What?" I replied incredulously.

"A breach of contract," Tank reiterated.

I simply shook my head in disbelief as Tank went on to explain. "A breach of contract occurs when one or more parties fail to fulfill their obligations under the terms of the agreement. This can happen in various ways, such as failing to perform where a party simply doesn't do what they agreed to do. For example, a seller might fail to deliver goods or services as promised or a buyer might fail to pay for them. In your case, because both names are on the titles, when you go to sell, they won't clear the title companies."

"But I'm not planning on selling either one of the properties."

"I know. However, because you're running a business that sells consumable products, you need to have licenses in Wisconsin as well as Federal licenses that require both signatures."

"Jesus!"

Tank continued. "There's another possibility and that's called 'breaching a condition' which refers to conditions essential to the contract. If a condition is not met, the other party can usually consider the contract to be breached. For example, a contract for the sale of a house might be conditioned on the buyer obtaining financing. If the buyer cannot obtain financing, the seller can breach the contract. Right now, with Tommie and Amy gone, you're really limited on the decisions you can make and any income must be put in reserve until the matter is cleared up, one way of the other."

"One way or the other? He's gone! He left the country! He abandoned the business!" My Minnie Point Badass was on the rise. Tank waited for more anger waves to calm before he continued. "There are some rules pertaining to when one business partner unexpectedly abandons the partnership. Unfortunately, you didn't put a dissolution clause in the agreement that would outline procedures for dissolving the partnership in case of a partner's departure. You also didn't put any buy-out provisions in the agreement."

"He's my god damn brother. I never thought this would ever happen."

"But it did!" Tank retorted. "What we need to do is assess the business situation. The farm is past due on last year's property taxes and no one filed state and federal income taxes."

"It's tough to do when you're locked in a cave."

Tank looked at me and offered in an empathetic way, "I know and you know and some branches of the government know, but the ones who collect the money don't know and all they see is a very ripe plumb ready for picking."

"Holy Shit!"

"George, I've begun looking at the financial implications including potential loss of revenue, increased workload, and changes in operational costs. Who did your taxes?"

"Wilco did them."

"So, we can't consult their tax people to understand the implications of the dissolution?"

"I don't have a clue who did the taxes. They were just done. With the building sold I have no idea what happened to all the income statements, tax forms or anything."

"How much wine is left?"

"I have no idea. I know that when the government took the sensor off the west cave, they put a lock on the door. I know there's still wine in the north cave where I was. I don't have any idea how much wine is in the other two caves."

"If it was all there, how much wine would there be?"

"Let's see...six caves with Barrique barrels that hold 225 liters or about 59 gallons each. Around 7,000 gallons which means 2,200 cases of wine. At $50.00 per liter, each case had a wholesale cost of $600 and a total value of a little over a million per cave for a total of roughly seven million if it's all there and none of it has spoiled and we still have the distribution."

"What do you mean distribution?" Tank inquired with furrowed brow.

"You have to realize the wine business is like the entertainment business in that it's incredibly subjective. You build a mystique through reviews where one false move and you've got a whole hell of a lot of vinegar and there's another winery to take your place. To build your reputation requires years of seducing the wine reviewers. Take a year or two off and the value of your wine can easily drop 90%."

"Wow! I had no idea. In other words, you need to reassure clients, critics and vendors of your commitment to providing ongoing services and products."

I looked at Tank and simply inquired. "How do I do that? I'm alone. I've got limited funds. I used to do business based on personal interaction around the world and most people think I'm dead."

Tank noted. "Another possible way is to start legal action under breach of contract. The problem is, Tommie and Amy haven't been gone long enough and you really don't know if they're ever coming back."

"In other words, for now, I'm screwed."

Tank shook his head 'no' and offered. "The third type of legal action is called repudiation. Here, a party indicates they won't perform their obligations under the contract. This can be done explicitly or implied by their actions or words. For example, a seller might tell a buyer they won't deliver the goods they ordered. Or, in your case, your brother doesn't show up to help run the farm and, therefore, you won't pay him his share of any profits you generate."

"OK."

Tank looked at me and noted. "There's one more." "What's that?"

"It's called 'anticipatory repudiation' where a party indicates they won't perform their obligations under the contract before they are due. This can be done explicitly or implied by their actions or words."

"How does this apply to Terrill B&B? My brother's gone. He almost killed me. Isn't that anticipatory enough?"

Tank looked at me and replied. "George, is there any proof he's gone? Is there any proof he's the one who zapped the lock on the cave? You can't do anything until you prove he's gone or tried to kill you."

"God Damn It! What do I do?" I said shaking my head in disbelief.

Tank took a deep breath and noted. "Legally, the consequences of a breach of contract can vary depending on the circumstances. You may be able to rescind the contract which means the contract is canceled and both parties are put back in the position they were in before the contract was made."

"I can't rescind the fact he's my brother. I can't rescind the fact we have agreements stating we're partners."

Tank looked down at the porch floor and nodded. "It's just one of the options and you're right, it's not a strong option. I'm just outlining what may take place. The second option is for you to sue for damages for monetary compensation. The damages may be compensatory, meaning they're intended to put Tommie, or the non- breaching party, in the position he would have been in if the contract had been performed. The damages may also be punitive, meaning they're intended to punish the breaching party for their wrongdoing."

"How in hell do I do that when he skipped the country and what about Amy?"

Tank shook his head and noted. "Well, that's the sticky part. With the pre-nup, she's entitled to half of anything you'd recover."

"Holy shit!"

"I know. The final option is seeking what's called 'specific performance' where you can ask the court to order the breaching party, namely Tommie, to perform his obligations under the contract. This is normally only available if the breaching party has unique or rare skills or abilities or if the subject matter of the contract is unique or rare."

"That's it?"

"That's it. All three are going to be long, drawn out legal matters that could take years."

"And what do I do until then?" "That's the other bad news." "What?"

"The retirement money you have in the bank and the Lighthouse are in both your and Amy's name and can't be touched without both signatures."

"So, I'm not back to where I was financially?"

"You are. However, you can't touch those funds without her signature."

"So how much money do I have?"

"Around a hundred thousand dollars but you owe property and income taxes on Terrill B&B."

"How much are those?"

"Around $35,000."

"You mean I've got $65,000 left?" "Yes!"

"That's all?" I offered as I shook my head in dismay. "Sorry, George!"

I looked at Tank and could see he sensed my frustration as I wanted to ask, 'why didn't you say something earlier?' However, I already knew what his response would be. I was in no mental shape for issues like this and so I held up my hands as if to stop him and simply said. "What do we do now?"

Tank had a forlorn look on his face and offered. "The ambiguity created may lead to disputes between you and Tommie, as well as you and Amy. These disputes could potentially result in costly and time-consuming litigation."

"In other words, I don't own the farm?" "Half, yes with Amy. All of it? Legally, no." "And the Lighthouse?"

"Same."

"What about the funds I received from the settlement with Wilco?"

"Amy has the right to claim half of those as well and they're frozen without both signatures."

"Simply because of the word "and" instead of "or"? "Sorry, George. Yes."

"What in hell do I do now?"

Tank took another deep breath and replied. "I'm going to have to do some digging but it could get messy."

I snapped. "You mean, my brother tries to kill me and my wife runs off with her mistress and I'm the one getting screwed?"

"George, I'm not saying that. What I'm saying is right now things aren't as absolute as they would have been had whomever wrote the pre-nup put the word 'or' instead of 'and'. You don't know who wrote the agreements do you?"

I thought back and realized that both of them were written by someone at Wilco as I leaned back in the old wicker rocker and shook my head in dismay and then noted. "They're gone.

They've left the country and no one knows where they are. They're they're missing persons. Don't I have some rights?

Tank looked at me with the same look the doctor had when I was informed I had cancer and noted. "Generally, a relative can't simply claim ownership of a missing person's property without legal proceedings. In most cases, a court must declare the person legally dead before their property can be distributed. This process involves a legal declaration of presumptive death, which often requires a certain amount of time to pass since the person was last seen or heard from."

"But they're not dead. Is that the Federal law or Wisconsin's?" Tank gazed at me and added. "Wisconsin law requires a waiting period of seven years before a missing person can be presumed dead. This means relatives must wait at least seven years from the last time the person was seen or heard from before they can initiate legal proceedings. However, this waiting period can be shortened if there's strong evidence suggesting the person died

in a specific incident, such as a natural disaster or plane crash."

"Well, the government reported they died in the plane crash." "George, do you really think that's what happened? If you ask the government to verify it, they'll deny it."

"Why?"

"First, because it didn't happen. Second, they don't want to admit they lied. Finally, because it would tip their hand about trying to find Derrick."

"What about Saint Martin?"

Tank shook his head and replied. "I looked into that and found out that Saint Martin, as a French overseas territory, has the same laws as France where the waiting period before a missing person can be presumed dead requires five years. However, like Wisconsin, this waiting period can be shortened if there's strong evidence suggesting the person died in a specific incident, such as a natural disaster or accident."

"But Amy isn't dead or at least we don't think so."

"George, we don't know that and the governments don't

know either. Therefore we can't go to court and claim she is without proof. In cases like this, generally, a relative cannot simply claim ownership of a missing person's property without legal proceedings. In most cases, the court must declare the person legally dead before their property can be distributed. This process typically involves a legal declaration of presumptive death, which often requires a certain amount of time to pass since the person was last seen or heard from."

"How long would that take?" "Three to five years."

"I'm screwed?"

"No, you just can't make any major decisions that will affect the value of the estate as it currently exists. What we need to do is have both properties surveyed to determine their worth and then put them in separate trusts. In so doing, you've established value and we can work from there."

"What do I do?"

"First, you've got your personal savings so you're not going to go hungry. Then, you can sell the wine and bourbon and start your new Wagyu herd. All you're going to need to do is put half the profits, if there are any, away for your brother and half of the other half away for Amy. It's really important you don't lose money. If you do, either one of them can come after you for breach of contract and claim the entire farm."

"What about Saint Martin?"

Tank smiled as if in relief and noted, "Well, that's some good news."

"What's that?"

"I've been able to convince the government to make me conservator of both the farm and the Lighthouse."

"What does that mean?"

"A conservator of property is a person appointed by a court to manage the financial affairs of the estate when it's unable to do so itself. You have the legal authority to make financial decisions on behalf of the estate such as paying bills and investing money but you can't sell the property."

"OK. That's good news," I replied.

Tank added. "I have a fiduciary duty to act in the best interests of Terrill B&B and must be honest, loyal, and prudent in my decision-making and remain subject to court supervision that may require I obtain approval for certain actions, such as making significant investments."

"And how do I fit in?" I inquired.

Tank smiled as noted, "It means **we** have the freedom to operate both until we get things cleaned up."

"Where do **we** start?" I asked.

Tank looked at me and added. "Right now, the Lighthouse is costing a lot of money each month just for maintenance and security. We need to transition it into something that generates income instead of expenses."

"How do we do that?'

"Find a management company down there and put it up on VRBO."

"And the farm?"

"My vote would be to create the two trusts. This would take any liability away from us while still allowing you to have a secured partial ownership and therefore control."

"How do we do that?" I asked.

"I can do it. It's not that tough. I've got all the papers and all you'll need to do is sign them when I'm done. Do you want me to be the executor?"

"Of course. You're the only ones, other than 'V' and Rodney I can trust." My mind was a whirling dervish when I then asked. "What about Melia's money?"

Tank raised his hands so that both palms were up and replied. "I'm certain the government has taken care of that when they put her in hiding."

I shook my head and realized I had a real mess on my hands. I had a farm worth millions where the wine, bourdon and cattle businesses represented potential viable income. I had a house on Saint Martin that was being called the jewel of the island. Both of which there was nothing I could do simply because, legally, I actually only owned half of them.

If I decided to sue, it would take years. It was then I realized, I needed to find Tommie and Amy and get papers signed giving me full ownership. But how in hell do you do that when I have no idea where they are and then whether they'd even cooperate or even if they were still alive?

I looked at Tank and realized he'd done an awful lot for me. I thanked him and promised I'd make it up to him when I could afford to. He shook his head in gratitude. It was then I noted that I felt my only option was to find Tommie and Amy and have them change the agreements from 'and' to 'or'.

"And/Or!" I'd created a phrase that had no meaning to anyone but me.

Doctor Roberts:

As I was going through my wallet and trying to figure out what I needed to keep and what I could get rid of, I looked behind by driver's license and found Doctor Roberts business card. My mind went back to Area 51 as I came to realize he'd actually saved me from insanity by making my return very gradual. I realized that in all the hubbub with the NIA and all, I never had the chance to properly say thank you.

I flipped the business card over and on the back was a handwritten phone number and the words 'call me if need be.' While I felt I was on my way to recovery, I had this feeling of regret that I'd never said thank you and slowly dialed the number on the back.

"Hello."

"Doctor Roberts, it's George, George Terrill." "George, how are you?"

"I'm fine. I'm doing better. I never had the opportunity to say thank you for all you did nor me."

"No problem, George."

"Doctor Roberts, I've been doing a lot of reading and learned an awful lot since we were together and I know now what all you did for me and again, I just want to say thanks."

"George, it's part of my job. Just like you have your foundation."

I paused and noted the Foundation had been closed. "I'm sorry to hear that."

"Well, a lot happened and, in the end, all the good we did wasn't good enough." I replied.

"Don't say that. You started a movement that really helped a lot of people."

"Thank you."

"How are you really doing?" Doctor Roberts asked in a very sincere way.

I didn't want to get into what was going on but he had a way about him that was able to pull things out of me as I replied. "Well, things are pretty good but not great."

"What's going on?" Roberts asked with a concerned tone to his voice.

"I've moved back to our family farm and, well, things are a lot more complicated than I thought they'd be."

"How?" Roberts asked.

"First my wife, Amy, thought I was dead and left the country with her mistress."

"OK, we talked about Amy and how she emotionally challenged you at times."

"Doc. I understand what happened and why she did it. I still love her but realize it might be in the past tense on her part."

"That's healthy."

"The issue is... the issue is when we were about to get married I asked for and got a prenuptial agreement."

"And?"

"I didn't have two nickels to rub together and her dad was rich and I didn't think I had anything to risk and wanted to show the world I didn't marry Amy for her money."

I heard a deep breath on the other end as Doctor Roberts urged me with "And..."

"Well, Amy put the Pre-nup together and I signed it without reading it. I figured I had nothing so what was the risk?"

"And now?"

" I should have read it because instead of 'or', Amy or whoever wrote the agreement used the word 'and'."

"Oh, boy!"

"I own half the family farm, but can't do anything with it because it all needs Amy's signature."

There was a long pause on the other end and then the Doc's tone changed as he explained. "George, few people realize either the legal or psychological consequences of the difference between the two words. I can't speak about the legal aspect but here are some of the consequences psychologically. While the choice between 'and' and 'or' might seem like a minor linguistic detail, it can have subtle psychological implications. Here are a few potential psychological consequences."

"Such as?" I inquired.

"First there are increased expectations simply because using the word 'and' means you're suggesting both conditions or actions are expected or desired. This can create higher expectations for yourself or others, leading to potential disappointment or frustration if one or both conditions are not met." "Second, there are limited options because 'and' can narrow down the possibilities by implying that only both conditions or actions are acceptable thereby limiting flexibility and creativity."

"I'm realizing that now."

Doctor Roberts continued. "This can cause increased stress simply because the expectation of fulfilling multiple conditions or actions simultaneously can increase stress and anxiety creating a sense of pressure or overwhelming limitations. In some situations, it can result in decreased motivation. If the conditions or actions connected by 'and' seem overwhelming or unattainable, it can decrease motivation and lead to procrastination or avoidance. Finally, it can lead to misunderstandings simply because, in certain contexts, using 'and' instead of 'or' can lead to misinterpretations."

"So, in other words, it can affect a person emotionally?" I inquired.

"George, there's a big difference between a psychological response and an emotional response."

"There is?"

Roberts offered. "Psychological responses and emotional responses are both reactions to stimuli but they differ in their nature and origin."

"What do you mean? I asked, now concerned that my own self-evaluation wasn't as apparent as I thought it was.

Roberts continued. "Psychological responses are cognitive processes that primarily involve thoughts, beliefs, and perceptions that are rational and logical and often based on reason and analysis. As such they are conscious and deliberate and can be controlled or modified."

"Emotional responses are what are called 'affective states' that primarily involve feelings and sensations that can be both intentional and automatic and, as such, both conscious and unconscious that normally precipitate physiological reactions such as increased heart rate, and sweating."

"All right." I replied wondering where this was going as Doctor Roberts continued. "In essence, psychological responses are more cognitive and deliberate, while emotional responses are more affective and often automatic. However, it's important to note that psychological and emotional responses can interact and influence each other. For example, a negative psychological thought can trigger an emotional response like sadness, and an emotional response like anger can influence cognitive processes like decision-making."

Doctor Roberts continued. "You need to realize George that using 'and' can create a sense of expectation or pressure. While at the same time create levels of disappointment and frustration, such that, if one or both conditions connected by 'and' are not met, it can lead to feelings of disappointment or frustration."

Boy, he had that right. I was frustrated because I couldn't move on with my life. At the same time, I was disappointed in myself for never reading the agreement in the first place. What a dolt!

Roberts continued. "When the word 'or' is used it can provide a sense of relief or flexibility. For example, saying 'I can either go to the beach or the mountains' suggests that both options are acceptable reducing feelings of stress or pressure. However, using 'or' can also lead to feelings of indecision or uncertainty where multiple options to choose from, can be difficult to decide which one is best." George, in my field of study, the choice between 'and' and 'or' have us believe they can influence emotions in various ways where using 'and' can create expectations and pressure, while using "or" can provide flexibility but also lead to indecision. The best choice depends on the specific context and the desired emotional outcome."

There was a pause and then the good doctor added. "George, I'm certain that whomever developed the agreement was only thinking of the good things and not what has transpired."

"Really, don't blame anyone including yourself. On your side, when you have nothing and someone puts a document in front of you where you believe you have no risk and, therefore, no potential loss, you sign it. It happens all the time. It doesn't mean you were stupid. It certainly doesn't mean you were naive. What it does mean is that you were, or make that are, in love with Amy and because of that, simply believed in the best of everything."

I didn't know if I should be relieved or even more depressed. I did know I appreciated the conversation as I noted, "Doc, I again want to thank you for the way you helped me and now I want to thank you for what you've shared tonight. I've felt like a complete idiot and appreciate the fact you've taken the time to clarify things. If you're ever in Wisconsin, I want you to come to the farm and go with me to the Forest. I'd love to get your opinion on what transpires when you experience what I and some others have felt and how it changed our lives."

"I'd like that George. Do me a favor though." "What's that?" I asked.

"Keep my card and number. I'd really like to know how this all turns out."

"I'll do that Doc, and, again, thank you."

I hung up the receiver on dad's 1970's phone, leaned back in his leather chair and realized Doctor Roberts had simply clarified the mess I was in, while making me realize I wasn't a fool, just a kid in love where the consequence of the word 'and' instead 'or' had created a compound/complex legal situation that could be rectified if I only knew how.

The Offer:

It was Sunday and after our call on Thursday, I didn't know what to expect from Megan. At precisely seven, I called her cellphone and she answered.

"Hi, how are you?" I asked, with a great deal of concern. "I'm OK," was her brief reply.

"Are you at the hotel?"

"No, Charlie's out of town. I'm at the house. Ellie and I aren't speaking."

"I'm sorry!"

"Charlie did exactly what you said he would. He left here, went to the studio and told Ellie I was the one who wanted to do it."

"Did you explain?"

"Ellie wouldn't listen. She said she always thought I wanted more than what we'd arranged. She said the photo above my bed was my way of...of seducing Charlie."

"I'm so sorry, Megan."

"I told Ellie, she was the one who took the picture. She was the one who made the statues. She...she...she well, she, let's just, let's just leave it there."

I had no idea what Megan was referring to but had an inkling and realized it was best to not ask. I could almost feel Megan's angst as I inquired, "Did you tell them you wanted out?"

"Yes, and they said they couldn't afford to buy me out and offered $50,000."

"Fifty-Thousand?" That's ridiculous."

"I know. My share of the mortgage is $400,000."

I guess Charlie wanted to screw Megan financially when he couldn't any other way as I inquired. "Do you have a copy of the agreement?"

"Yes."

"Can you scan it and e-mail it to me and I'll have Tank, my lawyer, look it over?"

Now Megan was crying as she asked, "What am I going to do?"

"Hang in there. We'll get you out of this."

Between rasps Megan added, "Friday, the doctors came to agreement with the hospital. The hospital takes over at the end of the month."

"What about you?"

"What do you think? I'm the odd person out." "That day?"

"I think so."

"What about the program?"

"What do you think? It's all about money and they don't see any revenue in the program."

"Bastards!"

Now the crying was getting intense as I waited for the first volley to diminish and then inquired. "Any form of compensation?"

"One month's pay for every year I was here. In other words six month's salary plus insurance."

"Tell you what. Hang in there and let me see what Tank comes up with. You know Charlie's schedule and do like I said and go to the hotel whenever he's going to be in town. It's only three weeks, then come back here and stay with me while you figure out what you're going to do."

The crying subsided as Megan asked, "You wouldn't mind?" "I don't and I'm certain the frogs and mosquitoes would like someone else to croak at or bite instead of boney old me."

Megan was calming down and inquired. "How are you doing?"

I paused to think what I should say and then replied. "I had one of my spells on Thursday but they seem to be getting milder. All my research indicates it can take up to five years to finally resolve all the issues."

"Have you been into Mineral Point?" "Nope."

"How did the haircut go?"

"Oh, boy. I forgot to send you the pictures. Tell you what. Hold on and I'll send them now."

I got my cellphone and clicked on the photos and sent her the before-and-after photos and then offered. "Promise you won't laugh?"

"Wow! What a difference? You really did look like a hermit."

"I know. Had I gone into town, all the townies would have thought that, too."

Megan paused and noted, "You've got to promise me, you'll go into town before next Sunday."

"I will if you promise to send me a photo of you. All I have are memories."

"G? PG? or "R?" was the reply with the girlie giggle that told me Megan was coming out of her funk.

"What no "X"? I teased.

"I'll save those for the frogs and mosquitoes," Megan teased. "'X' rated photos of frogs? I can only imagine what they'd be like. Yikes!"

We both had a good laugh that was the tonic we needed as I got serious for a moment. "I'm glad I have you in my life. Without you, I'd never laugh."

"George, the feeling's the same." "Have a good week."

"You, too, and I'll send you a photo a little later."

"Goodnight."

"I like that better than 'goodbye', don't you?" Megan noted.

"Yes." I said as I carefully placed the receiver on the base realizing I was probably the only person in Wisconsin who still had a beige, push-button, desk-top phone where the receiver still had a curly cord.

Sold:

The "G" rated photo arrived and I smiled. The week rolled by and then the next and then it was month's end where everything Megan forecasted came true. She was released and given her severance. She sent Ellie and Charlie a certified letter indicating she was exercising her option and offering her third of the house to them for $450,000 which they denied. Megan called and I got her in touch with Tank who told her to send him a copy of the agreement even though he wasn't licensed to practice law in Georgia.

Tank read the agreement and agreed with Megan. She had the right to offer her third to Ellie and Charlie and when they refused, put the house on the market such that Ellie and Charlie would be required to buy their own house. To do so, Megan placed the house on the market and priced it at $1.5 million which meant instead of paying Megan $450,000 and taking out a second mortgage, they would need to not only re-finance at a higher interest rate but pay more money.

Ellie and Charlie got cute and when there was a realtor open house, they trashed the place. Nothing permanent but just enough to make the place look like a mess. Unbeknownst to them, one of the 'realtors' was a friend of Megan's who took photos. Megan sent the photos to Tank and a writ was drawn up indicating attempted fraud by deception where the key point was that Ellie and Charlie were intentionally trying to reduce the value of the house to lower their own re-purchase price.

I remembered our lawyers in Atlanta and gave Dan Raskin a call. I explained the situation and asked if someone on his staff could help. We'd paid them a lot of money and it was a small favor. As is the case with so many people, Raskin had a case of amnesia when it came to who helped whom. Funny how money does that.

I told Dan I was asking for a favor. I told him that when my funds were released, he'd get paid. There was reticence on the other end and so I lowered the boom. "Listen Dan, we paid your firm twenty million dollars. All I'm asking is that you scare the shit out of two assholes by writing a single letter."

Raskin agreed and made sure it was sent on their best stationary and was remitted via certified mail. He sent me a copy and it would have scared me too in that it covered all the civil and then some capital crimes involved. Anyway, amazingly, 'E' and 'C' got the hint, went to the bank, used their equity and bought out Megan. After all the fees, remaining balance and crap, Megan walked away with $30,000. Whoopee! But that's better than buying a dead horse as dad would say.

That Sunday the call came through and Megan noted that all of her belongings were in public storage and she was at the hotel. Once again, I offered the choice of temporarily staying at the farm. While reluctant, and with her home family situation on less than wonderful terms, she agreed.

I asked Megan how she was going to get her belongings back to Wisconsin and she didn't know. She had her Lexus and the stuff she had was too much for her car or even one of those small U-Haul trailers you tow behind the car.

I tentatively offered to fly to Atlanta and help her load a rental truck and drive it to Wisconsin as fear churned within me that she'd say yes. Megan said she'd think about it which meant, 'no.' Instead, Megan rented a truck, loaded her belongings and then had the car attached to the back of the rental truck. She planned on two days from Atlanta to Waldwick with a stop somewhere in Southern Indiana or Northern Kentucky. I told her to call me when she got to the hotel just to let me know she was OK. She was and did.

Late the following afternoon Megan called from just south of Beloit and asked me the best way to Waldwick. I told her to take Highway Eleven west to Highway 23 and gave her directions and to call me when she got to Darlington which she did. I told her to come north on Highway 23 to Highway G west, turn right on Furnace Hill Road and it would be the fourth farm on the right.

It was just about dusk when I heard the truck on the driveway gravel. I took a deep breath and wondered if I was doing the right thing. Megan pulled in as I walked down to meet her. My God, the feelings I had in Atlanta flowed through my body as a trembler of apprehension made me quiver. I smiled and offered. "Welcome to Waldwick."

Megan looked weary as she presented a weak smile as I offered, "You look beat."

"I've never driven a big truck before and you know what, I never want to do that again."

"Is all your stuff in the truck?" I inquired.

"No, my hangar clothes are in the car," as Megan nodded towards the Lexus.

"How about taking your clothes in the house tonight and we can unpack the truck in the morning?"

"Can I take a shower?"

"Well, I don't know about that." I joked.

A soft smile made its way across Megan's lips as I made my way to the Lexus, opened the door and saw the entire back seat stuffed with clothes which were still all on hangars. I looked at Megan and inquired. "Why don't we do this? Pick out what you want to wear tonight, then tomorrow we can take our time. You're too tired and there's a lot of clothes here."

Megan nodded that she agreed and took the key fob and pressed the trunk release button. Pulling out a suitcase, she simply smiled as she was way ahead of me. With that, we made our way into the house where Megan placed her suitcase next to the front door before offering. "George, I really appreciate this."

"What are friends for?" I replied before inquiring. "Are you hungry?"

Megan nodded, "Yes".

"Tell you what, why don't you get freshened up and I'll make dinner. You have your choice. The upstairs bathroom has an old-fashioned tub with a plastic shower curtain around it. If you want, and this will probably sound weird, there's a shower down in the barn. Tommie had one of those massaging shower heads installed and it has one of those wands with the pulsating heads on it."

"Even in the winter?" Megan inquired. "There's infrared heaters built into the ceiling."

I'd forgotten to mention that, while we called it the barn, it was actually Su's lab area where Francis and Aristotle had their training facility. I also forgot to mention, it was where Francis and Aristotle had their weekly baths and was literally big enough to hold either two pigs or six people.

Megan thought it over and chose the barn. She retrieved a small overnight case she probably used at the hotel as I got the barn keys off the hook and we made our way to the door.

Passing the barn doors, we made our way to Su's lab and training facility. Upon opening the door, Megan let out a gasp. "This isn't a barn, this is a lab of some sort. I thought I'd be taking a shower where the cows used to be."

I sort of shrugged and was reluctant to tell her who used the shower last...two pigs. I explained what the lab was for, along with the training area and took her to the shower room, opened a cabinet and took out one regular and two over-sized bath towels along with a new bar of soap and shampoo and said, "I hope you like Porterhouse Steak".

"My favorite," Megan replied.

I excused myself and told Megan to take her time and then come back up to the house when she was done. I made my way back to the house, took Megan's suitcase and put it in mom and dad's bedroom and went back downstairs, went out in the back yard and started the Weber grill.

As I was setting the table on the porch Megan appeared wrapped in one of the over-sized towels with the smaller towel wrapped around her head. I walked back into the house as Megan opened the front door, smiled and glanced at where her suitcase had been as I noted. "I put your suitcase upstairs in the bedroom on the right."

With the big towel wrapped under her arms, it covered her torso and fell just below never-never land as Amy called it.

"Let me go get dressed." Megan announced. As she made her way to the stairs, I glanced and caught a peek at the bottom of her bare butt. I know I shouldn't have but some things never change.

A little while later, Megan appeared and exclaimed with a sigh of relief..."So much better."

I nodded, smiled and offered. "Porterhouse, baked potato, salad and some of the Terrill B&B Pinot Noir. I hope you don't mind the wine being chilled. I can't drink red wine at room temperature anymore as the warmth softens the taste."

"If you haven't been to town, how do you get your food?" Megan asked with a frown on her face.

"There was a lot here when I arrived and now I just order it on the internet and have it Ubered. They take my credit card and the delivery person leaves it on the front stoop."

"You still haven't been into town, have you?"

"Not yet. I've been waiting for a reason and she showed up today."

"Megan put the food on the plates and we made our way out on the screen porch. The warm breeze made it a wonderful way to end the day. As we sat looking at each other, I realized how beautiful Megan really was as our conversation dealt with the house sale, trip and future. I told Megan she was welcome to stay as long as she wanted and she was both grateful and I think a bit confused, not knowing where the relationship was going or how it would end. Quite honestly, neither did I.

It was nearly nine when we finished the bottle of B&B. Needless to say, there had been jokes about my visit to her house and the spilled wine she called Chateau Lafitte George and the statues out by her, or make that, former pool. There was no discussion of the clinic or the classes but then we'd talked about them on the phone and you can only talk so much in one night, especially when the number of nights together was open-ended.

Megan was trying to hide her exhaustion and cover the yawns when I suggested she head for bed and I'd clean up. I think those words were what she needed to hear as they set the parameters on where we were and what was happening between us.

"Good night!" Megan whispered. "Thank you."

"What are friends for?" I replied as I watched her make her way upstairs and heard the bedroom door close. It was then I smiled. It seemed good to have someone to talk to. Perhaps, it was what I'd been missing and was glad she was there.

Squiggly Bacon:

I've always been an early riser and so I got up, went out and disconnected the Lexus from the rental truck, went in the barn, got a four-foot-long piece of doweling and came back in the house. Megan came down all sleepy eyed and said, 'good morning,' wearing a white tee shirt that came down to the middle of her thighs. I smiled and asked her what she wanted for breakfast.

"Coffee?"

"Yes!"

"Eggs?"

"Please!"

"Bacon?"

"Yes?"

"Squiggly or crisp?"

"Huh?"

"Squiggly is when the bacon's not as crisp."

"How are you having yours?"

"I don't eat bacon or pork."

"You don't. Why not? Religion?" Megan offered with an inquisitive frown.

I told her all about Francis and how he was trained to communicate and what he shared with us.

Megan simply shook her head in disbelief and asked. "Why the bacon?"

"In case you liked it."

"You mean you bought bacon in case I liked it? What would you do if I didn't?"

"Put it out for the birds."

"You're one very special man, George Terrill."

I was a bit embarrassed by the compliment. It had been a long time since anyone said anything nice about me. I smiled and said, "I disconnected the Lexus from the truck. The ground is hard and so, instead of walking a dozen times from the driveway to the house, why don't you pull the car up to the front door and we can unload it that way?"

"Should I take my shower first?" Megan inquired.

"You can if you want to but it's supposed to be in the low nineties today and quite humid. My suggestion would be to wait until after we're done unloading the car and truck. Then, before we take the truck to Dodgeville, get cleaned up and we can eat over there. There's a Mexican restaurant which is as good as it gets."

"Mexican in Dodgeville?"

I looked at Megan and replied in my weak attempt to sound like a radio announcer. "Corralejo Mexican Grill is a vibrant gem waiting to be explored. Renowned for its immaculate cleanliness and welcoming atmosphere, this restaurant provides a feast for the senses. With generous portions, reasonable prices, and the option to customize your drink with a personal touch of tequila, Corralejo Mexican Grill stands out as a must-visit destination in Dodgeville for an unforgettable Mexican dining extravaganza."

"In other words, you like it," Megan replied with a smile. "Nope. I love it and it's been nearly three years since I've been there."

We had breakfast, without bacon I might add, and Megan got the Lexus keys and pulled the car up to the front door. It took us less than fifteen minutes to take all the hangar clothes out of the car and into the living room. With it as hot as it was, there was no sense keeping the front door open and the air conditioner running.

I got the doweling and saw the eyebrows curl in as I noted. "Instead of a dozen trips upstairs, we can load the clothes on the pole and take them up that way."

"You're one smart man, Mister Terrill."

I smiled and sort of shook my head. With Megan at the front and me at the rear, the first load went fine. We got overconfident and tried to add more clothes for the second load. Mistake! Half way up the stairs, all the clothes fell off and I felt like a fool.

"Not so smart?" I offered and we both giggled.

Picking up the clothes, we made it up to mom and dad's bedroom and put the clothes on the bed. I told Megan to put the clothes away and I'd take care of the breakfast dishes. Little did I know she had a method of organization first by clothing type and then color. She was way ahead of me when it came to organization. "I've got more clothes in the truck in some boxes," Megan announced.

"How many?" "Five or six."

"OK. Where are they located?"

"I loaded them last and so they're right behind the door."

"Great, I'll start hauling and you can begin putting them away. OK?"

I drove the Lexus back down to the driveway and opened the back of the truck. It was full. I saw the boxes labelled 'clothes' and began walking with one back to the house. With only five boxes and the rest of the stuff going in the barn, it made no sense to drive the truck on the yard.

It was only eleven o'clock and we already had what dad called 'Memphis Weather'... oppressively hot and incredibly humid... as beads of sweat formed on my forehead and my tee-shirt was already sticking to my back. I thought to myself, 'people always think weather in Wisconsin is bad. Yet living like this or with earthquakes and forest fires? We shovel our problems. They can have the rest.

It only took about 20 minutes and the clothes were all in the house. I brought the last box in and simply took it up to mom and dad's bedroom. All the boxes were taped shut and Megan used what we called security tape that had the nylon strings imbedded to make the tape stronger upon which Megan used a magic marker to label what was inside.

Trying to pull the tape off by hand would be a real pain and so I offered. "If you don't mind, I'll get a knife and open the boxes for you and then you can put the clothes in the dresser. Then I can remove the bottom tape so the boxes will fold flat."

"Sounds good," Megan responded.

I went to the kitchen, got an old paring knife and came back upstairs. Putting the first box on the bed, the label read 'tops' and so I carefully sliced open the tape as Megan took the t-shirts as we'd call them and put them in one of the empty dresser drawers as I slit the bottom tape and folded the carton flat.

With this procedure in place, we went through socks, more tops and then a box labelled 'undies.' I paused as Megan got this pensive look on her face and noted. "It's OK George, there's nothing in there you haven't seen before."

I opened the carton to a plethora of different 'undie' styles, fabrics and colors as Megan opened the top right dresser drawer and loaded the goods into their new home. I looked at the last box and the label was 'others' and had no idea what it referenced. I looked at Megan and she caught my drift and noted, "Mainly bras and things."

After the undie box, I guess I had permission to proceed, shrugged and slit the tape. Inside was yet another plethora of different colors, styles and shapes. I had no idea!

Megan caught my somewhat sardonic grin and inquired. "What's so funny?"

I looked at her and admitted that all the contents reminded me of Amy.

"Amy? Why Amy?" Megan inquired with a bit of a frown on her face.

"Because she hated wearing bras. I mean, the only time she wore one was when we had somewhere public to go and to the office. When she'd come home, the first thing she'd do is ditch the thing. She called them her 'holsters' and was never and I mean never, comfortable wearing one."

Megan grinned and I think was somewhat relieved as I continued. "Whenever we were home she'd go 'sans-a-bra' as she called it, and hardly ever wore one in France and definitely not on Saint Martin. If I remember, I think she did have one in France, just in case, but there was never one in Saint Martin."

Megan was smiling and said, "My kind of girl. They're so uncomfortable, especially in the heat."

I looked at Megan and jokingly said, "When it's this hot, you can run around naked for all I care."

Megan got a more serious expression on her face as she asked. "So, you wouldn't mind?"

"No! not at all, except when we go into town. You've got to realize Mineral Point is quite conservative."

Megan paused and leaned on the top of the dresser before divulging. "George, I'm a naturist."

"You mean a nudist?" I incredulously asked.

"No, not a nudist!" Megan said with a quite unyielding tone to her voice. "Nudists primarily practice in social settings that emphasize the act of nudity itself, without necessarily implying a deeper philosophical or lifestyle connection to nature. A naturist's beliefs encompass a broader lifestyle philosophy that values harmony with nature and a connection to the natural world to the point that the social aspect is secondary, if a factor at all, to the point that what you do or don't do is dependent on the social situation. In my case, my preference is to enjoy the sensations and not the socialization. This allows me to develop a way of life in harmony with nature, with the purpose of encouraging respect for myself, others and the environment."

After a long pause, Megan continued. "Because of what I do, or make that, what I did career-wise, I became ambivalent to the human body. Because of my 'journey' where I tried to find answers to questions I didn't even know I had, I needed to find something that would take some of the stress out of my life and inject a way to accept myself for what I am."

Megan inquired, "Is what I do for everyone? Hardly! This experience is for anyone who's craving the freedom to be themselves, without judgment or pretense, to allow them to cultivate a deeper sense of intimacy with the natural world and their own body, to heal trauma, shame and guilt and appreciate the raw beauty of their human form, including all imperfections, while awakening the untamed, primal aspects of their being as they embrace their natural instincts and desires."

"This allows them to foster a deeper connection with Mother Earth, accept all their emotions, and release the societal shame and disgrace attached to their sensuality and sexuality and lets them see their own beauty in a way they've never seen before."

"In so doing George, I had an awakening and a journey that allowed me to begin a self-directed retreat away from all that had bound me up in so many ways...materialism, self-centeredness, indifference towards others... all the things people retain as they grasp for that next ring up the ladder of success."

Woah! This was getting serious.

Megan added. "The more I looked, the deeper I got, until I realized I needed to unwind both physically and mentally. In studying ways to do so, I looked at Eastern religions and why people in Italy and Japan live longer and found the secret was not only what they ate but the fact they lived a life with less stress which was one of the reasons so much of my life was screwed up."

Megan continued. "There are so many reasons why these people live longer and fuller lives than we do. First, what they eat is rich in antioxidants, nutrients and probiotics without all the chemicals American food manufacturers are allowed to add to make its shelf life longer. Then, it's their lifestyle with regular physical activity, strong social connections and the one thing I truly believe in and that's stress management. Beyond that, they consider preventive health care to be a right and not a business."

Shaking her head somewhat in dismay Megan added. "When I went down the 'rabbit hole' as I call it, and finally hit bottom, I truly didn't like what I saw. Not the environment I was in, nor myself. In so doing, I looked at my values, practices and things that helped me unwind and realized I was at peace when I was enveloped in nature."

Wow, this was sounding more like Amy by the minute.

"I began practicing, Shin Rin Yoku, or forest bathing, which we've talked about. As I progressed and began relying on my senses beyond sight, the more I became attuned to my body and the sensory messages it was receiving that I literally had been cancelling out."

"With the house and yard and the way it was in Atlanta with both Ellie and Charlie rarely home, I had the opportunity to begin the process of assimilation in what I felt was total outdoor privacy. Like you and your Theory of Acclimation, I quickly became accustomed to full body sensory activation. In so doing, I became liberated to the point I now consider myself to be a naturist stemming from my desire for greater freedom, connection with nature and acceptance of my body and how it's freed from the constraints and therefore the stress I used to feel."

"So you want to run around naked?" I asked.

Megan glanced out the bedroom window and then back at me with a taciturn look. "No silly! That would be ludicrous. However, when circumstances are right, I find freedom and comfort in accepting my body with or without the restraints of clothing and appreciate the natural beauty of the human form and feel more connected to myself. It's been a journey of self-acceptance and overcoming my image insecurities as I now feel a deep connection to nature and believe I'm able to experience the natural world more intimately to promote mindfulness and a sense of presence in the moment."

Megan looked directly at me and continued. "This allows me to fully engage with my surroundings while being present and aware of my thoughts and feelings without apprehension or judgment simply by paying attention to the current moment, rather than worrying about the past or future. In so doing I believe I'm able to calm my mind and reduce my cortisol levels thereby helping me improve my focus and concentration, better manage my emotions and respond to situations with greater clarity to the point I'm actually experiencing reduced blood pressure and improved sleep."

"But why do you need to be naked to do all that?" I asked, not trying to start a debate but better understand the rationale.

Megan stopped folding the clothes, looked at me and added. "Many people don't need to. However, I must admit, I draw inspiration from naturalistic philosophies, believing that nudity is a natural state of being and humans should strive to live in harmony with nature. To this point I've assimilated, realizing that allowing all my senses to become involved is more effective in allowing me to reach my ultimate goal of tranquility and self-acceptance but doing so only in the right time and right place where I feel comfortable and not conspicuous."

Megan paused and asked, "have you ever heard of Walt Whitman?"

"Sure! My grandma used to get a box of his chocolates at Christmas. I didn't like them because you never knew which one you were picking and Grandma wouldn't let us take a bite and put the ones we didn't like back."

"No, silly, the poet!" Megan replied with a grin. Turning serious, she added. "I think I'm a lot like Walt Whitman who embraced life as a natural and healthy state. He once wrote, "Nature was naked, and I was also."

I looked at Megan, got serious and noted, "'Leaves of Grass' is famous. It revolutionized American poetry in several ways. First, Whitman pioneered the use of free verse, breaking away from traditional rhyme schemes and metrical structures allowing a more natural and conversational style, that captured the rhythms of everyday speech. Whitman's use of long, flowing lines, vivid imagery, and cataloging techniques created a unique and powerful poetic voice."

Megan appeared a bit surprised and asked. "How do you know so much about Whitman?"

"Because I took courses in creative writing where we needed to study great authors and poets, particularly those who changed literary styles and way to create expressions."

Megan looked at me and smiled as she continued. "As much as his structure, there's more to him than that. Whitman celebrated the individual and their unique experiences, emphasizing the importance of self-discovery and self-expression."

I smiled and thought of the famous line from 'Children of

Adam,' *"A woman waits for me, she contains all, Nothing is lacking, yet all is lacking, I know it, I feel it, I wait."* and wondered, is this what's happening to me?

Megan looked in my eyes and we connected as if her soul was speaking to mine as she added. "George, 80% of all our sensory information comes from what we see. 10% comes from what we hear. One percent from what we touch and 1% from what we smell. Yet touch and smell play crucial roles in our emotional responses, memories, and overall quality of life."

"What about the other 8%?" I asked.

Megan smiled and added. "I asked myself that when I first began studying and learned that the remaining 8% can be attributed to several other senses that contribute to our overall experience of the world. First is our *'vestibular'* sense, responsible for balance and spatial orientation that helps us understand our body's position in space to maintain equilibrium."

"Next, there's *'proprioception'* which is the sense that gives us information about the position and movement of our body parts to help us coordinate movements and perform tasks. Then there's *'enteroception'* which provides information about our internal bodily states, such as hunger, thirst, pain, and temperature that help regulate our bodily functions and respond to internal cues and finally *nociception* which is the sense of pain, which alerts us to potential harm and helps us avoid injury."

I certainly knew a lot about the last one, not only from a physical sense but social and emotional ones as well, as Megan continued. "Obviously, our sensory modalities can be somewhat blocked or even turned off simply by closing our eyes, plugging our nose or ears. The other four are autonomic and are there to help support the primary senses to create a sense of being and awareness of our own existence, identity, and connection to the world that was and continues to be influenced by factors such as culture, upbringing, and personal experiences."

Megan smiled a gentle smile and added. "With what I practice, I have an enhanced sense of self-awareness that allows me to recognize my own thoughts, feelings and sensations, as well as my self-identity, such that I now better understand my own values, beliefs and goals. Because of this I have an enhanced level of self-esteem by creating a positive view of myself and my abilities without being narcissistic. Finally, and the greatest gift of all, I now have a profound sense of connectedness and belonging to something larger than myself, in terms of my community, innate causes and the natural world."

What started out as a silly little mention of the oppressive heat turned into an exposition on life and self-discovery. While my original supposition about being naked had an initial lascivious slant, what Megan had simply done was debase all that had been drilled into my head by our society, media and advertising that always puts nudity on an erotic plane. Instead, I realized a degree of innocence and purity to what Megan purported.

Megan wasn't trying to titillate, she was trying to sustain a sense of internal peace and was, in one way, simply inviting me to join her in finding the one thing I needed more than anything else and that was harmony… internal peace for which I would be profoundly grateful as she continued. "When I'm in the mood and need to refresh myself, I like to be outdoors, if and only if, there's a sense of safety, security and privacy around me. When there, I want to close my eyes and keep them closed for at least thirty minutes."

"A half hour, why?"

"When we close our eyes, our other senses actually become heightened because our brain is no longer focused on processing visual information. Sounds become more distinct and focused which is why people often close their eyes when trying to listen intently to music or a conversation. Our sense of touch becomes more sensitive, which is why people often close their eyes when feeling textures or enjoying a massage. Our senses of smell and taste become more pronounced which is why people often close their eyes when smelling food or wine, or tasting a new dish. In essence, closing my eyes helps me appreciate the nuances of my other senses and allows me to relax and enjoy the world around me."

Megan paused and added. "While I'm in one of my meditative states, I focus on my breathing, noticing the sensation of the air moving in and out while paying attention to the sensations of nature around me… the breeze, the warmth of the sun, the sounds of birds and insects. If you do this, you can actually get to the point where you can focus on a specific part of your body and feel how nature is affecting a small part and therefore the whole."

"And you need to be naked to totally do this?" I asked, thinking back to Amy and how she told me so many of the same things.

Megan shook her head 'no' and noted, "You don't, but you also won't get all the same sensations. I used to be so uptight about my body and then realized it's simply a superstructure for my mind and soul."

"The more I ventured into mindfulness, the more willing I was to shed the last vestiges of modesty and accept me as me, nothing more, nothing less. I'm no longer aroused nor embarrassed by my body. It's there and the only caution I have is when my freedom is interpreted in a different way such as what happened in Atlanta. I don't totally blame Charlie. Perhaps I was sending the wrong vibes. I thought we were past that and, yet, what happened was deep, dark and dangerous."

I took a deep breath. I didn't want Megan to classify me with Charlie. We were just beginning. We'd only really been together a few times and I knew I needed to learn to trust Megan and she me, to do so, there would need to be positive experiences as we began to interact over a myriad of different scenarios. The goal was getting predictable, reliable and consistent and keeping promises to each other, not some of the time, but all of the time. There also needed to be open and honest communication like we were having, to the point we both were being understood and truly cared for each other by simply paying attention to each other's needs and perspectives. I vowed I'd start with small acts of trust and gradually increase as our relationship grew if, and that was a big if, Megan wanted to. Megan had seen me at my most vulnerable point in time, alone, afraid, literally crying out for someone, anyone, to simply give me a shoulder to lean on.

We'd stood in the bedroom with carboard boxes flattened as Megan shared her personal experiences and deep dark determinations. It was because we were both bruised, we were able to come together for I sincerely believed she understood me and I was beginning to understand her.

I silently vowed that our relationship would remain plutonic, perhaps forever, until we both garnered a point in our own and then mutual, existence where we trusted ourselves. It's only then that one can move beyond that first rung of a relationship ladder. To do so, I knew I needed to walk a fine line such that Megan never felt physically uncomfortable with me.

I also knew I needed to make sure she felt appreciated simply for what she was, a beautiful woman who'd chosen an old farmer to be, what I hoped, her best friend… that complex and beautiful bond between two people who share mutual trust, respect and affection for each other based on shared experiences, interests, and values where we could offer each other emotional support, companionship, and a sense of belonging.

As we stood there, I remembered back to somewhere where I'd read of the seven keys to lasting friendship... trust, respect, empathy, support, communication, shared experiences and acceptance. Where, in accepting each other's flaws, while celebrating their strengths, we became one. I realized it was going to be difficult getting over my own socialization and accepting her liberation and, yet, it was what it was and, at this point in time, the friendship and support of Megan superseded any physical need I could ever have.

Megan paused, looked out the bedroom window again and added. "I guess I reached a point of holistic well-being that's now encompassing my physical, mental, and spiritual health thereby allowing me to connect with a higher power or spiritual dimension."

The more Megan talked, the more I realized she was really a lot like Amy. I wondered if this could be the reason why I was so attracted to her. Like Amy, she was both my antithesis and my guide, showing me the path to self-acceptance. I don't know how many people in the world were into this but I now believed I knew the reason why Megan came into my life."

"Do you want to...uhh...do that here?" "If you wouldn't mind." Megan replied. "Where?" I asked.

"Perhaps, out behind the barn. You know, just a chaise lounge and a quiet place."

"It's OK with me but I'm worried about the neighbors."

"Neighbors?" Megan countered with a look of concern or was that surprise on her face. "They've got to be at least a mile away and no one can see us from the road."

"I'm talking about the flies. They still think there's cows around here."

"I'll take care of the flies if you don't mind me sitting outside meditating."

"I don't mind, if you don't mind." I offered. "And you don't mind if I'm naked?"

"I don't mind, if you don't mind." I repeated.

Megan looked at me and noted. "George, your theory of acclimation is so correct. Why don't we do this, why not take off all our clothes and simply look at each other?"

"Huh?"

"Within five minutes all the mystery will be gone and with it all the uhh... eroticism. You've seen the photo that was above my bed and my statue. I've seen all of you during physical therapy and then in the classes. If we just, you know, see each other, won't it take away the mystery and we can get over all the cryptic nonsense and get on with life?"

"You're serious?" "Certainly."

I was reluctant and yet it made sense and so I asked, "Can I think about it?"

"If you want to, but does that mean I can't be?" Megan asked.

"In other words, you want to, even if I don't?"

"Yes." Megan responded with a slight smile on her face. "If you really don't mind."

"It's going to be a little rough in January, don't you think? George, I'm not suggesting we parade around naked. What

I'm suggesting is that we get over it and when the time is right, neither of us takes it the wrong way."

I looked at Megan and frowned. "If you do and I don't, then there'll be that.. that gap. Yet, if I do and we both agree it's not anything prurient, the pressure will go away?"

"Uh huh. Acclimation, George! Acclimation."

"And we can, you know just be...I don't know... comfortable with each other?"

"Yes, George. Comfortable with each other, accepting that we are just two people who live together and accept each other for what we are."

"Well, OK." I reluctantly agreed.

"When you're ready George and not until." Gulp! "Agreed."

"Great! Then it's settled."

Megan put the 'other' things away as I slit the last bottom tape and folded the last of the boxes. In less than an hour, all her clothes were unpacked as was part of her life, arranged and ready to wear or un-wear for that matter and it felt good, really, really good to begin the transition from the notion of 'me' to 'we'.

Cardboard Boxes:

As I'd been unloading the back of the U-Haul, I noticed that Megan had packed everything else in cardboard boxes and thought to myself 'great for shipping but certainly not for storage'. On a farm, that's a big mistake simply because field mice think you brought them a new housing development.

I asked her how long it would be before she thought she'd be done upstairs. She asked why? "We need to drive to Platteville and buy some plastic tubs at Menards. If we store things in cardboard boxes, the mice will make nests in them. If we buy plastic tubs, whatever's inside will be protected from moisture and mice."

"Are you up for it?" Megan asked, realizing I hadn't driven in a long time.

I paused and replied. "I think it would do me good. A couple weeks ago Tommie's pick-up wouldn't start because mice made a nest in the engine compartment and eaten all the wiring. I went on Amazon and ordered a TRQ ignition coil, iridium spark plugs and a wire kit and changed the oil."

"In other words, a tune up?"

"Yup." I said in a self-satisfied way.

"I didn't know you were so handy, Mr. Terrill."

"When you live on a farm you'd better learn how to fix things or you'll go broke paying someone else to do it for you." I paused and then added. "Why don't you finish putting your clothes away and then we can go and have lunch at Culvers."

"Yummy! Other than LeDuc's Custard in Wales and Leon's in Milwaukee, I haven't had Culvers in a long time."

"OK. You finish and I'll make sure the truck starts and then, when we come back, unload the U-Haul and take it to Dodgeville."

Megan smiled in agreement as I think we both realized that so-far, things were working out pretty darn good.

We made the twenty miles to Platteville and Menards in a half-hour, went in and bought all twelve of the 105-Quart Industrial tubs with Snap-On lids they had in stock.

I bungee-corded the containers in the bed of the truck and put the covers behind the front seat so they wouldn't blow away. We made our way to Culvers where we pigged out on butter burgers, cheese curds and strawberry shakes. While eating, what caught my attention was how every guy in the place was eyeing Megan which certainly increased my ego simply because she was with me.

We got back to the farm a little after two and the hottest part of the day. I backed the U-Haul down to the barn and opened the doors. Between the heat, humidity and flies, I realized why I never wanted to be a farmer. I got the dolly and unloaded all the boxes, pulled the truck out and turned on the barn fan. It was still hot but the flies were being blown out the back door. Whoopee!

"What's in the big box?" I inquired.

"You didn't think I was going to leave my statue, did you?" "You mean...?"

"Uh huh," Was all Megan replied as a devilish smile spread across her face.

"What about your...uhh...portrait? "It's in the long box there."

I got all tingly when I realized that I was carrying a carboard box with the 3-D nude sculpture of Megan that had been beside her pool in Atlanta that had initiated a long and somewhat personal conversation of Megan's exploratory trip through self-realization.

I didn't think one woman who owned one-third of a house could have so much stuff but she did and it was nearly four by the time we were fully unloaded. I looked at Megan and she at me and I don't know who was wetter. Both of us were soaked in sweat as she inquired. "How far is it to the pond?"

"A little over a mile." I replied.

"Can we go for a swim?" Megan asked.

"Tell you what, why don't we save that for another day. We can take a shower and get cooled off and then take the U-Haul back and go out for dinner."

I think Megan was a little disappointed but I also knew the mile walk down and back in ninety-degree heat with all the humidity would mean a temporary respite and we'd need to take a shower when we got back anyway.

We put all the stuff in the new tubs while the only things that didn't fit were the Megan statue and her infamous portrait which were still in their cardboard boxes. I looked at Megan and inquired what she wanted done with the two. I knew the mice would have a field day with the cardboard.

"How about putting the statue down by the pond?" Megan inquired realizing it was the closest thing to her old pool."

"That will really make more than the frogs eyes bug out," I joked.

"What about my portrait?" was next in line for decision making.

"Do you want to put it in the house?" I asked and continued.

"Instead of the Playboy Magazines Tommie used to hide under his mattress, we can class the joint up a little bit. I know, how about in the living room over the fireplace?"

"Sure! Why not? Then, if company comes, we can really give them something to talk about," Megan giggled.

I countered. "Seriously, how about upstairs over your bed?" "You'd do that?" Megan asked, now getting concerned.

"If it's what you want, it's OK with me."

Megan looked at me and noted. "George, it was a different time and place in my life. I only brought it with me so that I didn't leave it behind. Can we put it in the storeroom in the barn for now? Perhaps someday?"

What started out with a degree of mirth evolved into an unpleasant memory for Megan and I felt bad. I was trying to make light of the two things and instead I simply blew it. Damn!

I locked up the barn and handed the keys to Megan so she could go directly to the lab shower. Once more, it was my way of reaffirming that our relationship was on a plutonic level. I went back to the house, climbed in the bath tub, closed the shower curtain and cooled off.I was standing in the bathroom and glanced out the window where, it wasn't long before I saw Megan walking up the sidewalk with a towel wrapped around her, as she made her way towards the house. It sure seemed weird to see her as she was totally oblivious and ambivalent to her surroundings as she opened the front door.

I didn't want to admit I was a peeping George and so I let it slide. It was then what small prurient feelings I had seemed different. Gone was any lust. I wondered was it me? Was it the fact that Megan and I had shared so much? Was it our comfort level with each other? I really didn't know.

I remembered sharing my mantra with her regarding 'The Theory of Acclimation' that simply states, 'Through repetition, what was once special becomes commonplace. What was once commonplace, through repetition, becomes mundane. And, what was once mundane, through repetition, becomes boring or meaningless.'

After seeing the sculpture, observing her risqué self-portrait above her bed, me being her 'model' at the urologic clinic and then running around naked at her house when I spilled wine in my lap, I concluded we were past the "what was once special" phase and were probably entering the commonplace aspect, but really didn't know if that was the case at all. What I did know was, I wasn't ready for any physical interaction. Yet, I was somewhat comfortable with the fact we were two adults who had become good friends who'd moved to the commonplace phase of our existence.

We got ready and headed for Dodgeville with me driving the U- Haul and Megan her Lexus. It's only seven miles and so we made it in around fifteen minutes the guy came out and inspected the truck, Megan signed the charge and we were on our way to Corralejo for our Mexican treat. My God, it was good! Very, very good as we pigged out and had one too many Margaritas simply because we bought a pitcher instead of two glasses.

When we finished, I was concerned about driving and

suggested we walk it off. Even in the heat, we made it out to Harris Park and simply enjoyed the simplicity of watching kids play on the swings that brought back memories of Derrick, 'V' and Melia and how our lives were always too busy for them to enjoy the simple things.

I looked at Megan and asked, "I hope I'm not getting too personal but do you ever regret not having kids?"

Megan looked at me and replied. "Yes. It's one of the biggest disappointments in my life. I always dreamed that Rick and I would have two kids and live happily ever after. After Rick, there's never been anyone with whom I wanted to share the majesty and joy with until I met you."

"But I can't...can't do that."

"I know," was all Megan said as she turned to me and kissed me on the lips.

I didn't know if it was the heat, tequila or exhaustion. At first, I was reticent and then felt the softness I'd forgotten as the kiss ended in a somewhat awkward way.

The ride back to the farm was quiet... too quiet. As we pulled in the driveway Megan shut off the engine and, as she turned to me, I returned the kiss. What I'd been fighting. What all I promised I wouldn't do, just simply happened.

We went in the house and Megan went out on the screen porch while I got a bottle of B&B from the refrigerator. Megan was sitting on the sofa and so I put the wine on the coffee table and sat beside her. I poured two glasses and we toasted each other in total silence. My mind was going crazy. I still loved Amy and wanted her back. Yet, here I was with a woman I was also falling in love with.

While the 'moment' was upon us, I knew I needed to clarify what was going on. I also realized it might totally change the dynamics of what was taking place. Yet, I also totally knew it needed to be done.

To change the dynamics, I noted I need to use the bathroom, went and did what I needed to do and came back and sat a little further away from Megan to create a completely different set of subtleties. For the next hour, I laid out all that was going on. Not only the cave but Tank, Doctor Roberts and finally the financial reality regarding why I needed to find Amy, I didn't want to hurt Megan, but also knew I needed to be straight with her.

I saw the disappointment in Megan's eyes and watched as her smile turned upside down. I knew I was hurting her and taking her expectations and curtailing them. Yet, it was something I needed to do before we got into anything neither of us could get out of.

Megan looked at me with doleful eyes and simply asked, "Where do I fit in?"

I paused and said. "I don't know. What I do know is that I'm falling in love with you, yet I'm still in love with Amy. I know I need to find her and have the documents signed that removes any limit on my ability to move on with life. I also profoundly know the last thing I ever want to do is hurt you."

Tears formed in Megan's eyes as she asked, "Why did you ask me to move in with you?"

"I thought you needed somewhere to go. I thought I was helping you."

"You are, but I need more than that right now."

"Megan, what can I say? What can I do? I'm broke, without the papers. I'm free, if they're signed. I can't do anything with the farm. I can't touch our investments. I... I don't know. I thought I was helping you."

"So, money is more important than me?"

"No, of course not. But how can I, or even we, survive?" "What do you think you're going to do?" Megan inquired in
a totally different tone.

"I've got to find Amy." "But how?"

"I don't know."

"And if you find her?"

"And if I find her, I'll have all the papers with me that will supersede our agreement and I can move on."

"How long do you think that's going to take?"

I was getting somewhat annoyed and replied, "I have no idea."

Megan was softening a bit as she inquired, "Right now, you think you're going to go to Peru and find her?"

"Yes."

"How?"

"I haven't got that figured out yet."

"How much will that cost?"

"I don't know."

Megan began to realize I needed a plan and so she offered, "How about visiting all the major cities in Peru and simply asking people. Finding Americans couldn't be that hard."

"But how?"

"Why not go on one of those sightseeing tours that take you to all the big tourist attractions and then ask around."

I saw it was a good idea as I replied. "How about tomorrow, you and I go on-line and see if we can find a tour?"

The emotional roller coaster came to a stop. Megan and I both had been up and then way...and I mean way down, without the thrill of the ride and now were getting back to where we started. I looked at her and realized I really was falling in love with her.

I yawned. She yawned. It was time for bed. We stood and I decided I needed to give her a support hug and pulled her close and felt her body next to mine. My hands went down to her waist as I leaned back and requested. "Please be patient with me. It's been a tough few years and right now I'm confused and afraid."

Megan leaned back and had a soft smile on her face as she looked deeply into my eyes and noted. "I'm a fighter, George. In you, I see a man different from all others I've ever met. I'm willing to work with you. I'm willing to help you. I'm willing to support you. All I ask in return is that you never hold anything back. Promise?"

"Promise!"

With that we kissed but it was different. This wasn't a passionate kiss. This was a kiss to seal the deal. What I thought of Megan went way up as I realized she was willing to help me find my wife knowing, in the end it might mean losing me forever.

"Tomorrow can we go to the pond?" Megan whispered. "Sure, why not?" I whispered back.

"Oooohkay!" was all Megan said as we separated.

"Now, go get some sleep while I put the glasses in the dishwasher."

Threes:

Wisconsin summer weather seems to come in threes. When it results in hot humid conditions you can expect day two to be no exception. It was hot! It was humid! It was the Florida weather that I hated. Even the flies didn't want to move.

Megan spent the morning applying for jobs. I spent the morning trying to figure out how to find Amy and Tommie. Around eleven I asked Megan if she was up for the walk and she nodded 'yes' while asking what she should wear. I simply shrugged as the question had never come up before in my entire life. When you're a farmer you wear overalls or jeans and always a baseball cap.

Megan got into some frayed denim shorts with holes that played peek-a-boo with her rear as well as a tank top as I handed her a Badger baseball cap. My biggest concern were mosquitos and so, when we made it to the barn, I told her I needed to get a can of 'Deep Woods Off' as Megan asked, "What's that for?"

"You," I replied.

"Really?"

"Oh, yah!" I responded in my very best Wisconsin slang as I handed Megan the can and she sprayed some on her arms and wiped some on her face then sprayed the front of her legs. She paused and asked me to do the duty on her shoulders and the back of her legs. Slowly, I sprayed the Off on my hands and spread it around. Next, I bent down and sprayed the back of her legs and slowly massaged the repellent all the way up to the bottom of her shorts. I was tempted to spray the Off in holes in her jeans as well but thought otherwise.

"I think you missed the inside of my legs." Megan noted as she took one-half step to the right so that I could do the inside of her thighs. Slowly, I rubbed the Off on my hands and worked my way higher until I was at the bottom of her shorts. I never thought applying insect repellent could be erogenous and yet, oh my God.

"How about you?" Megan asked. "Let me put some on your face."

Megan sprayed the Off on her hands and then applied the repellent carefully to my face and neck as I looked in her eyes. Then she sprayed some more on her hand and then began applying it to each of my arms starting at my wrists and working her way up to the edge of my t-shirt. First my right arm and then my left, making me realize that the inside of one's arms can be very and I mean very erogenous.

The spell broke when the Off can was empty which I put the can in the dumpster, thinking someday, through recycling, that can could be the hood on a new Cadillac as we began our walk. Along the way, I spoke of the farm and how George the First bought the land from Blackhawk and the story of the albino bear skin without mentioning it was in the trunk in the office.

Our first stop was at the family cemetery where I explained all the residents and how they were related and spoke of, Jake, my dog and Francis, the pig, and why they were there. Next, we made our way past the orchard and I explained how the original apple trees came to be as the Native Americans in Upstate New York picked the apples there, ate them here and threw the discarded cores into the field. I also explained how the apples were turned into hard cider during Prohibition by my great grandparents who also survived the Great Depression.

We crossed the unplowed field and, as we were making our way to the manhole cover where the foundation had stood, I explained the reason for the Foundation and all that we'd accomplished. When we made it to the manhole cover, I showed Megan how it was stamped a property of the U.S. Government and then went into detail about Simon and how he got his name...**S**uper **I**ntelligent **M**onitor **o**f the **Net**... and how we fought for the ten acres of forest and that Rodney and I had become such great friends.

While the previous day had been hot, this day made yesterday seem like Spring. The temperature had to be near one- hundred and the humidity just about as high as we finally made it into the welcomed shade where I outlined Skunk Hollow School and why it meant so much to our family.

We finally made it to the obelisk and sat on the bench as I detailed who great grandfather was and why he meant so much to me. Megan had spoken nary a word. She'd listened and allowed a sentimental old man to share his life. As we sat on the bench, a slight breeze caressed the trees and I knew it was great grandfather welcoming me back to reality.

After we'd rested, it was time to go to the Springs as I noted. "This is where George the First saved Rodney's great grandmother's life and why the land is sacred. We've always called it 'the Forest' and each generation has honored the sanctity of the area by leaving it as a natural habitat."

From the obelisk we began our walk to the Springs on a path I'd traversed so many times before. As we were but twenty paces, Megan held up her hand and beckoned me to stop. I thought she was having trouble with my pace or perhaps the heat. We stopped and I continued my expose. "For many, the Forest is nothing more than a group of trees and then the Springs. For others, including me, it's an area of profound majesty and mystery where I've gone throughout my life to find peace and tranquility in times of woe."

I looked Megan in the eyes and reported. "To explain the feeling I, and others as fortunate as me, experience whenever we go into the Forest is extremely difficult. Yet, without sharing what happens, you would never understand why the area is so important to me. When I enter the Forest, my internal subjective state of moods, emotions and/or feelings immediately begins to change, regardless of where they've been."

"As an example, if I'm experiencing fear, anger, disgust or sadness, they'll be compensated for and my mind will enter a period of profound tranquility that allows my body to simply relax and experience the majesty of totality. If, on the other hand, I'm in a realm of joy, trust or anticipation, the Forest takes away the edges and allows me to absorb my feelings by enhancing the sensations and positive emotions that I am experiencing.

Regardless of my feelings when I arrive, I become more introspective, experiencing the consequence of both within my soul."

"While the trees of the Forest demarcate the boundaries, the Springs give it meaning. The crystal-clear water bathes my soul in a sense of sincerity, decency, purity and innocence. Unlike anything I feel elsewhere, the Springs do so to the point that match my beliefs that our current world is flawed and can be replaced by a better place and existence, if only given a chance."

Megan looked at me with a totally different expression on her face. She was realizing I had a different perspective on life she'd never seen before that aligned with the persona she'd acquired in her 'journey' as she had called it and we were more alike than she'd initially perceived. While she'd ventured where, fortunately, few people ever go to find themselves, I was the one who'd been able to ponder all forms of existence and do so in a non-structured manner that actually didn't align with the truisms pontificated by any social edifice.

We made it to the Springs and paused to listen to the never-ending sound of the water trickling from beneath the rocks as it had done since before our family arrived nearly 200 years before as I continued. I explained the existence and convergence of the three ley lines and how they created the positive energy force that we felt and then added. "To me, the Forest is not a concept but an existence related to, but differing from, perceptions of heaven, afterlife and the Kingdom of God, where heaven is simply another place or state, and the afterlife is an individual's life after death. I believe the Kingdom of God can be anywhere as long as the traveler is willing to give of themselves and accept humility, generosity, compassion and forgiveness as the goals by which they live."

Megan glanced at me and smiled, slowly shaking her head, accepting that she was in a religious place where goodness prevailed where she began to see that her beliefs and mine paralleled each other in many ways as she summarized, "In other words, the Forest for you, is where the positive energy is so great that synchronicity can be felt, transmitted and processed into both emotions and behavior."

I smiled in agreement and relief, realizing she understood what I was talking about as Megan added. "For some people, like you, the feelings are profound because the energy is positively linked to your soul. For others, there is little or no feeling and, therefore, no emotion. No matter how strong the feelings, the connections are still there and that's why your family respects all there is."

I smiled again, nodded and added. "While visiting the Forest, the experience can be an opportunity that profoundly affects a person. Unfortunately, this is limited to a very few people and I hope and pray you're one of them. That's why I brought you here. I know of no other person besides myself who's gone beyond being affected and transcended into another realm that has changed me, challenged me and controlled me since I was a child."

Megan whispered, "We're someplace special. I can feel it, George. I've never felt quite like this before."

"Do you want to turn around and go back?" I inquired.

Megan firmly shook her head no and replied. "Just the opposite. I'm being bathed in goodness and it's the feeling I've been looking for but never found until now. George, for the first time in my life I sincerely feel good about me. George, about me!"

I looked and saw tears streaming down Megan's face as I asked, "Are you OK?"

Megan shook her head 'yes'.

The silence became deafening and yet I sensed I shouldn't speak. We simply stood in total silence as Megan took another deep breath, exhaled, took another deep breath and closed her eyes.

"Are you sure you're OK?"

A soft smile pursed her lips as Megan opened her eyes. "George, I've been looking for this my whole life. I've done so many, many things to try and find it. I've done things to the point I finally thought it would only take place if I was allowed to enter

Heaven. For the first time, there is profound peace within my soul and the goodness of simply 'being' has overcome me."

Megan looked at the water, then the bog and finally back at me as she noted. "I've been very lonely even when not alone. I've been sad when I should have been happy. I've never really felt joy. With Rick, I should have bathed in the majesty of love, only to always feel as if it wasn't there, with no sense of satisfaction, regardless of what I'd accomplished, what I'd given of myself. Satisfaction has always been fleeting. To come here and feel all that I've dreamt about and hoped for is now within me and is simply beyond anything I could have ever imagined."

I stood for a moment to allow Megan bathe in the majesty of serenity that accompanied her. As the spell broke, a broad smile returned to her face and I knew it was time to see if she could be baptized in the name of innocence where all her transgressions would be forgotten.

While normally I would get the tin cup to retrieve the water, I silently cupped my hands and gestured to Megan, visually instructing her to drink from the Springs, knowing that any sound from me could break the mystic spell that was transpiring.

Megan knelt down, duplicated my hands, dipped them in the cold water and placed it to her lips. For a moment there was nothing and then her body began to quake as she looked skyward. She arose, looked at me and simply shook her head. "God is here, George! God is here! I can feel him unlike no other time before. Perhaps, this is what the disciples felt when they met Jesus. Perhaps, this is what Jesus felt like when he was baptized by John the Baptist. God has forgiven me, George, God has!"

There was a long pause with deafening silence. The call of the birds seemed to dissipate and even the flies and mosquitos drifted away.

Megan paused as if in deep thought and then inquired, "Do you think I'm worthy of being baptized here? I never was as a child."

Oh my God. This had never been asked before and so I asked. "What do you want me to do?"

"I want you to bathe me in goodness George."

"But the water's really cold and it's too shallow to submerse you."

Megan shrugged and countered, "I know, but by pouring the pure water on my body, it will symbolize the death of my old self while providing my spiritual rebirth into a new life."

"Are you sure?"

"Yes, George. I'm totally sure. Please!" "OK."

Megan stood before God and me as I took the little tin cup and dipped it into the spring. God, the water was cold!

As I poured the tin cup on Megan's head I simply said, "I baptize you in the name of the Father, and of the Son and of the Holy Spirit."

"Now my body George, cleanse my body of all that's been done."

Once again, I dipped the cup in the Springs and poured the water on her right shoulder such that it dribbled down her back as Megan stood with eyes closed, looking up at where we all believe heaven exists.

As cold as the water was, Megan didn't flinch. Once again, I dipped the cup in the rivulets of purity and repeated the process on her left shoulder with no physical response.

"Now my back," Megan whispered and so, I repeated the process.

"Lower," as I poured the water on her legs.

"Now my front," Megan directed as I slowly poured the water on her chest.

"Lower," Megan noted and I poured the water at her waist.

Megan stood totally immersed, as she opened her eyes and looked at me with tears cascading down her cheeks and said. "You've given me one of the greatest gifts I could ever receive… forgiveness! You've shown me that my life is worthwhile, where all the times I wondered if what I was doing, what I was giving, what I was attempting was really worth it."

"Now,… right now… I can see and feel that I've been wrong. I didn't look inward but outward. I didn't accept myself for being me. And now, right now, George, I realize I was looking the wrong way and will always and I mean always be so, so grateful."

Megan brushed the tears from her cheeks, smiled another gentle smile and added. "This is a place of worship, George, unlike any I've been before. Not created by man but by God! Not as an interpretation of what we THINK Heaven will be like but an exclamation of the goodness He has created. I'll never forget today and all that's transpired, nor will I ever be able to thank you for bringing me here and giving me my life back."

I was humbled as we stood there and allowed the 'spell' to dissipate. It was then I looked across the shallow stream, into the bog and saw 'him', the great buck who'd traversed time and remained immortal. I whispered to Megan, "Look", as I nodded past the brook. With that, Megan's eyes slid across the horizon as the big buck simply bowed his head and quietly walked away.

Megan noted. "He came, didn't he?"

"Yes, Megan, he came and now you're free. Free of the past. Free to start again. He only appears when someone has seen the magnificence of goodness. He'll only stay for a moment and then be gone. He's been here as long as I've been alive, if not before. I didn't have any idea what was going to happen to you, but I wanted you to come to see if I could help you regain eternal peace. I needed to see how you would feel once you were here. I needed to make certain that what you felt was strong enough that you would accept what I wanted to share with you and that was the truth. Not about this or that, but about yourself, that you are a wonderful person who needs to learn to love yourself and in so doing have others love you, as well."

Megan's expression assured me that it was all right to continue as I added. "I don't know if you'll ever have the same feelings again. For some, it's a one-time thing. For others like me, the sensations come and go, as they react to my own emotions. However, I believe they're always here and that's why I keep coming back."

Megan looked at me and then at the springs and then back at me. She closed her eyes and looked towards the sky and simply said, "I'm forgiven. Thank you, God!"

I knew then, that Megan's life would never be the same. The guilt and anger that had corroded her soul and eroded her joy had been washed away. I sincerely felt that, from now on she would remain satisfied with herself. I also realized that whether we continued on together no longer mattered. Megan would always be internally happy for which I would be thankful for what I'd done.

It's honorable to admit one's mistakes, no matter how purloined they might be. It's more virtuous to accept that they have been forgiven and learn from those mistakes and, finally, it's even more righteous to never make the same mistakes again.

Megan was soaked as she stood totally indifferent to her physical existence but the intensity of both the moment and the weather was refreshing to both her and me. There'd been others but nothing like this. There'd been those driven to tears and those who simply walked away. There'd been Amy's mother whose last wish was to come here but never had there been the resurrection of a soul, an abdication of pain and an elimination of guilt as there had been for Megan who was the first person I knew who'd been cleansed of all the memories that had burdened her and made her sad.

Rocks:

The day was done and it was time to head back to the house. Back to reality where, along the way, the heat was almost unbearable as it sapped our energy and turned us into wilted flowers. Taking a different route, we came to the spot where dad, grandpa and great grandpa had simply piled all the rocks that had made their way to the surface when they plowed. Over the years, it had literally become some form of fence that reminded me of yesteryear.

As we made it to the pile, I remembered one of my careless days as a kid when I stepped across the assemblage into deep grass and sprained my ankle and had to crawl back to the house, tears in my eyes, pain in my ankle and embarrassment in my soul. Farm kids knew better than that!

I knew where we should cross and took Megan to the spot. I went first and then reached back to take Megan's hand in mine. As she traversed the rocks and we resumed our journey, our hands were still clasped together. I really didn't know if it was for physical or emotional security, nor did I care.

God, it was hot! By the time we made it back to the barn we were both soaked in sweat and streaked with the dust that had caked itself to the insect repellent. I looked at Megan and she at me and we both knew what we needed and that was a cool relaxing shower. My mind reiterated... 'Through repetition, what was once special becomes commonplace. What was once commonplace, through repetition, becomes mundane. And, what was once mundane, through repetition, becomes boring or meaningless.' Had we reached the point of commonplace? I wondered if we could become physical without being intimate. As had been the case with Amy, there would be a point in time when physical exposure no longer emoted sexual desire.

When you've bared your soul, when every deep, dark secret has been shared, can one then progress to a comfort point devoid of inference? Had my intonation regarding my love of Amy curtailed anything more than simply two people being physically comfortable with each other without the sexual consequence? I was about to find out.

We headed for the lab as I reluctantly handed Megan the keys and made my way back to the house where I climbed in the tub, pulled the curtain back and cooled off. It wasn't long until my body was back to normal and I got out and looked out the window in time to see Megan crossing the yard with a towel and another atop her head.

I slipped into a pair of old khaki shorts and made my way to the living room as Megan opened the front door and came in. Pausing, she unwrapped the head towel and casually stood drying her hair as she finally spoke, "George Terrill, this has been one of the best days of my life. In you, I've found the friend I've always wanted. Someone kind enough, generous enough and thoughtful enough to accept me as me, to understand my trials and tribulations and still accept me for me. I don't know where we are going. I do know, right now I don't care. What I cherish is the reality that you have accepted me and helped me conquer what's been within."

My God! Here she was pontificating wearing, only a towel as she pulled me in. For the longest time, we simply held each other as nothing more than two people in need, bound together by loneliness, realizing the battles ahead were not to be endured alone but with each other at our side.

The moment passed as Megan smiled and said, "Let me get dressed for supper."

My lecherous mind was a tizzy as I hoped she'd stay the way she was. Instead, Megan went upstairs slipped into a pair of shorts and a tank top, came down and asked. "What's for dinner?"

"Brats" I replied.

"Yummy! Are you going to boil them in beer first?"

"You bet...Spotted cow"

And so we spent the rest of the evening eating, sitting out on the screen porch, drinking wine and each other's glances.

Mud:

As noted, hot, humid days seem to come in threes and the next was no different than the first two. We had breakfast and then Megan went to her laptop and me to mine as we perused the day. Right before lunch, Megan came into the office and asked. "George Terrill, are we ever going to go swimming in the pond or do I have to run around naked in the yard under the sprinkler? You do have a sprinkler, don't you?"

I looked up and realized she was being mischievous and replied. "Well, I can get out the impulse sprinkler and you can listen to the wish, wish, wish...clickity, clickity, click or we can go down to the pond, and listen to the frogs tell you how deep the pond is which is 'knee-deep, knee-deep, knee-deep.'"

Megan got this devilish look on her face as she asked, "How far is it to the pond?"

"About a mile."

"Can we go skinny dipping?"

I thought about it and had it resurrect some fond memories. I didn't want the relationship to progress but also knew my theory of acclimation couldn't continue to take place if we didn't get more comfortable with each other without the erogenous aspect being involved.

"Yup! Just you and me and perhaps a few hundred mosquitoes biting us on the butt."

We had lunch, walked the mile and made it to the pond with Megan giggling as we pulled off our clothes and put them on the big rock grandpa pulled out when he dug the pond.

We went to the sandy area grandpa also put in, we called 'the beach,' and began wading in the cold water. "Yiikes! You didn't tell me the water would be freezing," Megan complained as the Greek malady called Nippless Erectus verified her allegation.

With that, I splashed her as she turned and began splashing me as the entire episode escalated into a full-scale water fight.

Soon we were both laughing so hard I thought I'd pee my pants until I realized they were laying on the rock.

Here we were, the two of us, chortling and cavorting, paying no attention to the rain clouds forming on the horizon. We paused our fun as my attention turned to the western sky as I proclaimed, "Jesus!". I mean it was starting to rain. Not a little bit! But so hard it was like what dad used to say... "a cow pissing on a flat rock."

"When you're naked and wet, what do you do? Your clothes and towels are already soaked. You don't have any shelter. The only good thing was the rain was warmer than the pond. There was no need to run as even the mosquitoes had headed for cover. I looked at Megan and began to laugh. God, it felt good, as I thought how dumb can two people be?

We headed for home in the deluge, with me assuring Megan I'd come back for our now-soaked towels and clothes. Totally naked, where shoes would have helped... I think. We made it through the forest and were crossing the empty cornfield as the mud squished between our toes while the rain pelted us from above. As we headed up the hill towards the house, Megan slipped and fell. I stopped to help her up. And, as she grabbed my hand, she pulled me down and slapped a great big glob of great Wisconsin pasture on my butt.

"This is war!" I countered as I grabbed my own handful and slathered it on Megan's chest as the transfer of slurpy, sloppy topsoil continued until we were both covered from head-to-toe.

When we both looked like chocolate snowmen, we stood, shaking our heads in total disbelief, laughing and laughing, then laughing some more, literally convulsing in glee, watching the rivulets of rain slither and slide down our bodies into the muck below.

Just then, the first crack of lightning erupted and the boom of thunder shook the ground. 'Holy Shit!' I thought. The beginning volleys had been something but they were simply sprinkles and pop-its compared to M80 firecrackers Mother Nature was tossing at us as torrent after torrent of rain catapulted its way down, turning our former mud pie into a literal swamp in a matter of minutes.

"We'd better get inside!" I hollered. With that, I grabbed Megan's mucky hand and we made our way to the lab where, instead of the cool shower the day before, we went in to simply wash off and warm up.

When you've slathered mud all over your body, it has a way of getting in nooks and crannies you don't think about. While doing one's 'front' isn't that difficult, doing your back can be a challenge. For this, Megan took the bar of soap, had me turn around and began using the soap to traverse my peaks and valleys. God it felt good to have someone provide a tactile sensation so long lost.

As she completed the journey, Megan motioned for me to turn around and simply repeated the process making certain every inch was covered in the soapy lather. While, at one time, this would have been some sort of erogenous escapade, simply having her take the time to envelope me in the purity of both thought and deed was found to be luxuriating.

As Megan finished, she handed the bar of soap to me and I duplicated her efforts beginning with her back and then her front until we were both void of the mud we'd acquired. As she stood lathered in soap, I nodded towards the small plastic examining stool in the corner that was used when Francis had his weekly bath. I moved the stool to the middle of the shower and told Megan to have a seat. She did as directed while I took the shampoo, put a dollop in her hair and slowly began massaging her scalp and then her shoulders.

It wasn't long until I began to observe her head tilt left, then right in total pleasure. For the next several minutes my fingers did the talking, tacitly telling Megan she was all right, while communicating a neural sense of pleasure that comes only when someone is showing you they care.

I then detached the removable shower head and began the process of providing an aquatic massage as the pulsating water provided a respite from the constant emanation which had been above us. Up and down Megan's body I went as she stood encapsulated in the pleasure that can only come when someone else is providing the indulgence. Try tickling yourself and finding out it's impossible, likewise it's the same for streams of water. However, having someone else focus those same streams can result in a sartorial-less experience that results in one profound tactile realization called bliss.

With our hair and bodies 'squeaky clean', we wrapped towels around ourselves more for heat than decorum and peered out the lab window at the torrent that came in wave after wave after wave, making muddy rivers flow between us and the house.

"We'd better wait this one out," I offered.

Megan nodded in agreement as we stood watching Mother Nature do her thing. Having been raised on the farm and seen nature at her best and worst, I knew storms like the one we were experiencing were great in intensity but short in duration representing nothing more than the edge of a weather front between the hot, humid weather and cooler, dryer weather to follow. Within fifteen minutes the front passed and an eerie calm replaced the tumultuous display God put on, as the sun came out to dry the glistening milieu that surrounded us. Like some grand finale to a wonderful fireworks display, the air cleared and with it the threat, as birds began chirping simply to tell each other they were all OK.

I looked at Megan and she at me as we both just shook our heads and smiled. Like little kids, we'd played in the mud. Like juveniles we'd risked our lives thinking we were infallible. Then, like two adults, we came to realize we'd created one more chapter of memories... something to look back at and smile, a quiet smile of the day we did what little kids do and threw caution and mud to the wind.

We made our way back to the house squeaky clean except for the new-found mud on our feet we didn't want to bring in the house. Standing on the porch, I looked at her and Megan at me and we simply unwrapped the towels and wiped our feet.

We entered the house and Megan took the towels into the laundry room only to come back stopping, looking at me, chortling "knee-deep," before heading up the stairs evoking yet another smile that cantered its way across my face for the silly girl who'd saved my life and made me thank God she'd arrived.

Acclimation:

'Through repetition, what was once special becomes commonplace. What was once commonplace, through repetition, becomes mundane. And, what was once mundane, through repetition, becomes boring or meaningless.' As Megan and I evolved into a syncopated rhythm of morning internet searches and afternoon adventures, it became even more apparent I needed to find Amy and determine my status martially, financially and emotionally. The hypothesis was Amy and Karen were somewhere in Peru and I needed to find them.

No matter how much I was enjoying the bliss that surrounded Megan and my friendship, wallowing beneath was the reality I needed to resolve And/Or or risk the farm and the Lighthouse as well as my half of the financial mountain that would make the difference between one strata of existence and another. The question became where to look?

Megan and I'd reached a point where we were open about our relationship and she accepted that I needed to resolve 'Amy issues' one way or the other. Being generous, Megan took it upon herself to become my consigliore in terms of creating a strategy to find Amy. I had a photo of Karen and Amy from those in Amy's personal file hidden in the Sentry box and was about to open the thumb drive when Megan came into the office. I was reticent but then realized she'd been totally open with me and so I held up the thumb drive and explained what it contained to which Megan simply shrugged her shoulders.

I knew what I had in my hands was quite personal. Yet, I also felt that if I was going to be totally, and I mean totally, honest with Megan, showing her Amy with Karen, at least in the... uhhh... public photos wouldn't be violating the sanctity of Amy's personal endeavors. With that decision, I inserted the thumb drive, went to the file entitled 'Karen' and opened the images.

Megan was standing behind me with her hands on my shoulders and commented. "Nice photos. What's in the other file?'

"They're a bit...uhh... personal."

"You mean?"

"Yes!"

With a flat-lined response that sounded almost analytical, Megan asked. "Anything in there that would allow strangers to better recognize either Karen or Amy?"

"I don't think so," I replied.

"You want me to look?"

"I don't think so," I responded.

There was a pause as my mind and morals played chicken with each other. Megan and I had promised we'd be totally open. Perhaps, if I shared the photos, Megan would see why my heart was broken.

I took a deep breath and slowly moved the icon over the electronic folder. Pressing the side of the mouse, the entire litany opened in a summarized list where you could barely decipher the tiny images. At this point, my conscience changed the equation and I quickly clicked the folder shut realizing I simply couldn't do it.

"Do you mind?" Megan asked.

I reluctantly shook my head 'no' as Megan leaned over, took the mouse and began going through the file as the images got more and more explicit. With no emotion, Megan found a close-up of Amy and Karen, zoomed in and commented that she'd take that one as a person's face might change over time, but never their eyes. There was no comment about what all Megan had seen and I didn't really know if it offended her, reminded her, or if she was simply indifferent to what she saw.

I took the photo and placed it in the 'photo' file, opened it, and zoomed in so that all we had were two faces staring back at us and pressed the print button as the image of Amy and Karen slowly made its way from its electronic cauldron to the paper it was printed on. I took it from the printer, looked at it and, for some reason, there was little-to-no emotional evocation on my part as the image had become nothing more than my passport to financial freedom before asking, "Now what?"

"Do you have any photos of your brother and his wife? How about Derrick?" Megan asked.

I never thought of taking photos of them with me but it made all the sense in the world, assuming they were all still together.

"Want me to check anything else?" Megan asked.

I thought, I really didn't want to show everything but was curious about the reason for the general file and so I slid the mouse over and clicked on it.

Megan took a look and sort of shrugged. "There's some really beautiful women here and I can see why Amy was attracted to them, but then, who wouldn't want to...? I mean, they're gorgeous!"

Megan caught herself and noted. "You've told me Amy was 'bi' and so I guess it was her way of... I don't know, stoking the fire. More than men, women can be aroused by both men and women. Whether or not a woman is aroused by photos of other women depends on her individual preferences and experiences. Some find photos of naked women to be sexually stimulating, while others may not. With this uhh...assortment, I'd say Amy was aroused, wouldn't you?"

"Yes, I guess so." I replied. "How about you?" Megan asked. "What?" I asked.

"Are you aroused by these photos?" Megan inquired.

Gulp! How in hell do you answer that? I paused for a moment and then replied. "In this situation, 'no'. Had I come across them any other way, 'yes'.

"Good answer George. It tells me you're normal." "What do you mean?" I asked, now concerned.

"If you would have said 'yes' or 'no' to both, I would have thought you weren't telling the truth. Instead, by saying that, in the context you saw them, you were 'not', but, had it been in another situation, 'yes', I think it was a quite normal reaction."

"How about you?" I asked.

There was a pause and then Megan answered. "I found some of the women to be quite attractive and some not visually appealing. Was I turned on by them? Not really. Anyway, not in this scenario."

I guess I had my answer, or did I? Megan's hands dropped from my shoulders and she returned to her laptop while I sat in the office chair and looked at the photos of the smiling faces. It was then I began to rationalize that Amy thought I was dead and emotionally left me to start life all over again. I, on the other hand, believed she was alive and that emotion was still within me. However, like a small candle whose flame was flickering, I began to believe that she too was literally, but not physically, dead as well.

Peru:

After a few days of strategic discussions, Megan broached the idea of taking a tour of Peru that visited all the high spots and taking the photos to share with the locals. We began looking at tour options and found one that would hit all the key cities and scenic spots in ten days. The challenge was the cost. It was $4,325 per person, based on double occupancy plus airfare, I knew it was more than I could afford. What was crazy, and what I learned after looking at other options, was the fact that all the tours and cruises booked that way where they charge for the room regardless of whether it's one or two guests.

Megan was aware of my financial situation and made an offer I couldn't believe. She noted that she had her severance pay and the profit from selling the Buckhead house and was staying with me for free. It was then she offered to pay my way. At first, I balked and then said only if she'd go with me.

"You mean you want me to go with you to help find your wife?" Megan asked incredulously.

"Why not?" I countered. "The only additional cost is going to be the airfare and it would do us both good."

Megan wanted time to think it over and finally saw the logic. I contacted Tank and asked him to draw up the papers needed that would allow for the resolution of the pre-nup such that Amy and I could liquidate the assets and split them 50/50. Two days later, Tank dropped off the papers and I introduced him to Megan whom I'd outlined and detailed as to what all had happened.

As I walked Tank out to his car he looked at me and noted, "George, everybody in town knows Megan's here. You know how things like this can get blown out of proportion. I'm your lawyer and also your friend and I highly recommend you come into town with Megan to stop the rumors."

"How did anyone find out?" I asked.

"You don't think people knew when you took the U-Haul back or the restaurants you've been eating at do you?"

Naive me never put two-and-two together as I remembered back to what I'd told 'V' that the Duke had offered... "Nothing is bad when it's no longer a secret."

As I went back into the house, Megan commented on Tank and how nice he was. I looked at her and spilled the beans. "People in town are talking. Tank thinks it's best if we go in and set the record straight. What do you think?"

"I think he's right. When do you want to go?"

I paused, looked at the floor and had a smile cross my face. "Let's wait until Sunday morning and go to church. That will really get the tongues wagging."

"Are you sure?"

"Yup, it would do them all good."

Megan looked at me and giggled before offering. "How about me wearing a micro miniskirt and my deep 'V' blouse, high heels and lots of make-up. If they're wagging I'm a hooker, I can give them a show."

"Ahhhh. I don't think that would be too good of an idea, Minnie Point is pretty conservative."

Megan got serious and replied. "George, I'd never do that but I do like the idea of going to church. It's been a long time."

"Then we can go to the Red Rooster for breakfast. Trust me, if we do those two, everyone in town will be in on it by Monday morning." Sunday came and I got out one of my best suits. Megan was dressed in one of her business outfits and we made quite the couple as we rode into town in her Lexus. We walked into church and sat about ten rows back on the aisle as I simply nodded at those people I knew, two of which were Ann Mitchell and her husband, Bill.

The good Reverend did his spiel and soon services were over as Megan and I made our way outside. It's amazing what people think when they believe your nuts and then to see you in church with a different woman they know isn't your wife. We made our way to the Red Rooster, went in and waited for a table to clear. Once again there were stares but then, I knew there would be and also realized it was going to take time for everyone to realize first, I wasn't dead. Second, I wasn't crazy... well maybe a little, and third, my wife left me because she thought I was deceased.

Tank and I agreed that he'd 'spread the word'. When I asked him what he'd say about Megan, he'd indicate she was a business associate visiting from Atlanta. It all made sense to me. I didn't know if it would in town but realized there was nothing I could do about it and The Duke was right, once a secret is known it can no longer hurt you.

After church and lunch, we went home and worked on making our tour reservations. When all was done, Megan provided her credit card number and we were set to go the first week of September. I sent a copy of the itinerary to 'V' and explained what was going on. He noted he hadn't heard from either Amy or Melia and asked how I was doing. I said I was recovering nicely but didn't let on that Megan was my roommate.

I thought about Peru and then Saint Martin and wondered if Megan would mind if we stopped and checked out the Lighthouse and arrangements for someone to manage the property. She thought it would be a great idea and so, once again, I called Tank and asked him if I needed to create management papers for the house and he said most legitimate companies already had them prepared. When I looked at the airfare, I almost pooped in my britches. Yikes!

Megan, dear sweet Megan, came to the rescue. She had over two million miles accrued from when she, Ellie and Charlie travelled and offered to use them so we could fly business class. I mentally made a note to make sure, when the funds were available, Megan would receive the first $50,000 as that was what it was going to cost just for the airfare and the tour for two people.

I wanted to visit Peru, not buy it. It's really neat pretending to give away pretend money you don't have as I thought of all the people who play the lottery and spend their time thinking about how they're going to spend it, where the odds of winning the Powerball jackpot is around one in 292 million while the odds of being struck by lightning in the United States in a given year are approximately one in 15,300. I shook my head in total disbelief remembering that a few days before we were running naked around in a torrential thunderstorm like chickens with our heads cut off, giggling like kindergartners at recess.

Megan worked her magic as all the reservations were made that gave us two weeks to get ready while making sure the house and facilities were secure. Even bucolic Iowa County had become less than pristine when it came to burglary. The day came and Tank was kind enough to drive us to the Dane County Regional Airport formerly called 'Truax Field', by those old enough to know better. We arrived in Chicago and waited for our flight to Lima. With two hours to kill, Megan booted up her laptop and checked the flight and our hotel reservation to make sure everything was as planned. Fortunately, it was.

We boarded and went to our seats. After having one's own jet, even business class wasn't that neat but sure better than being cramped back in economy plus or worse yet, economy minus for eleven hours. We both slept and were awakened by the flight attendant reminding us we'd land in about thirty minutes, which we did.

Our airplane conversation centered around logical places to look in case the tour resulted only in dead ends. We both concurred that the most memorable thing in Peru would be the Andes mountains that form a spine of rugged peaks that stretch from north-to-south with everything from snow-capped summits to lush valleys, as well as the rich cultural heritage. Megan noted that the Andes are the longest mountain range in the world, stretching approximately 4,350 miles from northern Venezuela to southern Chile and are also the second-highest mountain range after the Himalayas. In other words, as great place to hide.

We had a generalized target but no specific location. We felt that, if they were hiding, they would want to blend in and to do so would be in one of the mountain ranges but which one? The Peruvian Andes are divided into several distinct ranges, including the Cordillera Blanca, Cordillera Huayhuash and Cordillera Vilcanota.

The Cordillera Blanca would likely be the most logical because it's home to the popular tourist destination of Huaraz, offering a relatively developed infrastructure with hotels, restaurants, and transportation options. In addition, the climate in the Cordillera Blanca is generally milder than other parts of the Andes, with cooler temperatures and less rainfall. Because of this, Huaraz attracts a fair number of expats where English is spoken more widely and the transition would be easier due to the presence of a familiar community.

While it all seemed logical, I realized it was too logical. I kept looking at the options, realizing if we did find the right range, how would we know which peak, as Peru boasts some of the highest peaks in the Americas, such as Huascaran, the highest mountain in Peru.

I knew Derrick hated winter, which he got from his mother and so I was certain he'd avoid any area that had glaciers, particularly the Pastoruri Glacier. I also thought he'd not want to be in a valley for security reasons and would also want to be away from a tourist area which eliminated areas such as the Sacred Valley of the Incas, known for its ancient ruins and stunning scenery and one of the most popular tourist destinations in Peru.

I realized the challenge in front of us was like finding the proverbial needle in the haystack or the Badger football team winning the National Championship. Instead we concluded we'd take the tour and see what happened. Maybe, just maybe, we'd get lucky. Who knows?

We acquired our suitcases and went to customs where we were asked how long we would be staying in Peru as we only had booked one-way flights. I explained we were going on a tour with Insight Vacations and thought we might like to stay a few extra days after the tour as Megan offered our reservation confirmation with Insight. The reason seemed logical and we were waved through. In the airport lobby was a courtesy phone as Megan called the Hilton Lima Miraflores who indicated the courtesy vehicle would arrive in approximately twenty minutes.

Both of us having traveled extensively had learned that the American branded hotels were set to US standards. While not the most glamorous facilities, they normally always met what we were looking for when staying one night. The other big attraction was the fact that I could cash in 40,000 Hilton Honors points and stay for free even though we weren't where the tour began.

We were met by the Mercedes courtesy car sedan that reminded me of Germany. Megan then surprised me with her fluent Castellano or Espanol as she had a conversation with the driver who indicated it was a forty-minute drive to the hotel. The driver then excused himself as he called the Hilton and made arrangements for the bellman to be waiting when we arrived who whisked us directly to our top floor room.

As Megan was taking a shower, I read the brochure that pointed out the hotel had a rooftop swimming pool with two hot tubs and was in Lima's upscale Miraflores district just six blocks from the beach. After Megan was done, it was my turn. When I came out of the bathroom, I inquired if she wanted to go to the Executive Lounge as I was a lifetime Diamond member and were invited as their guests for á la carte Peruvian-American dishes as well as a drink in the outdoor roof-top terrace. Once again, all was free.

"Sure, why not?" Megan answered as I slipped into a sportscoat over my jeans to make us really look like American tourists.

We had a little food, two glasses of wine and then realized jet lag was coming on strong. We made it back to the room and for the first time ever, crawled into the same bed. As I was about to turn off the light, Megan turned to me and whispered, "Goodnight Moon," which sent my mind spiraling back to the kids and Pine Lake. In turn, I leaned over and kissed her goodnight. Not a passionate kiss mind you, but one of gratitude. Without her, this trip would never had taken place.

Morning came and we got ready to transfer to M'Gallery Manto Hotel to meet up with the Insight Tour group.

As I was checking out, Megan appeared and offered the

photos to the desk clerk while simply asking, *"Recuerdas haber visto a alguna de estas personas en tu hotel en los últimos dos años?"* which I learned meant, "Do you remember seeing any of these people in your hotel in the past two years?"

The clerk carefully looked at the photos. First Amy and Karen, then Derrick and finally Tommie and Su. At first, his facial expression was neutral until he saw Tommie and Su at which point, his eyebrows arched and I knew he'd remembered someone.

I know that hotel people are supposed to be discrete and so he slowly shook his head from side-to-side as if to infer none of the photos represented anyone he saw. I caught his drift and was prepared as I took the photos back, added a $50.00 bill to the photo of Tommie and Su and placed it on the counter with my fingers on the bill at which time I asked. "Are you sure none of these people look familiar?"

The clerk looked at me and then offered *"Recuerdo a la señora china porque era muy guapa, pero también muy nerviosa. Estuvieron aquí hace unos dos años,"* which Megan translated as, "I remember the Chinese lady as she was very beautiful but also extremely nervous. They were here about two years ago."

Megan looked at the clerk and asked *"¿Por qué no hablas inglés? Sé que puedes."*

The clerk then replied in English. "We are taught to speak Spanish first and only if the guest wants us to speak English do we do so."

I looked at the clerk and asked, "Why do you remember the lady."

The clerk paused, looked to make certain no one was listening besides us and noted. "First, she was very beautiful and with the white man. Normally, Chinese women are only with Chinese men. Second, she was very nervous like someone was following her."

"Do you know where they went?"

"No, I do not. We don't ask questions."

With that, I took my hand off the $50.00 and slid it across the desk. The clerk was nervous as he looked around again and quietly slid the fifty into his pocket. When you're only making about $500 per month, fifty dollars is a lot of money.

We now knew that at least Tommie and Su might be in Peru.

We didn't know about Derrick, Amy and Karen.

As we left the hotel, we had the same hotel courtesy driver take us to the M'Gallery Manto Hotel. As we pulled into their parking lot, Megan offered the same photos and asked the driver if he'd driven any of the people and that we knew that Tommie and Su had stayed at the Hilton. He paused and then affirmed he'd seen Tommie and Su with two ladies and a man at the hotel but hadn't driven them.

The driver noted he only remembered because the bellman had commented, *"Dama que ama a las damas,"* or "Lady who loves ladies," when he saw Amy holding hands with Karen in the elevator when he took them to their room. We now knew all five had stayed at the Hilton and Melia was correct, they'd come to Peru for which, Megan gave the driver an extra $20.00 as we joined the tour group.

The Tour:

The tour group was mostly couples, my age, in other words, old. They all seemed like nice people and it was interesting watching the eyes of the old guys as they took a look at Megan. I'm certain some of the women weren't too happy having such an attractive woman in the group but there was nothing we could do about it except hope they'd quickly realize how good of a person she really was.

The first stop was Casa Aliaga, which had been the home of the Aliaga family for seventeen generations, which is a colonial-style building located in the historic center of Lima in the Libre district and only a few blocks from the Hilton. We learned that the mansion was built on a huaca in May 1536, where the huaca was a religious location laid out by the Incas to express the cosmology of the culture and aligned astronomically to various stellar risings and settings as a way to tell time.

The original owner was Conquistador Geronimo de Aliaga while current owner is Gonzalo Jorge de Aliaga Ascenzo, VIII, Count of San Juan de Lurigancho, who wasn't home. I wondered if the Conquistador would be spinning in his grave if he knew the front of his house was on a city street with an ice cream shop on one side and a clothing store on the other. As we wandered through nearly 500 years of history I thought back to my Uncle Will and how he'd traced the Terrill family back to 65BC and thought...'rookies' to myself, although I must admit the house was really neat.

Megan had the 'family photos' as I called them on her phone but we didn't have a chance to show them to anybody. It was also my belief that 'the family' wasn't going to stay in Lima too long. Just long enough to find a safe place to live.

The next stop was the Museo Larco museum that has the largest collection of Pre-Columbian art in South America. Megan opted to go with the VIP tour guide to see the private collection while I sat on the patio and drank two bottles of Cusqueña, known for its smooth taste often associated with the country's rich history and culture. It was a very warm day and the beer tasted good, but still didn't beat Spotted Cow on my list of great beers.

We had a group dinner as all the pretenses began to melt, the questions of where are you from had answers including Virginia, California, Florida, England and Waldwick which got everyone's brows scrunched until I added Wisconsin.

The following morning, we flew to Cuzco and made our way to the Sacred Valley. My first thought was 'whoopee ding' until we got there and then it was 'holy shit!" The place was simply incredible simply because the Sacred Valley of the Incas, also known as the Urubamba Valley, offered a glimpse into the heart of the ancient Inca Empire. I first thought it was going to be like going to the Dells until we started looking around. Incredible! Simply incredible! We were herded to Ollantaytambo which was an Inca fortress known for its well-preserved stonework and terraced agricultural fields and gateway to Machu Picchu, as the train to the ancient citadel departed from here. On board, Megan and I had a couple of Chicha de jora which is a traditional Peruvian corn beer before arriving at the entrance to Machu Picchu which is a UNESCO World Heritage Site.

Having another one of those jaw-dropping moments, we saw one of the most iconic archaeological sites in the world, then went to Pisac that has some really neat Inca ruins perched high above the valley. Pisac is a town famous for its Sunday market... also, it seems when tourists arrive... with a wide variety of handcrafted textiles, jewelry and souvenirs that had Megan drooling. We had lunch at Altar Inca and were served Pachamanca, which is a pre-Hispanic cooking method that involves cooking food in an underground oven made of hot stones. The name comes from Quechua: 'pacha' means earth and 'manka' means pot or food. The ingredients we chose included pork, chicken and beef.

We took a pass on the Guinea Pig and Alpaca but did include potatoes, corn, beans, yucca, plantains, and chili peppers all seasoned with Huacatay which added a minty flavor, Aki panca, which created a smoky flavor, garlic, cumin and oregano that was wrapped in banana leaves and placed on the hot stones covered with earth to steam. Needless to say, it was the Inca's version of Cornish Pasty that I topped off with three extra-strength indigestion tablets from the pharmacy next door as I washed down with yet a couple more Cusqueña, while Megan went shopping.

That night, we stayed at Aranwa Sacred Valley Hotel and met Juan Carlos, the bartender. As had become part of our routine, Megan pulled out her phone and shared the family photos with Juan. Juan looked at us and the casual, friendly demeanor quickly faded. We knew something was going on but had no idea what. We also knew Juan couldn't talk about it then and we needed to come back. We told him we were on the tour and needed to complete the trip but would come back and meet with him and asked what day he had off. We needed to make sure he knew we were serious and slipped him a fifty and told him we'd be back.

We kept to the schedule of the tour, staying at Hacienda Huayoccari which was a quaint, delightful hotel with one of the most beautiful views you could imagine. With an incredibly friendly staff, magnificent rooms and incredible grounds, I could see why people fell in love with the place. I thought back to America and how contrived everything based on your socio-economic profile.

The following morning, we boarded the train that would take us deeper into Machu Picchu. The ride was simply awe inspiring and made the entire trip even more worthwhile. We stopped at Ollantaytambo ruins and visited an Inca temple made of pink granite whose windows are aligned to the position of the sun on the solstices making me realize, once again, that not all the world started in Europe. That night it was time for our goodbye dinner where all fourteen people who'd been strangers a few days before promised to keep in touch.

We made it back to Aranwa and signed an agreement with Insight Vacations denoting we were ending our tour there as we wanted to spend a few more days exploring the area. The tour people were quite nice and provided us with passes allowing us to take the train back to Cuzco whenever we wanted.

We checked back into the hotel, went to the bar, had a drink with Juan and made arrangements to meet with him the following day for lunch. I could tell by his facial expressions he was as 'nervous as a whore in church' that dad used to say, even though I don't think either of us ever saw one there other than a couple of politicians.

Information:

Precisely at noon, we met at a cantina and sat out in the courtyard away from any eyes and ears. What Juan had to share was more than we ever expected. Megan opened her phone and showed Juan the photos. The first one was of Amy and Karen as Juan politely commented *"dama que ama a las damas"*.

I noted. "Juan, the lady on the left is my wife. The woman on her right is her mistress."

Megan took her phone and found the photo of Tommie and Su as I offered. "This is my brother and his wife. He's my business partner."

Next photo of the family. "This is our family photo. The young man on the left is my son who lives in Wisconsin. The young lady is our daughter who is in hiding because some really bad people wanted to harm her. The young man on the right is our other son who we believe is here in Peru."

With my mention of Derrick, I saw the sides of Juan's mouth drop in fear as his eyes indicated he knew or had heard rumors about him.

I continued. "Nearly three years ago, there was an accident and my wife thought I'd been killed and the family had some problems they were afraid would end up harming them. When that happened my wife, her mistress, my brother and his wife and our son left the United States and we believe have settled here in Peru. When we were in Lima, we confirmed they had been at the hotel we stayed at. We are on this trip not to hurt them, but to have some papers singed so that we can get on with our lives. Can you help us?"

Juan looked around to make certain no one was watching or within listening distance as he lowered his voice and whispered, "Montaña del diablo".

I frowned, looked at Megan who offered, "Devil's Mountain."

"Devil's Mountain?" I asked looking at Juan who was now beginning to sweat profusely.

Again, Juan looked around before speaking. "Two years ago, the man you call your son came to our area and purchased a mountain top about one-hundred kilometers from here. Over the next year, he purchased a great deal of materials and hired many workers and built what many would call a fort with high walls and a large steel gate.

While the policía were suspicious and thought it was a cartel, there has been no drug activity and they have done nothing illegal that the policía can determine. They paid the workers a premium and have kept to themselves. The only problem has been some Chinese who came asking about them simply disappeared."

"What do you mean, disappeared?"

"They stayed at our hotel, paid for the room and rented a car. They didn't say where they were going. After one week when they hadn't returned, their stay was up and we went to their room and found all their belongings including their passports. That was over one year ago and no one has seen them since."

"What about the car?"

Juan didn't answer but continued on. "At first, all was fine and then things began to happen."

"Like what?" I asked.

"First there was an accident that involved the rental car. The policía said a Chinese lady was driving and she was killed. They noted that, even though the car burned, they were certain she was dead before the accident and the car had been rolled off a cliff and into a ravine."

I shuddered to think that Su was dead as Juan continued. "We reported the missing Chinese to the policía and they began to suspect they were the ones who killed the lady. No one knows who did it. The policía tried to question your son but they were told he had left the country in a private plane. Like all accidents or murders, time takes a toll and soon everyone here began to forget."

"Did my son return?"

"No one knows, except that, when he built the house, he had the workers create a place to land a helicopter and one day some of the people in the village saw a helicopter in the area which is quite strange."

"Anything else?"

"Yes. The mountain is called Devil's Mountain because anyone who goes there does not return."

"What?" I countered incredulously.

"Two of the local workers went there and never came back. After that, people were afraid and no one goes there anymore."

"What about my brother and my wife?" I asked, now with great concern.

One day, *Amante de la dama*... the lady with the light brown skin and an *hombre sin pene* came to the hotel. They'd come to town with your brother but came in while he was getting petrol for the car."

"Hombre sin pene?" I asked.

Megan politely interjected. "Juan probably means Karen." Juan clarified. "A lady in man's clothes with very short hair. As short as yours."

"What did they want?" I asked, now quite concerned.

Juan stared out into the street and then back at me and noted. "They came to ask if we knew someone who could drive them from Montaña del diablo to here so they could catch the train to Cuzco. They were aware the local villagers were afraid and that's why they came here."

"What happened?" Megan asked.

"They offered my cousin five hundred US dollars to bring them here."

"Did he do it?" "Si!"

"So, they came here?"

"Si! We warned my cousin to stay away but he did not listen. Instead, he went to see if he could work for your son. Instead, he, too, disappeared."

"I'm sorry." I offered as Juan continued. *"Amante de la dama and hombre sin pene,* which translated meant. "They got on the train and left and that's all I know."

"Do you think my son is still with my brother?"

Juan shook his head 'no'. One day a helicopter came again as one of the villagers was working in his garden and saw your son board the helicopter. We think he left and only your brother is there except, as rumor has it, he has many guards with guns and no one is willing to disappear simply to see what's going on."

"What about the police?" I asked.

Juan looked at me, shook his head and noted..."We are a poor country. People here don't have a lot. The policía are good honest people but they too have a difficult time. When they cannot prove there has been any problem and someone provides a little extra, what can one do except look the other way? The Chinese lady's accident. The missing Chinese. My missing cousin! They're gone, but no one can prove there was anything wrong and no one is willing to go up to Montaña del diablo."

We'd reached the end of the conversation. Megan opened her purse and handed Juan a U.S. hundred-dollar-bill. Juan looked at it and realized it was a lot of money and thanked us. I looked at Juan and assured him that what he had said would remain between the three of us. We all stood and he left. We walked to the train station and caught the train to Cuzco. Our glorious tour was over, in its place was fear and trepidation. Was Tommie really a killer? What happened to Derrick? Where did Amy and Karen go? Would we ever find them?

Cuzco:

The train ride to Cuzco was just as beautiful as the ride out to Machu Picchu where the only difference was the fact my mind was now wondering where in hell Amy had gone and why. We entered the city and took a taxi to the Hilton Garden Inn in City Centre simply because it was the only Hilton in Cuzco and we were using Hilton Honor points again.

We made our way to the front desk and provided identification as well as my Visa card for ancillary items. I hadn't used the card since before the debacle, as I called it, and so there was little thought about what all was on it. To my chagrin, the clerk came back and apologized saying, "I'm sorry, Senior, the card has been denied."

"What? That's impossible." I retorted.

"No sir, the message says that you have reached your credit limit."

I was incredulous as I replied. "That's impossible. I haven't used the card in nearly three years and the balance is on autopay every month."

"I'm sorry, Senior. Do you have any other credit cards?" Megan stepped in and offered hers and it went right through.

We got our bags and headed for the room. No bellman. No one to make us feel important. As we were walking to the room I expressed my embarrassment. "That's crazy! I know the invoice is on autopay and I haven't got a statement in three years."

Megan tried to calm me down as she inquired, "Do you have your password?"

"Sure, it DVMAG=5" "Huh?"

"Derrick, 'V', Melia, Amy, George equals five."

Megan then inquired. "Does anyone else have access to the card?"

"Yes, Amy. It was our common card, why?" "George, perhaps she's been using it."

I was getting royally pissed until Megan noted. "If she has and we can go online, we can see where she's been using it to see if she left a tracer for us to follow."

All of a sudden, I realized, in using the card, Amy had done us a favor. When we got to our room Megan opened her laptop, went to the browser, put in the Visa web address on the back of my card, added my number and then 'DVMAG=5' and sure enough, there was a complete summary of charges for six months that stopped nearly two months ago, superseded by a message that the bank account was overdrawn and funds could not be transferred. The paper trail showed that Amy had stayed one night at the Wyndham Costa Del Sol Cuzco in late June which corroborated Juan's story that his cousin took Amy and Karen to the train back then.

The next two charges were for $130.00 each on LATAM airlines. With 48 weekly flights, we checked and that was the cost to fly from, Cuzco, Peru to Santiago, Chile. The next charge was for $24.00 at the Doubletree Santiago - Vitacura and I knew Amy had dipped into our points to pay for the room.

I wondered why Chile? Megan Googled to learn same-sex marriage became legal in Chile on March 10, 2022 and they have the same legal rights and protections as heterosexual couples. We already knew that Peru tolerates and protects same-sex couples but doesn't currently allow same-sex marriages. Perhaps, the reason for the relocation was marriage. Perhaps it was to escape from Devils Mountain. We didn't know.

Digging a little deeper, Megan found an article about Santiago that reported. Santiago is a cultural powerhouse whose historic center is filled with world-class museums, stately theaters and palm-lined plazas. Key neighborhoods for travelers include Barrio Yungay for street art, Barrio Italia for shopping, Lastarria for strolling, Providencia for sleeping and Vitacura for dining. Come nightfall, neighborhoods like Bellavista and Barrio Brasil explode with energy as Chileans party until sunrise at clubs blasting everything from Latin rap to K-pop, EDM and Reggaeton.

The article noted "Santiago makes a great base as there's plenty to do within an hour of city limits. You can raft whitewater in Cajon del Maipo, swirl Cabernet in the Maipo Valley or snowboard at some of the biggest and best ski resorts in the Southern Hemisphere." The final paragraph put it all together that said "LGBTIQ+ travelers should head to Bombero Núñez street, which is lined in bars, clubs and performance venues where drag queens entertain into the wee hours of the night. When going out to dance, don't even think about showing up before midnight!"

While Cuzco was beautiful, we needed to go to Santiago and made reservations for the following morning to fly there. Five and one- half hours later, we landed. While Cuzco was 'quaint' Santiago was incredibly dynamic. What an incredible city, as we made our way to the Doubletree Santiago - Vitacura.

The only time I'd ever heard Chile referenced was for it's fine wine and also Chilean Sea Bass. Boy were we in for a surprise! Like Peru, the Chilean Andes represented another segment of the impressive mountain range, that stretches all along the western edge offering a unique blend of rugged beauty, diverse ecosystems, and cultural richness. At 2,700 miles long, the Chilean Andes are one of the longest mountain ranges in the world. Little did I know then that we'd end up seeing most of them. While the Andes in Peru were dormant, the Chilean Andes are home to numerous volcanoes, including active ones like Villarrica and Llaima.

In a world built 'upside down' in our American mindset, the farther south you go, the colder it gets to the point that the southern Chilean Andes are covered in extensive glaciers. When you get down to the southern-most region, you've got the Chilean Fjords which are as pronounced and dramatic as those I saw in Norway. I remember from my trip to Stockholm for the Nobel ceremony that the Chilean fjords were formed by glacial erosion during the Ice Age and characterized by rugged mountains and deep valleys. The Norwegian fjords were also formed by glaciers but they tend to be narrower and deeper but also dominated by mountains and valleys. What's really crazy is how the Andes affect the weather. Incredibly wet in some areas, the Atacama Desert, that lies at the northern foot of the Chilean Andes, is one of the driest places on Earth.

When we checked in, I attempted to use Hilton Honors points only to learn they'd all been used. It seems that Amy and Karen stayed at the hotel for an entire week. Once again, Megan bailed us out. Megan went to the Visa account to see if there were any new charges and there weren't. We had the right church, just didn't know which pew, as the credit card charge paper trail ended in Santiago, probably when Amy had the card rejected for hitting its limit.

I looked at Megan and wondered where in hell Amy would have gone. Did she and Karen get married? What was going on? I then realized, Amy knew someone in Chile and that was Pepe, our Oenologist who would come to Waldwick every three months to perform the Solera process of taking 25% of the top or youngest barrel of wine and transfer it to the one below and then take that blend to the next until he reached the fourth, or bottom barrel, that would then be bottled and sold.

"Where does Pepe live? Megan asked.

"I don't know. Everything was always done by e-mail." "How are we going to find him?"

"Well, Pepe is an expert on Pinot Noir. This means, he's probably from the area that produces that type of wine."

Once again, it was back to the laptop and a report on the fine wines of Chile which was broken down into three regions. The Central Region which included the Maipo Valley known for producing some of Chile's most prestigious wines, especially Cabernet Sauvignon. The Colchagua Valley famous for its Carmenere, a grape variety that thrives in Chile's climate that produces excellent Cabernet Sauvignon, Merlot, and Syrah and the Rapel Valley known for its diversity of wines, including Cabernet Sauvignon, Merlot, Syrah, and Sauvignon Blanc.

I shook my head 'no' as the only one that might be correct would be the Maipo Valley and we were running out of options.

Megan clicked on the Southern Region that summarized the Casablanca Valley known for its cool climate wines, especially Sauvignon Blanc as well as excellent Pinot Noir and Chardonnay and Leyda Valley known for its maritime influence, producing fresh and crisp wines, especially Sauvignon Blanc and Pinot Noir.

This option had the most potential but I thought we'd better check the final Northern region around Santiago that had the Aconcagua Valley known for its high-altitude vineyards, producing concentrated and age-worthy wines, especially Cabernet Sauvignon and Carmenere.

I placed my hands upon Megan's shoulders as she sat looking at the laptop screen and noted. "Dime against a dollar they went to the Southern Region."

Megan Googled 'Southern Wine Region' and the following appeared. "The Southern Chilean Wine Region or 'The South' is one of the five principal wine regions of Chile. It encompasses all wine-growing areas in the BioBio and Araucanía Regions and is composed of three minor wine districts; Itata Valley, Bío Bío Valley and Malleco Valley." I looked at the map and realized the 'south' was the southern wine region and not southern Chile where the glaciers are. The area is surrounded by the Andes Mountains to the east and the Pacific Ocean to the west and has a Mediterranean climate with warm, dry summers and cool, wet winters influenced by the Pacific Ocean to the west and the Andes Mountains to the east, that create a unique microclimate.

We had our marching orders. Now the question became how in hell did we get there? Megan went on line and sure enough LATAM flew to Temuco in less than 90 minutes for only $66.00 each. We booked a room at the Best Western Ferrat and the next morning were off to the airport.

Upon arriving, our mouths dropped open. We certainly weren't expecting the incredible beauty that surrounded us with a diverse landscape featuring rolling hills, forests, rivers, and volcanoes. The airport had the little brochures about what to see and do and the thing that stood out the most was the fact that the wineries focus on sustainable and organic viticulture, respecting the environment and local culture that made me think of Luke who'd planned our foundation facility with the same objective.

Now the question became, how did we find Pepe?

Itata Valley:

We rented a car and our first venture was into the Itata Valley where we went to all the vineyards where no one heard of Pepe. After about six tastings, I don't think either Megan and I could have carried on lucid conversation anyway.

The next day, we made it to BioBio Valley with the same results, except we drank smaller glasses of wine. Next, was Malleco Valley that motivated me to wonder if we should take the bus to Puerto Montt, rent a car and use it as a home base. Wrong! It was a five hour drive back to Malleco and so we stayed the night in Temuco.

The next morning, we set out for Malleco Valley with the intent on visiting all five primary vineyards. Viña Santa Cruz, Viña Maqui, Viña Trabunco, Viña Las Pizarras and Viña Alto Malleco.

We stopped at Viña Santa Cruz known for its high-quality Pinot Noir and Chardonnay first and inquired if anyone knew an oenologist by the name of Pepe. They were polite in saying, "no," but I didn't believe them. Something in the eyes, again. The next four provided the same polite answer and we were about to give up when we elected to take the drive to the higher elevations and visit Viña Alto Magnifico.

As I drove, Megan provided a summary of the winery from our hotel tour book that said. "Viña Alto Magnifico is one of the most interesting wineries in the Malleco Valley. Its location at high altitude allows them to take advantage of a cooler climate, which translates into wines with vibrant acidity and more defined aromas. The cold climate approaches the extreme of what is suitable for winemaking and the relatively short growing season limits what varieties growers are able to plant. The high rainfall of 1300 millimeters or over four feet per year, is a far cry from the semi-arid heartlands in the north of Chile, such as Aconcagua, or the warmer, drier parts of the Central Valley region."

"On the positive side vineyards enjoy more hours of sunlight than the more northerly regions, and the nights are considerably cooler than the days. This diurnal temperature variation slows the ripening period of the grapes, and as a result, the wines of Malleco Valley have a fresh, racy acidity that complements their varietal character."

"Malleco Valley's red volcanic clay and sandy soils are reasonably well drained – essential, given the area's high levels of rainfall. The lack of water held in the ground means the vines have to work harder for hydration and, as a consequence will develop less energy-sapping foliage and lower yields of grapes. The wines produced from these grapes have more-concentrated flavors and excellent structure".

"What makes Viña Alto Magnifico special? First is the altitude. Their vineyards are located at a higher altitude than the valley average, which significantly influences the ripening of the grapes and the expression of their flavors. The varietals can vary depending on the vintage. However, they usually stand out for their Pinot Noir, Chardonnay and sometimes white varieties, such as Riesling. The cooler climate of the upper Malleco area allows for wines with greater freshness and elegance, characteristics highly valued in Pinot Noir and Chardonnay. Finally, the focus on quality, such that it usually produces wines in smaller quantities, which allows them more rigorous control over the quality of each bottle where their Pinot Noirs tend to be elegant, with notes of red fruits, spices and sometimes a hint of smoke. The vibrant acidity makes them ideal to accompany white meats, poultry and soft cheeses."

Megan paused, looked at me and recited. "The name of the oenologist is Pepe Rodriquez."

Bango! We'd found our man!

Alto Magnifico:

We drove into the Viña Alto Magnifico parking lot, got out and walked into the visitor center. There was an elderly lady behind the counter who had a pleasant smile. I asked if she spoke English and she shook her head 'no'. Megan took over and told her who we were and that we had come to visit Pepe.

The old lady had a look of consternation spread across her face. Megan understood and said, *"Me llamo Megan y este es mi amigo, George. Venimos de Estados Unidos, donde creemos que Pepe trabaja para el señor Terrill como enólogo de Terrill B&B, donde viene cuatro veces al año para mezclar el vino"* or "my name is Megan and this is my friend, George. We have come from America where we believe Pepe works for Mr. Terrill as an oenologist for Terrill B&B where he comes to blend the wine."

"Si!" The old lady responded with a big smile on her face before adding. *"Pepe está en la ciudad. Debería volver en breve. Si quieres, puedo llamarlo y dejarte hablar con él."*

"What did she say?" I inquired.

"She said Pepe is with a friend and she can call him if you like." "Si!" I said in my most fluent and feeble attempt at Spanish as the lady nodded, turned, picked up the phone and called. A few seconds later she handed me the phone.

"Pepe, it's George. Yes, yes I'm fine. No, I'm not dead. I know, it was a surprise to me, too, that we were able to find you. Ok, let me ask my friend."

I took the receiver from my ear, looked at Megan and noted, "Pepe wants to know if we want to meet his friend and have lunch."

"Sure" Megan replied. "Ask him how long it will take us to get there."

I looked at Megan and reported he's at Viña Aquitania that we passed on the way from town. I then detailed the rental car we were driving to Pepe, gave the phone back to the nice lady, went out and got in our car. As I was driving, Megan took out her handy Chilean tourist guide and noted. "In 1993, Viña Aquitania pioneered the development of an innovative and successful wine project in Traiguén, Valle del Malleco, 650 km south of Santiago.

When there was no vineyard further south of the Biobío, Felipe de Solminihac in a visionary way, talked to his father-in-law, who was a farmer, to start the project and plant the first vineyards in the area, which would later give name to the name 'Valle del Malleco' of the Traiguén area and it started the entire wine industry in the area.

In 2000 the first SOLdeSOL Chardonnay wine was produced. Thanks to the quality of the wine, they obtained the recognition of the Ministry of Agriculture to expand the Wine Denomination to the South of Chile, creating the new name Valle del Malleco, Traiguén area. Two years ago, a new winery was created called Malleco del Magnifico that has become a powerful force in the Chilean wine industry.

"Pepe's having us come to a competitor?" I asked. "George, these people are all friends. They're all making a good living and are proud of their achievements."

We followed directions which wasn't hard as everything was just on the opposite side of the road and made it to the winery. Pepe was standing in the parking lot when we arrived. As I got out of the car, he came and gave me a big hug which made me feel good as it was great to see him. I introduced Megan and he gently shook her hand and then introduced us to Edwardo Gonzales, the owner of the vineyard who had us follow him into the house for lunch.

We had small talk and drank a glass of some of the greatest wine I'd ever tasted which, I had to admit, had more body than Terrill Pino Noir as Pepe explained to Edwardo our association and all about Terrill B&B. In a few moments, Pork Curanto accompanied by Milcao pancakes made from grated and mashed potatoes, lard and seasoning was served family style and oh boy, it was good!

Pepe couldn't get over that we came to visit. We hadn't shared with him our reason and wanted to wait until we were alone and not with a stranger. It came as a surprise when Pepe noted that Amy had been there with her 'friend' a few weeks prior and inquired about opening a restaurant in Puerto Montt.

"Did she say if she was going to stay?" I asked.

"No, Senior George. She and her friend said they looked around and thought it best to learn the restaurant business before trying their luck. I told them it was the smart decision as even in Chile, it is a tough business, especially in a tourist town."

"They left?" Megan inquired.

"Si. They were only here for two days and then departed." "Did they say where they were going?" I asked, wanting answers without tipping my hand.

"No! They just thanked us for our hospitality."

"So there not here?"

"Oh no! If they were, all of the town would be talking about the two...uhh...friends. Even with the new laws here in Chile, we don't see many couples as obvious as them."

We finished our meal and knew our journey had reached a dead end. We told Pepe we were planning on heading back to the States and he asked how we were going. We said by plane. Pepe noted he'd learned that in two days Cunard Queen Victoria would be in Puerto Montt. Pepe then asked Edwardo if he was still good friends with the Administrador de terminales.

Edwardo nodded 'si' as Pepe asked him to find out what the occupancy rate was on the ship before adding. "If you're planning on flying, you'll need to go to Santiago and then Houston and then Shecawgo and finally Wisconsin. I know, I've done it and it's a difficult journey."

Pepe added. "Normally, this time of year, the Queen Victoria sails at full capacity. However, if there's room, you'll be traveling on a segment of their annual 85-day cruise from Hamburg, Germany. The cruise already went to Florida, down the east coast of South America, around the Drake Passage and is now heading up the west coast. After Puerto Montt, it will then go through the Panama Canal to Fort Lauderdale. Take it from me, I've done it both ways and it's worth the few extra days."

Edwardo excused himself and returned with a big smile. noting he'd called his friend who contacted Cunard and learned the ship had an early disembarkation of a Princess Suite because someone became seriously ill and got off in Rio de Janeiro.

I looked at Megan and she nodded and I asked. "Could you please let your friend know we would like to travel with Cunard? Do you need a credit card for confirmation?"

Edwardo looked at Megan like she was from outer space. It seems that, when the Administrador de terminales calls and asks for a special favor for a special friend to the cruise line, the ship's captain not only has the red carpet rolled out, but its vacuumed and marked with a V.I.P. designation and the reservation is done on an honor system.

Lunch was done and we needed to make some sort of arrangements to go to Puerto Montt. What a wonderful day, where the hospitality was only exceeded by the incredible food and great wine. Even though we hadn't caught up with Amy, we knew she had been in Peru and left. We knew she'd been in Chile and was now somewhere else.

Puerto Montt:

The following morning, we went Puerto Montt and checked into the hotel. What a wonderful surprise. The city is surrounded by mountains, forests and lakes, providing a picturesque backdrop for visitors. We quickly learned that Puerto Montt offered a mix of Chilean and German influences, with a historic district that could have been in Hamburg, as well as a vibrant cultural scene. If we had more time (and money), the surrounding area offered plenty of opportunities for outdoor activities, including hiking, trekking, fishing, and kayaking.

Megan Googled the city and read, "Puerto Montt is considered the capital of the nation's Northern Patagonia province. The city was founded in 1853 after government-sponsored immigration brought Germans here to populate and develop the remote region. By 1912, a train linked Puerto Montt to Santiago, opening up trade and transport with larger cities. Beyond the city lies Chile's second-largest lake, Llanquihue Lake, watched over by the snowcapped volcanoes Osorno and Calbuco. On the lake's shores, villages boast endless delights, magnificent gardens and charming architecture from Old Europe."

I shook my head in disbelief. I guess too many westerns had me thinking it was either going to be a dusty little cattle town with the swinging doors to the saloon or perhaps a place for baby back ribs until we checked in to Hotel Cumbres Puerto Varas. Surprise! The hotel is a five-star resort whose accommodations were only superseded by the incredible service. We used the pool, had dinner and a couple of drinks and met some people from Germany, learning it was one of the highlight destinations for people from Europe because of its strong German heritage.

It being our last night in Chile, we decided to see the town and found it to be quite the tourist destination for the cruise ships, especially those sailing through the Chilean Fjords, where it's often considered a gateway to Patagonia with easy access to the region's stunning landscapes, seven national parks within driving distance and an incredible variety of wildlife. Our only regret was that we couldn't stay longer and promised each other we'd come back. My, what a wonderful, wonderful surprise!

Because it was a sightseeing stop, the Queen Victoria was in town until 5:00 PM and so we waited until mid-afternoon to board. Megan went to the Purser's desk and made all the financial arrangements and said it was like we were royalty. Edwardo's friend had made certain we were treated special. We knew there would be ten stops to Fort Lauderdale with the highlight going through the Panama Canal. Pepe was right, the cost was less than the Business Class airfare we would have paid simply because we spent all my miles coming down.

I hadn't been on a cruise since we went with the kids and Megan had never cruised. I hoped she wouldn't get sea sick and offered to get her some Dramamine patches for behind her ears. She said 'no' and the motion didn't bother her. We were going to be onboard for 19 days and so we settled in. We were also quite careful with our on-board charges as horror stories about runaway bills had always concerned me. The biggest surprise was the fact that our suite allowed us to eat in the Princess Dining Room where the chef prepared meals to match the area of the world in which we were traveling. Because South America has such a broad ethnic mix of European, African, Mestizo, South and East Asian cultures, the meals were an eclectic blend of different foods, tastes and pleasures. If that wasn't enough, we also had some of the best wines I'd ever tasted, some of which paled our own Terrill B&B to the point I vowed we needed to improve our offering, if I ever got back in the wine business.

We made it to Fort Lauderdale and, reluctantly, it was time to say goodbye to some of the nicest people and staff we'd ever met. As we made our way down the gangway, I noted that we were half way to Wisconsin and half way to Saint Martin and asked Megan, "do we go home or the Lighthouse?"

Megan recommended flipping a coin to determine where we were going which became a problem as I didn't have one. I mean who carries coins anymore? Megan opened her purse and took out a quarter. I called heads and it came up tails and Wisconsin and so we said "two out of three" and Saint Martin still lost. It didn't matter as we took a taxi to Miami and caught the $77.00 plus, plus, plus, afternoon flight on Spirit Airlines to Saint Martin where it seemed like I'd never left.

Mary Ann:

We arrived in Phillipsburg and took a taxi to the Lighthouse where I went to the security panel, lifted the cover, looked into the camera lens, pressed my right index finger on the print sensor and heard 'click' that opened the door to the tram. Whew! One never knows! Megan and I got in and headed up the incline as memories came flooding back to the day I was told to leave. The property, like everything else, was under the same order that had frozen all of our assets that took Tank six months to free and he was assured the right of occupancy had been returned to me. I hoped the two men who escorted me out kept their word about packing up our personal belongings and storing them until the whole mess was settled.

We reached the top and I pressed my index finger against the sensor and the door opened.

"Two locks?" Megan inquired.

"The first one was for the tram. This one's for the door and is linked to the other sensor just in case someone figured out a way to get up here without the tram."

I opened the door to the great room and switched on the kitchen light. The house was just as I'd left it. I told Megan to stay in the kitchen while I de-activated the security system which would then allow me to pull down the steel hurricane panels that covered the windows.

I put my code 120546 into the security panel, went to the control center and pressed the down button and heard the slight hum of the motors as the steel panels made their way down into their storage modules located below the main level of the house. With that, I flipped the switch and the pool light timer was activated. For three years, I'd had someone come and clean the pool every week. The last thing you want to do with a swimming pool is let it get empty or fill with debris and I'd spent money to keep it going even though we couldn't afford it. Now I was glad I did.

I came back to the kitchen as Megan offered, "The house is beautiful."

"Thanks, let me take you on a tour." For the next few minutes, I took Megan through the Lighthouse and pointed out the lights of Anguilla and why I designed the house the way I did. Next it was the upper level that consisted of the primary bedroom. The bare mattress was there and I knew we'd need to vacuum it to get the dust off the cover before making the bed.

Looking out, Megan noticed the balcony with the shower head as I noted that's where we took our showers.

"Even in winter?" Megan asked.

"Well, yes. We'd tough it out when those cold days happen and it only got up to 80 degrees."

I pushed the button and the false wall opened to expose the vault door. I went through the three-step security process again while telling Megan. "It's the same three permutations...eye, finger, numerical code, just in a different sequence. Using three different activators, we have six different combinations. If a person would somehow get the first three and then came here and opened the wall and tried the same sequence used on the tram, the door would lock for twelve hours and the security system would notify the police."

"So, you need to remember the sequence you used for the tram and not use it again?"

"Correct. When we had Wilco, you'd be connected to the security department. We had this as a back-up system in case we couldn't get through."

"Is it always the same series?" Megan asked.

"No, it's based on what I did at the tram which was eye, finger, code. Here I did code, eye, finger and viola, the door opened."

I motioned to Megan to follow me as we entered the vault. "This was designed to hold four people for up to six days with food, water and emergency power in case a hurricane hit. When we were here a few years ago, we were ready to use the vault, but the storm wasn't severe enough to challenge the house integrity."

We stepped inside as Megan's mouth dropped open and she exclaimed, "Oh, my God!".

I continued. "Unlike other vaults, this one has been carved into the side of the hill and we had steel bank vault panels put in like those on the cave back home. When you have well over a million dollars in fine wine and premium alcohol, you can't be too careful."

On the floor were several cardboard boxes that had been taped shut. Each one was labelled and dated and were ready for shipment in case we permanently lost possession of the Lighthouse. I pointed at the boxes and noted. "The men who came kept their promise as they put all our personal belongings in boxes." I looked at two cartons that were labelled 'Vêtements pour hommes' to which Megan recited "men's clothing." I looked at the next six boxes that said 'Vêtements pour femmes' and already knew they were marked 'women's clothing.' Megan looked at the six and noted, "it looks like Amy had a bigger wardrobe than you."

I replied, "Some of these are probably filled with Melia's clothes. She stayed here and felt none of the clothes were what she'd wear in Wisconsin."

I went to move one box but it was heavier than I planned and it was marked "Platos". I looked at Megan and inquired. "What, no Socrates?" which got a groan. Next was a carton labelled "Lino" which Megan politely told me meant linens. Whoever was told to put away all the personal stuff, really did a complete job.

"What do you want to do? Megan asked.

It was like moving day and so I suggested we bring the dish boxes as well as the linens and make the bed. "We can open the clothes tomorrow."

"You want to open all the clothes boxes?" Megan asked, somewhat concerned we'd be invading someone's privacy.

"Why not?" I countered. "Melia won't be wearing hers and who knows what's in the other boxes."

Before closing the vault door, I grabbed a bottle of Terrill Pinot Noir and then showed Megan the house security system and explained how the hurricane panels she saw went into place. I then noted how the tram worked and all the cool things the house included.

We returned to the main level and I showed Megan the other two bedrooms. One with a king-sized bed and the other with the bunk beds, each with half-baths to which Megan inquired, "What about showers?"

"Same thing as upstairs." As we went out by the pool, I pointed to the alcove with the shower built in and then took her over to the deck prow so that she could see how far up off the ground we were as I noted. "You'd have to be some sort of mountain climber to get up here as there's a six-foot angled edge to the deck they'd have to traverse."

"You thought of everything," Megan complimented.

We set about hauling and opening the linens and dishes and it seemed good to make the Lighthouse back to operational. It didn't take too long and we were done. Whoopee!

"How long do you want to stay?" Megan inquired.

"Well, let's see. I have nothing to go back for and all my bills are on auto-pay. We have satellite TV which means we can watch TV as if we were at home. Do you have anything to go back for?"

"Not really."

"We need to sign a contract with a management company for the house that means it will take some time before we get any listings. On top of that, it's getting cold in Wisconsin and will be in the eighties here. How long do you want to stay?"

"Hmmm!"

"My vote is we stay as long as we want. We both need more time simply to let sleeping dogs lie."

"Sounds good to me."

"Tomorrow, we can go to Carrefour and stock up on groceries. If it's all right with you, we can plan on eating out twice a week and cook the rest of the time."

"You've got it all figured out, don't you Mr. Terrill?"

"No, Ms. Egan. I'm playing it by ear until we get things resolved."

"What happens if Amy and Karen aren't here?"

"Then we keep looking, but my sixth sense leads me to believe this is where they came."

"If so, why didn't she stay here?"

"Because I erased all the entry codes when I left except mine. Which, by the way, reminds me, we should add you to the list in case you need to get in when I'm not here."

"Really?"

"Sure. Come with me."

We went back to the 'office' where I booted up the computer and waited for the security logo to appear. I looked into the camera, put my finger on the touch pad and added my code. With that, the screen changed and I was able to select "add member".

"Here, sit down and do exactly as the commands tell you to."

The first command was to look at the black dot on the screen. Megan did as directed and the computer recoded her retina. Then the screen changed and instructed her to put one of her fingers on the touch pad.

"Which finger should I do?" "That's up to you."

Megan looked at me, smiled, gave me the bird and pressed it on the touch pad with a mischievous smile on her face.

We watched as the screen showed it copying her fingerprint. Once again, the screen changed and told her to add a six-digit numerical code which she did.

The final screen appeared and took a 'photo' of her and indicated she had been authorized to use the full security system at the Lighthouse including all entries, as well as the computer and vault.

"What happens if you rent the house?" Megan asked.

I replied "When we rent the house, the guests will be provided a six-digit code that will open and lock the doors for the period of their rental but won't give them access to the security room or the vault which is why we installed the panel. Curiosity is eliminated that way."

Megan stood as I suggested she give it a try. We got in the tram and went to the base of the hill and got out. I locked the system and told her to go for it. One-two-three and the system responded.

"What happens if there's a power failure?" Megan asked.

"There are secret plans. But if I tell you, I'll have to kill you because, you see, I'm really... Bond... James Bond."

"Then which Bond Girl am I? Honey Ryder? Pussy Galore? Or perhaps Andrea Anders?" Megan smirked.

"Take your pick, anyone of them is fine with me." I countered.

Megan's smile appeared and she offered. "Let's see, Honey emerged from the sea in a white bikini. Pussy is famous for her name and was a formidable opponent turned love interest. Then Octopussy ran an all-women floating island and was the only Bond girl to have a movie named after her."

Megan paused, raised her index finger and said, "I know Jinx Johnson where she and James really get it on."

"I think of you more as Mary Ann from Gilligan's Island." I offered.

There was a pause and then Megan inquired. "Huh? So you don't think I'm sexy?"

"Mary Ann WAS sexy!"

"She was?" Megan asked with an incredulous tone.

"Of course. For her...uhh...visual persona, she wore short shorts or her famous red jumper that were a key part of her character's wholesome, all-American, yet sexy image. My only question was, why would she take all those clothes on a three-hour cruise?"

Megan simply shook her head as I got serious. "The big difference is that Mary Ann had so many other great qualities the Bond Girls never seemed to have that I see in you."

"Like what?"

I shrugged and thought of the Boy Scout Creed... 'trustworthy, loyal, helpful, friendly, courteous, kind, obedient, cheerful, thrifty, brave, clean and reverent, but couldn't envision Megan in the khaki pleated shorts with knee socks, Buster Brown lace-tied shoes and the neckerchief I had to wear and so I offered, "kindness and compassion, resourcefulness, optimism and dedication."

"Me?"

"Yes, you." I replied with a big smile.

Megan's bottom lip protruded as what started out as a lark turned into a compliment which was something I should have offered long ago.

Megan glanced at the floor of the tram and then at me and I could tell she was moved by what I'd said and then asked, "can I still be a Bond Girl?"

I pressed the button and tram began its slow descent as I...in my worst British accent, replied. *"Of course, my dear! I'm James Bond and you get to be Bond Girl number 69 in my next movie entitled, 'The Lighthouse' where you will be 'Lascivious Layla'* as I attempted to sing the chorus to Derrick and the Domino's... *"Layla, you've got me on my knees. Layla, I'm begging, darling, please Layla darling, won't you ease my worried mind?*

Megan giggled, shook her head, laughed, then raised her eyebrows and replied... "girl number 69? Lascivious? Oh my!" as she waved her hand in front of her face like a fan as she feigned embarrassment.

We got in and the tram began making its way back up to the house with giggles all around as the extent of the day began settling in. We'd started the morning disembarking from the cruise ship in Fort Lauderdale. Ubered to Miami International. Rode on Spirit Airways and made it to the Lighthouse. When the tram stopped, we got out and I went to the kitchen counter and flipped the switch on the instant wine cooler, set it at twelve degrees Celsius and slid a bottle of Terrill B&B Pinot Noir into the sleeve knowing that, in two minutes, it would reach and maintain the optimum drinking temperature. I wanted to see if the Terrill B&B was as good as the Chilean wine Pepe had for lunch.

Feeling grungy from the plane ride, Megan asked if she could use the pool. I replied, "Of course, it's my house."

Off went the clothes and in went Megan motivating me to join her and it sure felt good to be in my own pool, at my own house, with my friend until we both got 'pruned' that is.

I looked at my finger tips and saw the wrinkles, showed them to Megan and she adroitly noted 'pruning' was actually blood vessel constriction where your nervous system signals the blood vessels in your fingertips to reduce the blood flow to the area. As the blood vessels shrink, the skin loses volume and starts to wrinkle creating a pattern of ridges and grooves. My mind immediately went to the hilarious episode of 'Seinfeld' in the Hamptons where George gets caught with his 'pants down' and says it was 'shrinkage' because he'd been in the pool.

With a smirk on my face, wondering if 'shrinkage' was true and too shy to check, we got out, dried off, sat at the outdoor table and emptied the bottle of Terrill Pinot Noir.

The Chilean wine was exquisite but, from my memory, I thought the Terrill Pino Noir had a little more body and therefore not susceptible to 'pruning'.

Ahh! To be a Sommeliers as I lifted my pinkie finger in self-exclamation as we finally headed for bed, where I don't think the sheets were even up to our chins before we both were sound asleep.

Cartons:

Morning came and I decided we needed some good French pastry. I got in the Rover and went over to Orient Beach to Good Morning, got fresh croissants and brought them back to the house, arriving as Megan was just getting up.

When you've been travelling from country to country, the amount of clothes you pack are spartan to say the least. I think I had three different changes and Megan perhaps four and none of them designed for Caribbean casual. For me, it was no big deal. I still had my clothes at the Lighthouse. For Megan, it was an issue, yet stored in the vault were boxes of Amy and Melia's clothes.

We had breakfast and I suggested we open all the boxes. "Even the women's clothes?

"Sure, why not?"

"Even Amy's?" Megan asked as if we were invading Amy's privacy.

I looked at Megan and appreciated her sense of propriety as I

replied. "Some of them were Melia's. If they fit, why not wear them? No one else ever will."

"You don't mind?"

"Heavens, no. I never saw Melia in them and they've only been worn a few times and I think they'll fit. It's up to you."

Another box was labelled *'livres, photos, papiers'* and I knew it meant books, photos and papers and decided they could wait for a rainy day.

Megan opened the first box and saw what appeared to be Amy's clothes. Megan gasped as she thumbed through Amy's dining attire and read off the labels. "Stella McCartney, Donatella Versace, Phoebe Philo and Carolina Herrera! My God, Amy has good taste."

"Ah yes she did or does." I replied.

Megan opened more 'Amy' boxes and simply shook her head in disbelief as she thumbed through clothes by Simone Rocha,

Molly Goddard, Victoria Beckham and Sandy Liang as she opined, "She's got expensive taste."

Megan carefully folded the clothes and put them back in the appropriate boxes and then opened box number three that contained panties as well as Amy's favorite short shorts, ribbed undershirt and string bikini that brought back fond memories as Megan proclaimed, "Reality!"

I offered. "Amy loved to wear those shorts and the undershirt she kept from when she came here to die."

"And she wore them in public?" Megan asked with a frown on her face.

"Sure, why not?" I incredulously responded.

Megan simply shrugged as she saw a different side of me that I don't think she ever considered as she opened the fourth box that certainly had to be Melia's. Inside were two horse collar dickies, three pairs of shorts, one romper, two halter tops, two hankie tops, which were literally triangles of rayon cloth with strings on them, as well as two mini- skirts, one pair of elevator sandals and one pair of gold big hoop earrings. Finally, there was the yellow button-up- the-front jumpsuit. Megan looked at me and asked, "How old is Melia?"

"Why?" I asked.

"These clothes look like they're from the sixties."

"Oh, there was a store in Phillipsburg called 'Retro Clothes' and I think that's where she bought them the day she got her tattoo." "Melia has a tattoo? Megan incredulously asked. "You said

she was always so conservative."

"I guess so. I never saw it because it was placed in 'Never, Never Land.'" I replied.

"Never, Never Land? You mean like 'Peter Pan symbolizing the desire to escape the struggles and expectations of life."

"I don't know why Melia called it that, she just did. Perhaps it's an allegory to why placing it there is so private and personal."

Megan let out a, "Hmmm," to let me know she was either a bit embarrassed to see what my daughter had been wearing or realizing Melia was a little more liberal than I'd detailed as she continued taking the clothes out of the box.

Next was a pair of cut-off shorts, artfully distressed with frayed threading along both the front and back, revealing just enough skin to add a touch of allure. Megan simply offered a knowing nod before setting them aside—a clear indication that she intended to try them on.

Megan reached into the bottom of the box, looked at me and then looked again. Inside were the infamous itsy bitsy, teenie weenie and OMG swimsuits I'd seen the photos of.

Megan held up the brown teenie weenie as her head bobbed favorably. Next was OMG which consisted of nothing more than three tiny triangles and some strings and commented. "If Melia's conservative, I'd like to know what the liberals wear down here."

I looked at Megan and politely announced, "In many instances, simply a smile."

"You don't mind if I try these on?"

"Not at all. I don't think Melia's coming back. If she does, after two kids, I don't think she'll be wearing those. If you find something you like, we can wash it and you can wear it."

"You don't mind?" "Not at all?"

"Let me try on the shorts and one of the tops." "OK"

Megan came out wearing the shorts and the white dickie as she inquired. "Well?"

"I think you look great."

"Why did you call this top a horse collar?" Megan asked as her hand slid along the edge of the dickie. "I've never seen clothes designed like this before."

Forgetting Megan wasn't a 'farm girl', I elucidated that when plowing was done by horse, they wore a padded leather collar that went around their neck and down over their chests to distribute the pull on the horse.

The term dickie initially referred to false blouse front as a fabric insert worn to fill in the neckline of a jacket or low-cut dress. As times changed, in the 60's, instead of the horizontal bandeau, the vertical wrap became popular with women as a top that consisted of one piece of cloth that simply went from a waistband up and around their neck and down again.

This design allowed for full exposure of a woman's back, arms and shoulders with basic coverage of their breasts. With the sewn cassette or channel hem that allowed for string to be inserted that tied in the back, the wearer could adjust the width of coverage anywhere from somewhat modest to quite revealing.

Next, Megan did her 'fashion show' in the swimwear which is what she needed most. Itsy Bitsy didn't fit very well. Teenie Weenie looked great and I was certain it would be Megan's choice.

Finally, it was OMG and OMG. If Megan told me she was going to 'hang out' at the beach, she certainly would have two options. It's funny, we'd become quite 'accustomed' to each other. Yet, when she put on OMG it was more tantalizing than all the times I'd seen her in her birthday suit.

All that was left was the yellow nylon jump suit. When Megan came out, I almost choked as my mouth dropped open wondering if Melia really wore that in public. It left nothing, and I mean nothing, to the imagination and realized why Jack and Melia's first child was born nine months after she and Jack came here on vacation.

With two pockets strategically positioned on the chest and buttons all the way, and I mean all the way down, the front could be open or closed depending on the mood. I thought for a moment and realized, it was quite indicative of when young women appeared to be more self-confident than they've become. With the jump suit fully buttoned, I guess it was conservative, even though still revealing. However, with all the buttons undone, yikes! The big surprise came when Megan turned around and there was nothing but a thin layer of yellow that stole the show.

"I looked at Megan and asked, "You'd wear something under it, wouldn't you?"

Megan had a devilish smirk on her face and countered. "Perhaps. The only problem is the legs and sleeves are too long.

"You could get it altered." I offered.

"And you wouldn't mind?"

"Again, Melia's gone and it was simply a part of her life back then. If you want to, we can find a seamstress and have it done."

"OK." Megan said, somewhat surprised by my offer and the reality I was probably a little more liberal than she thought I was.

Megan asked if I wanted her to open the man's box. I told her 'no', I'd do it and got down on the floor and proceeded to sort out the shorts, shirts and shoes I hadn't seen in years. For men, the only thing that ever changes are the width of ties and that's one thing no one, outside the managers at the Dutch Hotels in Saint Maarten, ever wears.

As I was getting to the bottom of the box, I came across my post-surgical bathing suit, commonly known as a Speedo, which Lucille actually made to ride much lower and much briefer to the point I was embarrassed to pull it out.

Megan glanced at it, smiled and incredulously inquired. "You wore *that*?"

I nodded "yes" and detailed. "When we came here after my surgery and I was still in recovery, I had my choice, a suit like this that didn't show the dribbles and drips or not going swimming."

Megan nodded in assurance that she understood as she then inquired, "And now?"

"Again, the entire aspect of acclimation." I proposed with a tone of total indifference.

"You'd wear that now?" Megan incredulously inquired. "Sure, why not?" Acclimation removed the reservation.

The boxes we brought from the vault were all opened. As we stood, I looked at Megan and, in an effort of equanimity offered, "Wear what you want. There'll always be some negativity in our world as well as pushback, just as there will always be people who chastise us and our relationship. People will have different ideas regarding what we're all about. Those people really don't matter. It's about whether you like yourself and I like myself and we care for each other."

My head cocked to one side as I continued. "You've become

my best friend. Without you, I don't know how I would have survived. I know it's not perfect. I do know whatever happens, the world will go on. The weak will fall and yet we… you and I… will be standing together simply because the world is more or less a fixed thing and, externally, we've adapted ourselves to it and not the world to us!"

"We can please ourselves or we can please others. Emotions will constantly change... but our friendship and memories will always be there as one!"

Megan's hand reached out and grasped mine. Without word, she looked in my eyes as her chin tilted down in contemplation and then rose up such that our eyes met again. It was then that she began to speak. "George, we both need each other right now. We both have hills to climb and by walking hand- in-hand, we have each other's strength to rely on. That's what makes this so special. We've unraveled so many of the questions people use to take years learn about each other."

Megan looked down at the floor and then at me as she continued. "We've done so to the point you and I can stand face-to- face and look into each other's heart and realize where we're at. It's somewhere few people ever go...a place so good, so pure, so innocent... a place called acceptance, devoid of the physical fallacies that pervade so many others."

The spell was broken and we simply hugged each other. Once again, not an amorous overture but one of acceptance as my mind took me back to when things were good with Amy and me, and the fact it had taken fifteen years for our relationship to reach the same comfort point where we accepted each other for what we were. Nothing more! Nothing less! And that was good!

How grand, a place to be where there's acceptance. A location in time and space where you know each other, respect each other and above all else, believe in each other and the goodness therein.

I thought back to my marital treatise... *attraction, association, communication, understanding, trust, compromise and forgiveness*... and realized Megan and I were getting really close to being 'there'.

The moment passed as Megan looked at me, giggled and inquired, "Well, are you going to wear that thing or not?" as she glanced at the bikini in my hand.

Tattoo Who:

Pausing, Megan looked at me and reluctantly asked. "What do you think of tattoos?"

I shrugged my shoulders and replied, depends upon what, where and why?"

"I've always thought about getting one."

"You have?" I asked, somewhat surprised.

"Yes. Most women my age have at least one.

"What and where?" I asked.

Megan shrugged and replied. "I don't know... something, somewhere... small and unobtrusive. The most popular places are the wrist, ankle, shoulder and back but I'd want it to be something for me and those I wanted to see it, when I wanted them to see it and not some sort of... I don't know... advertisement.

I thought of Amy and the rose but didn't want to say anything as I replied. "It's your body, and you can do what you want to," as I thought of the melody to Leslie Gore's song *It's my party and I'll cry if I want to."*

"What would you think of me if I did?"

"It's not what I think of you, it's what you think of yourself. Ultimately, the most important thing is that you feel confident and beautiful. If you feel good about yourself, it will shine through and that's what's attractive to me."

"Aww! You're so sweet, George. "Perhaps something in what you called 'never, never land', like Melia's."

"If that's what you'd like, go for it." "Really. If I get one, will you get one too?"

"Yes, I want a big one on my face, perhaps my eye lids or neck. How about 'LO' on my left lid and 'VE" on my right? "

"You're kidding, aren't you?" Megan cringed.

"How about a naked lady on my arm?" I countered. "With the word 'mom' underneath?"

"You can have a live one on your arm any time you want, Mister Terrill. Anytime you want."

I got serious for a moment and asked, "Do you really want one?"

Megan smiled and shyly nodded 'yes.'

"OK, let's go for it."

"Really?"

"Sure, why not?"

"Oh my God!" Megan squealed and continued,

"Right here?

Right now?"

"Well no, not right here and now. You don't want me doing it, that's for sure. All I can draw are cows and pigs. We need to go into Phillipsburg. There's an old guy next to the hardware store whose supposed to be really good."

"You're serious?"

"Yes! I'm serious."

"What do I wear?"

"I don't think it's going to matter depending on where you get your tattoo."

Megan smiled and offered. "I like Melia's idea, that way it's just for you and me."

"I'm not getting one." I countered.

"I didn't mean it that way, dummy," Megan noted, all jingly with excitement.

I called and found out the tattoo parlor opened at ten and so we made our way into Phillipsburg, went inside and saw wall after wall of different designs. Just then, this little old man came out and smiled and asked who the tattoo was for and whether we'd given it careful consideration. Megan said 'yes' and offered, "something delicate and feminine."

The old guy detailed the entire wall of designs with everything from astrological symbols to flowers. When I saw the red rose I literally quaked to think Megan would 'join the club' and choose what I'd seen so many times before. Instead, she saw a small, four-color Monarch butterfly. I wondered if it was the same one Melia had. However, I said nothing as I saw Megan's eyes light up as she asked me, "Are you sure it's OK?"

"It's fine with me." I replied as I shrugged my shoulders in emphasis.

Megan and the little old man went into his studio and pulled the curtain closed. As I sat there, I began to wonder if Megan's choice was symbolic of her life.

Like the caterpillar, she'd gone through metamorphosis... breaking down her body, mind and soul and reorganizing them into the structures of a kind, gentle, giving person, where the transformation took place within the protective casing of friendship without pressure or ulterior motive.

As I sat there, I decided to look at all the options the old man had and came across the gender symbols for man and woman, where the symbol used in science for a male is a circle with an arrow pointing diagonally upward at around one o'clock representing the shield and spear of Mars, the Roman god of war associated with masculinity.

Then I examined all the zodiac symbols as I made my way through all the different iterations until I came to June 21-July 22 and the symbol for cancer resembling two circles or spirals connected by a curve, while also symbolizing the nurturing and protective qualities of the zodiac sign. My intent was simply filling time and then the urge came as I wondered if the old man could combine the cancer symbol with that of the symbol for men to create 'male cancer' as a prostate cancer symbol.

Megan came out with a huge 'shit-eating grin' on her face, although I don't know why it's called that as most people who'd eat shit wouldn't be grinning.

"Can I see it?" I asked.

"Later, Mister Terrill, later! How about you?"

I looked at Megan, then at the old man and inquired whether he could put two symbols together. The old man assured me he could as we went to his computer and simply merged the two.

"You mean like this?" he inquired. I nodded 'yes'.

"What size?"

"About five centimeters or two inches." "Where would you like it?"

I'd thought about it, remembered about where my prostate had been and indicated "lower back".

Megan's mouth dropped open. Conservative George was about to be inked as the old man and I went into his studio and fifteen minutes later I came out with my one and only tattoo.

"Let me see it." Megan asked.

"I'll show you mine if you show me yours," I joked.

And so it was, both Ms. Egan and I were now 'inked'. And yes, she'd placed the small butterfly precisely in a spot meant for welcoming eyes and approving glances that could be sequestered except when Megan wanted it to be.

It was then I realized why I was so attracted to Megan. She was the 'good' Amy I'd loved for thirty years without... so far anyway... the 'bad' Amy who broke my heart.

As we walked out to the Rover, Megan stopped, turned and gave me a big hug and simply said "thank you."

Having invested two hours in Megan's and my body modification, it was time for a late lunch and we decided to go 'local' for the day and simply returned to Anse Marcel Beach Restaurant below the Lighthouse and got somewhat fancied up with Megan wearing Melia's black shorts and white horse collar top with me in khaki shorts and navy-blue button-down collar polo shirt from Collars & Company.

I thought we made quite the pair until I saw the glances. It was bad enough when Amy and I would get the 'stare' simply because she was mixed race. I never expected it for Megan and me simply because I'm older than her. Yet, there it was and I know there were whispers behind our back with the term 'trophy bride' being bantered about in numerous conversations.

Megan caught the gist of what was going on, excused herself and went to the ladies' hut a little east of the restaurant. While she was gone, I had a moment to reflect on our relationship. For the first time since Megan moved in, the thought had indirectly come up regarding why we had a celibate relationship, other than the assumed lingering commitment to Amy.

We'd bathed together, swum together, slept together and kissed goodnight but had never been together, together. In so doing, I had no guilt feelings while the entire process of acclimation had taken place that removed any erogenous inclinations to the point we were both comfortable with each other in all other aspects.

Other than that first 'encounter', our relationship had been one of friendship as my mind went back to what I learned in the hospital about interpersonal, cross-gender attraction between people that can lead to friendship instead of romantic relationships. With us, it seemed the process was different from perceptions of physical attraction that we're able to flourish without turning sexual. In trying to understand how it could be that we traveled together, periodically slept in the same bed and everything else, I'm certain most people would wonder why we'd never been intimate? Half of it I knew was my subconscious insecurity after my prostate surgery. The other half I believed was Megan's reluctance to violate the sanctity of my love of Amy which I felt was a noble deed to say the least.

I remembered that interpersonal attraction is a major area of research in social psychology related to how much we like, dislike or hate someone that can be a force between two people that tends to draw them together while still resisting separation.

At the base of Megan and my relationship were two very lonely people without immediate friends who bonded, not only out of financial and emotional need but social, as well. One truly is the loneliest number and to simply have a friend with whom to share each day was a magnificent way to recover from the travails we both faced.

Once again, acclimation had allowed the normal bounds of propriety to erode to the point we were physically comfortable with each other without messing it up with sex. In other words, just like it had become with Amy and me.

The food was incredible and I was glad we only had the short walk to the tram and then back to the Lighthouse. It was only two o'clock and so Megan announced she wanted to get some sun.

For the next two hours we both lay out relaxing and enjoying the weather and got to examine each other's acquired body art which, I must admit, in my case, was quite personal and Megan's exquisite. Mine was simply the combination of the two symbols located on my lower back. Megan examined it and told me she thought it was quite 'tasteful'. I don't know how it would taste, but it certainly was personal as it showed both the symbols for cancer and man and therefore men's cancer.

As for Megan's, people were right, the old guy was truly an artist. Instead of a one-dimensional Monarch butterfly, not only was it colorful, but he'd added shading beneath the wings to make it look like it had landed on Megan as well.

As we lay there, Megan realized something seemed to be bothering me. After a pause, she asked, "George, can I be frank with you?"

"Well, I like you as Megan. I don't know if I'd like you nearly as much if you were Frank." I joked.

"No silly. That's not what I meant."

"I know, I was just joking. What is it?"

Megan looked at me, paused and then expressed, "The reason we get the 'look' is because you appear much older than you are."

"What can I do about that?" I asked.

"Well, first let's begin with your skin. You don't have any wrinkles and we won't need to work on that. However, if you begin to moisturize your face, it will help keep it hydrated and looking its best.

"Really?"

"Uh huh. Then there's your hair. Quite honestly, your hair style looks like it's from the forties. A new hairstyle can help freshen up your look and make you look your age."

"OK and where do I go to get that?" "The kitchen chair."

"You mean you can cut my hair?"

"I helped pay my way through my undergraduate program cutting guy's hair."

"OK." I said with a smile. Anything would be better than the buzz cut Tank's wife did and it sort of sounded sexy."

Megan paused and I thought I knew what was coming next as she added. "I know that your six months in the cave and all the stress you've been under has affected you. I also know that the one area it shows the most is your hair color.

I saw photos of you with Amy and the kids before the... uhh... 'incident', and your hair was light brown and then, since you came out of the cave, it's mousy grey."

"I thought it was just me getting older." I countered.

"It could be." Megan replied, as she added. "However, stress can contribute to graying of hair by triggering the release of a hormone which depletes the stem cells responsible for producing melanin, the pigment that gives hair its color. Chronic stress like you've been under, can increase oxidative stress in the body, leading to an imbalance of antioxidants and free radicals that can damage cells, leading to a decrease in melanin production and gray hair."

Antioxidants and free radicals, isn't that what the hippies demonstrated about in the sixties? Instead, I simply asked, "So you think I should dye my hair?"

"George, a lot of men are doing it, why not you? I'm not saying do anything drastic. I'm suggesting washing away the grey and going back to the light brown color I saw in the family photo when you looked twenty years younger."

"Anything else?"

"You're in great shape simply because you exercise regularly and we're both eating healthy diets. Getting enough sleep is also important for both our physical and mental health which I believe we're getting."

"What else?"

"The other area I really think will help is figuring out how to manage your stress levels. I would really like to work with you on some basic relaxation exercises. You know, Mindfulness, shin rin Yoku and Wim Hof, periodic massages, as well as going for long walks again."

I nodded and realized stress was taking its toll to the point I was looking older than I was. If I wanted the stares to stop or at least decline, I needed to take Megan's advice.

Megan paused as if to infer there were more things she was reticent to add. I looked at her and noted. "Look, everything you've told me haven't been criticisms, they've been suggestions which I appreciate. If there's more, please share them with me.

"OK, I think you need to dress in clothes that fit well and flatter your physique. Right now, your attire screams 'old'. If you wear colors that complement your skin tone, you'll also look younger."

I had what I had at the Lighthouse that had been there for over twenty years. At home, I had closets full of designer clothes I'd simply stopped wearing somewhat as a rebellion to the life I'd led.

I thought of Melia and me in Dubai when the hoity toity designers did the spectral scan of Melia and chose colors to accentuate her skin tone and realized Megan was spot on and so I inquired "Is there anything I don't need to work on?" somewhat overwhelmed by all the recommended changes.

Megan added. "First, you maintain good posture and then the one that steals every woman's heart is your outgoing personality, punctuated by your smile. George, your smile's infectious. Keep smiling. Keep laughing. Keep putting a smile on other people's faces simply because it makes them feel good to believe you think they're important."

"Where do we start?" I asked.

"Let's go to the pharmacy and buy some skin cream, hair clippers and then the right hair color."

"You're sure?"

"I'm positive." Megan offered with a smile.

"We can pick the stuff up on our way to dinner and start tomorrow." I noted.

"OK." Megan replied as she simply leaned across the chaise, gave me a kiss and whispered. "I think you're going to be even more sexy than you already are!"

Shazam! What a way to entice a guy into making changes he once thought would never happen.

We got out of the pool and it was our "happy hour" where a couple of glasses of wine set the mood. It being Tuesday, I knew we needed to go into Grand Case for 'Ti Moune's Night' which is Creole translates to 'little house' or 'small home' often used to refer to a cozy and intimate gathering or event. However, in Grand Case it means live music, dancing, street vendors and a festive atmosphere.

Megan dipped into Melia's clothes and was wearing a black, long-sleeved romper tailored from a supple, stretch fabric, featuring a meticulously structured princess-seamed bodice. Its square neckline, adorned with delicate rhinestone embellishments, was elegantly framed by diagonal seams that traced a sculptural path from the bust to the shoulders and waist, accentuating its sophisticated silhouette that added a touch of elegance to the attached flowing shorts that accentuated Megan's long legs.

On the way, Megan explained, "Rompers typically feature short hemlines, ending at the upper or mid-thigh, creating a playful, casual look while the same style bodice with pant legs is usually called a jumpsuit" She, then, had to explain that a bodice is the upper part of an outfit, typically extending from the waist to the neck."

We stopped at the store to fill our little red plastic basket with all kinds of make-George-look-younger items...skin cream, hair clippers and scissors, Clairol, you name it and every male eye in the place was on the gorgeous shopper in aisle number ten.

We made it Grande Case and had a great time having dinner at Le Pressoir where, instead of a shot glass of rum, they left the bottle as their way of saying 'welcome back Mister Terrill.' It had been years since I'd danced and so it took a few shots to get me going, but dance we did all the way up Boulevard de Grand-Case and what I remember of it, we sure had fun.

As we were heading back to the car, I stuck my head in Auberge Gourmand to wave at Pasquale and the crew and saw big smiles as their friend, George, had returned. It was then I remembered the last time I was there and how embarrassing it was when all my credit cards were denied and Pasquale said the meal was on him. One should never forget goodness. One should never ask for sympathy. One should always cherish good friends.

The time and dancing had taken the edge off the rum so that I could make the drive back to the Lighthouse. While it's less than two miles, the last thing I needed was an accident and the drive was always more than challenging.

First, was getting out of Grand Case and past the salt marsh with numerous inebriated celebrants making the simple task more challenging than it normally was.

Next, was going east on the N7 which meant having idiots on motorcycles flying by. Next, it's the round-about with five entrances that's enough to challenge any driver.

Next, was making it to the road to Marcel Cove and the climb up Pigeon Peak with all its twists and turns and then back down on the ocean side with even more twists and turns.

Finally, was making one's way through Le Domaine Anse Marcel Beach Resort parking area and putting the Rover in the garage literally adjacent to the beach restaurant and taking the hot tram up to the Lighthouse. Whew! Twenty minutes to go two miles. Glad we weren't in a hurry.

Sleep came early. "Goodnight moon!"

Waking up came early too and so we got up, decided to go for a walk and went down to the nearly-empty Orient beach. We parked on Rue Caye Baie and walked towards the ocean.

We made our way down to Plage Naturiste and turned back. My watch said it was nearly eight when we got back to Avenue Des Plages and stopped at Good Morning for croissants then went back to the house as Megan began what she called, my 'renovation' where I assumed getting your hair dyed was just like having it washed except sitting a little longer.

Wrong!

Megan went through all the steps and when she was done, told me she'd see me in 45 minutes as I sat, feeling like a fool looking at nothing, wondering what in hell did I get myself into?

Ding! I got up, went in the bathroom, looked in the mirror and 'tah dah' the old man had vanished, replaced by a suave, debonair, aristocrat. All I needed was a pipe and an ascot I'd be mistaken for royalty, or anyway I thought so.

As for my new clothes, they were going to have to wait. I had a closet full of custom-tailored suits, sportscoats, pants, dress shirts and shoes, I'd simply abandoned and now realized clothes really do make the man.

I'd forgotten what the Duke had always preached that first impressions matter where well-fitted, tailored clothing conveys competence, reliability, and respect that boosts one's self-assurance. My time in the cave had taken that away, and it was time for the old... make that former... George to reappear.

Phases:

Morning number three meant both of us on the computer. Megan looking for a job and me, first whittling down my options in terms of management companies for the Lighthouse. As it was nearing noon, I asked Megan what she wanted to eat.

"I don't know. What are my choices?"

"Well, the competition is incredible. If you don't serve good food, you're not going to last very long. Because of this, the quality is almost all the same, it's the scenery that changes."

"What do you mean?"

"Depending upon where you eat determines what you're going to see."

"Huh?"

I offered. "My Theory of Acclimation' comes into play here simply because of the popularity of Orient Beach Club that was founded in the 1960's as a clothing-optional resort and quickly became known as one of the most famous nudist destinations in the Caribbean. Through their liberal standards, where today's Perch Bar and Grill's sign says, 'No shoes, no clothes, no problem!' what would be considered extreme elsewhere is simply commonplace to the point, levels of acceptance are much broader on the rest of the beach than you normally find on another island."

"Starting with total nudity, as you head northwest you see the impact of European standards where, 'beyond the rocks,' as it's called, means topless women are accepted. It's not as prevalent as it was when I first started coming here. What's changed is the brevity of bikini bottoms where what was once commonplace, through repetition, became mundane. And, what was once mundane, through repetition, is considered conservative today to the point the term 'half-assed' has nothing to do with ability and more to refer to coverability."

"So, you have graduation from completely covered to totally nude as you head from end-to-end?" Megan inquired.

"You got it. Because the beach is crescent shaped, from the ocean, it's sort of southeast to northwest but on the scale of things who really knows? On the landward end you have Waikiki, KaKao and Bikini Beach restaurants who cater to an older and more mature group as well as the cruisers, who are usually more conservative."

"How do you know what to wear and what's considered proper?" Megan asked.

"Basically, by women's cover-ups," I replied. "Huh?"

"It took me years to realize it's women's cover-ups that make the difference."

"What?" Megan inquired somewhat incredulously.

"On the northwest end, women's cover-ups are primarily long and opaque. In the middle you have Wai and Kon Tiki which get a little trendier and a younger crowd where the cover-ups are usually more transparent."

"Then what?"

"Then you come to the buildings we used to own that are literally adjacent to Plage Naturiste where you periodically see cover-ups but most of the time it's simply swimwear. However, even the women who are topless sunbathing beach-side, put on their cover-ups when they come into the dining areas."

"Food?" Megan asked.

"You name it. It's always good. Some of the best lunches are the seafood salads and fish tacos. All the places on the northwest end and mid-beach are what I consider restaurants that serve good drinks. In the Plage Naturiste area, they're mostly bars with good food. It doesn't sound like that big of a difference, yet, it makes all the difference in the world when it comes to attitude and attire simply because things are more liberal due to the fact they have a different point of reference next door."

"What's your favorite?" Megan inquired.

"For food, my favorite is where we ate lunch yesterday at Anse Marcel Beach. Beyond that, it depends upon my mood as I like them all."

"What really matters is what you want to experience. If you want the more a conservative atmosphere we can stay on the northwest end. If you're into a more 'European' experience, the restaurants down by Plage Naturiste provide great food and a different mindset."

"What do I wear?"

"Whatever you want or nothing at all. That's what so different."

"How do you know what's proper and where?" "That's determined by what are called the rocks." "The rocks?"

"Yes, there's a set of rocks that touch the water. On the ocean side, where Plage Naturiste is, if you're wearing a bathing suit, you're somewhat condoned. Northwest of the rocks, if you're not wearing a bathing suit after 8:00 AM, you can get a ticket. On both sides, women go 'European' or topless on the beach and no one cares."

"Why eight o'clock?" Megan asked.

I replied. "Early morning risers are allowed to walk the beach in any form, or lack of attire, with no hassles or consequences." I didn't think it was proper to share that it was part of Amy's daily routine to walk the beach and immerse herself in total Shin Rin Yoku.

"The constables put their foot down at eight simply to keep the beach open to more conservative people. Because the majority are European, they don't consider toplessness to be the big deal it is in the States.

I paused, reflected, smiled and then added. "There used to be a restaurant called Pedro's that was at the rocks that was the melting pot from both sides who simply mingled together where everyone got along. It was the only establishment where topless women were never asked to cover up. What was crazy would be to watch a naked couple from Plage Naturiste walk up to the edge of the restaurant, put on their bathing suit bottoms and come in for lunch."

"What happened to Pedro's?"

"Hurricane Irma literally washed Pedro's away on September 6, 2017. The storm made landfall as a Category 5 hurricane, causing widespread destruction to the island, infrastructure, homes, businesses and the local economy."

I continued. "What really made it devastating was not only the sea swell, but the winds. Because the eye went right over Saint Martin, you had 160 mile-an-hour winds from one direction, then the calm, then the same winds at the same speed from the opposite direction. The storm was so strong it blew salt water on top of the hills and killed all the vegetation. Images we saw looked like the island had been bombed and when things were slowly getting back to normal, Covid hit and no tourists came for two years."

I lamented. "Pedro's had the best grilled chicken! When Irma was coming, no one thought it was going to be that bad and so the people at Pedro's simply battened down the hatches. When Irma hit that night the storm surge reached heights of approximately ten feet on top of which were ten to twelve-foot waves. Imagine being hit by a wall of water twenty-two feet high, enraged by winds of 160 miles per hour. It was devastating!"

"In the morning, the destruction became apparent as Pedro's literally ceased to exist except for the green painted steps that go down to the shoreline that are still there as a reminder to never mess with Mother Nature."

"So sad!" Megan offered.

"Pedro's was so eclectic, people from all over the world would have their picture taken at the edge of Plage Naturiste where there was a sign that read: *"Nudisme Autorise"* which translates to "Nudism Authorized" in English as a reminder of a time when they probably got a little more liberal than at home. Tens of thousands had their picture taken in front of it, would have lunch and send photos to the restaurant where Pedro's had a bulletin board with hundreds of photos on it and music playing, as well. After Irma, the staff noted they'd lost over 10,000 pictures whose memories were simply washed away."

I'd become quite laconic and needed to get out of the funk and switched back to note, "We have our choice depending more on attitude than taste."

"What about you?" Megan asked, somewhat inferring to my preference.

I replied. "Well, I go topless all the time and no one seems to care."

"What about down at Plage Naturiste?"

I just smiled as it was one of Amy and my little secrets. "Any stores?" Megan asked.

"You have the hat ladies who walk the beaches and there's a couple of bathing suit stores and one that rents aquatic adventures."

I paused for a moment and then thought I'd better warn Megan about Lucille's as I added. "I'm certain Melia's bathing suits came from a place called Lucille's which is down by Club Orient. The lady that owns it has been called the only woman who could sell bathing suits to nudists and ice cream to Eskimos. If you go in, you WILL walk out wearing one of Lucille's assortment. Word has it she has a seamstress who makes most of the suits while you wait and has all the current styles available."

Megan's brows uplifted as if in anticipation. "You mean custom made swimwear?"

"Yup!"

"Can you just buy bottoms?" Megan asked.

"I guess so. In fact that's what I bought," I joked.

"And when do you get the suits?

I added. "You go in, select the style and fabric, have lunch and a couple of drinks, and either go back then or the following morning and the suit is ready for you. I've heard she has twenty different styles and over two hundred different fabrics to choose from."

"Interesting."

The word propinquity entered my mind. I remembered it referred to the concept of physical or psychological proximity between people, meaning the closer you are to someone in terms of location or shared experiences, the more likely you are to develop a relationship or bond with them; essentially, the more likely you are to become friends or develop a connection.

At first, there's normally a physical attraction enhanced by a positive level of responsiveness. In Megan's and my case, we were both 'recovering' and built this non-intimate wall between us even though all other aspects had come into play. I also remembered this being a natural human tendency to develop tight interpersonal bonds with the people or things that are closest to us and this was certainly the case.

As I sat in the chair, I remembered one theory called 'the interpersonal attraction principle.' In this concept, social psychologists identified several factors that influence why people are attracted to each other including affection, respect, liking, friendship, as well as, a physical partnership. Very similar to an exposure effect, here, the more a person is a receptor of a stimulus, the more the person will like or dislike (social allergy) what stimulates them where, through repetition, the stimulus becomes less and less intense.

When I was pondering life and my relationship with Amy, I learned that similarity is a crucial component of interpersonal attraction simply because people are strongly attracted to those common to themselves in physical, intellectual and social levels, which can encompass everything from physical characteristics to life goals, ethnicity and appearance.

In Megan's and my case, it was the circumstances that brought us together that went beyond the physical elements. Our relationship, at least, on my part, is one where we are attracted to each other because of our demographics, attitudes, interpersonal style, social and cultural background. Then, as we got to know each other, determined our personalities, interests, activities, preferences, socio- economic status, communication, social skills and above all else, loneliness are mostly the same. Whew! That's a lotta things to have in common.

I felt, with all that happened, and how Megan stepped in to

literally save me from myself, my attraction evolved in a positive manner and then into a more profound sense of caring to a degree that, even though I still love Amy, it has been more intense than what I experienced with other people and came without the emotional challenges associated with my wife in terms of her proclivities.

The question then became, what has differentiated my caring for Amy and Megan? I thought about it and surmised that caring is a feeling of concern and affection for another person. It's a willingness to help and support, even when it's not convenient or easy and is an important part of any relationship and a way of showing that you value them and are committed to their well-being. Caring for Amy had been a life-long endeavor. Never knowing how her mental state was going to be. Never really accepting her physical needs, while doing everything I could to justify them. Never understanding what it's like to be mixed race and from profound wealth had also been things I worked on to try and acquiesce our marriage. I did my best and am willing to keep trying... I think.

Caring for Megan as a friend had been easy simply because some of the things she experienced, I too, had done, to the point she'd become a critical part of my life and attempt to regain a sense of happiness. When I was in Atlanta and she opened up about her past meant she trusted me and respected all that I am. In so doing, we both laid bare our inner souls to the point there aren't many more secrets to hide and we simply became comfortable with each other.

I realized that, without caring for Megan, I'd be emotionally flat-lined to a point of indifference as I had when I literally was a hermit with no peaks... only valleys from which I'd finally begun to climb out.

My mind wandered as Megan carried Melia clothes up to our bedroom. While she was gone, I resolved that caring could, in its purest form, be classified as 'passion'...a passion for life, a passion for love and a passion for Megan, not currently in a physical sense but a point of greater value and, therefore, the chance of a greater loss and sorrow.

It was then I realized that, without Megan I was only a shell, walking, interacting, functioning in a world like some plastic snowman sitting on our Pine Lake neighbor's lawn at Christmas. There, but not really...glowing, but not really...dynamic and three dimensional... but only as what I represented and not what I truly am that provides dimension.

Megan glanced at me and smiled and I knew then that she, too, cared to the point we both appreciated each other simply because we wanted to fully integrate ourselves to make both of us better and, hopefully, make each other happy... to think, feel and act... in such a manner we could both walk away from life's challenges better, more positive and in some way moved by being together.

I looked at the beautiful, vivacious woman knowing that, like my association with Amy, people were asking why? Why is she with him? He's so much older. Is she his trophy girl? They just don't understand and so, right away, their mind goes 'there' simply because they don't realize that sex is really only touch… the closest of all touch and it's the touch we're all afraid of and something we chastise others for when it doesn't fit within our own social, emotional or cultural realm. Yet, to touch another person can be the most rewarding of all emotions when there is commitment and passion involved.

It doesn't matter who the person is or how old they are, as long as both people sincerely care for each other. But what about when there's no physical passion? What then? Can a man and woman really be as close as Megan and me without... without the intimacy everyone whispers and automatically assumes is there?

Enie Menie Minie Moe:

Instead of making a choice, we decided to drive to Orient Beach and simply go down behind the restaurants until we found one Megan liked. As we neared the edge of where Pedro's had been and the new buildings existed, Megan was amazed at how many cars were parked in the lot.

"Why are there so many cars down here?" Megan inquired. "You thought only a few people went to the nude beach?" "I had no idea. I thought a few, but this is crazy."

Just then a parking spot opened up right behind Chez Leandra and I took it as I asked, "Is this OK?"

Megan shrugged her shoulders and almost gleefully said, "Sure why not?"

Facing the ocean, Megan looked right towards what I still called Club Orient, then at Chez Leandra and Le'String next door and decided we could have 'just one' drink before lunch'. While not nearly as famous as its predecessor, Chez had, for all intents and purposes, replaced Pedro's and their glorious grilled chicken, ribs and lobster but had become even more famous for the integration of those from both sides on the 'rocks' where no one seemed to care.

We went in and 'Z' the owner saw me and smiled. Coming over to me he noted. "Mr. Terrill, what a wonderful surprise. We heard you had been in an accident and now you are here."

"Thanks 'Z'. You know how things get blown out of proportion. I'm fine."

"Est-ce ta fille?" 'Z' inquired, as Megan blushed

I sensed it was some sort of comment and so I reported. "This is Megan Egan, a business associate of mine from the States. We've come to inspect our property and find a property manager." "I see." 'Z' offered with eyebrows raised and a gleam in his eye as if to say 'you devil, you' before asking. "Are you joining us for lunch?"

I looked at Megan and she nodded 'yes' and so 'Z' took us to a table under the roof but at the edge of the sand so we could do some people watching and then asked, "Dirty Lemonade, if I remember correctly?"

I nodded 'yes' without letting on it was Melia's favorite and not mine, but still made with lemonade, vodka and rum.

"Wow! you weren't kidding about the people." Megan mentioned.

"What do you mean?" I asked.

"I mean, first lot's more people than I would have imagined. Second, you're right about the attire. Anything goes."

I paused and then added. "During lunch, 'Z' requires proper attire which means cover ups. During happy hour which starts at three, unless things have changed, it's 'come as you are' and the place is packed where the term 'bottoms up' takes on two meanings."

"We'll have to come back for Happy Hour." Megan offered and then asked, "Where's Lucille's?"
It was two doors down as I inquired. "Do you want to go there?"
"Yes, please."

"After lunch?"

"That would be great."

The server came and took our order as we shared a crab salad that was simply out of this world and then our second dirty lemonade which was already having it's effect. As we were finishing 'Z' came over and asked, "How is Melia doing? We haven't seen her in a long time. We all cheered for her on that TV show. She really has a beautiful voice and those songs...I remember when she sang 'Daddy' and then the 'Solider Song'. George, you must be so proud."

"She's married and has two kids and doing fine." I lied.

"And what about crazy Annie?" 'Z' inquired as he smiled and shook his head.

"She's married, too, and lives in California."

"Those were the days my friend. We still have guests come in and ask if Crazy Annie has ever returned." 'Z' said as he shook his head in disbelief and then asked. "Would you like a chaise on the water's edge?"

"Perhaps, another time." I replied. We have some business to attend to. That is, after Megan visits Lucille's."

"Oh, boy. I hope you have room in your car for all she's going to sell you." 'Z' laughed, shook my hand, politely nodded at Megan and disappeared to resolve another one of the day's small problems.

I looked at Megan and inquired, "Are you ready?"

Megan had a grin on her face as we stood and simply walked the twenty paces to the den of iniquity called Lucille's.

As we walked in, for me it was as if time had simply stood still. Virtually every square inch of the walls was covered by bathing suits plus racks and then even bins. Suit after suit after suit all waiting to be filled by someone from somewhere who never thought they'd ever be wearing one of Lucille's famous *'Barely There Swimwear'*.

Lucille had to be in her late fifties and had put on a few pounds. Her jet-black hair had added some white highlights, supplanted by one of the most infectious smiles you could imagine that literally lit up the store.

As her latest 'victim' was placing her newest acquisitions under her arm, Lucille looked up, saw me, smiled and then smiled some more. Thanking the lady for her purchase, Lucille came from behind the counter and over to Megan and me. Being, at most five feet tall, she looked up at us, nodded, smiled again and then added. "Mr. George. What a wonderful surprise. We all thought you, you had passed away."

I returned the smile and noted, "Well, the rumors weren't true. I'm here."

"My, what a wonderful surprise and who's this fine lady?"

I politely noted. "This is Megan Egan, my business associate. We're in the process of looking for a management company for our property here on Saint Martin. When Uncle Frank died and all that transpired, we haven't had time to find someone to replace him."

Lucille got serious as she lamented. "You'll never find someone to replace Frank or Julia. They were two of the finest people I ever knew, along with Doctor and Mister Williams. You know, I say a prayer for them every week in church and light a candle in their name."

Lucille was touching my heart but I was glad there was no mention of Amy. Catching herself, she looked at Megan and announced. "We have over five hundred suits here to meet your needs. In addition, we have over two hundred different fabrics and twenty different styles as well. Megan, you look like the type of person who enjoys fine things, let me show you what we can do especially for you."

I knew right then and there the bait had been placed and the hook was in Megan's mouth. It was time for me to exit left and let the ladies do what they like to do. I looked at Megan and said, "I'll be back at Chez Leandra. Why don't I let you two be alone?"

Lucille, being Lucille, had to get in the last word as she said, "Mister George, we have new styles for men, too, and can also make custom swimwear just for you."

"Not today, Lucille. Perhaps before we leave, but not today." With that, I walked back out into the sunshine and the ever-changing mural of humanity who made their way along the shore as if in search of something called happiness and back to 'Z'.

"Do you have any open chaises?" I asked. "Of course, for you Mister George, follow me."

"By the way, my associate is in with Lucille. When she comes looking for me, can you show her where I'm at?"

"Most certainly and how about another dirty lemonade?" "Sure, why not?"

A short time later as I sat gawking at the passersby, the server came and asked me if I was interested in yet another Dirty Lemonade to which I simply nodded yes. About an hour later, Megan came and woke me up. It seems I'd fallen asleep.

"So how was Lucille's?"

"Oh, my God. She's incredible."

"Did you buy anything?"

"Are there fish in the ocean?"

"Where are they?"

"They're being made. I can't believe custom made swimwear."

"How many did you buy?"

"A few."

"A few?"

"Uh huh."

"What's cool is I bought tops and bottoms I can mix-n-match. That way, I've got more variety."

I simply laughed and shook my head and asked when they'd be ready as Megan replied, "Tomorrow morning."

I guess that meant that we'd be back at Chez Leandra and Orient Beach once again. Little did I realize we'd be back and back and back for happy hour virtually every day we were in Saint Martin.

"Seinfeld":

We had a quiet dinner at home, watched Netflix and reruns of 'Seinfeld', that supported the social fact that two people of different genders can be friends, as yet another bottle of Terrill B&B was opened. At ten, it was time for bed and we crawled in as Megan whispered, "Goodnight Moon."

"Goodnight Moon," I replied as a soft smile permeated my heart and lips.

Sunrise awakened me and I got up, got out of bed and dragged a comb across my head. Went downstairs and had a cup. Waking up, I realized I was late. Not for the Beatles but for walking the beach. Oh well, tomorrow will be another day.

"Around eight, Megan got up and came downstairs asking, "What time does Lucille's open?"

"Around ten, why?"

"I tried on Melia's suits again and they're a bit large, I really need to get my new ones."

Large? I didn't think that was possible. How could three triangles be too large?

"Tell you what. How about a cup of coffee? Then we'll go to Good Morning and sit out with all the old French guys, have some pastry and then Lucille's?"

"What should I wear?"

"You mean to Good Morning?" I said, somewhat incredulously. "It's an outdoor cafe. Wear whatever you want."

Megan returned wearing Melia's ripped denim short shorts and a rayon hankie top as she simply inquired. "OK?"

"You're fine." In fact, she was more than fine, to the point the old codgers were in for a morning treat that wasn't coming from the bakery.

We had our coffee, checked email, then drove over to Good Morning. As we parked in the angular parking lanes and got out, every male sitting outside turned and mouthed *'Putain de merde'* or 'Holy Shit' in French.

We went into the small bakery and ordered chocolate eclairs and Espresso and went out to one of the empty tables. Megan shrugged her shoulders and elicited a slight smile of satisfaction and noted, "I love it here."

I almost replied "And I love you," but caught myself. Don't go there George. Don't go there!

As we finished our treats and headed for the car, I could feel every male eye watching Megan with regret the show was over. 'Oh well, maybe tomorrow,' I thought to myself.

We made it to Lucille's and I stayed in the car. It was too late for the morning walk and too early for lunch and so I thought we could go back to the Lighthouse as Megan came out with a bag with *Lucille's Barely There Swimwear* logo on it.

We went back to the Lighthouse as Megan needed to check in to see if any of her job inquiries had responded. With Megan on the laptop and me with nothing to do, I sat in the living area and looked out at the pool. It's crazy what you think about when you're simply sitting and waiting. My thoughts went to how the island had changed. In the thirty years we'd been coming I guess there had been a slow evolution. However, when you go three years without visiting, you really notice how different things really are.

It seemed as if the French side had been 'Americanized' and was more commercial than before, to the point it had become more of a mirror to the Dutch side than an antithesis. What was once a quiet, almost sleepy environment where the French came to relax, and you went to dine, had become more frenetic, where you went out to eat.

In having Terrill B&B, I quickly learned the difference between fine dining and going out to eat lies in the level of formality, service and cuisine. While still available in Grand Case where there remains a high level of formality with an unwritten business casual dress code and etiquette, those located near Orient Beach had literally become more casual as they morphed into 'come as you are' restaurants.

In Grand Case we enjoy attentive waiters and waitresses who anticipate your needs that highlights gourmet food, often prepared with high-quality ingredients and innovative techniques. While still a long way from phony baloney elegance and sophisticated ambiance, those in Grand Case remained a step above a standard restaurant in terms of food and service. Do you pay more? Yes! Is it worth more? Yes.

I then wondered what happened? Was it Hurricane Irma who washed away the innocence? Was it the aggregate sum of so many like me who'd come and fallen in love with the lifestyle that's punctuated by tolerance and warm smiles? Perhaps it was Covid that curtailed visitors and simply eroded those who built their businesses on a passion while the real business people survived.

Rumor had it that the beach restaurants wanted to hire more renowned chefs, but none of them wanted to be associated with a beach restaurant except at Anse Marcel.

It was now late morning and we agreed to sit out by the pool for a couple of hours. Megan in her 'total tan' mode and well... me too. I guess the mud bath and shower had removed more than mud. Around 3:00, I asked Megan if she wanted to go back to Chez Leandra and she said, "Sure," and asked which suit she should wear.

I shrugged and replied, "whichever one you feel most comfortable in."

"How about half of one?" Megan teased.

As we were driving to the beach, I realized that, with my imagination or make that anticipation of what was in Lucille's *'Barely There'* bag, I'd created some erogenous impulses that were cavorting through my brain, as I thought to myself, 'that's not what's supposed to be happening, George! Not now anyway.'

Three or perhaps four Dirty Lemonades later, served with lots of laughter and some 'observations' of others imbibing and it was time to head back to the Lighthouse.

Dinner was salad and an early bed. I don't know if it was me, the booze or all the fresh air, but I was sleeping like a baby...

wait, babies wake up every three hours crying with wet or dirty diapers... make that like a teenager... they're the only ones I know who can sleep twelve hours without getting up to pee.

Agents:

I'd done my due diligence when it came to property management companies and examined pricing for similar properties based on the time of year. All I needed was to have the representatives come and give me the sales pitch.

I scheduled a morning and asked Megan if she wanted to be there. She chose to go into Philipsburg. With traffic a nightmare only superseded by total lack of parking, I suggested she take a taxi which she did.

I had the management companies scheduled for nine, ten and eleven while allocating 45 minutes for each one. I planned on taking them on a tour of the house, showing them the comps and then detailing pricing. I knew we were late regarding listing for the upcoming season, but felt we could still generate some revenue.

The first guy was simply a jerk. High pressure and full of B.S. who treated me like I was some sort of idiot. I named him 'Slick Willy' and thought, "Adios Amigo!" Gee, I guess I did learn some Spanish is Chile.

The next two were ladies. The first one had to be in her fifties and had a power point that provided a summary of the services including renting, cleaning the house and pool, landscaping and security. It was nice but there just wasn't the excitement I was expecting. I think the company had their hands full with the clients they had and were a little 'too big' for me.

I felt like Goldilocks as the third lady was professional and started by detailing her background in real estate. Her name was Delphine Anjou and was about as French as you could get. During her pitch I noted she was providing virtually the same services as the first lady at the same rate of commission. Where she had me was the fact that she marketed the homes outside VRBO resulting in a higher net income when someone went direct. She then showed me some samples of her web sites and also the placements she had on vacation sites and I was impressed.

I looked at the contract, read it and wondered if I should sign it right then and there. Being cautious, I read out loud every paragraph and allowed Delphine to explain anything I didn't understand. It was then I wished Amy was there. She was the lawyer in the family, not me.

As we were finishing our review, I heard the tram making its way up from the parking lot. I offered Delphine a soft drink as the door opened and Megan walked in with two shopping bags, one labeled 'Affordable Department Store, 16A Back Street, Phillipsburg'.

"Whew!" was all she said, as I introduced her to Delphine.

Knowing she needed to start all over, Delphine went through the entire spiel as I looked at Megan to watch for facial expressions. It was only when Delphine proposed having Megan sign the agreement, so she'd be able to continue on at the discounted commission rate if something happened to me. I put one-and-one together and realized Delphine assumed we were married.

It was then Delphine went for the close. "This is one of, if not the finest home on Saint Martin and will command one of the highest rentals. As such, I am willing to reduce my commission by twenty-five percent if you sign today."

Not one to jump into things, I told her I'd sign it if I could date it two days hence. This would give me time to make sure it was what I wanted to do. Delphine countered and said one day and I agreed. At least I had 24 hours to get out of the deal if I got cold feet which is really tough to do when the average temperature year-round is eighty degrees.

Delphine departed as Megan showed me the clothes and gifts she'd purchased. I smiled as I thought of her generosity and wondered if she bought anything nasty to send to Charlie and Ellie but knew better than to make any snide remarks. Time was healing the wounds and it was best to let sleeping dogs lie.

Megan had an 'inimitable' smile on her face and noted, "Give me a minute," as she went in one of the bedrooms and came out wearing a white, ribbed-cotton tank top 'undershirt' with narrow shoulder straps we called *'wife beaters'* in college that had oversized armholes for greater mobility resulting in a looser fit that allowed the sides of her boobs to show.

Megan then matched the *wife beater* with a pair of shorts, over- sized sunglasses and a white 'SXM' labelled baseball cap.

"Well?" Megan asked. "You look great." I offered.

Feeling the edge of the armhole of the undershirt with her left thumb, Megan noted. "I really didn't think I'd ever wear anything like this, but now I've got one on, I can see why Amy is so fond of them. I mean, they're so comfortable. I got the three-pack of white, black and maroon. Then the store had Mini Rodini baby tees from Sweden. I mean, wow! In girls XL, they're practically tailor made."

Holding up one of the Rodini's, Megan proudly noted. "They're all the rage in Atlanta because you've got a lot of flexibility with high waisted clothes."

"Where'd you get the shorts?" I asked, trying to elicit some polite form of interest.

"At the same store. They were on sale and so I bought three pair of 'boy shorts' to go with the tops."

"So you bought boy's shorts?" I asked.

"No, they're called 'boy shorts' because they're modeled off men's boxer shorts. However, they're made of thinner, more form- fitting fabric and have a more unisex styling."

"I don't understand."

Megan, stopped and noted. "Unisex clothing was a baby-boomer reaction to the rigid gender stereotyping of the 1950s, which itself was a reaction to the roles imposed on men and women during World War II."

Wow! I wonder if mom was involved in that? Not my mom! Well, anyway, not the mom I knew where the only time the word hippie came up in her vocabulary was when another lady had gained some weight.

Megan added. "In the 50's the term "gender" began to be used to describe the social and cultural aspects of biological sex simply as a tacit acknowledgement that one's sex and gender might not match."

"You mean like Amy?"

Megan nodded 'yes' and continued. "Unisex clothing of the 1960s and 70s aspired 'to blur or cross gender lines'; ultimately, however, it delivered 'uniformity with a masculine tilt.'"

"So 'boy shorts' are literally shorts for women that are designed like those for men?" I deduced.

"Yup. However today you can find designs that are more feminine if that's what you prefer. While boy shorts usually have a mid-rise waist and available in different lengths, I like them low-rise with shorter inseams that make them really comfortable."

Megan turned around to let me see the back and then asked. "You don't think they're too short, do you?"

How does one even respond to that? Do you mention that they're a bit 'cheeky'? Little did I know, Megan had just acquired what would become her go-to everyday ensemble—three wife-beater undershirts and three pairs of shorts, effortlessly mixed and matched into nine different combinations, always paired with her sunglasses, SXM baseball cap, and sandals.

Having listened to my expose on the different cover-ups based on where women were on Orient Beach, Megan excitedly offered. "I bought some cover-ups too. Let me show you."

First was a tribal print, deep V-Neck opaque dress that was quite conservative. Then Megan held up what she called a 'Pareo' which was simply a large piece of brightly colored cloth she said could be wrapped around her waist and worn as a skirt, up higher as a dress or even a shawl.

Next was a beige textured, open-weave romper, that was semi see-through to allow both a little sun and some errant glances to get in. Finally, there was a backless long sleeve, mesh cover up that was more like a sheer t-shirt that would leave little to nothing to the imagination.

I could see Megan's logic followed the social evolution of the beach. The tribal print and Pareo for Anse Marcel and the more conservative northwest end. The romper for the mid-beach area and finally, the t-shirt for down by rocks.

The next day, with the wheels in motion, in terms of renting the house, it was back to our daily routine as we'd sort of 'hit the groove'. Morning would mean either eggs, Frosted Flakes or something from Good Morning and then respites to our respective computers.

Having looked at all the football scores, weather in Wisconsin and all the other 'stuff' I had one question I needed answering and that was why women...namely Megan, was so interested in my opinion regarding what she was wearing. I guess I should be happy that Megan wanted my approval. It had been a very long time since that ever came up at the Terrill house.

I went on line and found all kinds of articles regarding why women were so focused on what they wore. What I learned was, in our liberated... well, somewhat liberated world... women have the opportunity and therefore the right to dress however they choose without judgment or criticism. What's interesting was the fact that what they choose to wear isn't only about self-expression, it can be about social signaling where clothing serves as a form of non-verbal communication that the wearer wants others... namely me... to see. It was then the cartoon 'bulb' lit up over my head as I was realizing our 'plutonic' relationship was morphing into a romantic phase, where, by asking if her outfit is 'OK', Megan was sending a message to me. Duh!

Late morning would mean tan time, then lunch, followed by Chez Leandra for happy hour. Dinner meant one of the gastronomical delights twice each week.

We'd been on Saint Martin for over a month and were getting 'comfortable' in terms of not only our routine, but each other. It was interesting to see how things changed at Chez Leandra while they remained the same. The facilities, staff and management remained constant. The variables were the guests.

Each week would see a new rendition with those who'd watched their vacation time evaporate only to be replaced by "newbies" as we called them. In total there are 39 airports around the world that have direct flights to SXM or Sint Maarten, including eleven US cities, two Canadian, two European and nineteen central and South American with an average of two million air passengers per year or around 165,000 per month on nearly 1,500 flights. Needless to say, there would be new faces who needed to assimilate or regain the verve of the culture.

It's amazing how easy it became to identify where the newbies were from. Casual, laid back and somewhat initially aloof, meant Europe. Uptight, constrained, impatient and demanding meant American. Really aloof meant South America with money, lots and lots of money. The Europeans were always the first to soften. It normally took about two or three days but then jet lag would do that to anyone.

Americans either melted or became socially aggressive where they expected more and faster than anyone else. With the environment as 'casual' as it was, you could tell the gawkers from the participants as the male gawkers would stand with mouths open trying to harvest all the images to take back home to brag about to their friends. What was really cool were the repeat Americans who got the vibe and came to relax and enjoy... to erase the pressures they were under at home and simply accept a lifestyle and attitude that wasn't tied to a clock or dollar bill.

As we morphed into 'regulars' we realized one of the constants was the weekly turnover and the subsequent assimilation process where the faces changed, but the percentages only varied slightly. Club Orient was inhabited probably by 85% European and represented Chez Leandra's major customer base. It's a little over nine hours from Paris to Princess Juliana Airport with flights every day and so, with the in-flow and out-go of participants, peak season never really had a weekly increase or decrease, just a slow, smooth osmosis from one group to the next depending upon the time of year.

Some weeks, would be more dynamic than others where one or even a few people would ignite the atmosphere and change the mentality. Other weeks, would find a more subdued group simply because no one 'let go'.

As we spent time there, we became more comfortable with the mores of the place, meaning literally seeing a wide range of dress or undress that was all simply accepted. It was fun watching the transition as the newbie's would be reticent until they realized no one cared and would then liberalize themselves as they blended in, providing a cheap thrill until they too acclimated.

Such was our case as we began deferring our afternoon home tan time by getting two beach-side chairs and watching the world go by. At first, Megan was a bit cautious and it took a few days before she morphed into a true European mindset regarding what she did or didn't wear. With her transition, she became totally oblivious of stares and gawks as lecherous Frenchmen and cruisers surveyed the afternoon's options.

As for me, the same acclimation took place but from a different perspective. What had been titillating became commonplace as I, too, became ambivalent to the attire, or lack of, regarding our 'chaise neighbors' as we called them, enjoying the sun, sand and sea where the only difference was they were counting days of freedom and liberation and we had none.

We'd been gone over two months. It was nearly Thanksgiving in Wisconsin. The pace we set had been such we'd both recovered from the pain and agony we'd been exposed to. The question became, 'When do we go back to reality, or did we?'

Everything was great until the next day when my phone rang and it was Delphine. "Mister Terrill, we have a problem."

"What's that?" I inquired.

"The agreement you signed was for exclusive representation."

"That's right."

"Mister Terrill, your house is already under contract with another management company."

"That's impossible," I countered.

"Sir, we run checks to make certain all of our efforts don't result in someone else earning the commission."

"And you're saying the house is under contract with another company?"

"Yes. It was signed two months ago."

"Who signed it?" I asked, now both irritated and concerned. "I don't know."

"Well, I don't believe it. The house is in my... " It was then I knew what was going on...Amy and Karen had come back from Chile and listed the house.

"Do you have the name of the listing company?" I asked.

Delphine provided it and I wrote the number down. In addition, I went on VRBO and saw old photos of the Lighthouse and realized what was going on as I shook my head in dismay and swore I'd get even.

I had Megan call the management company using her US cellphone so that they would think she was calling from the states. She indicated she was interested in the Lighthouse for Christmas week and was told it had already been rented. She asked about January and was told that all of January through March had been rented to one family. Megan thanked the lady and hung up and shared the news with me. To say I was pissed was an understatement. I was playing by the 'And/Or' rules while my wife was playing be some underhanded method she learned in law school.

We spent the night watching Netflix and were about to go to bed as it was almost ten. Megan decided to take one last dip and went out to use the pool. Out of nowhere I heard the doorbell ring as someone pushed the button at the base of the tram. It had happened before when some kids thought it would be funny or drunks thought it was a short cut over the hill. I heard the lower level door open and someone on the metal stairs. I didn't know whether to grab a butcher knife, hold my ground or call the police. I opted to forget the knife and simply stood there as the door opened.

"Holy shit!"

Surprise:

I don't know who was more shocked, Amy or me. We'd found her and she had the shock of her life. Her dead husband wasn't dead at all. I looked at the woman who'd been my wife for thirty years.

Amy was thinner than the last time I saw her as I peered at the somewhat sullen face and saw where small thin wrinkles had begun to appear around her eyes and mouth while her hair was cut in the same 'boy cut' style she had when she accidentally got stoned with the nurses.

As Amy stepped into the dining area, the chandelier light brought her into focus and I noticed that her almond skin had darkened which I attributed to the weather. While still trim and, for a woman her age, still quite muscular, Amy had still aged more than I'd expected.

Perhaps it was the leukemia. Perhaps all the pressure she'd been under. Perhaps, just perhaps, it was the fact she no longer had the T-cell transplants to rely on. I thought of telomeres and the Hayflick Limit and wondered how they came into play.

As we stood there, almost frozen in emotional space, I glanced at Amy and she at me and one would have thought we'd been apart for a decade instead of three years. My eyes examined her for any signs of acquiescence to the phase of life we'd entered. Instead, it was as if Amy was still trying to be twenty something and not the age we'd both become.

There was a pronounced pause as we both tried to regain our composure as I observed the woman I still loved, but now in a completely different way. Was it her or the fond memories that came to the forefront? Was it the long-gone laughter and mirth that had faded like a winter sunset? I really didn't know. What I did know was the reality that Amy was fighting time and had positioned herself as a warrior against which we all must face... aging... and how, with each and every day, the rose of youth withers until it too becomes nothing more than a memory.

When you're young, you always try to look older. When

you're no longer young, some people keep trying to look youthful to the point of the absurd. At a point when they reach that juncture and it's time to look their age, they try to pretend and it simply doesn't work anymore. For some, it's in their forties. For others their fifties, For a very few, their sixties.

I glanced at Amy and wondered why? Why was she still dressing like she was 21? What was once an amatory ensemble consisting of a too-tight, t-shirt that showed everything, and I mean everything, as well, as short, short, short-shorts, the outfit made Amy look out-of-place in a world so focused on youth. While still very attractive, her choice of dress expressed a totally different message to the point Amy simply looked desperate, discordant and sullen, not only because of her attire but because her once infectious smile now remained upside down, buried beneath the ravages of misery. Was she really trying to simply 'hold on' or was it all for Karen?

My memory took me back to the thumb drive I'd discovered from which I put the thematic thread together. With her relationship with Karen, I perceived that Amy was the submissive and needed the power exchange she experienced to simply validate her own demeaning self-concept. For a moment a wave of pity rushed through my mind. I perceived that Amy was dressed the way she was, not because she wanted to, but because it was Karen's fantasy to have a young woman she could control.

The thought lasted only an instant, much like a strobe light that sends flashes zooming through your mind and makes you wonder. I blinked and simply stood there, frozen in reality until I heard, "George?" with Amy inquiring in disbelief.

"Yes, it's me."

"George, you're...you're alive." "Yes I am."

"But how?"

"I wasn't the other person in the car with Langdon. I was in the cave. You know, the cave Tommie tried to kill me in."

"What?" Amy asked with an incredulous tone.

"You heard me. He came and probably used a laser pointer to burn the lens so that I was locked in the cave."

"You're crazy!" Amy retorted in a now defensive tone.

I looked at her and wondered if she was just in one of her 'moods' as I added. "I went crazy, Amy. I went insane! It seems being locked in a cave all alone for SIX MONTHS has a way of doing that to a person."

"Oh, my God. We all thought you were killed in the car accident."

"No shit! That's why you tried to collect my life insurance.

That's why you escaped with Derrick." "George, you don't understand."

"What don't I understand, Amy? Tell me what." I challenged.

Amy looked at me, then at the floor and then at the ripples out in the pool before answering, "We all thought you were dead. The government threatened me with sedition because I signed Derrick's documents. I had to do something."

"That's why you ran away with Karen."

Amy's eyes grew wide as she realized all that had transpired was coming to fruition as she replied in an almost monotone. "Yes, Karen did leave with us. You need to understand George, Karen took care of me after the stem cell transplants." There was a pause and then while nodding in the affirmative Amy repeated what she had said as if to remind herself..."Karen is the one who cared for me."

"Tell me about Peru." I demanded.

"We needed to go somewhere and Derrick learned we could live in Peru and the government couldn't come after us."

"And ...."

"We moved there, lived in Lima for a while and then Derrick bought some land and we moved there."

"Montaña del diablo," I countered as Amy's mouth dropped open.

"How did you find out what it's called?" Amy asked almost incredulous to my knowledge. "Simple. We went there." "We...Who?"

Just then the slider opened and Megan walked in. Amy glanced at Megan, looked at me and put two-and-two together as she emotionlessly offered. "Hello Megan."

Megan looked at Amy and gently replied, "Hello."

It was like two boxers meeting before a fight. The emotions were there but not the anger and also, without any malicious emphasis, just a cold, dark, dank acclimation of the other's existence.

Without another word, Megan physically excused herself as I looked at Amy and said. "It's not what you think."

"What do you think I think, George?" Amy said in a very tacit way.

"You know what I think and it's not the case. You left. You ran away. You, broke my heart. Megan was almost raped in her own house, lost her job and I needed someone...anyone to help me recover and she's been that person. I thought I'd never see you again. I thought it was over. What should I have done, Amy? Tell me what I should have done?"

Amy shook her head in dismay. "So you hooked up with another woman!"

"Just like you, Amy. Just like you." "What do you mean by that, George?"

"You know what I mean. You left Devil's Mountain and went to Chile with Karen. Why Amy? Was it because, in Peru, as a same sex couple, you were protected while in Chile, you could get married. Didn't you get married Amy?"

Amy's eyes were filling with tears. She was despondent as she replied. "You don't understand."

"I do understand. I understand that right now you're a bigamist married to me and Karen at the same time."

"But I thought you were dead."

"But I'm not. And that's why I'm here Amy. That's why we've been trying to find you."

Amy shook her head in disbelief and so I continued. "When you used up all the Hilton Points on the hotels in Santiago, you started using the credit card we had in both of our names until you hit the credit limit. I have to thank you for that, it gave us the leads we needed to follow you."

I continued with my finger pointing directly at her. "When you maxed out the credit card, I thought we'd lost you until I remembered Pepe and knew you'd be going there and so five weeks ago we had lunch with Pepe and he indicated that you and Karen were scoping out the area because you were thinking about opening a restaurant in Puerto Montt."

Amy knew the proverbial goose was cooked and so she began to calm down. She looked at me and moved a little closer as if to indicate some sort of softening of her stance. She looked at the floor and then me and said. "George, I love you. I've always loved you. I always will. I truly thought you were dead. I sincerely thought I was going to prison. I didn't want to go with Derrick but I was afraid."

I too began to cool as I replied. "I understand. What I don't understand is why, when we were planning our life together, you did what you did?"

"What?" Megan inquired as if shocked that the subject was brought up.

"The pre-nup."

"The pre-nup? That was your idea." Amy retorted.

"It was my idea but not the part about using the word 'and' instead of 'or'." I countered.

"What?" Amy challenged, now almost incredulous.

"Yes, you put 'and' in the pre-nup which means that everything, and I mean everything, is locked down and I can't move an inch. I can't buy anything, sell anything, do anything and am in a world of hurt."

"So, that's what this is all about. It isn't about finding me because you love me. It's because you're broke, just like you were when I met you and you need me to change everything so that you can lead the life I gave you!"

"You gave me? You gave me? What did you give me Amy? Tell me one thing you gave me that I didn't earn."

Amy just shook her head and replied. "Money! Money! It's all about money!"

"No, it's not Amy. It's about equity. It's about living up to what you agreed to. You're the one who created the agreement, not me."

"But you signed it."

"Yes, I did, because I loved you." It was then the word went into the past tense and it shocked me as I added. "I did it because I trusted you."

Bitterly, Amy responded. "You did it because you had nothing to lose."

"I had everything to lose...everything," I countered.

Just then, the sound of feet on the metal tram stairs echoed through the open door that interrupted what was quickly getting out of hand. I paused, Amy paused. Megan returned from the bedroom as Karen walked in with her mouth open in total disbelief. The years had been quite good to Karen. I thought she had to be in her early forties but had maintained her looks and still had light brown hair that, like Amy, was shorter than it had been the last time I saw her.

Karen looked at Amy. Karen looked at Megan. Karen looked at me and whispered. "I thought you were dead."

"I'm not. It seems my brother wasn't proficient at murdering me."

I watched as Karen's eyes closed as if to ponder her next comment and then she offered. "Now what?"

"Well ladies, we have a problem. it seems your marriage in Chile..."

Karen's mouth dropped open as she looked at Amy and challenged. "You told him?"

I replied "No, she didn't tell me. Megan and I figured it out. When we asked ourselves, why in hell would you go from Peru to Chile? We couldn't answer it until we read the laws about same-sex marriage in Peru and Chile."

Both Amy and Karen shook their heads in dismay as I continued on. "Congratulations! The problem you have is that

Amy and I are still legally married. Trust me, in trying to clear up this mess, I learned that one is not considered dead in the States until missing for seven years and five years in France and, therefore, Saint Martin."

"I know you don't think I'm the brightest bulb on the Christmas tree but I'm smart enough to know American law where the consequences for an individual who assumes their spouse is deceased and then marries another person, only to find out their first spouse is alive, can be severe and the person is called a bigamist."

I looked at Amy and continued. "Amy, you already have a warrant out for your arrest and they can add criminal felony charges where you could face additional imprisonment, fines or both. Then, if you want, I can demand an annulment of your second marriage because it's based on a fraudulent belief. Then there's the legal challenges related to property division, taxes and other issues such as signing a contract with no legal right simply because the Lighthouse is garnered in my custody."

"Why?" Amy asked as if to challenge the decision.

"Because you skipped the country and technically, you're trespassing in MY house. The final problem you have is that there's an extradition agreement between Saint Martin and the US."

Amy seethed. "The pre-nup agreement says that we own it together, George."

"That's right, except, if you look at the deed, I'm responsible for the safety, security, maintenance and wellbeing of the property and not you, simply because you were chicken shit and skipped the country."

Megan just stood there with her mouth agape. She'd never seen the Minnie Point bass ass side of me and it was coming full force and finally spoke. "Stop! Both of you stop! Say what you mean and mean what you say. Just don't be so mean when you say it. All George is trying to do is resolve the open issues so that everyone can go on with life. Right now, George's hands are tied. He can't even rent the farm land without Amy's signature. We've spent the last three months trying to find you simply to put closure on this entire situation. If that's wrong, I don't know what's right."

Megan continued. "Amy, you once loved George to the point you carried his children. You lived together, loved together, laughed together and cried together. You thought he was dead and the last words you ever sent to him are frozen on his computer which simply say 'I love you.'"

"Over the past few months I've come to know a man who only wants to go on with life who has been saddened by the greed of his son who tore his family apart. A man who took what little money he has to simply try and find you. Not to hurt you. Not to embarrass or condone you but simply to put closure on a chapter no one foresaw. No one could have planned for this, that's for sure."

Megan's tone softened as she added. "In the end, all of this... all of it, comes down to two simple words... 'and' and 'or'. Simply by putting 'and' instead of 'or', nothing can be done. Amy, by changing the document, when everything regarding the sedition issue is resolved, you, too, will be free. You'll have half of everything that's currently frozen. Your bank accounts, your investments, the farm and this house."

"If you two want to sit and argue about it and lose everything, including your love and respect for each other and the life you lived, then go for it. I don't know about you, Karen but doesn't it seem ridiculous to be fighting over something you already have that can't be used simply because you're too damn stubborn to admit you both made mistakes?"

Amy looked at me and I saw she understood. I looked at Karen and realized she too was hurt. I glanced at Megan and realized just how good she had become at tolerating a level of drama that no one should ever have to experience.

There was a pause and then Megan spoke again. "Amy, the choice you need to make is not about yesterday but about tomorrow. If you want to punish George, don't sign the documents and you'll both lose. If you want to punish Karen, go back to George and ask for his forgiveness and the two of you will be very, very wealthy with all the perks that come with money. If you want to stay with Karen and sign the papers and decide your life together means opening the restaurant in Puerto Montt, you'll have more than enough money to open the finest restaurant in Chile. What you do is up to you."

I was about to say something but before I could, Megan continued. "George, you too, have a decision to make. If Amy sees a future with you, would you take her back? If she wants to stay with Karen will you allow her life to go on and only remember the good times? Finally, if she doesn't sign the papers, will you look at life and simply move on, perhaps go back to Home Depot where the most important thing is that you'll be happy? It's not money. It's not luxury. It's about sincerely feeling wanted, needed and loved."

I looked at Megan, raised my fingers and said, " I have one more option, Megan, and that's being with you," as I realized Megan had taken all the winds of anger out of everyone's sails.

We'd been standing for nearly an hour. I was exhausted as I inquired. "I know it's none of my business but where are you staying and what are you doing?"

Karen offered. "When we came back from Chile we thought Saint Martin was too...too familiar and went to Saint Barths."

I looked at the two of them and noted. "You know, if the United States has sufficient evidence to support the bigamy accusation and, if Saint Barths agrees to the extradition request, the accused person can be returned to the United States to face trial?"

Amy replied in a much softer tone. "George, I didn't think you were alive. As for the Derrick matter, I know you've been exonerated. I also know that the government is really trying to find Derrick."

I looked at her with an incredulous look and offered. "If Megan and I could find you, don't you think the government has already found Derrick?"

"They might have, but he's not on Devil's Mountain."

"What?"

"No. He slipped out and is gone."

"Who's doing all the bad stuff in Peru...missing persons... crime?" I asked.

"Who do you think?" Amy retorted.

I paused and realized there was only one other person and that was my brother as I replied, "Tommie?"

"And Su," Amy added.

"What? I thought Su was killed in a car accident."

Amy looked at me and shook her head as she questioned. "Didn't everyone think you were dead too?"

"So, my brother and his wife are alive and living on Devil's Mountain?"

"Yes, and they've associated themselves with some really bad people. All they're interested in is power and money and they've begun working with a cartel."

"Drugs?" I asked.

"Perhaps. I don't know. What I do know is that Karen and I didn't want any part of it," Megan offered.

"Why?" I continued.

"Because the bad guys want their money back...all of it and they're the only ones who can provide it. As long as Tommie and Su keep making payments, they're safe. The minute they stop, they're dead."

"Holy shit!" I exclaimed as my hand went to a chair back for both physical and emotional support. "What about Derrick?"

Amy offered. "No one knows. The heat is on from both the U.S. and the bad guys."

"Where do you think he is?"

"George, we honestly don't know. The last anyone saw of him was when he got in the helicopter and took off from Devil's Mountain."

"Whose helicopter was it?"

"No one knows."

"Where do you think he is?"

Amy paused and then noted, "Venezuela, Cuba, Nicaragua,

Bolivia." Any one of them would protect someone with a lot of money and the one thing Derrick still has is a lot of money."

It was nearing midnight and the end of a day I'll never forget. I looked at Karen and Amy and began to feel sorry for them and asked, "would you like to stay here tonight?"

I believe Amy was shocked to think I'd make such an offer but she was still my wife.

I looked at Amy and noted, "we've got your clothes in cartons in the vault, do you want me to get them out? "

"Please."

I went to our bedroom, opened the wall, unlocked the vault and got the boxes out. Megan came up and offered to help me bring them downstairs as we interrupted something Karen and Amy were sharing in a low voice.

Amy looked at the cartons and asked if we could put them in the guest bedroom. We did.

All of us had experienced a long day and realized no one was in any shape to continue. We excused ourselves as Megan and I went to our bedroom while Karen and Amy adjourned to the guest bedroom.

What a day! What a night!

Walk/Talk:

As had been the case every time I came to Saint Martin, I was up early. I quietly got out of bed and made my way downstairs. Sitting at the kitchen table was Amy. She, too, had always been an early riser. She'd opened her box of casual clothes and was wearing her Saint Martin 'outfit'... boy's white ribbed undershirt and old khaki gym shorts.

I poured water in the Keurig and got a cup of coffee. Before sitting, I asked if it would be all right if I sat with her. Amy silently nodded it was OK. I sat, looked at her and saw a sad person staring back and didn't know how to begin.

I looked at Amy and commented, "I like your new hairstyle. It reminds me of the time when you accidentally got stoned with the nurses."

Amy shook her head as a weak smile crossed her face before replying, "Karen is the one who likes it."

Wanting to add a little levity to the conversation I added. "Remember when you woke up the next morning, ran your hands through your hair? Had this OMG look on your face? Went in the bathroom and came out in total shock?"

Amy shook her head and smiled. It was good to see her smile. It had been so long as I continued. "Then you came back and asked me if you looked like a boy and I said 'yes' and so you took off your shirt and said, 'if I'm going to look like a boy, I'm going to dress like a boy,' and wanted to go to Chez Leandra for lunch."

Now Amy was beginning to giggle as I concluded. "You were so funny. It was like watching an episode of 'I Love Lucy.' I almost peed my pants laughing."

Amy had her infectious smile as she countered. "Didn't we 'compromise'? Didn't we ride over to Orient Beach with me only wearing just my shorts?"

"Yes!"

"Those were the days, Georgie! Those were the days."

I paused and then confessed, "I really think it would have been better if Megan hadn't saved my life."

"George, that's a horrible thing to say." "Look at all the trouble I've caused."

"It's not your fault, George." Amy paused and then looked out the window and commented. "I used to love it here. Now I don't know."

"I feel the same way." I replied.

Amy looked at me and then offered. "I think I'm the one who should have died a long time ago. If I had, you'd be happy and none of this would have taken place."

I shook my head, looked at the table and then at Amy and commented. "If you had, my life would never have been as good as it's been. Without you, nothing would have mattered."

"But look at all that I've put you through."

"Peaks and valleys! Peaks and valleys." I replied, thinking of my mom and how she would always say it.

Amy looked at me and inquired. "Do you think Megan or Karen would mind if we went down and walked the beach? It been so long?"

I paused to evaluate the consequences and then said I thought it would be all right while adding. "I do think we should leave a note."

Amy got a piece of paper from the junk drawer in the kitchen and simply wrote, "George and I have gone for a walk to talk things out. Thank you for understanding."

Amy and I rose, went to the tram and took it down to the Rover, got in and drove over to Orient Beach. For November, the weather had begun to clear and it was going to be a sunny day.

We parked the Rover behind Lucille's and got out. It had been over three years since we walked the beach and time and all the issues had made both of us a lot more reserved. We began our walk as all the reticence I'd had simply disappeared. It was like old times.

I remembered the first time Amy convinced me to go with her 'au natural' as she called it and how nervous I was. I remembered all the relaxation things she did. I remembered laughing and thinking about tomorrow and how happy we'd been.

As we walked, I saw a piece of driftwood that had come in with the tide and walked ahead to pick it up. As I bent down, the back of my t-shirt slid up and Amy saw my tattoo.

"When did you get that?" Amy inquired.

"What?"

"The tattoo."

"A few days ago, why?"

"I never thought you'd ever do it." Amy said as she shook her head in disbelief. Did Megan make you do it?"

"No. It was my idea." "What is it?"

"The zodiac sign for cancer and men put together." "Prostate cancer! Good choice. Good location." Amy offered.

Wow, a compliment just as the tip of the sun was breaching the horizon.

Amy took a deep breath, locked her right hand around her left wrist, raised her arms above her head, stretched and commented, "A new day! A new beginning!"

Retaining her upright yoga position, Amy provided the opportunity for me to examine the outline of her entire body where, for the first time since who knows when, she aroused me.

My glances started with her outreached hands and made their way down her arms. I looked at the now-protruding semblance of her breasts as my eyes journeyed down her torso, rib-by-rib until I got a glimpse of where the little red rose was hidden beneath her shorts. The little red rose that had been put there for me. The little red rose that brought back so many memories of love and laughter... of simply being together where time stood still as we traversed the peaks and valleys of each other in a time of innocence, a time of confidences where the only thoughts were good thoughts, not of today but only tomorrow.

My God, why now? Was it intentional? Was it her way of enticing me? Or was it simply one of those things Amy did to maintain her mind and body?

I wanted her. I wanted her right then and there. My mind convulsed in sensual urges. I wanted to take her out deeper in the water and do what we'd done before, quietly, silently sharing each other in our own escapade that had been our own little secret culminated in sly glances and wicked smiles we shared as we had each other.

The glance was over in a flash as Amy's hands returned to her sides and my mind went back here and now as I didn't know how to interpret what she was saying and simply decided it was nothing more than her elocution that she'd always pronounced when the sun began to rise.

As we walked, Amy's eyes focused on the sand in front of us as the warm water gently lapped at our feet. After a few steps, she noted. "I really thought you were dead and it was the saddest day of my life. You, George, have been my guiding light. You've been what has made my life worthwhile. My only regrets are the things I said last night. I was angry. I was upset. I was wrong and I hope you'll forgive me."

When you live with someone for thirty years, you know when they're being sincere and I realized what Amy was saying was coming straight from the heart as I countered. "I got too emotional last night and said things I shouldn't have and owe you an apology. It's just been so...so difficult these past few years. I really never knew how good we had it until it all went away."

We kept walking and talking about all that had transpired, then the kids and finally Megan. I didn't know how to start and so I began at the beginning. "Amy, Megan saved my life. She was the one who responded to my calls for help. First, in the cave and then when I was all alone and literally a hermit, afraid of anything and everything."

Amy paused for a moment and then added. "I can see that she's important to you."

I didn't know how to take Amy's response and so I added. "You need to realize, I went over a year without seeing another human being. I moved into the farm house and simply existed, wanting nothing more than to die but never brave enough to do it. It took me all that time to even turn on my laptop and then another month before I opened my email. It was then I found your note and it simply broke my heart."

"Oh, George, I was so...so sad."

"Melia explained what happened and I thanked God you were still alive."

"I'm alive." Amy interjected. "I'm still at risk but doing OK." We were nearing 'the bend' as we'd called it and I continued.

"Melia told me how Karen had taken care of you and that you two were together. I understand Amy. I really understand."

Taking a deep breath, I looked back at where we'd walked and saw, like life, that our footprints were slowly fading in the sand and continued. "As I started to heal, the only person in my life was Megan simply because she cared. Then, when her practice was sold and she lost her job, I offered to let her stay with me until she found someplace else. She was living with a couple and the husband decided one day to force himself on her. In a matter of weeks, she lost her job and the security she once felt and I guess I felt sorry for her as we were two people all alone."

I didn't know how to explain Megan's and my relationship and so there was silence for an extended period of time as we listened to the breeze and saw the Sawgrass moving with the wind, highlighted by the sound of the small waves lapping at the shore.

Finally, I knew I needed to explain further. "Megan and I have had a deep relationship but it isn't intimate. We eat together, do things together, are comfortable with each other but nothing has *'happened'.*"

"Do you want it to?" Amy asked.

Before I could open my mouth, she interjected. "George, it's OK. If it's what you need, go for it."

"But!"

"But what?"

"But, I've always been faithful to you."

 "But I haven't with you." Amy retorted.

"I know, Amy. I know."

Amy stopped walking, looked at me as I added, "I was going through our old papers in the security box and found the thumb drive." "Jesus!" as a river of pronounced fear roared through every nerve in Amy's body.

"I shouldn't have looked but I did. I'm sorry. It was private but it was there and I thought you were, you were gone forever."

"You saw everything?" Amy inquired with an emphasis on 'everything'.

"Everything!" I replied.

I really didn't know how to begin or what to say and so, instead, I simply looked in Amy's eyes and began. "Amy, I've loved you from the moment you stepped out of the UPS truck. I've loved you more than life itself. While I was locked in that cave, all I thought about was being with you. When I was finally free, my only goal was to find you and tell you how much you meant to me but you were gone and with it you took every single thing I believed in. Every single thing I held beyond reproach was challenged. I gave you my word… make that my vow… no, make that a covenant... that my love was greater than anything you could ever do, ever be or ever say that would take that away."

"When I found the thumb drive and saw what was on it, it was only then that I began to understand. Before that and for thirty years, I never realized what you endured. I never had any idea the depth of feeling and the profound sense of internal strife you tolerated. It was then, that I began to seek out why it was that you thought so little of yourself."

"But I don't…" Amy interjected as I raised my finger as an indication for her to allow me to continue.

"Yes, you do my love. Yes, you do. Perhaps it's the challenge of being a tri-bi. Perhaps it's the reality of living in the shadow of two of the most incredibly dynamic people in the world and attempting to measure up to those standards. Yet, it's always there. It's always been that you never thought yourself worthy of anything, simply because you've always believed you were inferior that has been reinforced so many, many times by so many people."

I paused and watched as some early morning strollers passed by and then continued. "When I watched those videos, I saw it. When I saw how you desecrated yourself, denigrated yourself and, in some ways, humiliated yourself simply to prove to yourself you weren't worthy of being you, it was then, after all these years, I realized just how deep the scars were, how profound the pain, how inexplicably great the agony has been."

Tears started cascading from Amy's eyes. I'd hit a tender spot and, for the first time ever, I was explaining what I'd seen and more importantly, what I felt as I continued. "I now see that you have internalized the negative stereotypes and biases about your race, orientation and mental health that have led to low self-esteem and feelings of inadequacy."

We stopped as if to allow me to reach deeper into my soul as I added. "Amy, I've seen and witnessed your bipolar disorder. I've experienced your mood swings, your anxiety and your depression and now understand the consequence of the added complexities in terms of navigating your multiple identities and, for the first time, realize the challenges you faced."

"While the kids and I tried to do everything we could to be a 'normal' family, I can only imagine the difficulty you had in finding supportive communities and understanding from others that lead to your feelings of loneliness and isolation where you did everything in your power to debilitate your own self-concept. My greatest regret is that I couldn't have been a greater help."

I put my hands in Amy's, not in a romantic way but one of a conciliatory nature and added. "To know that I could never REALLY satisfy you was something I was willing to give up simply because it was you. I can only imagine the challenges you've faced navigating your desires simply because of family, societal and personal as well as the complexities of your own identity."

"In the end, I saw the exposed you. The one without the shield. It wasn't pretty and it certainly wasn't what I wanted to see. Yet, for the very first time, I saw the real you, the person who has experienced a life of trauma filled with discrimination, prejudice, and microaggressions that I now believe you've never been able to escape."

"What you did. What you are. What you can be is so incredible, if only you learn to love yourself. However, if you continue without that self-love, I'm truly afraid it will lead to trauma and PTSD, if it's not already there."

I don't know if it was embarrassment, fear, resentment or a total collapse of Amy's inner self but she almost convulsed right then as her hands went to her mouth as if in prayer and she whispered, "I'm so sorry," as she began to cry.

We stopped and I pulled her in to give her a shoulder to cry on as I repeated. "It's all right! It's all right! It's all right."

Amy pulled back with the most sorrowful expression on her face I'd ever seen as she shook her head, looked down at the water and then at me and offered. "I'm so sorry!!!!"

We simply stood and allowed the tsunami of grief to roil within her as regret simply shuddered within her body. Finally, she looked at me, looked again at the water, then back at me and simply asked, "Will you ever forgive me?"

I took a deep breath as if to allow the pain to be diluted and then noted. "Amy, I knew who you were when I married you. I knew the challenges you faced. I accepted it all. The only things that really, really hurt were the little red roses. Yours was meant for me! "I'm so sorry." Amy assured me as tears welled in her eyes.

"Mine is for you and only you."

I waited for the emotional tidal wave to calm and then added. "For all our years together, I accepted that you had other 'needs' and validated it by the fact the 'others' provided things I never could and then you broke my heart."

"How?" Amy asked in a meek and almost crying way.

I looked at the ocean and out to sea and proclaimed, "When you were with Michelle and the guy. That's when you broke my heart."

Amy almost convulsed on the spot to the point I took her hands in mine and added. "You made a vow. You assured me. You had... you had always made me feel as if I was the only man."

Amy looked at the water again and simply shook her head before noting. "George, I love you. I always have and always will. I don't know how you can still love me after all I've done."

"But I do." I replied.

"I know. I can feel it and it makes me feel incredibly guilty." "Why, George? Why do you still love me?"

"Because you've always made me feel 'complete'." "What about Megan?"

"I don't know. I love her too, but in a totally different way." "What are we going to do?"

I released Amy's hands and looked down at the gentle waves and then admitted. "As for me, I'm tired, really, really tired. I've given everything I can to you simply because I have and will always love you."

There was a pause to allow me to collect my thoughts knowing this was one of the most critical conversations of my life as I added. "Our lives have changed. Our paths are no longer parallel and yet I love you more today than yesterday but not as much as tomorrow. However, I also now know that neither of us will ever be truly happy with each other."

There were tears in both of our eyes. We both knew we'd reached the end of the road. They say you can love someone so much you begin the hate the love and you can also hate someone so much you begin to love the hate. I knew neither of us wanted to get to either spectrum and that, if we were going to spend the rest of our lives making up for what we tried so damn hard to create, we needed to do so with someone else.

"What now, George?"

We stopped walking and I looked at Amy and replied. "I have

no idea. The only thing I know is that we can't fight each other. If we do, neither of us will win."

Amy looked up at the brightening sky as if for guidance and then at me and finally replied. "I agree but what are we going to do?"

"I think we need to join forces and go after Derrick. I think we need to teach Tommie Terrill a lesson. I think! I think, that's what we've got to do."

"What about Karen?" Amy asked.

"Nothing has changed has it? You have Karen and I have Megan. All we need do is make sure they realize this is a fight for all of us."

Amy inquired as if in statement form. "And you want to stay with Megan?"

I countered, "And you want to stay with Karen?"

It was at that point in time, a pact was made. We would live the lives we were living but fight together to regain what had been ours.

We made it back to spot on the beach where we'd turn to get the Rover and paused. I looked at Amy and she at me and then we hugged. Oh my God, it felt so good, so God damn good to feel her in my arms. We stood pressed against each other and I could feel her, all of her...her body and her soul as if, by osmosis, all that we'd shared had been internalized.

As we stood there, Amy's hands slid down around my waist as she pulled me in even tighter as she whispered. "I don't want to let go. I don't want to let go. I love you, George. I love you."

While most people would love to hear those words, they tore at my heart. I was in love with both women, yet I knew I had to make a choice in order to be happy. It could no longer be Amy **and** Megan, it had to be Amy **or** Megan. I had to decide. I had to decide. I simply had to decide as the chorus of Pure Prairie League's 1972 song hit me.

Amy, what you wanna do? I think I could stay with you
For a while, maybe longer if I do
Fallin' in and out of love with you Fallin' in and out of love with

you Don't know what I'm gonna do
   I'd keep fallin' in and out of love with you

We lightly kissed, got in the Rover and made our way back to the Lighthouse and took the tram up the hill.

As we emerged in the house, two sets of concerned eyes were upon us as Amy politely said, "Good morning", and smiled at Megan and Karen.

Ouch:

The four of us spent the morning discussing our situation, ultimately realizing we were stuck with Amy's management company for the season. I decided to call Delphine and explain what had happened. With the ferry to Saint Barth's running seven times daily, including a 17:30 departure, Karen and Amy had time to figure things out before leaving.

We had lunch at Anse Marcel and returned to go over every option one more time. Each repetition drained the emotion from the conversation until we settled on a simple agreement—to keep in touch.

When it was time for Karen and Amy to leave, Megan and I offered them a ride to Philipsburg, giving us more time to talk. Before heading out, I printed the agreements Tank had drafted and handed them to Amy. I told her to look them over and emphasized that, no matter what, we needed to resolve things to get the liquidity we both desperately needed.

At the Green House parking lot near the ferry dock, we all got out and exchanged polite goodbyes. I knew rush hour traffic would be a mess, so Megan and I wasted no time heading back to the Lighthouse. The ride was quiet, the only sound coming from the tires against the road.

I knew I had to share my morning conversation with Amy. Without hesitation, I began. "Amy and I had a good talk. I told her how much she meant to me. But I also told her I was in love with you."

Megan's eyes moistened, and she let out a soft sigh of relief. I continued. "We agreed we needed to get our money back from Derrick and move on."

"And you're sure?" Megan asked.

I looked at Megan. She saw it in my face—I wasn't. I didn't say a word, but I didn't have to.

There was a long pause before I admitted, "Megan, we were together for thirty years. She only left because she thought I was dead. She's done things that would normally end a relationship, yet I tolerated everything. But now… now that she and Karen are gone, I feel relieved. And I'm incredibly happy you're here with me. I know it's not perfect."

I continued. "I know it's not what you want to hear. But please, just give me some time. I promise, I won't hurt you. I vow to always be honest. Just… understand where I'm at."

Megan reached across the console and gave my hand a squeeze. She didn't need to say anything. She understood. She was willing to stand by me as I navigated the mess in my head.

As we drove out of Philipsburg, I broke the silence. "Well, what do you think?"

"About what?" she asked. "About those two."

Megan stared out the windshield and said, "Karen is probably an L3-L4."

"A what?" I asked, confused.

"There's a test called the Graffenberg test."

I remembered the thumb drive and Amy's report mentioning that an L4 meant little to no interest in the opposite sex. "Why do people take those tests?" I asked, skeptical. "Aren't they a waste of money?"

Megan gave me a knowing look, her upper lip curling slightly. "Do you ever weigh yourself?"

"Sure, every week." "Why?"

"To see how much I weigh."

"In other words, to quantify your physical existence." "Yes."

"These tests are similar," she explained. "They aren't about changing who you are. They help you understand yourself better. It's like shining a light on why you feel certain things or why you're drawn to certain people. There's nothing wrong with gaining insight—it's empowering. It helps you understand yourself so you don't feel conflicted or question your feelings."

Her words started making sense.

"There's nothing wrong with being gay, bi, or anything in between. Just because Karen identifies as L3-L4 doesn't mean she won't occasionally be attracted to men. It just means her heart is happiest in a certain place."

"But it's weird, isn't it?" I asked.

Megan shook her head 'no' and retorted. "Nearly one-in-five U.S. women and 6% of men have had a same-sex experience. Why do you think it's weird? George, society is becoming more accepting. Sexuality isn't just black and white—it's fluid. Young people today get that. Exploring who you are is a normal part of figuring yourself out."

Megan shrugged, a small smile playing on her lips. "It's interesting, isn't it? In same-sex relationships between women, there's often a real emphasis on emotional intimacy. It's a much more communicative experience, you know? More about connection."

"And, well," she paused, "because it often takes women a bit longer to reach, *that point*, sex between women can involve a lot more foreplay, a wider range of stimulation, and a slower pace and can definitely feel softer."

"So, it's…better?" I asked

"It's not about being better," Megan countered. "It's just different and there are actually some real reasons behind that. For starters, women in same-sex relationships tend to focus a lot more on emotional connection, which makes things feel more intimate, slower, and in tune with each other's needs. Plus, they're usually more open about discussing desires, boundaries, and pleasure, which can make the experience feel even more comfortable and fulfilling."

"Another big factor is that women, on average, take longer to reach a high level of pleasure than men. Because of that, it naturally involves more foreplay, more variety, and a slower pace, which is probably why people describe it as gentler. And let's be real—without the pressure of male satisfaction being the "goal," the experience tends to feel more exploratory, relaxed, and focused on mutual pleasure, rather than rushing to the finish line."

"And so once women...uhh...try it, they stay there?" I asked. Megan had an incredulous look on her face as she replied.

"Hardly George! Exploration isn't a one-way street. In two-thirds of all same-sex experiences, 75% of women identify as straight afterward. Men, though? They're more likely to identify as gay or bisexual after similar experiences."

I must have made a face as Megan countered. "You're left- handed, right?"

"Yah."

"Ever tried writing with your right hand?"

"Of course."

"And?" Megan countered.

"And what?"

"It didn't make you right-handed, did it?"

"No." I admitted.

"Exactly. Exploration doesn't always change who you are—unless you want it to."

I was in a hole and the only way to get out was stop digging and so I decided to switch topics. "So there's more than one test?"

Megan nodded. "There are several. The Kinsey Scale ranges from zero to six—zero being completely straight, six being fully gay. Most women fall somewhere between zero and three, meaning they have some degree of fluidity. There's also the Klein Sexual Orientation Grid, the Sell Assessment of Sexual Orientation, the Storms Scale, and the Graffenberg Test."

She continued, "On the Graffenberg scale, zero represents an equal attraction to both sexes. The further you move toward L5, the stronger the same-sex inclination. The further you move toward R5, the more heteronormative you are."

"In other words, the further from zero you get, the more defined your preference?" I asked.

"Exactly."

Megan hesitated, then admitted, "We were required to take one in my Clinical Psychology course. I took the Graffenberg test—I scored an R1.5."

I shared Amy's result: R0.5.

"So… bi, but with some guilt attached," Megan concluded. "Sounds about right," I said. "So, you don't think Amy should feel

as guilty as she does?"

Megan shook her head. "Heavens, no. If I could talk to her, I'd tell her there's nothing wrong with who she is. The real tragedy is her self- deprecation."

Megan sighed and continued. "Where it gets complicated is her bipolar disorder. Bisexuality is just a part of who she is. Bipolar disorder, though—that's something that needs professional help. I could help her with self-acceptance, but I can't fix that."

There was a pause before she added, "While you and Amy were down at Orient Beach… Karen hit on me."

"What?" My jaw clenched.

Megan raised her hands in defense. "Relax, George. It wasn't about her being a woman—I don't think Karen is interested in love. I think she's a predator."

A wave of concern for Amy washed over me. "Why do you say that?"

"All the signs are there," Megan said. "She builds trust, manipulates, and exploits vulnerability. Amy's looking for emotional security. Karen's looking for a trophy. That's the problem—not their sexualities."

I shook my head, stunned by how well Megan had figured it all out.

"How do you know so much?" I finally asked.

Megan stared straight ahead. "Because I've been there."

She let that sit for a moment before adding, "And in some ways…I still am."

Ouch!

The Bottom Drawer:

We made it back to the Lighthouse and I pushed the call button as the tram trundled its way to the bottom.

Megan went to the guest bedroom and stripped the bed. It was as if she wanted to rid the house of all memories. Folding the blanket, she went to the dresser and opened the bottom drawer assuming that's where the blanket had been. Instead, Megan found several articles of clothing.

Coming out of the guest bedroom she inquired. "George, has anyone else been living here?"

"No, why?"

"I opened the bottom dresser drawer to put away the blanket and found some clothes."

I thought and then asked. "Men's or women's?" "Women's."

I thought for a moment and went through all the iterations. Because we had House-On-The-Hill as our guest house, no one used the Lighthouse except Amy and me. Then it hit me, when we were here before, there had been a hurricane and the two nurses who'd been so kind during my stay in the hospital came one week and when the hurricane was about to hit, we had them come from H-O-H and stay with us.

I looked at Megan and replied. "We had two house guests named Reggie and Sam or Samantha who were staying at our guest house. There was a hurricane and so they stayed three days with us here. What did they leave?"

"Some shorts, tops and rompers."

"It's been four years, and they never called or asked for them."

"What do you want me to do with them?"

I shrugged. "I don't know. I guess, get rid of them unless there's something that would fit you."

With Megan already wearing some of Melia's clothes, I hoped she didn't mind.

Megan went back to the guest bedroom and tidied up.

After the drama of the day, I asked. "Tell you what, why don't we go out tonight?"

Megan's eyebrows lifted in expectation as what she'd inherently wanted seemed to be just beyond the horizon when she inquired, "where do you want to go?"

"LeTaitu," I replied. "It's quiet and perhaps we can sit on the upper level and have a quiet dinner."

"How should I dress?" Megan asked.

"Not too dressy, but not what you'd wear to the beach."

Megan went to change and selected one of the girl's outfits consisting of a tan one-piece romper with large white polka dots that consisted of a demure cut, highlighted by a cinch-tie waist, and cross- over bodice that tied behind her neck. As was the case with most casual Caribbean rompers, the legs were loose fit and the inseam was quite short such that it accentuated her legs.

I remembered the night Reggie wore it to Auberge Gourmand, smiled and exclaimed "Wow! Ms. Eagan, you look **fantastic**."

"Thank you Mister Terrill." Megan replied as a smile of pride spread across her face.

When it was time to go, we got in the Rover and made it to the restaurant where we parked the car and walked in. It was late, even on a Friday night, and most of the dinner crowd had already departed. The restaurant was closed on Saturday and Sunday and there was only one table on the lower level that had a couple still eating. I surveyed the scene and saw the table on the upper level. Dark, quiet and very, very personal. Just what I remembered.

Philippe, the owner greeted us with his normal pleasant smile and was about to direct us to one of the lower tables when he caught my eye as I motioned towards the table up above. He smiled and took us to the table that had a white table cloth covering all the nicks and scratches that happen to tables and people in this thing called life. Whenever we'd gone out to eat, we'd always sat what I called 'married style' or across from each other, I thought it would make a tacit statement if I sat next to Megan which caught her by surprise.

We ordered a bottle of wine and when it came, eye contact with Philippe communicated I'd call him when we needed to place our order. As we sat there, the other couple departed and we had the restaurant to ourselves where the only noise was the sound of our hearts beating, telling each other that everything was all right. I knew I needed to calm any emotional waves that had turned to whitecaps with all that had transpired over the past two days.

I looked at Megan and asked, "Are you, all right?" "I'm fine," Megan lied.

"Honestly, are you, all right?"

"George, we started out on this journey to do one thing and that was find Amy. We found her, isn't that what you wanted?"

"Yes, but I also didn't want to **not** have you   "

"But you do have me. You can have me any way you want." Megan countered in a quite taciturn tone.

My God, where was this going? I was trying to tell Megan I really needed her and she was telling me that she wasn't satisfied with the level of our relationship.

I looked deep into Megan's eyes. I held my breath for an instant and then finally countered. "This is really getting complicated. I... I have really deep feelings for you but I also still have feelings for Amy."

"I know. I can see it. I can feel it."

I didn't know what else to say and so I asked. "Do you understand?"

"I think so," Megan responded. "I just know that right now, I have feelings for you that are, I believe, much stronger for you than yours are for me."

We ordered and quietly played with our spaghetti. It seemed strange to be eating Italian food in a French restaurant but it was some of the best I'd ever eaten. Slowly, the night was making its way into yesterday. I glanced down and saw that the outdoor lights had been turned off and kitchen lights had darkened. Like any gracious host, the restaurant hadn't begun its slumber simply because we were there.

As the overt symbols of commerce dimmed, the soft glow of the flickering candle on our table assumed the role of both illumination and mood creation as it softly painted a landscape of two lost souls, creating lopsided shades that highlighted the majesty of our friendship. My right hand slowly slid across the table as my fingers gently grasped Megan's left hand such that our bodies, hearts and souls became connected. I paused and then whispered. "I don't think I've ever mentioned how beautiful you are."

Megan's head tilted down as if embarrassed and then looked at me and softly replied, "Thank you."

"Not only physically, but deep inside," I offered. "Even with... even with what I've shared with you."

I looked at Megan and became conciliatory as I noted. "Megan, what you did, you did for a reason and I am not worthy of judging you. As it should be, we all have shadows within our soul and no one has the right to flash the light of judgement until they've been there themselves."

I looked at the table and then back at Megan, took an extended breath, slowly shook my head in regret and frankly admitted. "I think I've taken you too much for granted. You and only you, saved my life in many ways and I will always be grateful."

Megan looked in my eyes and we both remained silent as no words were needed as if to indicate some sort of demarcation. As we stared in each other's eyes, reality peeked its persistent head as Phillippe came around the corner, climbed the few steps and brought us back to that instant in time called 'now' as my hand quickly returned to my lap.

It was then I realized, we'd over-stayed our welcome and was a bit perplexed. We'd taken advantage of the hospitality and I felt guilty. In a compensatory mode, even with money tight, I knew I needed to leave a major tip and dug into my wallet and placed a one-hundred Euro bill beneath my plate as a way of letting

Philippe know it was one of the finest dining experiences I'd ever had.

We walked out of the restaurant and stopped to allow a car go whizzing by. Megan looked at me as I said, "I have an idea."

"What?"

"Instead of going back to the house, if we go to the beach, we can look up at the stars that are normally washed out by all the lights. The sparkles will only last a couple of hours before the moon rises and they'll be gone."

"Is it nearby?" Megan inquired. "Just around the bend."

Megan added, "We can look at the stars and hear the waves as well? Neat!"

As we got to the Rover and I opened Megan's door, I declared. "You get so much out of so little. So much joy! So much pleasure! So much fun! That's what I love about you. I mean, look at tonight, we're here and simply going to look at the stars. How many people ever do that anymore?"

Megan nodded in a positive way as I drove the few blocks towards the condos at Mont Vernon and pulled into the grassy residential parking lot by the tennis courts. We slipped out of our shoes and walked around Etang Chevrise, the small estuary that filled with sea water from high tide and some grass-covered sand dunes I thought would block the light and let us enjoy God's majesty as we reached the beach.

I looked left at the rocks where the turn-around was where Amy and I had been that morning as Megan and I began the slow trek towards the bend. As we were walking, I pointed out Polaris or the North Star, then Sirius and added that it was also known as the Dog Star, because it's the brightest star in Canis Major or the 'Big Dog'.

"See that bright white dot?"

"Uh huh."

"It's the brightest star in the southern constellation of Centaurus and the third brightest star in the night sky. It's the closest system to Earth. Just a shade over four light-years away.

Much like Sirius and Polaris, it's actually a multi-star system, consisting of Alpha Centauri A, B, and Proxima Centauri."

For a long moment we stood in silence having reached the zenith of interaction. I wanted to caress her. I wanted to make her feel I truly wanted her. Instead, certainty reared its ugly head and I knew we needed to move on.

'Lead us not into temptation!' my mind pronounced and so I pulled back as Megan turned to face me. God I wanted her. Not here! Not now! I begged myself. Instead, I put my right hand in hers such that I was on the water side and we started walking again.

"Let's keep walking." I offered.

With each step, the degree of primal insistence dissipated as we made our way down the shore. Reaching Bikini Beach where the light pollution from the restaurants quickly dissolved our starlight theater, I suggested we turn around and walked back a few hundred paces until we'd regained our personal solstice, stopped for a minute as Megan walked into the water with the placid waves lapping just below her knees. It was then she raised her arms to the ocean and let the breeze caress her body. "Come on, George, this is GREAT!" She announced.

I paused until Megan came back, took my hand and lead me into the water as she looked up at the stars and simply announced, "Let's be free, George! Free of all the past that's locked us up and made our world so...so restrained."

Perhaps it was the words. Perhaps the magic of the stars. All I know is that Megan and I stood hand-in-hand for what seemed like an eternity, letting the breeze caress our bodies as the upper limb of the moon broke the water's horizon, gradually dominating our attention. Gone were the stars, washed out by the prevalence of the moon as it began to cast its glow upon the waves. Somewhat like resurrection, the bright, white light erased the darkness that surrounded us. For the longest time we stood in total silence... spellbound, engrossed in an almost religious spectacle of sight, sense and sound.

Looking at the moon, I gradually slid behind Megan and

placed my hands on her hips with my chin on her shoulder as we became one body in unison, linked together by raw emotion. My hands went around her waist as she took hers and covered mine. For what seemed like an eternity, we simply stood, locked together until my lips met the right side of her neck and I kissed her as a soft, gentle expression of approval.

Megan's head arched to the left as if to indicate she wanted more and so, once again, I placed my lips upon her neck and shared my intensity.

"Megan whispered. "It feels good to have you touch me."

We were both breathing deeply as Megan turned to allow me to look at her with the moon over her shoulder and then it happened. We kissed. Not the polite or gentle kiss that had crossed our lips before, but a deep, passionate kiss I knew I wouldn't – couldn't stop. It had been so long and it felt so good. *My God, what was I doing?*

Megan' hands went behind my neck as mine went down to the small of her back as I could feel her muscles tense. I pulled her in until I could feel her breasts pressing against my beating heart. God, it felt good. So good! So, so good!

Without hesitation, we remained in a position of concurrence to the point we were in unison, breathing staccato breaths...in/out, in/out, in a syncopated rhythm such that I could feel her body telling me that her pleasure was my pleasure, her excitement my excitement, her arousal mine and only mine.

My hands made their way down until they pressed against her bottom such that I felt Megan's nervous shiver of anticipation as I pulled her in. Oh my God, it had been so long and it felt so good! My mind strived to capture each nuance and every neural quiver that accentuated my own pleasure as my hands pressed against what had only been in my imagination to make it a reality.

'Don't let go! Don't let go! Don't let go!' I silently pleaded with myself as the remaining ache of isolation slowly made its way from deep within my soul to the final vestiges of my body, freeing me, at last, from the captivity of simply being the number one.

As if the placement of my hands was some sort of release,

Megan took a deep breath, leaned back such that her face was in front of me, looked in my eyes, turned her head a little to the left and pressed her lips against mine and she slid her tongue in my mouth. I could feel her. I could taste her. I could sense every nerve in her body as she and I became we.

For an extended period, we simply kissed, deep passionate kisses. The mouth. The lips. The side of Megan's neck as her head tilted back in pleasure. Again, our lips met and then our tongues and we began again with even greater intensity.

Oblivious to the world around us, it was the sound of others walking the beach and sharing a memory that broke the spell. Fortunately, we were off shore and our passion remained our own and yet, the insipience that we were not alone reminded us that reality was upon us. Passion is a tender fruit. When it's ripe, it's succulent. To share one's passion is an ephemeral dream that lasts but a split second and then is gone.

Here we stood, knee deep in the sea and each other, totally indifferent to the world around us. Neither of us wanting to stop and yet, after what seemed like eternity where our mouths had experienced bliss, the intensity reluctantly waned as reality rose its pilfered head.

I looked at Megan and she at me as a post-partum kiss proclaimed acclimation. Acclimation! Neither of us wanted it and yet the reticence of reality overcame our carnal delight and we knew it was time to begin walking back from whence we came.

I brought my hands to my side as Megan's arms released my neck and we simply looked at each other nodding, smiling, knowing, accepting, relishing we'd taken one step closer to what I think we now both believed would be our consequence.

The moon was now in full force and it's brightness created obtuse shadows that designated our way back towards our inevitability. So it was, two people who trusted each other, respected each other and valued each other, who had first become friends, now solemnly knowing that no matter what happened, our bond would be forever.

We turned and began our walk back, hand-in-hand to certainty, silently rambling until we reached the rocky outcrop that represented the turning point in so many junctures and lives. It was there we stopped, stood and listened to the melodic rapture of the incessant waves touching the shore while looking out at the glistening moonlit water as the elegant white beams of night immersed Little Key and Ilet Pinel in a sparkling aura of purity.

I looked at Megan and she at me. We turned, such that we stood side-by-side, hand-in-hand and silently witnessed God's majesty... two lost souls, now found, who journeyed together from some now-distant point called loneliness to a tiny spot upon the earth that simply evoked serenity.

As that moment came to an anti-climactic end, we turned and kissed again - not only as a physical interaction but an evocation of our trust, belief and respect in each other.

After a dozen heartbeats Megan looked at me, smiled and shook her head before giving me a perfunctory kiss. My God, I really was in love. Yet, I was so, so afraid. What would happen if the good Amy returned? What would I do then? Who would I hurt? Would it be those I loved or only me?

With the air thick with introspection, the moment passed as we both realized we'd ventured far enough in several ways and quietly made our way back to the Rover.

We got in and I looked at the dash clock and it read 2:17 AM. I started the vehicle. As I drove, Megan closed her eyes with a gentle smile embracing her lips. As Megan's mind drifted off into her realm of one, I wondered how could this be? I'd been so emotionally vigilant. Yet, here I was, throwing caution to the wind, realizing I was no longer sheathed in a mantle of guilt.

I now knew that, what had been painfully sequestered inside of me, had finally come to fruition while glancing at the sleeping woman nestled next to me, made me smile.

We made it back to the Lighthouse and I gently touched Megan to awaken her. "Sweetie, were back. Time to go to bed."

Sweetie? I called Megan 'Sweetie'.

With that, Megan looked at me, stretched, smiled, reached out and pulled me in as we shared one of those moments one never forgets when propriety is bellowing don't... stop... don't... stop... that transforms into... Don't stop! Don't stop! Don't...!

Saint Barths:

As noted, I'd erased all the security passes except mine when I left the Lighthouse and was the reason why Amy had never been able to get in. After seeing her with Karen, I realized that's why her clothes were still in boxes we'd put back in the vault.

I knew I needed to meet with Amy again to create a strategy against Derrick and also find out what happened to my brother simply to understand why he'd changed. Amy noted that she and Karen had rented a small house on Saint Barths facing Anse Des Cayes and she needed to move out when it became 'in season.'

Amy also told me Karen was working as a server at Restaurant Le Manapany and she was working at Poupette St Barth, a high-end women's clothing store, located on Rue de la Republique in Gustavia where, when we had money, she'd shop, simply because it was known for its chic and stylish women's clothing.

I knew her day off was Friday and that would not be a good day to visit as we had no idea where their cottage was. I also knew that Tuesday-Thursday were bad days as the ships came into port because St. Barths is a popular destination for the luxury cruise ships. Add to that, the store was popular with the Cruise Directors who got great discounts for sending their female passengers there looking for the latest in French fashions and best 'deals' in the Caribbean.

This meant we needed to go over on a Monday and try to arrive when the store was about to close. With four boxes of clothes, I was tempted to take the ferry and then realized when Wilco went down, Peggy and Paul bought out the ownership to the dive business and perhaps I could get them to help us out.

Sure enough, I got hold of Peggy, explained what was going on and she said it would not only be good to see me, but for all that we'd done for them, she'd be honored to return the favor.

The following Monday was agreed upon and we went to Oyster Pond and rode with Peggy the 25 miles to Gustavia.

Peggy asked if we wanted her to wait and I told her to head back and we'd take the ferry.

Dropping us off at the Gustavia dock, which was literally across the street from the store, Peggy said good bye and so all we needed to do was haul the boxes over to the store.

Megan looked at the tranquil bay with all the yachts and was hooked as she proclaimed. "Wow, what a beautiful city."

I nodded, smiled and noted. "We almost built our house here but wanted to be close to our other house in Saint Martin."

"You have another house?" "We had. " I corrected.

"Why Saint Martin?" Megan asked.

"Because that's where Megan's mom was from," as I realized how many times family and memory altered the course of life.

Not knowing if Amy would be there, Megan stood outside the store as I went in. Amy saw me and her eye's grew wide as she came over and whispered "What are you doing here?"

"I have your clothes and thought you might need them." "That was stupid."

"What do you mean?"

"Are you trying to get me fired?" "Why?"

"I can't bring clothes in here. The manager won't allow it." "I thought we were doing you a favor."

"Who, you and Megan?" Megan asked in a somewhat snappish tone.

"Of course."

Amy shook her head in dismay, looked at me and noted. "I'm done in thirty minutes. Go across the street to the ferry terminal waiting area. I'll come over there then."

So much for doing Amy a big favor as Megan and I took the boxes back across the street and stood under the metal canopy and waited. About forty-five minutes later, Amy crossed the street and I could tell by the look on her face she was in one of her 'moods'.

"What were you thinking?" she tersely asked as she walked up to Megan and me.

In the past I would have been meek, mild and gentle but Amy had no right talking to Megan that way as I responded. "We thought we were doing you a favor."

"Well, you're not."

"Ok. Understood. Do you want your clothes or don't you?" "I don't need them."

"OK." I picked up one of the boxes and headed for the retaining wall and was about to drop them in the water when Amy yelled. "What are you doing?"

I spun on my heels, looked at Amy and let her have it. "We try to do something nice. We pack up your shit and haul it over here so that you and your wife can have your clothes and instead of being grateful what do you do, you make a big fucking issue out of it. We knew which day would be the slowest. We knew what time the store closed. We did EVERYTHING to accommodate you and what do we get in return? The same shit I got for thirty-years. No thanks! No gratitude! Just more of your self-serving bullshit! You can take your clothes and shove them right up… "

Megan screamed. "STOP! You two, stop right now! This isn't why we came. You two are acting like children. Not even little kids would act the way you two are right now."

Holy Shit! For the first time ever, Megan raised her voice. I stood in shock. Amy stood in shock. We both looked at each other and realized we'd simply over-reacted.

Amy went first. "You're right. I'm sorry. I want to apologize to you, Megan. I'm sorry." Amy looked at me and had a forlorn look on her face. "George, I'm sorry. I shouldn't have. I… I've had a bad day and I shouldn't have taken it out on you."

I looked at Amy and sensed a true level of remorse. What could I say? I shrugged my shoulders and quietly noted, "it's all right."

As the air calmed, Amy looked at the two of us and offered to take us to their house as she noted, "Karen is working the dinner shift and we can take a taxi. The last ferry doesn't leave until nine and so we can have some time to talk."

We all nodded and I stepped out into Rue de la Republique and hailed a taxi who was just down the block. We all got in, as the taxi driver put the boxes in the trunk. Upon getting in, Amy told him, *"Rue DeGaule, Anse de Flammands,"* and we left downtown Gustavia for the ten-minute ride.

We arrived at a spectacular villa and paid the taxi driver as Amy asked him, *"Pourras-tu venir chercher mes amis à 20h20 et les ramener au terminal des ferries ou dois-je appeler un taxi?"*

Megan looked at me and said, "Amy asked if the driver could come back at 8:20 and take us to the ferry terminal."

"You speak French?" I asked looking at Megan.

"Oui ainsi que l'allemand, le portugais, l'italien et l'espagnol."

"Huh?"

Megan smiled and noted "As well as German, Portuguese, Spanish and Italian."

"Really?"

"I was going to be an English teacher and once you understand basic grammar and tenses, it's simply memorization which, for me, after all the anatomy and physiology was quite simple."

We walked into the gorgeous three-bedroom villa that had a large pool that opened onto the beach. We stacked the boxes in the living room as Amy excused herself and changed out of her upscale designer work clothes and into a casual top and shorts. It was then I realized how important clothes are to the overall image. She'd gone from looking suave and debonair to just plain vanilla.

Returning, Amy pleasantly asked, "Would you like some wine?"

"That would be nice," Megan politely answered.

"Do you want to sit outside? Until dusk, it's quite nice but then the mosquitos come out."

"We adjourned to the deck and sat in the chairs. As we sat, I turned to Amy and asked. "Can you tell me how Tommie and Su ended up on Devil's Mountain and why Derrick left?"

Amy looked at Megan and then me, paused and noted. "George, Tommie really went off the deep end. He's vicious, ruthless and corrupt. Derrick and Tommie had a huge argument and Tommie threatened to notify the Fedarles and try and get Derrick extradited back to the States."

On what grounds?" I asked. "Drugs mainly."

"They're into drugs?" I inquired.

"Tommie? Yes. Derrick? No."

"My brother's selling drugs?"

"Not selling, producing. Cocaine is a derivative of the coca plant which Tommie is growing. He then is probably selling the cocoa leaves to a broker who then has the alkaloids, extracted and processed into various forms, such as powdered and crack cocaine. Knowing Tommie and Derrick, I'll bet they're also processing the plant to make more money"

"Jesus."

"Where's he getting the money?"

"Derrick has money transferred in every month from his bank accounts."

"In the Caymans?"

"Hardly. While you would think that, most of Derrick's money is in Chile?"

"Chile?" I asked totally surprised by the answer.

Amy continued. "Chile is a wonderful country and they're doing everything they can to help people and ensure it remains a democracy. To that end, the government introduced a data protection law in 1999, titled, 'Law No. 19.628 Protection of Private Life 1999'. While Chile was the first Latin American country to have a data protection law, the lack of official regulatory authority, in addition to low fines, made it a relatively obsolete legislation."

"The 2018 amendment changed that when Chile designated data privacy as a human right. Hence, any organization found to be insufficient in its data protection practices can be held liable for human rights abuse. With this human rights amendment, it's really difficult to follow fund transfers."

"So, Derrick has his money in Chile and you and Karen went there?"

"Yes."

"To get married?"

"Yes."

"And?"

"And to set up partnerships to protect his investments."

"Why didn't Derrick go?"

"George, he's a wanted man. Crossing any border automatically, not only gets your passport, but your face scanned and it goes into an international database. Phony passports don't work when it comes to people the US government really wants when they've got your picture. He was safe in Peru because there's no extradition agreement with the US government. Not safe in Chile because they do."

"He's still in Peru?" I asked.

"No. He's long gone because of Tommie." "Where is he?"

"No one knows for sure."

"Yet, he keeps sending money to Tommie?"

"George, Derrick is greedy and looks at Tommie as an investment and he's willing to take the risks while he makes even more money."

It was all making sense. Tommie obviously knew Pepe from Terrill B&B and connected the dots between Derrick and Pepe. In so doing, Derrick had a legitimate way to launder his money. Dime against a dollar, Derrick owned or was a primary stockholder in Viña Alto Magnifico and so I asked Amy. "Why did you and Karen really go to Chile?"

Amy looked at Megan and then me and responded. "We saw the handwriting on the wall and wanted out. I've had too many sleepless nights worrying about the US government to start worrying about the Peruvian or Chilean government's as well."

"All of Derrick's money is in Chile?" Amy looked at me and replied. "Hardly. You have to realize Derrick is too smart for that. While he has a substantial amount invested in Chile and wineries, he maintains funds in non-CRS countries."

"CRS?" I inquired as a frown creased my forehead.

Amy's legal background readily appeared as she added. "The Common Reporting System or CRS allows entire countries to mandate their banks to share financial data with other nations to keep tabs on their citizens. It means that the 'undisclosed' Swiss bank accounts the media likes to talk about, for the most part, no longer really exist."

"CRS requires banks to perform financial information-gathering and reporting, as well as participate in the automatic exchange of information to help fight tax evasion and protect the integrity of tax systems. So far, around 120 countries, including most tax and offshore banking havens, have signed up and most are already exchanging data."

I looked at Amy and asked, "So banks must ask you what country you're a tax resident, and they no longer accept 'nowhere' as an answer?"

Amy shook her head 'yes' and replied. "Banks never understood the perpetual traveler or digital nomad concept, but CRS elevates their suspicion to a whole new level. Today, being a resident of nowhere is quite challenging from both tax and operational perspectives. For the wealthy, the answer is increasingly difficult to create a base and secure a tax residence certificate in a country that doesn't tax them even if you're a perpetual traveler. However, there's a possible workaround in the form of non-CRS countries."

"How?" I asked.

"If 120 countries are taking part in CRS, that means there are 75 who aren't. Many of these countries are places you probably wouldn't want to visit, let alone bank in. However, a few quality countries have yet to take a proverbial sledgehammer to their own tradition of banking secrecy."

Amy paused, took a sip of her wine and continued. "What makes the government so interested in Derrick is the fact that, not only did he steal a lot of money, US citizens and resident aliens are subject to a separate set of tax residency rules called the Foreign Account Tax Compliance Act or FATCA."

Amy took another sip of her wine, leaned forward and added. "Under these rules international banks report information on American account owners to the U.S. government and the Internal Revenue Service."

"While that would seem like a way out, almost every country that doesn't report under CRS still reports under FATCA. As a US citizen, it's Derrick's responsibility to report his annual accounts through form FBAR and possibly Form 8938. When you're a US citizen, it's your responsibility to report all foreign accounts."

"What about in Peru?" I asked.

Amy shook her head 'no' and I now realized why Tommie was there and Derrick had departed as Amy added. "Residents of some countries are also required to report foreign bank accounts, even if the information isn't automatically exchanged. If you live in a developed country, chances are you have some obligation to report your offshore bank accounts, even if the bank doesn't do it for you."

"In other words, Peru," I surmised.

Amy nodded 'yes' and continued. "As an example, the difference between, say, a British citizen and a US citizen is that the British citizen can declare themselves non-resident in their country and move to a nation that doesn't require reporting if they wish. On the other hand, a US citizen must renounce their citizenship to achieve that, which is something none of us has done... yet!"

"Where's the money?"

"Many Canadian and U.S. expats move to the Dominican Republic, some getting permanent residence permits that require deposits in Dominican banks. While expats may be concerned about banking in developing world institutions, the Dominican Republic is one of the non-CRS countries with decent banking."

Amy added, "Derrick had me do research and I found out there are a lot of banks and savings institutions in the Dominican Republic, many of which are locally owned. However,

Scotiabank, which is a sizeable Canadian player in the region, has a presence there and continues expanding its local operation."

Even though we were in her house, Amy looked around as if to make sure no one was listening and noted. "The other place is Guatemala, which is often overlooked, as a destination for Central American expats and, according to Derrick, has been very cooperative in terms of his 'investments' as he calls them. Local Guatemalan banks like Agromercantil and Azteca Bank who dominate the market, although banks like Citibank also have a presence."

I raised my hand to indicate I needed to ask a question and inquired. "So, if I've got this right, Derrick has investments in Peru and Chile and deposits in the Dominican Republic and Guatemala?"

Back to Amy. "That I know of, but there were always people coming to Devil's Mountain to talk 'business.' that I didn't know who they were or where they were from."

"What about my brother?"

"He's the reason Karen and I left Peru. He's really gone crazy and literally has an army of guards around him."

"Why?"

"He's paranoid, George. He's in way over his head. The only reason Derrick allows him to continue is because it was Tommie's plan we used to get out of the States and he's a good farmer now raising a different type of crop. Beyond that, Tommie's doing everything he can to simply hang on to what he's got. He knows the bad guys still haven't forgotten and want to get Su and we both know he's dealing with some really bad people on the other end."

"In other words, mister big isn't so big after all." "You got that right."

Just then, the back gate opened and Karen walked in from the beach. The restaurant was just a few hundred yards down from the house and within walking distance. Karen stopped, looked at Megan and me, then at Amy, and tersely asked, "What are they doing here?"

So much for 'welcome to our humble abode' as I looked at my replacement.

Amy looked at Karen and abruptly replied, "They were kind enough to bring my clothes from the Lighthouse."

Megan had been quiet during the entire conversation and finally spoke as she noted. "We thought it would be nice to bring Amy her things before the rentals began. If we were wrong, I'm certain both George and I would like to apologize."

The comment seemed to defuse the tension as I looked at my watch and noted it was 8:10 and the taxi would arrive soon. It was then I broached the real reason why we came as I asked, "Any progress on the agreement?"

"Not yet, there's some points I need to study. I'll have it to you soon."

Like so many other promises in life. I found the words to be hollow and the promise just that, a promise. I didn't want to begin an argument but knew what I needed to do.

At precisely 8:20 we heard the taxi horn, stood and thanked Amy for the hospitality as she thanked us for bringing her clothes, we nodded goodbye towards Karen and headed for the ferry and back to Saint Martin.

Ferry:

When Megan and I boarded the ferry, I suggested we stand outside so we could talk. You never know who's in listening distance whenever you speak and Amy had shown me she wasn't being totally truthful and, certainly, not innocent.

As we stood on the deck I asked Megan what she thought and she simply shrugged her shoulders and so I began. "First, when you're a sales clerk and your wife or whatever she is, is a waitress, how can you afford to live in that house? Second, why would Amy share so much information about where to stash cash unless either she and Derrick had a disagreement and she wanted to get even or to throw us off Derrick's track? Third, why wouldn't she sign the agreement? She has to know I'm going to have the house income put in an escarole account until everything is settled."

We had three different sets of circumstances and I knew the only one I could handle was item number three, freezing the assets, getting out of Saint Martin and heading home so that I could figure things out.

I looked at Megan, smiled, hugged her as if to show my support and asked, "Are you ready for some winter?"

Megan reluctantly nodded 'yes.'

To assure her we'd be back, I told her to simply pack her clothes and we'd put them in the vault. No one except Megan and me had the right three-step combination and so all the booze, wine, clothes and memories were going to stay there.

"When do you think we can come back?" Megan asked.

"If the listing is legit, April. The weather's really great and it can be our preamble to summer."

Megan smiled as it seemed as if I was making the longer commitment she needed.

The following morning, I contacted the Lighthouse management company and requested a meeting. Two hours later a Mister James Kincaid arrived and we sat in the living room to discuss all that was happening. I'm certain he thought he was there to get canned. Far from it!

Kincaid was of Caribbean descent which means a little bit of African, a little bit of Spanish and a little bit of Inca or Miya blood thrown in that created a medium brown skin that accentuated his broad smile that lit up the room. While Megan and I were in shorts, Mr. Kincaid was wearing a white shirt, tie with black pants and light tan blazer with shoes shined to the point you could almost see your reflection in them.

As we sat on the couch, Megan provided tea and I offered, "Mr. Kincaid."

"James, please."

"James, I'd like to show you some documents and then allow you to determine our course of action. As you might not be aware, Mrs. Terrill and I are legally married."

"Who is Mrs. Terrill?"

"The woman who signed your contract," I replied. "Mrs. Terrill didn't sign the agreement."

"She didn't?"

With that, Mr. Kincaid opened his briefcase and offered a copy of the management agreement signed by Karen Wilson.

I looked at the signature and was simply incredulous. First, Amy had Karen sign the agreement to hide her tracks as she knew her signature would expose her to possible extradition. Second, by having Karen sign the document when the government had awarded the house to the trust of George and Amelia Terrill meant that Karen was acting as an agent and legally, if my legal understanding was correct, would mean that Amy and Karen considered their marriage legal and, therefore, Amy was a bigamist.

I put the document down and noted. "Look, Mister Kincaid, this is getting really complicated and I believe we have an issue here. First, the ownership decree and legal trust was created in the United States and is in effect regarding the Lighthouse. Second, my wife assumed I was dead and married Ms. Wilson in Chile where, unless I'm wrong, even though the second marriage took place outside the United States, it was done before the first marriage ended in death or divorce and is therefore not considered legal in the United States. Consequently, Ms. Wilson had no legal right signing the contract."

There was a very pregnant pause as I'm certain Mr. Kincaid was wondering if I was telling the truth or simply applying a very thick layer of pure, unfiltered bull shit to the entire matter and so I offered. "Why don't we do this? Why don't you create a trust or reserve and put all funds received until the matter is resolved?"

"I would, except we've received payment in full and it has been disbursed to Ms. Wilson already."

I took a deep breath and asked if he could possibly provide a copy of the check.

Mr. Kincaid noted that no check was paid and that the funds were remitted electronically to a bank account.

"Where's the bank account?" I asked.

Kincaid looked at me and then noted. "That's what was strange. The bank account was in Guatemala."

"What?"

"Yes, we normally transfer funds to French, Canadian or

U.S. banks and had never remitted the funds to Guatemala before."

"And it went through?"

"Yes."

"Tell you what. I'm willing to resolve the issue on all ongoing business IF you provide the routing number to the Guatemala bank."

"I can't do that," Kincaid replied.

I looked at our visitor and politely noted. "Then, Mister Kincaid, you are in a world of hurt as you accepted and remitted funds without authorization of the true owner which is me. When you leave here, I'll be on the phone with our attorneys here on Saint Martin and we'll not only seek reimbursement but a termination of your realtor's license. Your choice, one set of numbers or a whole pile of shit you'll never get off your shoes."

"But you don't understand, Mr. Terrill."

"What don't I understand?"

"I could lose my license if I give you that information." "What YOU don't understand, Mister Kincaid, is that if you don't you WILL lose your realtor license and I'll do everything in my power to shut your entire company down."

My Minnie Point badass had had enough as I stood and looked down at Kincaid. "Well, what it's going to be? And if you give me a bogus number I'll sue your ass for fraud."

Kincaid's fingers splayed as he mentally examined his options and then clarified. "I give you one set of routing numbers and this all goes away?"

"And you keep the listing for the full contract period." "And no one will know the number came from me?" "What number?"

"What about next year?" Kincaid asked. "You mean that number?"

"OK. I'll get the routing number and we're done."

"Make sure whomever has rented the Lighthouse maintains it with normal wear and tear. If it's abused, I'll be back and won't be alone."

"Mister Terrill, the couple who rented the house are long-time clients of ours in their seventies who are celebrating their 50th wedding anniversary. They chose the Lighthouse so their children and their families could come and visit during the winter. We've never had a problem with them in over ten years."

I nodded and let out a sigh of relief and added. "They know the rent doesn't include the garage or access to the vault, correct?" "Yes, they understand and, if you look at the last page of the

agreement, you'll see those delineations are included."

Mr. Kincaid stood and we shook hands as I inquired. "You'll call me within the next two hours with the routing number, correct?"

"Yes, sir," as Megan pressed the call button for the tram and it arrived at the door.

Fashion Show:

With the presentations done, we realized it was time to return to reality and so, as had always been our custom, I called and made reservations at Auberge Gourmand for dinner.

"What should I wear?" Megan asked.

"In my opinion, it's the best restaurant on the island and the clientele is a little more upscale." I replied.

Megan went upstairs and came back and inquired, "how about this?

"One of Reggie's?" I asked as Megan appeared wearing an apricot color sleeveless and backless bib romper that was cut more like the denim overalls grandpa used to wear on the farm except with elastic straps, waist and ruffle sides with a hem sitting high enough to reveal a peek at her lower silhouette. What was really 'different' was the fact that, with Megan's arms raised, the romper's bib design subtly revealed the outer curves of her bust, adding an alluring touch to its elegance."

"Dressy enough?"

Before I could respond, Megan said, "I've got another option, tell me what you think."

Megan went back into the guest bedroom and came out wearing a chocolate brown, ribbed short sleeve romper with a deep V-neck and turn down collar and four buttons down the front that was also cut quite high, offering a bold and revealing look."

"That's nice." I politely commented considering the romper looked more like a leotard than something you'd wear to a fancy restaurant, even in Saint Martin.

"Two more!" Megan announced as she turned and went back in the guest bedroom only to return wearing a creme color, six-button, romper that looked like it was made out of suede while cut in the same style as the brown suit with a very minimal design ending high on her upper thighs.

If it wasn't for where we were going, it would have been my pick as Megan noted "Last one!", went and changed and came back wearing a deep V-neck, floral print romper with long sleeves highlighted by a bow knot in front. As she did her pirouette I saw the deep backless expanse that created a bold and fashion-forward look by dipping low enough to reveal the natural curve of her lower back. What made the outfit 'dressy' was the double layer ruffle hem that, while actually shorts, made the romper look like a mini dress with a gorgeous and vintage look.

Megan knew by my smile, I liked the final option as I began to realize she was trying to seduce me and was doing a great job.

Dinner was wonderful and so were all the positive glances Megan received as we made it back to the Lighthouse in time to use the pool one last time before packing away all the clothes, including those Megan found.

Brrr!:

The next afternoon, it was time to head home. I had a sour taste in my mouth about Amy and Karen but realized there was nothing I alone could do about it. What can I say about the flight? Long, boring and then 'holy shit' cold weather. Brrrr!.

We landed in Madison and Tank was there to meet us. Thank you, Tank. On the way to Mineral Point, I filled him in on all that transpired only leaving out stuff that could get him in trouble.

It was good to get home and it was like time stood still. Everything was as we left it, which was great news. I promised Tank we'd go out to dinner and also, I'd make it up to him when all this was resolved.

Megan went upstairs to unpack the gifts she brought back while I went into the office/study/dining room and made the call I knew I needed to make.

"Hello!" It was the same incredible voice who'd impressed me from the first day we met. By far, and I mean by far, the most intelligent person I'd ever known. All Peter needed was a question he couldn't answer and a little time and he would be an expert on the subject as I replied. "Hello Peter. How are you doing?"

"I'm doing fine, George. I didn't expect to hear from you. It's been, what? Over two years?"

"About right. It's taken that long to get myself back to an even keel."

"And now you're OK?" "I'm getting there."

"What's going on?" Peter asked with a probing tone to his voice.

"I need your help."

"Anything exciting?"

"Perhaps. Also, it could be quite lucrative."

"Nothing illegal?"

"I don't think so, but then, I'll leave that up to you."

"What's going on?"

"When I was locked in the cave, Amy thought I was dead and ran away with her mistress."

"I heard that."

"Before we got married, I requested and she provided a prenuptial agreement."

"I remember that."

"Well, she tried to cash in and then I tried to cash in and both of us found out that instead of the word 'or', they used the word 'and' in the agreement."

"Holy Shit!"

"Now everything is locked down and we just spent three months trying to find her." I noted.

"Who's we?" Peter inquired.

"When I had my cancer surgery, I went for physical therapy and the physical therapist and I got along to the point that, when she moved to Atlanta, I went down and did two classes for her for the spouses of men who were having prostate surgery."

"OK."

"She's the one who actually saved my life because I contacted her when I was locked in the cave."

"I remember."

"Well, her job was eliminated and she came back to Wisconsin and needed a place to stay. Everything has been totally above board and she's been my room and travel mate as we went looking for Amy."

"And you found Amy?"

"Yes. It wasn't easy. She and her mistress, Karen, were in Peru with my son and brother because Peru recognizes same-sex couples. Then, they left and went to Chile because that country not only recognizes, but allows same-sex couples to get married."

"So, Amy married the woman and you're still alive?" "That's only one part of the problem. We followed Amy to

Saint Martin and she and Karen are living on Saint Barths."

"OK." Peter replied as I could tell he was placing all the puzzle pieces in the right place in order to see the picture.

I continued. "Her wife, or whatever you call her, rented the Lighthouse and collected over $75,000 for the winter."

"And she had no right doing that?"

"Correct."

"And you want your money?"

"No, I want all of Derrick's money that I'll split with Amy if she signs the And/Or agreement."

"And you want me to help?"

"Yes."

"How?" Peter asked.

"Instead of putting the money in a separate account, it appears Karen deposited it in one of Derick's accounts in Guatemala which they appear to be using to pay for the house on Saint Barths as well as living high off the hog."

"And so, you want me to transfer the money, correct?"

"Is it possible?"

"George, anything is possible. It's just that it's illegal as hell."

"I know and so one's tracks need to be covered and that's why I called you."

I sensed a great deal of reservation on the other end and then, "George, you gave me the start in life I needed. You made my life possible. You helped me in every possible way and I owe you. The only thing is, I don't know how we could do this."

"I do."

"How's that?" Peter asked.

"Who's sleeping in my back yard?" "Are you sure we can wake him up?"

"Peter, all we need are the two of us to go down into the silo and provide the recovery codes at the same time."

"And when we're done?"

"If we can wake him up, can't we put him back to sleep?" "But we're going to need some sort of routing number." "I've got that."

"You do?"

"How did you get that?"

"Do you really want to know or would you rather just be accused of seeing if you could get Simon back awake only to realize he was inert and couldn't be awakened?"

"You've got this all figured out."

"Nope, you see there's also money in the Dominican Republic and, perhaps elsewhere we don't know about that I also want. If it's possible, I want Simon to slowly drain the accounts while still having the accounts showing a full balance."

"Why?" Peter asked.

"So that when I let the Feds in on where Derrick and Tommie are and they arrest them, they'll think they've still got all their money when in fact they've got none. Without money, they'll have no power. Without power, they'll have no protection. Without protection, there'll be no bloodshed. Do you think it can be done?"

There was a long pause as I knew Peter was examining all the permutations before replying. "I don't know, breaking into banking systems shouldn't be too hard even with all the new security platforms. Maintaining a balance while withdrawing money might be a challenge. I do know who can do it if the reward is great enough."

I replied. "I think I know who can too. Tell him all of his gambling debts will be paid in full and he'll have an annuity set up so that he can maintain a respectful life again. What's really important to me is that you're not involved. You've worked too damn hard to get the clean slate and I don't want to risk it."

"Thank you, George."

"I wouldn't be asking, but I hate being screwed especially by my own wife, brother and son."

"You think Amy's in on this?"

"She has to be. How else would she know to use Karen's name on the wire transfer so she wouldn't divulge her location?"

Twiddling Thumbs:

A few days passed and it was Thanksgiving week. There had been no word from Amy and I thought I'd given her enough time. I waited until dinner and then asked Megan what she wanted to do for Thanksgiving and she simply shrugged as I suggested, "Let's go out."

"Sounds fine by me."

I still had a few connections and so we went to Campo Di Bella in Mount Horeb. As always, the home-grown food was spectacular. However, I believe Megan's mind was on her family and how she'd been disowned by them.

The weekend was spent watching the Badgers play Minnesota and then the Packers. I was just happy that Megan liked football as much as I did. With Amy it was never in her interest.

Two weeks passed and it was coming up on my birthday. As we were sitting at the kitchen table, Megan got a slight smile on her face and inquired. "Mr. Terrill, I believe you have a birthday coming up, don't you?"

I nodded 'yes.'

"Well, Mister Terrill, I would like to treat you to a very special weekend."

"You don't have to do that." "I know, but I want to." "OK," I replied.

"How about Eno Vino in Madison?"

I smiled and thought of the great food and the fact they had been a Terrill B&B customer as Megan then asked. "How about we make it a weekend and stay at the Edgewater?"

"Really?" I responded somewhat incredulously. "Yes. I think we need a break."

"You're serious." I really needed affirmation. "Uh huh!"

Megan watched as a broad smile made its way across my face as she added. "We can make it a special weekend. Just the two of us."

I nodded as my smile grew even bigger.

Thursday morning came and we got in the truck and headed the fifty-two miles to Madison. Along the way, the radio was on Sirius XM and the Billy Joel song "Vienna" came on. As we sat in silence, the lyrics dug deeper and deeper into my psyche.

Slow down, you crazy child You're so ambitious for a juvenile But then if you're so smart
Tell me why are you still so afraid? Mm Where's the fire, what's the hurry about?
You'd better cool it off before you burn it out You've got so much to do
And only so many hours in a day, hey
Slow down, you're doin' fine
You can't be everything you wanna be before your time Although it's so romantic on the borderline tonight, tonight Too bad but it's the life you lead
You're so ahead of yourself, that you forgot what you need Though you can see when you're wrong
You know you can't always see when you're right You're right
You've got your passion, you've got your pride But don't you know that only fools are satisfied?
Dream on but don't imagine they'll all come true, ooh When will you realize Vienna waits for you?
Slow down, you crazy child
And take the phone off the hook and disappear for a while It's all right, you can afford to lose a day or two, ooh When will you realize Vienna waits for you?
And you know that when the truth is told
That you can get what you want or you could just get old You're gonna kick off before you even get halfway through, ooh Why don't you realize Vienna waits for you?
When will you realize Vienna waits for you?

It was crazy that, just like when I came home from Saint Martin after the total collapse of our company and lives, it was a random song on the radio that made me understand life wasn't as dramatic, nor as bad, as I thought it was. Before it was Simon and Garfunkel. This time, Billy Joel.

As the words became mentally digested, I realized the song is a reflection on the passage of time and the allure of youthful dreams suggesting that, while it's tempting to cling to the carefree days of youth, it's important to embrace the present moment and appreciate the journey. I thought Vienna was a symbol of a romantic, idealized past and Joel was telling me to let go of yesterday, cherish today and honor tomorrow.

I glanced at Megan and realized she'd become my today and perhaps tomorrow. We made our way across John Nolen drive, up Broom Street to Wisconsin Avenue, parked the truck in the hotel garage and checked in. Knowing it was one of my favorite hotels, and particularly the view of Lake Mendota, Megan made certain we had a top floor room overlooking the vista that, even on a chilly December day, whispered, "welcome home."

We got situated and, with only a four block walk to the Square and State Capitol, we journeyed there and went inside the incredible edifice. At first memories of the kids and then Amy pilfered my pleasure until I realized why I wanted to come here. As we stood in the middle of the portico I looked at Megan and inquired. "Do you really want to take it to the next level?"

Megan looked at me and simply shook her head and replied. "I've wanted that since the first day I met you. Are you sure?"

"I'm sure, if you are. It's not going to be easy. I've got an awful lot of baggage but also realize life needs to go on and I want it to be with you. Monday, I'm going to go to Tank about drawing up the divorce papers."

"Why now?" Megan asked.

"To celebrate my new year and begin a new life," I replied.

Saturday, to celebrate my actual birthday, we went to Miles Teddywedgers and got pasty. Megan had heard about them adnausium but it wasn't until that first bite that said it all. Needless to say, the rest of the weekend revolved around simply being together. Happy Birthday, George!"

The following Monday I called Tank and asked him if I should draw up the divorce papers. Tank inquired, "And the reason?" I told him pick one and read off the Google page I had in front on me. "In Wisconsin, the only grounds for divorce are that the marriage is irretrievably broken and there's no chance for reconciliation."

Tank added, "While Wisconsin is a no-fault state, the reasons that lead to this irretrievable breakdown can vary widely. Some common factors include incompatibility such as the differences in values, goals, or lifestyles which can make it difficult for couples to maintain a healthy relationship."

"Check!"

Tank continued "Communication problems leading to misunderstandings, resentment, and a breakdown of trust."

"Check!"

"Infidelity."

I simply giggled at the absurdity.

"Financial difficulties."

"I guess so!"

"Domestic violence."

"Nope!"

"Substance abuse."

"Don't think so."

"Then you would need to serve the papers."

"How would I do that? She's living in Saint Barths, I think." Tank got serious. "George, here's the problem. Even though Wisconsin is a no-fault state, one of the ways to prove a marriage is irretrievably broken is to demonstrate that one spouse has abandoned the other. If a spouse disappears without notice or communication, and the other spouse cannot find them after a reasonable amount of time, this can be considered abandonment.

The problem is you found her."

"Yah but!"

Tank countered. "George, simply leaving the marital home isn't enough. The disappearing spouse must have the intent to abandon the relationship. If they have a valid reason for leaving, such as seeking safety or medical treatment, this may not be considered abandonment."

"What about thinking I'm dead?"

"Wow. That's a real challenge. Amy can say that she didn't abandon you, you abandoned her."

"Holy shit!"

"The problem isn't the separation as much as the estate. If we can prove she left you, you'll get a greater share than if she can prove you left her."

"What about the fact that she married another woman in Chile?"

"Well, that's another story. Do you have actual proof?"

"She admitted it."

"And what if she says it isn't true?"

"But I've got a witness."

"Megan?"

"Yes."

"And who's living with you now?"

"Megan."

"And so, she's got a vested interest in affirming the fact?"

"I guess so."

Tank paused and then added. "George, if a married couple in Wisconsin has a pre-nuptial agreement that outlines how their property will be divided in the event of a divorce, they need to follow the terms of that agreement."

"We do. It says everything is to be split 50/50"

Tank responded "I'll need to really examine the agreement again to see if it's valid and enforceable. If so, it will override the state's default property division laws. I've done these before and there are the general steps that a couple with a pre-nuptial agreement must follow in the event of a divorce. You both need to review the agreement and make sure you understand the terms and how they apply to your current situation."

"We did that in Saint Barths." "Was anything put in writing?" "I gave her what you prepared." "Did she return it?"

"No, and it's been over a month."

"Did you disclose assets and debts? Both of you should do that to ensure the agreement is being followed correctly."

"How can we do that when, other than the farm, it's all either locked down by the government because she's been indicted or taken by our son?"

"Then you've got a real pickle of a situation." "What do I do?"

"Negotiate if necessary and see if there are any disagreements about the interpretation or application of the agreement so you can try to discuss a resolution."

"We did that! That's why I had you draw up the papers." "And she did nothing?"

"Nothing."

"And you've tried contacting her?" "How?"

"You said she was living on St. Barths, do you have her address?"

"I know where she lives and where she works. If I serve her at work, she'll go off the deep end. Maybe Megan remembers the address or perhaps we can Google it. We went to her house. Do I have to go there to divorce her?"

Tank simply said "Nope," before adding Wisconsin has jurisdiction over a divorce if a person is a resident of the state. This means that the Wisconsin courts have the authority to hear the resident's case, even if the other party is living elsewhere.

"What do I do?"

Tank paused and then replied. "My recommendation is to try and contact her. If, she remains reticent, then prepare and file the necessary documents which would include a complaint for divorce, summons and other supporting documents."

Tank continued. "Once the papers are filed, you'd need to have Amy served with a copy of the summons and complaint. This can be done by hiring a process server or by certified mail."

"And, if she does respond?"

If Amy chooses to respond, you'll need to file a response to her answer. Finally, you might need to attend court hearings throughout the divorce process, such as a hearing to determine temporary orders or a final hearing to finalize the divorce."

"Wow! This is more complicated than I thought."

"George, you're doing the right thing to ensure your pre-nup agreement is valid and enforceable. Then, if necessary, have me help you navigate the divorce process. If you don't, you could lose everything."

I simply replied. "Then at least this entire mess will be in the past and not hanging over me. I just want it over."

Bart:

Home life was becoming more complicated. Megan's severance was about to run out. I was broke. Christmas was just around the corner and Amy hadn't responded. I thought I needed to go to Saint Barths and confront her but had no money and no place to stay.

I called Peter and inquired about what we needed to do. He said we needed to meet with Bart and talk things over. I agreed and drove to Lodi where Bart had moved after his divorce. What a sad story. To have everything, including a gambling addiction and lose everything including Cindy, his wife, custody of his two kids and, most of all, his pride.

I arrived at the house and Peter's Mercedes was already there. It seemed funny to see his luxury car and my pick-up sitting side-by-side in a house that had been Bart's parents with the wheelchair ramp leading up to the front door.

I rang the bell and Peter appeared and whispered, "Come on in but don't be shocked."

To say the house was a mess would be an understatement. Empty Pizza Pit boxes littered the floor and the living room had been converted into one electronic playground with at least six big screen monitors and multiple keyboards, arranged so that Bart could move from one console to the next.

I looked at Bart and realized he'd put on weight and probably hadn't had a bath in a couple of weeks as his now-grey stringy hair was only overshadowed by his unshaven beard and spotted clothes.

I walked over and stuck out my hand as Bart and I shook. I looked down at the beaten man and said, "It's good to see you," knowing it would be the biggest lie I'd tell that day.

"George, Peter says you have a problem." "Yes." I concurred.

"Peter says Derrick has hidden all your money off shore and you want to get it back."

"Correct."

Bart continued, "Peter also said you want to do it slowly so that he doesn't realize it's taking place."

"Yes."

"Peter said you have a routing number to a bank of Guatemala where the deposit on the Lighthouse went."

I nodded, pulled out the piece of paper with the routing number on it and handed it to Bart.

Bart noted that there were usually three sets of numbers for each account. The first set consisted of the 9-digit universal bank routing code of which the first four digits identified the Federal Reserve Bank that processes the transaction and the last five, the Routing Transit Number, or RTN, that identifies the specific bank or financial institution. Next, there is normally a ten-digit bank account number. Finally, there's usually a six-digit number to identify the specific transaction.

Bart looked at the numbers, turned and pressed the keys on his computer and the Guatemala bank's logo came up on the screen. Bart did something else and, 'holy shit,' he was looking at all the bank records and pointed to the account while noting, "Here's where the money went. The account has nearly twenty million dollars in it."

I nodded as Bart shut down the computer and noted. "We have less than sixty seconds before the bank's computer will identify any intruder and begin its security protocol."

"Then what?"

"Their bank would do an automatic reverse search and our ass would be grass and they'd have the lawnmower."

"What did all those numbers show you?" I asked.

Bart continued. "Once inside the bank records and then the account, you saw a lot of other numbers. These were transaction reports where you not only got the funds transferred but which accounts they came from or were transferred to that includes not only the country but the bank and the specific account."

"All we need to do is harvest the data, break into the transaction info to-and-from each bank and then keep searching from there. In the end. I can build a complete summary of where the money is, where it came from and where it has gone."

"Why can't our government do this?"

"They probably can, except it's as illegal as hell."

"Can you do what needs to be done in less than a minute?"
"Not with my equipment, even though it's the fastest on the
market today because I've enhanced it." "So we're screwed?"

"Hardly." Bart commenced. "All it means is that we need a faster computer who can break in, do what needs to be done and get out in less than a minute."

I remembered back to when the Mad City guys broke into the CDC to try and save Dr. Marie's life and murmured, "Simon."

Bart turned his wheelchair around and nodded that Peter and I should sit. We moved some of the papers and empty pizza boxes off the couch and did as directed as Bart continued. "The issue isn't breaking in. The issue is getting the money out. If we break in and start withdrawing funds, each night when the computer does its audit and examines its net increases or reductions, red flags will pop up and it won't be long until they do an account-by- account audit and it will quickly stop."

"So, we're blocked?"

"No. Not at all, What I need to do is get in their system and create another account and then transfer the funds from Derrick's account to the new one that will then move it to another and then another and then another."

"Why so many?"

"Because most binary computers being used by banks are designed to only search three levels and then report the funds missing. Banks don't have quantum computers and therefore, it would take weeks or months for them to do what we can do in the matter of seconds. In order to really mess with them, I'll create a dozen bogus accounts five levels deep."

"What do you mean, 'five levels deep?'" I asked. "Twelve to the fifth power or 248,832 possibilities." "Huh?"

"You're heard of 3D chess, haven't you?" "I've heard of it," I replied.

Bart looked at Peter who was smiling and continued. "3D chess is played on a three-dimensional board typically shaped like a cube, with each level representing a different plane. The rules are generally similar to traditional chess, with some modifications to accommodate the additional dimension where pieces can move up, down, and diagonally between levels, as well as horizontally and vertically on each plane."

"The big difference is what is called 'castling' where the king and castle can move diagonally to a rook on a different level. The additional dimension introduces new strategic possibilities and challenges, requiring players to consider more factors in their planning and decision-making."

Bart continued. "Now take the game from two levels to five levels and perceive it as a maze where the bank's computer would need to find the right gate for each level before it could continue on and do that on all five different levels. If I build in defense mechanisms that provide false leads, it will really screw with them to the point it will take well over a year for their fastest computer to make it through the process only to find the money is gone."

"But how?" I asked, totally perplexed.

"First, we need to go in and harvest all the transactional data. Then we need to create a new account that would allow us to begin to transfer the funds."

"But wouldn't the bank catch on?" I asked.

"George, you need to realize, the routing and account numbers used are a fixed set in terms of the number of digits. All we need to do is hide another number in the account setting that would activate at a certain time. This would make the last digit account inert and we'd have access to the money."

"What do you mean 'inert?'" I asked.

Bart continued. "The accounts will literally have the same numbers except for some hidden delineation that the human eye and computer can't detect. I can do this by using what is called a micro dot which is smaller than the sharp end of a needle and place it between the last two account numbers."

Bart looked up at me and offered. "Computers are programmed to look for and recognize certain images in terms of the keystrokes used to create them. By using a non-analogous keystroke, the computer won't recognize what we've done until the signal is given and the non-analogous symbol becomes the same as the numbers except virtually invisible to the human eye. When this happens, while looking exactly the same, the accounts will be different. When the bank does the end-of-day audit and the net funds stay the same, the bank's left hand will think the right hand simply added a new account."

"How do we do that?"

"Not a big deal." Bart offered.

"What about all the other accounts?"

"People are not as finite as computers. This means when they open additional accounts that communicate with each other, there's going to be some common thread between them."

Bart paused and then dumbed it down for yours truly and added. "The only way to do this is to use a computer who can be programmed to search for the commonalities within all the banks first in Guatemala, Chile and the Dominican Republic and then see if there's any links elsewhere."

"Do other people do things like this?"

"There are only a very, very few computers fast and sophisticated enough to do what we want done and do so at the speed necessary to avoid detection and one of them is Simon."

"We need to activate Simon?" "You got it."

"But he's under a manhole that says "U.S. Property". I warned.

Peter interjected. "The manhole cover says 'US Property'. It doesn't say anything about not entering, nor what lies beneath."

I simply shook my head at the conniving brilliance of these two who were looking at the 'project' as they began calling it as just another day at the office.

"How long will this take?" I inquired.

Bart looked at Peter, shrugged and noted. "Now that I've got the routing information and still have Simon's programming protocol, give me a couple of days and we should be set to go."

"Two days?" I inquired in almost disbelief. "Well, I don't want to rush it." Bart replied.

"If the program works, how long do you think it will be before we have the information and do the transfer?"

"That depends on Simon. If he's simply inert and you get him up and running, perhaps five, maybe ten minutes."

"Jesus!"

Peter noted. "George, it's going to take longer to get Simon operable. He needs to be unlocked and we need to have coolant and then we need to run some testing. I don't believe anyone has been down in the silo since the day I was there."

I looked at Peter and then at Bart, smiled and said. "You seem to have forgotten, we always kept an emergency supply of coolant at the lab in case the Linde delivery guy didn't make it."

"And it's still there?"

"I saw the canisters a few weeks ago."

There were smiles all around as Peter and I stood, shook hands with Bart before noting, "I owe you for this."

Forlornly, Bart responded. "You once saved my life and I blew it. I've gone through re-hab and am no longer gambling. I only want to get my life, wife and kids back."

"You have my word, I promise."

There was a deep stare as Bart replied. "I know I do and that's why I'm willing to help you. Without you, this shit hole would have been forever and now you're giving me a chance to do something good."

"One last question," I offered. "Were you ever involved with the cartel?"

Bart looked at me, before stating. "Without you, this shit hole would have been forever. You gave me a chance to do something good which I never forgot. They tried and even threatened me. The government came and talked to me and I told them what I'll say to you. 'On my mother's grave, I never helped them in any way."

"That's good enough for me," I noted. "That's why we're here," Peter offered.

The Surprise Call:

Peter and I went out to the cars where he stopped, looked around and said, "George, this better stay between the three of us. Don't tell anyone and I mean anyone. If we get caught, we're in deep shit and you don't want to take anyone else down with us."

"No one?" I asked.

"No one." Peter replied.

"Agreed." And then we hugged and shook hands.

I got in the truck and headed for Waldwick trying to figure out how in hell I could keep what was going on from Megan. I mean, she already knew what I wanted to do. She was with me when I found out everything. Yet, I also knew that if she learned went south, she'd be an accomplice and I'd been through that with Amy and didn't want it to happen again.

I made it home, got out, opened the barn doors and put the truck away. I thought, 'Damn, one of these days, when I get some money, I want to get a remote garage door opener!'

I went in the house and Megan was working on her computer. I went up behind her as she turned and looked at me and asked, "How did the meeting go?"

I paused and just couldn't do it. I couldn't keep the secret from her and so I said. "It was great seeing Bart. He's going through re-hab for his gambling. I explained what was going on and he said he'd see if there was anything he could do."

"Was Peter there?"

"Yes. He said the same thing."

"And what do you think is going to happen?"

"I don't know. I do know that the more I learn the more pissed off I get. Derrick not only screwed those in his Ponzi Schemes, he took Amy and my money."

"What's next?"

"I don't know. I do know it's a lot more complicated than I thought."

"Do you think you have chance?"

"Megan, we have a chance." For the first time I used the word 'we.' Was this a Freudian slip or something I wanted to communicate?

Megan looked at me and a soft smile crossed her face as she recognized my reference. I think it made her feel secure. Something she needed right then, simply because I hadn't told her about my conversation with Tank regarding Amy.

It was nearly Christmas and so I went up in the attic and got down all of our old family decorations. With little money, we both agreed no presents. I knew I wanted to do something and had an idea. I knew Megan's parents lived in Waukesha. I knew how old they were and that her dad's first name was Frank. There wouldn't be too many Frank Egan's on Google and when I put his name in and scrolled down, I found his and Megan's mother's phone number.

The next morning Megan said she was going to Dodgeville to get groceries and queried if I wanted to go along. I told her, "No," I had some computer work to do. Megan nodded as if she understood and went to the barn. I looked out the window until the truck pulled out of the driveway and made the call.

"Hello."

"Mr. Egan?"

"I don't want any! Can't you telemarketers leave us alone. Jesus Christ, we're getting a dozen a day. Whatever happened to privacy?"

"Mr. Egan, I'm not a telemarketer. Please don't hang up."

"Huh?"

"No, Mister Egan, I'm a friend of your daughter's." "We don't have a daughter."

"Mister Egan, yes you do and her name is Mary but everyone calls her Megan, including me."

"Our daughter left us," Egan replied.

I knew I only had one chance and so I went for it.

"Mister Egan, have you ever made a mistake? Have you ever done something you deeply regret? Megan did and today she has a broken heart. Not because of what happened but because of the hole in her soul since her family disowned her."

"But you..."

"Yes, I do. I know because she told me everything. She told me about the mistakes she made. She told me how much she regrets the choices. But most of all, she regrets that you and Mrs. Egan have removed her from your life. I see it! I feel it! I know that it's been the one thing, above all else, that she wishes for Christmas."

"But..."

"I know, Mister Egan, that you and Mrs. Egan are religious people. I know you believe in Jesus. I know, deep down, you accept that Jesus represents four key characteristics...humility, generosity, compassion and forgiveness. Isn't it time you begin to be compassionate towards Megan? Isn't it time to forgive? Mister Egan! "

"Call me Frank."

"Frank, I know of no greater gift Megan could get this year than to see her mom and dad, to hold them, to love them and, above all else, to be honored simply by having them call her their daughter. I know it will be a challenge. I know that for a few moments there will be discomfort. But beneath the challenge and discomfort there will be what we all need at this time of year and that's love."

There was a long pause on the other end and then I added. "The birth of Christ symbolizes a new beginning. Can't this Christmas be that... a new beginning for you, Mrs. Egan and Megan?"

"Who are you?" Mr. Egan asked.

"As I said, I'm a friend of Megan's. A friend who thinks the world of her. A friend who only wants to give her the greatest possible Christmas gift and that's love. Not love of me but love of her family."

I could literally feel the tears on the other end. "What's your name?"

"George Terrill."

"The Nobel Peace Prize winner from Pewaukee?" "Yes, sir."

"The man who saved so many lives?"

"Well, I hope and pray my foundation did and I can add one more."

"Mister Terrill, did Megan ever tell you what I did before I retired?"

"No, sir, she didn't."

"I was a counselor at Ethan Allen School for Boys in Wales."

"I'm familiar with the school, sir."

"I know you are. We have photos of some of our students on our Wall of Fame that you and the Derrick Williams Foundation saved. I remember Peter Arnold and how he came and played chess. I remember what a difference your foundation made in the lives of those kids. Mr. Terrill..."

"George, please."

"George, my wife and I are pretty basic, conservative people and what we learned about our daughter went against everything we ever taught her."

"I know, but didn't you also teach her forgiveness and all I'm asking is to give her another chance."

There was another pause and then Mr. Egan asked if I could wait a moment as I heard him call to Mrs. Egan. "Marsha, come here. There's a man on the phone who wants to talk to you."

"Who is it Frank?" Mrs. Egan inquired as I listened. "Let him make your day as he has mine."

"Hello."

"Mrs. Egan, my name is George Terrill."

"The man from Pewaukee who won the Nobel Peace Prize?" "Yes, Mrs. Egan but that's not what I'm calling about."

"Ok?"

"Mrs. Egan, Megan and I have become good friends. In so doing she's shared the saddest thing in her life and that's not being able to be part of your family anymore. She loves you and Mister Egan. She doesn't know I'm calling. All I'm asking, not for me, but for her, is for you to allow her back into your lives."

I sensed crying on the other end and then in a somewhat raspy voice, "Did God send you?"

"I think so. I believe so. No, I'm certain he did. " "How's Mary doing?"

"Well, other than the pain of being left out, she's doing pretty good. I know that what I'm about to propose is quite dramatic and I don't want an answer right now. However, I'd like to invite you and Mr. Egan to dinner in Madison where you'd be able to begin to heal the wounds. If possible, somewhere around Christmas and I'd like it to be a surprise. Please don't answer now. Please think about it and if you and Mister Egan agree, send me a text and I'll make the arrangements. I know of no other present I could give Megan than the love she has for you and you for her."

"That would be nice, Mister Terrill. That would be nice. How's Mary doing?"

"She's fine. She's fine. She just needs to have her mom and dad back in her life."

"Oh, thank you Mister Terrill. Thank you for calling. Frank and I will talk it over and send you a text. Do you have a day in mind?

"You tell me to date and time that will be convenient for you and I'll make all the arrangements and let you know. I thought we could meet for dinner in Madison and have it be a surprise."

"That would be wonderful and thank you again."

"Thank you again, Mrs. Egan. I hope to hear from you soon." I looked out the window and saw the truck coming up the driveway.

It seemed funny to see Megan driving a pick-up truck when the Lexus had always been 'her' car.

I began to smile seeing the tailgate down with the tip of a Christmas tree dangling out the back of its bed. It was then, Simon and Garfunkel's lyric...'a time of innocence, a time of confidences' wandered from my brain to my heart as I realized time has a way taking mountain tops and using them to fill in the valleys below simply to make things smoother, better and not quite so dramatic.

Merry Christmas:

December was quickly melting. Not weather-wise but by the calendar. The day after my call to the Egan's I received a text indicating they'd love to have dinner with Megan and me. I texted what night would be convenient in Madison and they replied that they were both retired and told me to pick the night.

I knew I wanted it to be special and so I called Graze in Madison which had been the Duke's favorite and one of Terrill B&B's best customers. I asked to speak with Tory Milner who had been a James Beard Nominee for Best Chefs 2011, Winner, Best Chefs 2012, Semifinalist, Outstanding Chef 2016 and Semifinalist, Outstanding Chef 2019 who'd become one of my favorite business friends.

It was then I thought of the show "The Bear" and the realization how difficult it is to not only succeed but become great in the restaurant business and the person on the other end inquired, "May I ask whose calling?"

"Please tell Tory it's George Terrill from Terrill B&B." "Mr. Terrill, we thought "

"I know but, like Mark Twain said 'The reports of my death were greatly exaggerated.'"

The phone picked up and it was Tory. "George?" "Yes, Tory, back from the proverbial grave." "Back in business? I'll take all you've got."

"That's what I'm calling about. I'm not back, yet, but still have some inventory."

"What vintage? Tory asked.

"Five-year old Pinot Noir and ten-year-old Terrill bourbon." "Pinot? Oh...my favorite year. I remember we had a wet spring, cool summer and lots of rain before it got cold early and the leaves didn't fully mature so you got a much more vibrant body. That was the year when everything was just right and you ended up with harmonious balance of fruit, acidity, tannin, and complexity."

"You've got a great memory, Tory."

"I have to, it's what my customers expect."

I paused and then decided to let it all out. "Tory, I need a big favor."

"For you name it."

"With my dying and all that happened, I'm a little short in the money department right now."

"OK," Tory replied as I could sense a slight scent of exasperation.

"I'm willing to trade a full case of Terrill bourbon and a case of Terrill Pinot Noir for dinner for four."

"What?" Tory asked, almost in shock.

"Here's what's going on. You might know that Amy left the country and well, everything we had together has been frozen by the government. Over the past few months, I've been helping a good friend who has had family problems. I'm trying to help mend my friend's fences with her parents and would like to have a dinner for them as it's been a few years since they've been together."

"You want to trade a case of bourbon and some of the finest Pinot Noir on earth for a dinner?"

"Yes."

"George, first, the friend must be someone very special but then you always have had a big heart. As for the trade, the answer is 'no', the dinner will be on me."

"You don't have to do that."

"George, when we were first starting out and needed a helping hand, your father-in-law came to the rescue. Then, when we got too big for our britches and started losing customers, it was your turn. If I remember correctly, you advanced us three or four cases of wine to tide us over. The restaurant business is a small world and if I can't help a friend in need, then I'm certainly not a friend indeed. When do you want to have dinner?"

"Between next week and Christmas. You name the day and I'll have my friend and her family there. By the way, it's a surprise as it's my Christmas present. Tory, I'll never forget this. Can I bring two bottles of wine? One for our table and one for you?"

"That you can do. That you can do. Let me transfer you to Caroline so that she can check the reservations."

"Thanks, Tory."

With that, there was a long pause and Caroline picked up and began. "Mr. Terrill, we're quite busy but tell me which night you prefer and let me see what I can do."

I knew better than to ask for a Friday or Saturday and so I picked December 19th or the Thursday before Christmas.

"Would you prefer Mr. Williams' favorite table? "You don't have to do that."

"Mr. Terrill, the generosity between you and Mr. Williams, as well as your humility, has never been forgotten."

I thanked Caroline and texted the Egans with the time, place and address.

Two minutes later I got a smiley face and we were set.

A week went by and then, as Megan and I were eating dinner, I asked if she'd like to go out for Christmas dinner and she thought it would be special. I asked if Graze would be OK and Megan looked at me as if I was crazy before replying. "George that's one of the finest restaurants in the Midwest."

"I know," I replied.

"And also, one of the most expensive." "I know. But I think we deserve it."

"Do you think you can get a reservation?"

"One way to find out and that's to call. I'll do it tomorrow night."

The next night, I went to the office and made the pretend

phone call. It's amazing how good you can make a fake call when you already have the answer. I came back into the living room and noted, "We got lucky, they had a cancellation for next Thursday night at seven. Is that OK?"

"You got in?"

I nodded 'yes' with a smile.

The days dragged by and then it was Thursday. Megan got all spiffy and I got out my navy-blue pin-stripe suit and my all-time favorite custom loafers. As I came down stairs Megan lit up like one of the bulbs on the Christmas tree and noted, "Well, aren't you the handsome one, Mr. Terrill?"

"Well, don't you look ravishing, Ms. Egan?

We agreed that the pick-up truck would sort of pop the cork on fancy-schmancy and so we got into the Lexus and made our way to Madison arriving at 6:30. I thought 'what in hell do we do for thirty- minutes' when I remembered the Wisconsin State Capitol puts up a large Christmas tree every year decorated with ornaments made by school children from across the state.

For some reason, I also remembered the tradition began in 1916 and, as is always the case in Madison when there's politics involved, some people wanted it called a 'holiday tree' until so many people told them to f--k off that now it's just one of those things Wisconsin is known for.

Being literally across the street from Graze, we parked the car and made our way into the rotunda to find a tree that was simply spectacular adorned with ornaments that were cute, creative and, in many cases, incredible simply because you knew they came from the heart and not some factory in China.

We examined the tree and I noted the painting on the dome over 160 feet above us looking down on the countless visitors who'd made their way to simply see the majesty within. I checked my watch and realized we needed to go to Graze. As we walked in the door, Megan saw her mom and dad who turned, smiled and simply said, "Merry Christmas," I stepped back to allow the emotional faucets to turn on as tears streamed from Megan's eyes as she simply said, "mom, dad... oh, my! Mom, dad, this is the best Christmas present I've ever received."

Megan turned to me, looked at me, smiled at me and shook her head, too moved to express words as I offered. "It's nice to meet you Mr. and Mrs. Egan." I looked at Caroline who had a huge smile on her face and asked, "Caroline, can you please show the Egans to our table? I need to get something from the car."

I simply walked back to the car, opened the trunk and took out the two bottles of Terrill Pinot Noir which, because it was 24 degrees out, were already chilled and walked back to Graze.

I went in, handed the wine to Caroline and told her one of them was for Tory as I saw beaming faces all around our table.

My dream had come true, I'd put the spirit of Christmas in the lives and hearts of three people who spent the night talking and talking and talking only to be interrupted by great food, great love and a lot of laughter.

As it was getting late, Mr. Egan reached for his wallet and I simply shook my head 'no' and noted. "Next time! Merry Christmas." We adjourned and made our way to the entrance as I helped

Mrs. Egan on with her coat and Frank helped Megan with hers. There were hugs all around as we walked out into the cold December air and felt the soft tingle of the light snow that had begun to fall.

Mr. Egan looked at me, shook my hand and said. "This is the best Christmas I've ever had."

I looked down at the sidewalk, looked up at Mrs. Egan and simply said, "Merry Christmas."

With that the Egan's went to their car and Megan and I went to ours. I opened the door for Megan and she got in. I walked around, opened the driver's door and, as I slid in, Megan leaned across, gave me an extended kiss and simply said, "I love you."

I looked in Megan's eyes and genuinely replied, "And I love you, too. Merry Christmas!"

Visiting an Old Friend:

With it being the holiday period, I didn't expect things on the invasion front to be active and was surprised when the day after Christmas Peter called. We'd agreed to keep the conversation in code. I'd learned my lesson in the past and so we spoke in generalities."

Peter noted. "Well, George, I think our friend was able to assemble your Christmas present. I was wondering when I could come and we could take a walk down memory lane?"

"Whenever you'd like," I replied.

"How does tomorrow sound? The weather appears to be just about right."

I hadn't realized that Peter wanted a day with moisture-filled stratus clouds that might develop enough moisture to turn into nimbostratus clouds for heavy winter weather.

It took me a while to realize Peter was concerned about spy satellites and our plan of visiting Simon. The reason for wanting nimbostratus clouds is because they act as barriers to electromagnetic radiation, including the satellites used to capture images. While some advanced satellites may be able to penetrate thin clouds or use radar to detect objects beneath them, they're not able to see clearly through thick, dense clouds and we wouldn't have to worry about someone taking our picture when we lifted the lid on what was actually still ours.

I asked Megan what her plans were for the day and she indicated she was meeting her mom for lunch. That was good news. Once again, hand on a Bible and swearing she knew nothing of what transpired was great protection for her in case it ever came to that. It was also good news that Megan and her mom were rebuilding their lives once again.

Peter arrived just as the snow began as light flurries. We made our way to the manhole cover and saw 'US Government Property.' Peter simply took some sort of key and released the lock. We took the ladder we'd carried and lowered in down into the silo.

We climbed down into the darkness as tremblers cascaded my body. It was the first time since I was freed from the cave and my claustrophobia was settling in.

"You OK?" Peter inquired with a concerned tone in his voice. "I'll be fine. It's just, well, you know," as I took a deep breath and flipped on the flash light.

As I took the light beam and focused on the walls, I saw the carbon footprint near the opening from where the bad guys had used some sort of bomb to blow up the facility. I turned the light beam down towards the floor and realized it was as if time stood still. Simon was simply asleep and all we needed do was turn him on, make sure the communication dish was intact and have Simon work his magic.

Peter went to the control panel and marked down all the readings. He then used his hands to check all of the welds between the sections of copper pipe used to transfer and blend the hydrogen and nitrogen. In the silo corner was a cabinet Peter opened and took out what looked like a twenty-pound propane BBQ tank.

"What's that for?" I asked.

"I hook it up to the system and allow the pressurized air that has a colorant in it to be expelled. If there are any leaks, the colorant immediately leaves a stain on the welds and connection points to the coolant tubes and I can see if there are any problems."

Peter hooked up the tank and I heard a 'whoosh' and saw nothing. Peter smiled and said, "We're all clear."

Phase one was done. We knew that, because Simon had survived the blast intact, we could get the helium and nitrogen tanks and wait for Bart to give us the go-ahead.

As I climbed the up ladder, I realized it had really had begun to snow and looked down at Peter below and said, "I think we should wait. It's really beginning to snow and the ladder will be too slippery." Peter looked up and saw my hair was already wet and nodded in agreement. Instead we climbed out, pulled up the ladder, put the US Government manhole cover in place, re-set the lock and headed for the barn.

"Well, at least we know Simon is safe and sound," Peter offered. "I think we're going to have to wait until the next cloudy day."

"What happens if it snows, won't they be able to see our tracks?" I asked.

Peter shook his head and nodded his agreement and simply said, "Shit!"

Peter said goodbye and I went in the house as the snow was really coming down. Beyond aborted plans to move the coolant into the silo I was concerned about Megan. She'd taken the Lexus with rear wheel drive and I knew the roads would be slippery.

I called her cellphone and got no answer. On the fifth ring her recording came on. "Hi, this is Megan, leave me a message."

"Hi, it's George and I'm worried about you. Call me."

Ten minutes later the phone rang and I leaped to get it and quickly asked, "Where are you?"

"I'm in Milwaukee with mom."

"The roads are terrible. I think you should stay with her tonight if she doesn't mind."

"Just a minute."

I heard Megan talk with her mother. "George says the roads down there are really bad and I should stay with you tonight? Would you mind?"

Her mother replied, "Of course not."

Megan came back on and I noted. "I heard. Call me in the morning."

"OK. Goodnight. Love yah!" "I love you too," I replied.

For the first time in over six months, I was all alone in the house and I really didn't like it!

The following morning, I got up to a total white world as ten inches of snow had clobbered Iowa County. I made my way to the barn, put on my boots, climbed aboard dad's old tractor, rolled over the front loader and attached it, went out and spent two hours 'playing' in the snow, clearing it out to the highway and around the mailbox.

We pay high property taxes and there's not much we get for it except great snow removal. I guess it's one way for the county to show something for our money.

I'd just finished working when the county plow went by and, of course, put a three-foot-high pile of now-dirty snow in front of the driveway. I got back in the tractor, went out and cleaned it up. As I was finishing I saw the black Lexus coming up the road and a smile spread from ear-to-ear, Megan had made it home.

Megan pulled into the barn and said she had to pee. We'd had a phone in the barn since God knows when and so I called Peter to make sure he got home OK. He picked up and said it took him over two hours to go the fifty-two miles to Madison but he made it.

We talked about 'Big Brother' watching who would be able to see footprints out to the silo. I told him I had an idea. I could either do like great grandfather and dad used to do and hook log to the back of the tractor and pull it through the snow smoothing any footprints such that, from space, everything would look nice and white.

Even for the genius on the other end, it seemed like a great idea as the spy satellites we thought might be watching would see a flat plane and not footprints in the snow. Then I had another idea. We had snowmobiles and I could make all kinds of tracks which would make it look like were out having fun. I also noted I still had the sled I used to take my dog Jake for rides in and we could put the coolant tanks in that. It was a better idea and I could teach Megan how to snowmobile as she'd never done it before.

All we needed do was figure out how to have Megan out of the house for the day. I remembered Megan's birthday was January 17th and so I asked Peter if that day would work and he said it would. I went on line and purchased two gift certificates for full day massages, skin care and pedicures at Elevation Salon & Spa in Madison. One for Megan and one for her mom. With

Elevation opening at 10:00, I knew she'd leave around 8:30 as it was located in downtown Madison.

The Saturday before Megan's birthday, I went into town and bought a small birthday cake with one candle and brought it home and cooked steaks on the grill. When dinner was done, I gave her a funny birthday card and had her open it and see the certificates and watched her face light up.

"Why two?" Megan asked.

"One for you and one for your dad." I joked.

"My dad?" Megan countered incredulously.

"Well, I thought..." and then I started to laugh and admitted, "I thought you'd like to invite your mom."

"Oh, how thoughtful," as Megan got up from the kitchen chair, came over and gave me a deep kiss and said, "You didn't need to. I get a present every day I'm with you."

Wow! What a nice thing to say.

January 17th arrived and I kissed Megan goodbye and told her to have a good day. She left and fifteen minutes later, Peter arrived. We got into snowmobile suits, hooked up the sled, loaded the canisters, road two-to-a-sled, followed some of the snow trails Megan and I'd made that magically had gone right over the manhole and headed for the cover.

We arrived, Peter unlocked the lock, went down the ladder and I began handing him the canisters of helium and nitrogen one-by-one until the sled was empty.

I quickly put the manhole cover back on the silo and went back to the barn. With no sled in sight and no additional tracks, no one would know Peter was there. An hour later, I went back, removed the cover and Peter appeared and reported. "All systems go."

Simon was in the process of awakening. We knew it would take two days before he was ready to be activated as he had a self- diagnostic system that Peter initiated. Unlike binary computers, Simon, as a quantum computer, generated a lot of heat. In so doing, he needed to go through his cooling protocol to make sure he didn't overheat and malfunction.

We knew that, if all systems were operational, Peter and I would need to go back into the silo and use our security system to literally turn Simon on. Peter departed and I told him I'd see him on the 19th.

Megan came home and walked in the house with a perplexed look on her face.

"What's going on?" I asked. "You tell me," Megan replied. "Why?"

"Why, George, because I passed Peter on the way home and there was a strange car parked up on the road."

"Holy shit!" What do I tell Megan?

I looked at her and told her she needed to sit down. I then told her my biggest concern was her safety and security and thought the best thing was for her to know as little as possible.

"About what?"

"About what's going on." "Tell me, George. Tell me!"

I then decided I needed to tell her the entire story. I began with Amy and I turning over the business to Derrick. I explained that Amy had been going to the Wilco office and signing papers that allowed the government to accuse us of sedition. I explained that with the sedition, all of our accounts were still frozen and, as she knew, Amy had put the word 'and' in our pre-nup instead of 'or' which meant everything there was frozen. So far, there wasn't anything she didn't already know.

Megan nodded as if she knew the story. I looked at her, took a deep breath, pondered how I should go on and then began. "When we were on Saint Martin and I met with the property manager, I gave him an ultimatum, either provide the routing number for the Lighthouse payments or I'd shut him down and he'd be out of business. He agreed and provided the bank routing number."

"When we met with Amy and Karen, I realized that Derrick had not only taken all the Ponzi money, he'd figured out a way to take Amy and my money as well and even if Amy did sign the And/Or agreement, there wasn't anything there which is why Amy hasn't responded."

"When we came home, I called Peter and explained and we went to Lodi and met with Bart who described how banks work and what he thought we could do to get our money."

"How much money?" Megan inquired. "Mine or total?" I asked.

"What's the difference?"

"My money, which is half of Amy and my estate, is around three billion dollars."

"Oh, my God!" Megan responded.

"The total that Bart's been able to find is spread in about a dozen different banks in seven different countries and is about eighteen billion dollars."

Megan's mouth dropped open in disbelief as she repeated "Eighteen billion?".

I nodded and continued. "Bart thinks we can transfer all of Derrick's, Amy's and my money into one secure account if we do it in a way that he's figured out where he hides a virus in each of the bank accounts and then, in one instant, have all of them transferred into our account."

"Eighteen billion dollars?"

"Yes!"

"But how?"

"Well, here's the tricky part. All the banks have security systems that are activated when they sense any invasion that lasts for more than sixty seconds. With the world the way it is, it happens literally every day. The only way to enter is to have an incredibly fast computer who can break in less than a minute, place the virus and then go back another day and transfer the money."

"And that's where Simon comes in?"

"Yes. So, first we needed to see if Simon was operational, which he is. Then we needed to install enough coolant to keep him running for seven days which is what Peter and I did on your birthday." "Peter was able to put Simon in a reverse memory mode and right now he's literally back to where he was, memory-wise, the day he was installed. Now, Peter needs to go in and reactivate his memory and restore where he was three years ago when he started the self- erasure program."

"You think all the data's still there?"

"Sure, Simon actually didn't erase anything, he just put it all in a sub-memory category that requires two of the three of us...Peter, Luke and/or me to activate at the same time."

"In other words, all the power Simon had, is still there?"

"Yes."

"And the car up on the road?"

"I don't know. It could be the good guys or bad guys." "What happens if it's the bad guys?"

"Then you need to get out of here and let Peter and me face the music."

Megan looked at me and noted. "George, I'm not leaving you."

"But..."

"George, we're in this together."

Walker:

Winter in Wisconsin can be a real challenge. The snow can last for months or, if you're lucky, there can be days warm enough to melt the snow before you get blasted again. When I was a kid, the winters seemed longer and more severe. With global warming, we get a couple weeks of the really cold stuff and then it warms up to the point you'd almost think spring was just around the corner when, in fact, you knew better.

Bart had the virus ready and had scanned all the banks to find out Derrick's web of money was in five other countries, not just Guatemala and the Dominican Republic. With each week, he'd audit the accounts to see money flow in and then some go out.

I hadn't heard from Amy and was pissed about that while the weather hit bottom with below-zero temperatures forecasted for the next seven days. Megan and I were getting along fine and that helped but I sure needed to get my hands on some money.

The car on the road scared me and I guess it showed. I called Peter and asked if he thought I should let the government in on what we were doing. Peter was quite reticent but then when you've been screwed over by the system as many times as we had, I guess there was a reason.

After a somewhat lengthy discussion, I told Peter I wanted to do a 'what if' with Agent John Walker of the CIA and tell him what was going on. When Peter, Langdon and I were in the Arboretum, it was Walker who really helped a lot.

At the time, it seemed weird to have the CIA involved until I did a little research and found out that, while the CIA's primary mission is to gather intelligence on foreign governments and entities, the CIA has been involved in domestic issues such as counterintelligence where they identify and counter foreign spies and agents operating within the United States in both terrorism and counterterrorism operations and do so both domestically and abroad. And finally, domestic surveillance where groups perceived as threats to national security are scrutinized which would certainly fit what was going on.

Peter thought about it and I could see his wheels spinning. Peter finally said. "I think I'm understanding why the CIA and not the FBI. The FBI primarily focuses on domestic law enforcement, including investigating federal crimes, terrorism, cybercrime and civil rights violations and has the authority to arrest individuals and conduct investigations, while it collects intelligence on threats to the United States from within the country, such as domestic terrorism and criminal organizations."

"What I think we have here, George, is the government realizing that the FBI reports to the Department of Justice while the CIA is a division of the Department of Defense and someone, somewhere has begun to realize that getting hold of Simon would have had profound international implications that could affect the nation's security. While the FBI is a great organization, I think dealing with Agent Walker makes more sense and I agree you should call him."

The following morning, I dug out Walker's business card and called him. "Mr. Walker, this is George Terrill. I don't know if you remember me or not."

"Mister Terrill, how could I ever forget? You were Agent Langdon's friend. What can I do for you?"

"I'd like to talk with you but don't want to do it on the phone. Is there any way we can get together?" "Important?"

"Critical!"

"Are you still living on the family farm?"

It scared me to think they knew that and I answered, "Yes". "Do you want to meet there?"

"I prefer not."

"Because of Miss Egan?" "Yes."

"Is it something you don't want her to hear?"

"No, I just think it's better if we meet somewhere. The less she knows, the safer she is."

"Understood."

"How about meeting at Fitzsimmons Park? You know, the one nobody ever uses."

I smiled to think back about how Rodney and I, along with Charlie Birdsong, used the park as a way to beat the county when they wanted to use the Forest to create yet another public park as I said, "OK. When?"

"Tomorrow morning at ten?" Walker offered. "I'll see you in the morning." I replied.

Megan came into the office and I looked up at her and must have had a strange look on my face as she inquired, "What's wrong?"

Whew! I let out a deep breath and told her that I was meeting with a CIA agent in the morning.

"CIA?"

"Yes. He'd been on the case when the bad guys were chasing me and I called him. I can't go on, not knowing who was parked up on the road."

"Are you meeting him here?"

"No, at the Fitzsimmons Park tomorrow morning at ten." "Do you want me to go with you?"

"Just the opposite. I want to keep you out of this as much as possible to protect you."

"From what?"

"From everything...the bad guys, the government...me!"

"You?"

"I'm poison."

"No, you're not, George. Don't ever think or say that again." "But look what I've done to your life," I countered.

"My life? My life? You've made me feel wanted and needed.

You rebuilt the bridge between my parents and me."

"But what about all this?" I asked as I spread my arms wide to express the magnitude of the problem at hand.

"Peaks and valleys, George! Peaks and valleys." My God it could have been mom talking.

Needless to say, I didn't sleep well that night and was up before sunrise. I looked at the thermometer out the kitchen window and it said 'six degrees'. 'Welcome to Wisconsin,' as my mind meandered south to Saint Martin and the people living in the Lighthouse.

At 9:30 I kissed Megan goodbye and headed for the barn, got in the truck and made my way to the park. Walker was already there and he motioned for me to get in his car.

I opened the door, felt the warmth and simply shook his hand.

"Good to see you, " he offered.

"I'm still so sorry about Agent Langdon. Do you have any clues?" I asked.

"We do," as Walker went into his professional mode of only saying what he had to and continued, "What do you have for me?" "I know where our son is and where he's hidden all the money from the Ponzi scheme."

"And?"

"What do you mean, 'and'?"

"George, we know that, too."

"You do? Then why don't you do something about it?"

"What can we do? He was in Peru and moved to Ecuador and then Chile and now back to Peru."

"You know all this?"

"Yes."

"Do you know where he's hiding all the money?"

"Yes."

"What the...?"

"George, Derrick is a small fish in the big sea. We want to get those he's working with."

My mind went into overdrive. I had no idea what Walker was talking about and so I asked, "Who?"

"Some really bad people, George." "Drugs?"

"Among other things and he's working his way up the chain of command."

"And so, you're waiting for him to get to the top and then what?"

"Sorry, I can't answer that."

"Does this have anything to do with my daughter and why she's being hidden?"

"Yes."

"Have you been staking out our house?" "No comment."

"No comment, then this conversation is done."

"George. It was really smart waiting until a really cloudy day to open up the manhole and visit Simon. Peter Arnold is really, and I mean really, intelligent. He just never thought there would be a core in the manhole cover that would sense motion and when it was disconnected from the base, set off an alarm."

"Who would have thought of that? And so, it was someone from your team and not the bad guys watching the house?"

"I didn't say that."

"I did and I'm relieved, so we're not being threatened."

Walker's facial expressions changed dramatically as he offered. "Intel has intercepted some messages that the bad guys know you're trying to get Simon operable and they're going to come for him."

"But they can't operate him," I retorted.

"They don't know that."

"What about my brother?"

"Small potatoes, but still someone who's gone rogue. He doesn't seem to care who he hurts or how."

I looked at Walker and flatly stated. "Look, I don't care what happens to Tommie or Derrick. All I want is this to be over."

"You mean the $3.3 billion that's locked down because Amelia, your wife, if she's still your wife, intentionally put the word 'and' instead of 'or' in your pre-nup?"

"Yes but I'm willing to collect all of Derrick's money and give it back to those who lost it in the Ponzi scheme."

"You mean the $15.3 billion in all the foreign banks?"

"Yes."

I was incredulous to think he knew everything I wanted to tell him.

Walker added, "If I had my way, most of those greedy bastards wouldn't get a dime. Half the money never hit their books and no taxes were ever paid."

"You think the money is hidden cash?"

Walker shrugged and changed the subject. "George, I don't set the rules. We leave that to the politicians who say that when money is recovered from a Ponzi scheme, it's typically distributed to the victims in a process known as 'restitution'.

"How much?" I asked.

Walker responded. "The remuneration is dependent on several factors including the jurisdiction where the scheme was perpetrated which, in this case, is Wisconsin and the amount of money recovered. While fifteen billion sounds like a lot, we're not sure if it's all from the Ponzi or if your son squirreled money away from somewhere else."

"Who gets what and in what order?" I asked, now concerned that I'd get the short end of the stick.

Walker continued. "George, we know you got screwed and I think I have a way to make sure you get what you've got coming, fair and square. If, after we take your portion out, the recovered funds are insufficient to repay all victims in full, they'll be distributed proportionally based on the losses suffered."

"How long will all this take?"

"It depends on the complexity of the case where more complex cases require more time and effort to determine the appropriate recipients and amounts and that also determines your reward."

"Reward, what reward?"

"There's a reward that's taken off the full amount recovered."
"How much?" I asked, totally surprised and not wanting to sound greedy.

Walker looked at me, shrugged and noted. "The average percentage for a recovered Ponzi scheme to the person who helps the government recover the funds can vary significantly and there are several factors that can influence the amount including the complexity of the case and value of the recovered funds. Larger recoveries like this, generally lead to larger rewards as determined by the quality and significance of the information provided where the more helpful and valuable the information, the higher the reward."

"Do you have a guesstimate?"

Walker paused and then said. "Look, we know you've been to hell and back. We appreciate all that you're trying to do and we consider you to be a victim and not a perp. While there's no definitive average percentage, rewards can range from a small percentage to a substantial portion that's ultimately determined by the authorities handling the case and there's no guarantee of a particular percentage."

Walker paused and then added. "We all know what you've done and also know that, if what we think you're planning works, it will be because of you, this case is solved. My vote would be 40%. Others probably would say that's too much and go for 20%. Take the average and you're at 30%."

My mind quickly did the math. Remove the $3.3 billion that's Amy's and mine which leaves $15 billion. 30% would be somewhere around $4.5 billion. Add that to my half of the $3.3 billion and my worth would increase to around $6 billion. I guess I could afford groceries on that as I simply asked, "Where do I fit in?" "Tell me what you and Peter, as well as Bart, have planned."

I looked at Walker, sat for a moment and listened to the engine in his car idle and the soft sound of the blower on the heater. I looked at Walker and finally said. "We have a plan to infiltrate all the banks, put in a virus, add a secret account and take all the money and deposit it in one account that would then ricochet to another account and then another and another while putting in blocks and hurdles along the way."

"George, it's been tried before."

"We know and we're aware that the security systems block anything that tries to invade in more than sixty seconds simply because it takes that long for a binary computer to determine the legitimacy of either the transaction or a byte of information. By using Simon, we cut the entry time to milliseconds."

Walker shook his head and exclaimed. "If this works, you're talking about being able to literally screw up the entire global system of banking."

"We know and that's why, when we're done, Peter is going to program Simon into a deep sleep that won't allow anything or anyone to activate him for at least one-hundred years."

"Including you? "Including us." "Then what?"

"We wait for the temperature to cool and withdraw the funds. I take what's Amy and my money, and forward the rest to you."

"That's it?"

"That's it."

"What would you do with the reward money?"

"Until a few minutes ago, I didn't know there was a reward and so I'll have to think about it."

Walker paused, looked out the car window and then at me and warned. "Right now, there's clear and eminent danger to you and your girlfriend."

"She's not my girlfriend. She's my friend, OK?"

"Whatever. The bad guys don't know that she's an innocent and you need to protect her."

"Me! What about you? You're the ones who screwed up my life and now you want me to protect her."

I could tell Walker didn't like the allegation as he turned to me and retorted, "And who's protecting Melia and your grandkids?"

He had me there as I cooled down and apologized. "Sorry!" "You got any guns at the house?"

"A shotgun and deer rifle." I replied. "Know how to use them?"

"I'm a farm kid," was all I answered. No farm kid worth his salt doesn't know how to use guns and do so safely.

Walker looked at me and said. "We've had you under a level three surveillance. Now I'm going to apply to have it raised to a level one."

"What's the difference?" I asked.

"You've had a bird above watching, as well as the manhole cover sensor. If it's all right, I want to activate cameras on your house, the barn and then on the manhole that will be under 24-hour surveillance. In addition, if it's all right with you, I'd like to store some drones in the lean-to on your machine shed."

"For what?" I asked.

"If the bad guys are coming, which we believe they are, we'll have surveillance and then, if they get in the open, we can use the drones on them."

"What do the drones do?"

"You really don't want to know. I'll tell you this, when we're done, what they did to Langston means we're going to get even and all that will be left of the sons-a-bitches will be some small white spots on the earth."

"OK. I want this over. I want to get on with my life. I... I'm not cut out for this kind of stuff."

"We know George. I read your file from when you were out at '51', Doctor Roberts said you were one of the inherently kindest and most generous men he'd ever met. We want it done. You want it done. Can I count on you?"

"Can I let Megan, Peter and Bart in on what's going on?"
"Peter, yes. Bart, no."

"Why not Bart?" I asked.

"Once investigated, always a suspect."

"What about Megan?"

"We prefer not but for a different reason."

"What's that?"

"We don't have her profile and are concerned she'll get the shit scared out of her and that's the last thing you need right now."
"OK," I agreed, wondering how I was going to justify the cameras.

Walker must have been reading my mind as he noted. "George, the night you went to Graze for your birthday, the cameras were installed. All we needed was your approval to turn them on."

"You've got it."

Walker reached behind his seat, pulled his laptop from the seat-back pocket, turned the computer on, logged in, went to a file and, Bango, screens appeared showing the Terrill farm as well as the entrances to the winery caves.

"Holy shit!" I exclaimed and then asked, "what happens at night?"

"The cameras have dual lenses such that they see during the day and then when it gets dark, they have night vision, as well. Our computer is constantly surveying for any motion and then identifies what it is. I need to have you and Miss Egan go for a walk when you get home. As you're walking, the cameras will do a body scan and memorize your features and even your gait. If anyone else comes along, the computer will identify that they're not either of you and notify security. If it's the bad guys, they'll activate the drones until confirmation. If it is the bad guys, you can say 'goodbye.'"

We'd reached the end of our conversation. I reached out to shake Walker's hand as he noted, "I've got a couple of presents for you in the trunk."

We got out and he opened the trunk to expose a whole bunch of equipment you'd never find in the back of another Chevy and then two cases. In the first was a Glock and a box with fifty rounds with it. The second was an assault rifle and two-hundred rounds.

Walker handed the guns and ammo to me and noted. "This is just in case our security isn't good enough, fast enough or thorough enough. Remember to always try and stay at least ten feet away from the bad guys so we can use the drones if we have to and carry the Glock with you wherever you go."

Next, Walker handed me what looked like two old-fashioned pagers and noted. "Whenever you or Miss Egan leave the farmhouse, wear this on your belt. Press the button once and the bird will zoom in on where you're at. Press it twice and we'll be on our way."

This was getting serious as I took the guns and put them in the truck. Looked back at Walker, nodded, got in closed the truck door and simply exclaimed... "fuuuuuuck!"

Sharing:

I made it back to the house and, as always, couldn't keep a straight face. God, I'm glad I don't play poker.

"What's up?" Megan inquired.

"Well, we might have visitors."

"Really? Who?"

"Bad guys!"

"Oh-my-God!"

"I met with Agent Walker and he explained what's going on and let me know there's a risk. I wonder if you should go and stay with your parents until this is resolved."

"Do you really want me to?" Megan inquired.

"No, I want you to stay with me but I also want you to be safe."

"

How bad is it?" Megan asked.

"Let me show you," as I brought the guns in the house.

"Oh, my God!"

"Do you know how to fire a gun?"

"Never done it."

"Well, my dear, time to learn. Beyond that, we need to walk out to the silo so that we're scanned. The entire farm is now under video surveillance and, by the way we walk, the computer will do a profile and if someone else walks on the property security will be notified."

"Scanned? How? Where?"

"First, there are cameras in position around the farm and out by the silo. Then the satellite will watch for any and all movement on the farm."

"I had no idea."

"Neither did I," I replied.

We got bundled up and walked out to the silo. During our walk, I explained all that was going on, not only in terms of the CIA, but with Simon and what the plan was as I watched Megan's mouth drop open in disbelief and then, I believe, in fear. I noted,

"If the bad guys come, press the button on the pager twice and make sure you're more than ten feet away."

"Why?"

"You really don't want to know."

"You mean...?"

"Pooof!"

"George, I'm scared."

"You're not alone." I exclaimed in total agreement,

We walked back to the house and I got the guns. I pulled a bale of really old hay from the barn and put a white sheet of paper on it. Looking at Megan I noted, "The idea is to shoot for the paper. The best thing with the pistol is to use two hands. The normal reticence is to not shoot to kill. Reality is, either you kill them or they'll kill you."

I went behind Megan and had her aim the gun at the paper. Her first shot went somewhere out in the field. She never even hit the bale of hay. I nuzzled in until my chin was on her shoulder as I felt her body up against mine in a way that was enticing. My God, what a stupid time to get horny!

I whispered in her ear, take both of your hands and aim at the target. Now take your right index finger and put it on the trigger. Slowly squeeze the trigger and don't jerk it! BAAM!

Megan's hands jolted up and she exclaimed, "holy shit!"

We walked the ten feet to the paper and there was a hole in it. I smiled. Megan smiled as I said, "OK, let's do it again except a little further back."

From fifteen feet she squeezed the trigger and BAAM, another hole in the paper.

"Easy Peazie, Lemon Squeezy!" Megan whispered.

"Good girl. Now it's time for the rifle. You need to remember, it's an automatic which means as long as you've got your finger on the trigger it's going to keep shooting and don't put it up to your ear, it's too loud and always shoot from the hip because there will be a spray of hot casings."

I stepped back and Megan did as she was instructed... bam, bam, bam, bam, bam.

Megan lowered the gun as I went up and wrapped my arms around her waist, pulled her in and noted, "You're a real Annie Oakley."

Megan looked at me and said "Who's that?" making me realize there was certainly an age difference between us. Darn!

Hunkering Down:

While the government put cameras in strategic locations, we went to Menard's and bought six of the motion activated outdoor lights. If anyone came near the house or barn, the lights would turn on and it would look like Camp Randall on a Saturday night.

"Now what?" Megan asked.

"If we leave the house, we're supposed to wear the pagers. Press it once and the satellite will activate and zoom in. Push it twice and who knows what's going to happen but I don't think it's going to be too pretty."

It was agreed, we weren't going anywhere and our only visitor was going to be Peter and perhaps, some racoons looking for dinner. I called Agent Walker and told him when Peter was going to arrive and what color vehicle he would be driving. I explained that Peter needed to check Simon to see if he was up-to-date. If he was, Peter was going to load the virus software and hook up Bart's computer so that Simon could be activated from Lodi.

Peter arrived and, as we were walking out to the silo, I explained all that had transpired with Walker and the security components. Peter shook his head and admitted. "I should have known it was too easy to get into the Silo. A strong set of magnets would have neutralized the magnetic field."

"Peter, I'm glad you didn't. Now we have the government on our side and it's time for the showdown. I'm tired of being afraid, tired of Amy and me having the issues we have and I'm tired of being broke."

We got to the silo and Peter opened the manhole cover and climbed down the ladder. Looking up he said, "All clear here. This will only take a couple minutes. You keep an eye out to see if we have any visitors. If we do holler 'Echo', 'Echo', 'Echo'."

I stood literally frozen in fear and thanked God when I saw Peter climbing the ladder just as something went whizzing by my head.

"Get down, George! Get down!"

I dropped onto the frozen ground, pulled out the pager and pressed the button twice.

"Shit!" I exclaimed as I crawled towards the hole. "Where's the gunfire coming from?" Peter hollered.

"The Forest" I screamed.

"Press the buttons!" Peter commanded.

"I pressed the button twice and pulled out my cellphone, pushed speed dial and called Walker.

"What's up?" Walker inquired.

"Incoming!" I screamed as I ducked down.

"From where?"

"The woods."

"Are you wearing a hat?"

"It's winter, what do you think?"

"Take it off and put it up, but watch your hand."

I was on speaker phone and Peter heard the directions and handed me a broom he'd been using to sweep up the dirt and dust. I put the hat over the bristle end and stuck it up out of the hole.

Bam! The broom was knocked out of my hand as the straw splintered and my stocking cap began top burn.

"Holy shit!"

"Can you reach the manhole cover?" Peter asked.

"I think so."

"Be careful!"

I inched myself across the ground until I felt the edge of the manhole.

"Drop down head first and I'll hold you." Peter commanded realizing if I stood up to come down feet-first I'd be a sitting duck.

I did as I was directed and was glad Peter was strong enough to hold me.

Peter crawled up the ladder and slid the cover tight while putting it in the locked position, taking the splintered end of the broom stick and jamming it in so the cover couldn't be removed.

We stood for an instant and then heard...boom, boom, boom followed by total silence as my phone rang and it was Walker inquiring, "You ok?"

"Yeah, but my new Badger stocking cap has a hole in it," I lamented.

"Better than your head. We'll have a chopper there in fifteen minutes. Don't open the hatch until I tell you to."

"Don't worry about that. What happened?"

"What are you talking about? Nothing happened that I know of."

It was Walker's way of telling me this was a classified mission. Fifteen minutes later we heard the roar of the chopper blades and the phone rang again. It was Walker who simply said..."All clear."

Peter unjammed the cover and we opened it up to the acrid smell of phosphorous. On the ground were three white spots still steaming from where it appeared the interlopers had been.

I looked at Peter and he at me as Peter shook his head and simply said, "Bastards".

We climbed out of the hole and were immediately surrounded by military in full combat gear who wanted to make sure we were unaccompanied and OK. I assured them we were except for the poop in my pants.

Walker called and said "That was a close one."

"You don't have to tell me. Does this mean it's all over?"

"I don't think so, George. You guys need to do what you need to do and then we're going to really close up shop. Once the bad guys realize there's no benefit and no opportunity and you've got the military on your side, they'll leave you alone."

"Why do you think they'll come back?" I asked.

"Two reasons," Walker offered. "First, we surveyed the area and there's no car parked anywhere. Someone had to drop them off. Second, how did they know that today was the day you were going to visit Simon?"

I cringed when I realized something was amiss. The only people that knew what was planned for the day were Bart, Peter,

Walker, Megan and me. I did a mental check-down of the group and the only one who didn't completely meet the loyalty criteria was Megan. Could it be she was on the other side?

"What about the white spots?" I asked.

"Whatever you plant in the spring will probably grow a little taller, They simply got an extra helping of fertilizer, didn't they?"

House Guests:

We were escorted back to the barn and Peter simply let out a deep sigh and shook his head before noting. "I never thought it would get to this."

"Neither did I. Giving me guns was one thing. Having people shooting at us scared the B-Jesus out of me."

As we were standing there two black Chevy Suburbans with deeply tinted windows pulled in the driveway. The door opened and Walker got out of the first vehicle, came up to us and shook his head before saying, "Sorry guys, we wish we could have captured the perps but they were too much of a risk. The biggest white circle was someone who had explosives and we think he was going to blow the hatch."

"Why didn't they do it before?" I asked.

"Because they don't know how to reactivate the computer, If they did, they would have taken it then."

"What do we do now?" I asked.

Walker looked at me and noted, "Until further notice you're going to have house guests."

I looked and saw four guys who weren't smiling who made even Walker look tiny get out of the second Suburban as Walker added. "They'll be here until this matter's closed. Any idea how long before you can harvest the crops?"

I must have had a frown on my face that Walker noticed and he reported. "The name of the mission is 'winter harvest.'"

Peter looked at Walker and replied. "Simon's 90% operational. He needs two more days to collect and sort all the data he'd stored. Bart has the virus complete and we'll need to plant it."

"When?" Walker inquired.

"Well, we sort of have a sentimental day coming up. It's not the same calendar day, but then neither is Washington's birthday." I looked at Peter, turned to Walker and said, "Super Bowl Sunday."

Peter added. "We can make it look like we're having a Super Bowl party. I can sneak out and add the security code to Simon. After that, Bart can do everything from his laptop."

"In other words, we have ten days until the deed is done?" Peter shook his head 'no'. "Ten days until we plant the virus.

It will then take at least a week to infect the computers and then we need to make sure it's in place."

"We can do that if you want us to," Walker offered.

"I don't think that's a good idea. Too many chefs can spoil the broth," Peter replied.

"Then what?" Walker asked while looking at the four men milling around as if they'd never been on a farm before.

"Then, when we see we're in, we'll add the program that will take about six days to transfer the money from each account to the accounts Bart has set up. Then we need to move the money again and again, as we gradually consolidate the money into one final account before we transfer it to the US Treasury. Once it's there, it's up to you to have your team protect it."

"When do you think this will happen?" Walker asked. "Beware of the Ids of March," Peter replied.

I interjected. "March 15th famously known for the assassination of Julius Caesar in 44 BC and soon to be recognized as the day one Derrick Williams will certainly never forget."

Walker got back into his leadership mode as he noted. "The men are prepared to sleep in the barn."

"No need!" I replied. "We have the lab that's heated, with complete bathroom and shower facilities."

"One of them will be on watch at all times. They know this is of national importance and have been briefed concerning the risks at hand. I'd like to introduce you to them. Would you mind if Megan can also be introduced so they know who they're protecting. Also, George, neither you or Megan should leave the property. Understood?"

"Understood."

Megan had been looking out the window and I motioned for her to come out of the house. It took a few minutes for her to put on her coat and come out. I introduced her to Agent Walker and he, in turn, had the four soldiers report their names.

Walker then asked. "Would you mind if two of the men surveyed your house? Also, they'll probably pull the shades down so no one will be able to see where you are."

Megan nodded 'yes' and two of the soldiers entered the house and we watched as the window shades were lowered. About ten minutes later the two emerged and indicated "All clear," as they had scanned the house for listening devices.

Walker shook hands with Peter and me, turned to Megan and noted "I'm sorry for the inconvenience, Ms. Egan. We hope this will be a short-term situation."

"Thank you, Agent Walker," Megan replied.

I took the four guards to the lab and unlocked the door. I showed them where they could bunk down and the security system that was in place when Francis was there. I think they appreciated the gesture as it sure beat sleeping out in a barn in Wisconsin's January weather.

Officer Nelson asked if we could visit the barn and I agreed. We went in and I turned on the lights. Nelson asked to go up in the south loft.

I offered. "The barn was built by my great grandfather and it's orientation has significantly impacted its function and durability. Great grandpa knew he needed to have the barn doors face south to maximize sunlight exposure to help dry hay and grain more efficiently as well as warm the animals and minimize moisture buildup simply to reduce to mold and rot. He then built the machine shed to the west to protect the cows and equipment from prevailing winds and did it on a slope to ensure proper water drainage to help prevent flooding and keep the barn dry."

Nelson looked at me and replied. "Mr. Terrill, I was raised on a farm down by Boscobel."

I shook my head and realized I must have sounded like the village idiot and said, "Sorry," as I laughed the first laugh of the day.

"It's Ok. Would you mind if I moved one of the barn slats a little bit so that we can keep an eye on the field and the manhole cover?"

"Not at all."

"We'll put it back when we're done."

"Tomorrow, we're going to put some small land mines around the manhole so you and Mrs. Terrill need to keep away."

"Mrs. Terrill?" I thought Amy wouldn't be coming here anytime soon and then realized he was referring to Megan."

"Landmines?" I inquired.

"Landmines and perimeter sensors. If anyone or anything comes with one-hundred yards of the manhole, we'll know and will call in all sorts of defense mechanisms."

I must have had an incredulous look on my face as Nelson added. "Sir, this project has an Alpha One classification and we need to do everything possible to secure the area. My clearance grade isn't high enough but I do know whatever is in that hole has to be incredibly important to have the resources in place that are being deployed. Can you also make sure that Mister Arnold is aware and that he doesn't get too close unless we clear the area first.?"

"I'll call him and tell him."

"No sir. Whatever you do, don't use your phone or computer for anything associated with Winter Harvest. It could be how the perps are getting their information."

I was feeling guilty for even thinking Megan was involved when Nelson noted the risk and fact that the satellite focusing on the manhole, plus drones, plus high-altitude flights.

Nelson looked at me and reiterated, "Sir, I really don't know what's in that hole. All I know is that this is the highest level of security I've ever been associated with. You can be assured any incursion will be met with a level of resistance and force most non- combat personnel don't know exists."

I blew the air out of my cheeks, looked at Nelson and thanked him for protecting us. I wanted to shake his hand but didn't know if that was permitted. I was about to leave when a thought occurred to me and I asked, "What about the north side of the house?"

"Sir, we'll have perimeter sensors located all the way out to the road tomorrow. Tonight, there'll be a guard posted with night vision goggles for your safety and security."

"Thank you, Sergeant." "You're welcome, sir."

Lodi:

Perhaps it was the failure of the mission the day before, but the sun came up and all was calm. Thank God!

For four days, nothing happened and Megan and I were going stir-crazy. I got a call on my burner phone the CIA had provided and it was from Walker. He noted that DNA of what little remains of whomever it was that got zapped in the field turned out to be Caucasian males, in other words, mercenaries.

I thought that was good until Walker reminded me that it expanded the suspect universe to literally include virtually every white male in America over the age of twenty-one, thereby limiting the prospects to just under 70 million, give or take a few.

So much for feeling good. Walker asked if I'd heard from Peter and I said 'no'. Walker then reported he was concerned about Peter and Bart's safety and had requested permission to provide them with the same type of protection Megan and I were receiving. This was when I realized this was getting even more serious.

Two hours later the burner phone rang and it was Walker. "George, I've got some bad news."

"What?"

"Bart's house in Lodi caught fire last night and he's believed to be dead."

" What?" I said in total disbelief.

"We don't know. All I know is that the house burned to the ground and it looks like arson."

"Jesus!"

"What about Peter?" I asked, now profoundly concerned. "He's missing."

"What?" I replied with an incredulous tone. "Our agents went to his house and it's empty." "Oh, my God!"

Fear rambled through my entire body. Without Bart no one could set off the viruses and transfer the money. Without Peter, we couldn't get Simon operable as he was programmed to require two sets of identification within sixty seconds and the only three people who could do it were Luke, Peter and me as I asked Walker, "What do we do now?"

"Pray."

I looked at Megan and she could tell there was a problem she asked, "What's going on?

"Bart's house burned and Peter's missing."

"Oh, my God!" Megan replied as her hands went to her mouth as a sign of dismay,

I looked at Megan and added. "Without the two of them, the whole deal is going to fall apart."

"What did Walker say?"

"Pray," I replied in a very somber tone.

I thought about the options and simply shook my head. No matter which way I turned, it looked like a failure.

I was about to give up when I heard a vehicle in the driveway. I looked out and it was Peter's Mercedes with all four of our 'neighbors' surrounding the vehicle. In the passenger seat was Bart. I don't know who was happier them or me.

I went out without my jacket nodded to the guards and said, "Good guys," as they looked at me and wondered if I was telling the truth.

Peter got out, went to the back and got out Bart's wheelchair. Opening the passenger door, Bart slid across and positioned himself.

I got Walker on the phone and did a Facetime so Walker could see Peter. Walker then noted "All clear" as Nelson took a photo of Peter while the facial recognition app. recognized him.

Peter nodded at Bart and told Nelson he was an integral part of Winter Harvest. Nelson put a phone to his ear, spoke to someone, did another facial recognition, nodded and pointed towards our front door while asking, "Do you need help getting Bart into the house?"

I was literally shaking, not because of the freezing weather, but simply because my prayers had been answered as we made our way into the house.

"Where's Susan?" I asked Peter. "I sent her on vacation."

"Someplace warm, I hope." I replied. "Someplace safe," Peter replied. "What happened?" I asked.

Peter looked at Bart and noted. "Bart was working on the internet and came across some interesting conversation and learned they knew who was involved in Winter Harvest and they were going to kill us both. He called me and we had a little surprise for them!"

"What happened to Bart's house?"

"Well, we sort of set a couple of booby traps and whomever it was that went in there, certainly didn't come out."

"But your house!" I exclaimed to Bart.

Bart laughed and offered. "Heh, it was old and full of a lot of bad memories. I'll claim it on my taxes."

"What about Winter Harvest?" I asked.

Bart replied. "It's all on my laptop and that's right here. Now we need to call Agent Walker again and I'll give him a list of things I'm going to need. Where can I set up shop?"

I pointed to the office and made sure Bart's wheelchair would fit. I got out the burner and called Walker and put him on the phone with Bart who gave him a list of monitors, keyboards, modems and external hard drives he needed. He also noted that we needed a parabolic dish put on the roof so that Bart could link up to a satellite system to make sure no one was able to intercept his transmissions.

After Bart's call, we all adjourned to the living room and realized we'd be spending the next few weeks together. We came up with a few 'house rules' and settled in. Boy, it was good to see those two as I thought they were goners and with them our entire plan.

Houseguests:

The following day another black Suburban arrived and was filled with all the equipment Bart needed, as well as four watches that had tracking devices in them. It was then I realized this was moving to the next level of serious.

Megan was becoming quite the cook and would make a list of groceries for the four of us and our 'four Amigos' as I called the security team, where each day one would drive to the Piggly Wiggly in Dodgeville to get supplies.

On the fifth day, Peter indicated it was time for he and I to go back into the silo. This meant a tactical team was needed to identify where the land mines were placed and create an electronic barricade around the manhole so that no one could capture any signals Simon was about to elicit.

Everything was timed and, with military precision, we made our way out to the manhole, unscrewed the cover and climbed down inside. Peter estimated we had five days of helium and nitrogen remaining which meant we needed to get things going if we were going to do what needed to be done.

We went to Simon's auxiliary control panel as the one that had been up in the silo when the building was there had been blown to bits by the bomb.

"Well, here goes nothing." Peter said as he lifted the plexiglass panel, put his right ring finger on the glass and heard a click as he pulled back to allow the sensor to do a retinal scan and then facial recognition.

"It was my turn and, as yet another form of security, we'd programmed the identification sequence requiring my face, then my finger, then my eyes meaning there were six different permutations where only one would work. If they even had the right people and it wasn't done in the correct sequence, the entire system would shut down after three tries. I faced the sensor, put my left pinkie finger on the screen and then moved in for a retinal scan at which time I heard 'click' and we knew Simon was now active.

"Simon, can you hear me?" Peter inquired.

"Yes, Peter and it's good to hear your voice. It has been four years, nine months, twenty-six days, three hours, fourteen minutes and seven seconds since we last spoke."

Peter was all smiles as he knew Simon had only been sleeping as he said, "Simon, George is here."

In a somewhat monotone voice, Simon greeted. "Hello, George. It has been over six years since we spoke how are Amy and the kids?"

"They're fine Simon. Thank you for asking." I didn't want to go into details.

"I learned that Melia was on some television talent show and watched all of her videos. You must be proud."

"Thank you, Simon. I am."

"Why has Amy left you George?" Simon asked with a degree of concern in his voice.

"It's a long story Simon. There was an accident and she thought I'd died."

"I'm sorry to hear that, George." "Thank you, Simon."

Peter interjected. "Simon can you please run a transmission diagnostic, we need to determine the status of your outgoing network."

"Most certainly, Peter. Just a moment. In what measurement form would you like my response?"

Peter responded, "How about dBM?"

"In other words, a logarithmic unit representing the power relative to 1 milliwatt?"

"Yes, please," Peter replied.

There was a brief pause and then Simon responded. "I've measured the transmission parameters three different ways including the spectrum analyzer, signal strength indicators and RF power meters. All but the SSI's are reporting 100%, which are indicating 94% capacity and could be because of something blocking my transmission antenna or damage to its edge. I'm sending a diagnostic signal now to determine the status of the dish."

We waited for a moment and then Simon continued. "The southeast corner of the dish has some sort of obstruction. It could be a large tree root or boulder. I cannot tell."

"Will it affect your transmission speed?" Peter asked.

Simon paused and then noted, "My calculations indicate I'll be able to transmit as 97.4% of maximum dbm's. Is that fast enough?"

I could see Peter thinking through the process. With the dish buried and unobtrusive, It would mean we'd need to go to the hidden site and dig down to find out the cause. Instead, Peter inquired. "Do you still have a way of shutting down that part of the dish so that you can increase the dbm's elsewhere?"

Simon replied. "Yes, I can do that but you will have a blind spot on the transmission footprint."

"If we send multiple bursts, how long would you need between bursts to fill in the blind spot?"

Simon replied, "With a fourteen-degree null in the signal pattern, I would need approximately 243 minutes, twelve seconds between bursts to allow for the earth's rotation based on its current axis."

Peter looked at me and noted. "That's four minutes resulting in message duplication. This would result in all the security systems sensing a breach because they're set for sixty second recognition factors with alarms for duplicity."

"In other words, we can't do what needs to be done?" I asked. "No, it means instead of one blast like Bart developed, he's

going to have to segment it to hit some of the security systems at one specific time and the rest, without the first also receiving the signal, and do so at the proper interval. It he's off by one second, the entire thing could blow up in our face."

Simon's receptor was still on and he heard the conversation and replied. "Peter, I am able to split time differentials into microseconds and take the aggregate signal and compensate for the variance. All I will need are the coordinates for the receptors and will also need to know the intensity of any solar flares on the day of transmission."

"Solar flares?" I asked.

Peter realized he had to dumb things down and noted. Solar flares are caused by the sudden release of magnetic energy stored in the sun's corona which is the outermost layer of its atmosphere. This energy is built up as magnetic field lines that twist and tangle and are often accompanied by coronal mass ejections (CMEs), which are large clouds of plasma that can travel through space and impact Earth's magnetic field which can disrupt satellite communications, power grids and navigation systems. Simon can adjust for the earth's rotation in terms of his transmission footprint. However, because he's doing so in microseconds he'll need to make sure there aren't any electro- magnetic disruptions that could affect the data being transmitted."

"And where do we get that data?" I asked as Peter pointed at Simon and simply asked him to calculate the potential solar flare instance for Sunday, February 10th. Simon quickly responded with a clinical summary that noted that the intensity of the solar flares would be minimal and would not affect high-speed electro-magnetic transmissions in the Western Hemisphere during daylight hours.

Peter then inquired. "What about the Southern Hemisphere?" "The Caribbean, Central and South America?" Simon asked. "Correct?" Peter replied.

"On February 10th of this year, the areas will not be affected by high density solar flares to a degree that would disrupt electromagnetic transmission."

"Thank you, Simon," I offered. "You are welcome, George."

Peter activated Simon's response sensors and programmed them to exclusively receive signals from Bart's laptop for only one day and then return to an inert position. We shut off the lights, climbed up the ladder and put the manhole back in place. Within minutes, "the boys" returned and reactivated the land mines. With the helium and nitrogen levels indicating five days of cooling before shut down, we really had no choice besides accepting

Simon's offer of segmented transmissions based on the earth's rotation.

As we were walking back to the house, I mentioned to Peter. "Isn't it incredible to think we have the greatest and, also, the worst possible technology in the world in one source? Something so great it can help save the world while, at the same time, also so great it could destroy it?"

Peter said nothing as I added, "Besides that, it's also tragic to think that in a few days, we're going to have to put Simon to sleep and do so in such a manner that no one, including us, will be able to activate him for a hundred years."

There was no response from Peter as we trudged through the fields as if we'd just attended a friend's funeral. It was then I thought of Francis, Jake, mom and dad and realized, in a few days, Simon would be, for all intents and purposes, dead and no one alive would be able to bring him back to life as reality hit home and I self- lamented, "All this for nothing except money, power and control. How sad! How incredibly sad!"

Bits and Bytes:

Peter and Bart had a conversation that could have been in Lithuanian for all I knew as they discussed what we'd learned from Simon. While I might be... make that... completely dumbfounded by their discussion, they both knew exactly what the other was talking about and it was concluded we could load Simon with the virus and have him release it on Super Bowl Sunday as planned, doing it from the house.

Bart simply went to the computer and did whatever it was he did with all kinds of dots and dashes, lines and squiggles, more dots and letters and even some more dashes that he called programming. He popped the USB plug of an external hard drive into his laptop and we watched the icon slowly make its way across the bar indicating the loading percentage. There was an incredible amount of data that needed to be transferred and it took nearly ten minutes to complete the task. Whew! We had what we needed. Now all that was left was to go back to Simon.

We waited until the next day as were certain the 'boys' weren't too happy to undo what they'd done the day before in terms of the land mines. We apologized and they seemed to finally understand.

It was around noon as we made it to the manhole cover. Something didn't seem right. Perhaps it was because I'd noticed how the words on the cover "US Government Property" were facing the day before and were now at a different angle. I held up my hands and noted. "Peter, something's wrong."

"What?" Peter asked as a frown spread across his face.

"When we left yesterday I came up the ladder first and was standing where you're standing and when you closed the cover, the words 'US Government Property' were facing me, today they're not."

"You remember that?"

"Yes, simply because Simon isn't the government's property, it's ours. Our agreement with them was to share the data not the computer."

"Do you think someone opened the lid and went down inside?" Peter asked.

"Somebody did something." I replied, wondering why. "What do you want to do about it?" Peter inquired.

"I don't know." I responded, shaking my head. "Should I open the lid and see what happens?"

"Let me call Walker first." I suggested as I pulled out the burner phone and called the agent.

"Walker here."

"Who went down in the silo yesterday?" "What are you talking about?"

"When we left yesterday afternoon, the embossed words were facing towards me. Today they're facing the other way. What happened?"

"George, I think you're imagining things."

"No, I'm not Walker. Either fill me in or the entire deal's off."

Peter stood staring at me. It had been a long time since he'd seen me royally pissed. There was a pregnant pause and then, so Walker could hear me, I said to Peter, "Let's get out of here. They no longer think we're valuable commodities."

"Hold on!" we heard coming from the speaker. "Hold on George. Don't do anything you'll regret."

"Regret? Regret! Are you kidding me. I've been regretting the entire thing. You seem to misunderstand, we're the GOOD GUYS, not the bad guys. Now either you tell me what's going on or, by God, we'll mess this thing up so bad you and your team will be working security detail at O'Hare. Do you understand?"

There was a very long pause and then Walker said. "George, don't do anything rash. Don't go down in the silo. Don't do anything until we sit down and talk, but we need to do it face-to-face and not over some telephone."

"What the f   ?" I exclaimed.

"I'll be at the house in two hours. Go back and wait for me. Don't do anything!"

I took a deep breath, looked at Peter and reiterated what Walker had said. I knew we had no option and silently, walked back to the house.

When we opened the door, Megan and Bart knew right away something had changed. Bart looked at Peter, saw his expression and simply asked, "What happened?"

Peter looked at Bart and then Megan and finally said, "Walker's on his way. Something's come up he didn't want to discuss on the phone."

We all sat and waited until the black Suburban rolled into the driveway as I stated, "This better be good."

Walker came up the front porch stairs and I opened the door. He looked at the four of us, no handshake, no nod, and then at the floor and simply said, "I think you'd better sit down."

"Why?" I asked, while looking at Bart and Peter for support. "There's been a change of plans," Walker noted.

"What do you mean?"

Walker became very disquieting as he announced, "Well, someone higher up doesn't want you to go through with what you're doing."

"Why?" Peter asked in an incredulous tone.

"Because it's much bigger than you think and much greater than simply getting your money back."

"So, in other words, I get screwed because someone 'higher up' thinks we're too small of fish and he's gone whale hunting?" I lamented.

Walker nodded 'yes,' as I added. "Let me see if I get this straight. Someone with a higher level of authority is willing to sacrifice our lives, Bart's house and my wellbeing, because he thinks he can get a bigger gold star after his name and move further up the ranks?"

Walker pursed his lips and nodded in a positive manner as he looked at the floor.

It was Peter's turn and so I stood back as I knew this was going to be incredible. Peter looked at Walker and began. "What's going on here is that someone, somewhere has finally figured out how critical Simon is to national security and they now realize that shutting him down would mean five to ten years of R&D to even come close to what Simon can do now."

Peter continued, now in a more agitated tone. "Someone, somewhere understands and accepts that we were simply the bait... insignificant individuals played until we got to the point where we were on the cusp of success and then they realized, 'holy shit,' they've figured out how to beat the global financial system which everyone thought was impenetrable."

Shaking his head in dismay, Peter added. "Someone somewhere said 'Woah, we can't let a few billion dollars stand in the way of maintaining relations with allies and adversaries and so what if it means the demise of a man, his family and friends?'"

Peter looked at Walker and simply asked, "Do you know anything about fractals?"

Walker shook his head 'no'.

"Well, Agent Walker, let me explain. Fractals are infinitely complex patterns that repeat themselves at different scales. This property is known as self-similarity. Fractals can be found in nature, such as in the branching patterns of trees, the coastlines of continents and the structure of snowflakes. They can also be generated mathematically using simple algorithms. Fractals have applications in various fields, including computer graphics, data compression and physics and, are also currently used to model complex phenomena, such as turbulence and chaos theory."

"Now let's say that a really intelligent, I mean incredibly intelligent computer figured out how to use fractals on living beings as simple as a virus. You know, like the Corona Virus, the one they called Covid so the media didn't have to say so many words."

"OK," Walker replied as his expression turned grim.

"Now, let's say the computer could take that virus down to one-one-thousandth of its size...you know... a sub-atomic level."

"And?"

"Let's say, when it got there, the computer made one tiny change. You know just a tiny change to its DNA?"

"OK." Walker replied with an even more concerned look on his face.

"Now let's say, at the same time the computer created an antidote for the virus and determined how to mass produce it and put it in, let's say, drinking water, letting everyone, including the chemists, believe it was the fluoride added to strengthen teeth."

"Yes."

"Now let's say the computer re-built the virus with the fractal change in it and someone simply let it go."

Walker's face grew grim as Peter continued.

"The virus would spread and kill millions. You know, like the seven million who died from the Corona Virus. Only those who'd been inoculated would be safe. Instead of bombing an enemy, instead of shooting an enemy, instead of capturing an enemy, you'd simply have to bury the enemy."

"Oh my god!" Walker replied.

"This is why the government wants Simon. They realize, he knows. He's figured out Fraktaline and they want him as the next weapon of war and they think by screwing George they'll have the grand prize and that's world domination without firing a single bullet, dropping a single bomb or negotiating with a single person."

Gulp! Was all I could do. I simply had no idea that, what we'd created for the good of man, could be his demise.

Walker paused, looked at all of us, took a deep breath, exhaled, looked at Peter and then at me and noted. "You're right on all but the last little bit and that's screwing George over. The government is willing to compensate George, you, Bart and Megan for all that you've done."

"How much?" I asked as my empty wallet slid around in my back pocket.

"We'd like to offer you each a million dollars."

I simply shook my head in disbelief and retorted, "A million dollars? A million dollars? Last time we talked it was six billion dollars."

"Well, things have changed," Walker replied. "What?" Peter asked.

"Derrick Terrill made the mistake of getting involved with George's brother and has been arrested in Peru on drug charges."

"So, we lead you to the water and you take a drink!"

"Not me, George, the Peruvian government."

"What?" I asked.

"Yes, it seems your hot-head brother took out an undercover agent on a deal gone bad and he, too, is in jail."

"Sounds like Tommie," I replied as I simply shook my head in disdain.

Walker continued. "With them gone, the drug situation's, level of attention, has declined."

"What about the money?" Peter inquired. "Well, it's sitting there and frozen."

"Why did someone go down in the silo?" I asked.

Walker looked at me and offered. "We needed to see how far you'd progressed. When we learned you were about to install the financial virus, we thought we'd made the antenna inoperable, instead Simon figured out how to use it."

"How do you know all this?" I asked now concerned about what all they'd heard.

"You don't think those watches you're wearing were really just locators, do you?"

Jesus! We'd been played and it was then I looked at Peter and simply asked. "How about you?"

Peter smiled, looked at Walker and shook his head before replying, "Agent Walker, the one thing you didn't take into consideration was the fact that I never trusted you. You see sir, while you've been thinking we were getting ready to do the deed, the deed's already done."

"What?" Walker questioned as a dour look spread across his face.

Peter simply looked at the floor and said. "Do you really think when I went down in the silo with the coolant, I wasn't ready to program Simon? Come on, what do you take me for?"

Walker stood in disbelief as Peter continued. "By the way, when your detonation team blows up a building and you want it to look like the bad guys did it, you should have them come back and put some of the carbon on the inside of the silo. Leaving the walls clear was the first sign you'd it done."

"What?" Walker feigned.

Peter looked at him and simply shook his head. "Your demolition team blew up the foundation buildings to make it look like the bad guys did it. They had two objectives. The first was to shut down the foundation and make the bad guys think you destroyed Simon, which, I now believe they do. And second, to hide Simon's existence to give your nerds the chance to see if they could break the code so that the defense department would have a new weapon of mass destruction."

Walker stood shaking his head as if he'd been caught with his hands in the cookie jar as Peter added. "We know who came to Bart's house and we now know that no one's missing. You came to see what the progress was made but you made a very big mistake thinking we didn't know it was your team who took the shots at George and me and conveniently missed."

"It was you who then put the men out there, not to safeguard our lives but keep track of our progress until we completed what you wanted, which is the ability to do what we've done... simply be able to take the money and power from whomever you want whenever you want without firing a single shot."

"The problem, Agent Walker, is you waited too long. It's done. All done, and, to ensure no one alive today ever uses the power of Simon for anything but good, you shouldn't have let George and me go into the Silo yesterday."

Walker had a sick look on his face as Peter continued. "Then, after we left, you sent the wrong person in to check the status of our project. Whoever you sent believed they saw an active computer and attempted to break into it to see what we'd accomplished. Instead, they pushed the wrong button and in so doing, actually activated the deep sleep mode to shut Simon down for a hundred years where even Simon's tri-delta security system can't break into the memory and reactivate the system even if we wanted to."

Peter looked at Walker with disdain and continued. "What you now have is a bunch of wires and chips that are inert and can't be restarted. The financial virus is in place and you can't stop it."

With a somewhat sarcastic grin, Peter continued. "Soon, the money will go from one bank to the next, to the next and then the next and someday, all eighteen billion will magically be deposited in an offshore account where, with one small instruction, 65% will be deposited in the US treasury to be used 'for the good of all Americans' the politicians will say.'"

Walker simply shook his head in disbelief as Peter continued. "As for the program that allowed Simon to break into the banks, that code is locked with Simon and was written specifically for him and there's no way you can get it."

"What about the hard drive you were taking into the silo today?" Walker inquired.

Peter looked at Bart, smiled and said, "Bart, why don't you put it in your computer and let Agent Walker see what we were going to load into Simon today."

Bart smiled, turned his wheelchair and we all followed him to his laptop. Bart inserted the USB cable into his computer and all kinds of dots and dashes, lines, squiggles and letters and then even some more dashes appeared.

Peter looked at Bart and asked, "Do you want to do the honor, or do you want me to do it?"

Bart smiled, shook his head to reflect indifference and simply pushed the button that converted all the code into audio signals and visual images as the melody to "Three Blind Mice" began to play as the intro song 'Three Little Beers', released in 1940, considered one of the best episodes that features the Three Stooges as three beer delivery men who get into a series of comic mishaps with Curly going, 'Yuk. Yuk. Yuk.' while slapping his forehead.

Peter looked at Walker and simply noted, "If you want a copy of the software, Bart can dub one off for you. I don't know if whomever it was who wanted to screw us will get as big of kick out of it as we did recording it off YouTube."

Peter paused, pulled the USB connector out of the laptop and said. "better yet, you can take this as evidence."

Walker looked at the four of us and really didn't know what to say. Peter was still on a roll and offered. "Tell you what, you simply have the Justice Department drop the sedition case so that George can close out the 'And/Or' issue to the point George can get on with his life and Bart will press the little button and woosh, all that money will be deposited in the U.S. Treasury."

"And if we don't?" Walker countered.

"You're out the money and we'll make it known your agency was responsible for the arrest of Derrick and Thomas Terrill and you broke into their personal, private and secure accounts and simply transferred the money which got lost in the transaction."

"Who's going to believe you?" Walker disputed.

"How about the banks who lost the money. How about the governments who are our allies? How about all those who got screwed by Derrick when they learn you took their money?"

Walker paused for a moment and then responded. "How about this, WE crack the case. WE learn where the money is and WE go public and reward those who lost in the Ponzi scheme 65% of what they lost with anything left over going into Social Services?"

I looked at Peter and Bart. They'd done all the work and it was my turn to speak. "I'll agree as long as there's a formal understanding in writing that we honorably served our country and are pardoned for any wrong doing. As for the WE part, I don't want the publicity. Instead, you can say that you and the agency broke the case and were able to recover twelve billion dollars that's being refunded to those who lost money in the Ponzi scheme with one billion dollars donated to prostate cancer research in America."

A warm expression came across Walker's face as he realized we'd come to an agreement where everyone would win. He'd be rewarded for his diligence. The Ponzi losers would receive some compensation. Amy and my 'And/Or' issue might be resolved if the sedition charge against us was dropped while Tank, Peter and Bart would be compensated by me for their efforts. As for Megan, I had other plans which I wanted to keep as a surprise.

"I'll need to get this approved by the Department," Walker advised.

"Do they really have any choice?" Peter countered.

"Not really, but then you never know. It's amazing what happens when it's not your money."

I replied. "Tell you what, why don't the four of us meet with whomever, if need be?"

"I don't think that will be necessary," Walker assured us.

"How long will it take and what about the interest that's being accrued on the money?" Bart asked.

Walker shook his head and suggested we determine what should be done with the interest and we all agreed it should go to spinal cord injury research in Bart's name.

Walker headed for the door, stopped and looked back and inquired, "Really one-hundred years?"

"Yes," Peter replied.

Walker finally smiled and noted. "That's really good news. I'll make sure it gets out. That should take any ancillary pressure off George that might still be out there."

That was the best news of the day as far as I was concerned. Super Bowl Sunday arrived and just as Bart and Peter planned, Simon began the 'procedure'. Needless to say, there was tension on the Terrill farm as we knew the funds were going to be removed, then moved and moved and moved again and finally placed in one highly protected account somewhere on

March 15th. The Id's of March arrived and Peter called to note, "Mission Accomplished". Derrick Williams had lost over $18 billion that was hidden so deep and so far that even the U.S. government couldn't

find it.

Peter waited a day and then called Walker and gave him the 'good news'. We'd done our part and all that needed to be done was to have the Federal Government provide the pardon and it would be over.

Anxiety:

A week went by and it was March 22nd, Good Friday. I was getting anxious to say the least. I called Peter and he said neither Bart nor he had heard a word about the pardon. All I knew was it felt good not to be afraid, at least of the bad guys. Megan was in Madison and the only sounds in the house were those of the refrigerator humming and the slow crackling of the fire I'd built in the fireplace.

I was getting anxious. My thought was, it was going to be even later in the year when the phone rang and it was Agent Walker. "George, good news. Everything you wanted is being approved. I've been instructed to tell you the Justice Department is dropping the sedition charges and your assets will be unfrozen."

"When?" I asked, not trying to appear anxious.

"Next week, simply because the news cycle is at one of its low points and they want this to be a low-key event."

"What about the And/Or?" I queried.

"There's nothing we can do about that, George. It's a civil matter."

"Understood. What's the other news?"

"Your brother and son have been released. Don't ask us how. All we know is they opened the doors and let them go."

"What?" I asked incredulously.

"We don't know. All we do know is they're free." "Am I at risk?"

Walker got a soothing tone to his voice and assured me. "I wouldn't worry, they're not coming back to the States. If they do, they'll be arrested at the border."

"I thought this mess would be totally over."

"We did, too, but we don't have any control over what the Peruvian government does. I mean, they're good, honest people and really legit but your son and brother must have some damn good lawyers."

I thanked Walker and asked him to let me know when it was formally settled on the sedition deal as I needed to do some celebrating.

Walker noted. "I thought some good news might be just the right thing to help you get back to normal."

Good news? Half good news! No sedition, thawed but still somewhat frozen assets. Almost wealthy, but still dirt poor. I sat in the living room and tried to figure out what to say to Megan.

After a 'spell', I heard the tires crunch on the gravel went to the window and watched Megan walk across the lawn towards the front door. I scrutinized her gait and then her facial expression. I glanced at her glove-covered hands and surveyed her legs as they took one step and then the next. I sat there and listened to the 'click' of the front door and felt the cool rush of Wisconsin March air as she entered the house that made its way to the fireplace to set off a few crackles as if to say, "Welcome home!"

I stood and intercepted her before her coat even came off. I think by the look on my face she knew something was up.

"How was your shopping?" I asked in a very cordial way. "Frantic."

Megan replied. "Every place was crazy."

"I had a phone call."

"You did."

"Uh huh!"

"From whom may I ask?"

"Agent Walker."

"And...?"

"Good news... bad news. Which one first?"

"Good news," Megan replied as she slipped out of her coat.

"The good news is all the sedition charges are being formally dropped."

"That's wonderful."

"Two sets of bad news."

"Two?"

"Yes. First the 'And/Or' is a civil matter and the Feds can't do anything about it."

"OK, but you'll still have 50%, right?"

"Yes, but there may be challenges," I replied.

"You said there were two bad news things, what's the second?" Megan said as she hung up her coat.

"Derrick and Tommie got out of jail."

"What?" Megan responded profoundly incredulous. I shook my head and replied. "Don't ask me how."

"How?"

"I don't know. All I know is they're free."

"And you have all of their money?"

"Yup! Or at least a lot of it."

"Now what?"

"I know they're not coming back to the States."

"Why?"

"Because, they knows there's a federal warrant out for their arrest."

"What are you going to do?"

"What are we going to do?" I replied.

"We?"

"Yes, you and me."

"You mean like... together, together?"

"If you want to be."

"Oh, George, you know I do." Megan replied as tears began

forming in the corners of her eyes.

"You don't mind being with someone accused of being your father?" I asked.

Megan got a smug look on her face and mockingly noted, "They say that incest always starts at home," to which she simply giggled as I gasped at the thought. Not with Megan but otherwise. Gross!

"I've still got the...you know, other issue on the table and so I don't know when or how, but the question of 'if' has been removed if it's all right with you."

Megan looked at me and smiled, and in that moment, everything shifted. We embraced, yet it felt different—deeper, more profound. It struck me then that we'd built our relationship in reverse. We'd become friends first, not lovers.

There had been moments—an "incident" that blurred the lines—but at its core, our relationship had always been rooted in something more profound than physical connection. It had been a bond of trust, shared experiences, and unwavering support. I had never required romance from her, nor she from me. We had simply been companions, walking side by side through life's trials, learning to understand and respect one another.

Perhaps it was everything we'd been through. Perhaps it was the closeness we'd developed, the familiarity that made this next step feel less like a revelation and more like an inevitability. Somewhere along the way, without realizing it, our connection had deepened. On my side, at least, it now carried a vulnerability I hadn't acknowledged before.

Yet hesitation lingered. Was it the lingering shadow of my surgery? The ghost of Amy still haunting my heart? Or was it simply the helplessness that came with so much change? Whatever the reason, I knew one thing for certain—the burden of uncertainty was lifting. With the weight of my fears no longer pressing down, my feelings were finally returning to me.

Megan had seen me at my weakest and most broken point. And yet, she'd stayed and accepted all of me.

We stood, frozen in thought, simply holding one another. Her body pressed against mine, warm and reassuring. I had no idea how long we remained like that, letting the quiet between us settle into something solid and unspoken.

All I knew was that it felt good. Really, really good.

To be wanted. To be needed. To be loved.

As our embrace ended, I exhaled and said, "Do you think we could go to the forest tomorrow?"

Megan studied me for a moment, then nodded. "If you want to."

"I do." I hesitated, then smiled. "But first, there's something I want to show you."

Curiosity danced in Megan's eyes. She asked "What is it?"

I took her hand and said. "Something very special."

Megan followed me to the kitchen, where I poured two glasses of wine as we went back in the living room and I set the wine on the coffee table.

The flaming log crackled as I placed another log into the fire. Then, with a quiet confidence, I led her into the office.

At the cedar chest, I spun the dial, unlocking the past. Lifting the lid, I reached inside, carefully removing the protective wrapper that concealed the history of the Terrill family.

Megan's breath caught.

"Oh my God."

I glanced at her. "What?"

"It's... it's gorgeous."

Slowly, I unfolded the white bear skin, running my fingers over its thick, spotless fur. "Is it all right if I tell you the story of my family?"

Megan nodded, her voice hushed. "Please."

We returned to the living room, where I spread the bear skin on the floor before the fireplace. Nodding to Megan, we got down and lay upon the soft fur with the fire casting flickering shadows as I began the tale.

I told her of my Great-Great Grandfather, of the bear he had slain to save his and my Great-Grandmother's lives, and of the moment the bear's spirit had transcended into him. I recounted how the skin had once been traded for the very land that became the Terrill farm, and how, upon Blackhawk's death, his descendants had been entrusted to return it to our family. And finally, I revealed how it had remained a sacred relic, passed through generations, cherished by those who had come before me.

Then, I shared the greatest secret of all. "In my immediate family," I murmured, "only my son, V, has ever seen this—until tonight. He is the chosen one. And that," I said, my voice softer now, "is why I am called 'Little Spirit.'"

Megan listened in reverent silence, her fingers gently caressing the fur. I watched as something in her shifted, as she absorbed the weight of the story, the legacy, the sorrow and triumph woven into the threads of my family's past.

We sipped the wine and then, as the firelight flickered, casting dancing shadows, Megan stood and shed her sweater with the soft wool whispering against her skin. Then, her jeans followed, pooling at her feet. With each piece of clothing that fell away, the fire seemed to burn brighter, hotter, until only the warmth of its glow touched her bare skin.

I followed, drawn by an invisible thread. There was no rush, no hesitation. We'd been naked before, yes, but this was a different kind of unveiling. Not just flesh on flesh, but a breath-held meeting of souls, a silent promise, acknowledging the journey that had brought us here.

As we lay upon the bearskin, my hands traced the landscape of Megan's body, memorizing every curve, every softness, every valley. She trembled beneath my touch—not from hesitation, but from something deeper, something raw and powerful.

The fire crackled as shadows danced along the walls. And in that moment, as we lay entwined, I watched the transformation unfold before me.

Megan quivered—not in fear, nor pain, but in something greater. A moment of surrender, as if the sorrow of Blackhawk's life was passing through her, only to be replaced by something pure. Peace. Unadulterated peace.

In my heart and in my mind, she was no longer just Megan. She was part of something larger now, something ancient and unbreakable.

As we lay together, our breaths mingling in the quiet, the woman who had once been just my friend became something more. What had been **you and I** faded, and in its place, there was only **we**.

Our lives, once separate, had melded into one—woven together in the warmth of the fire, the weight of our shared past, and the unspoken promise of what tomorrow might bring.

The silence stretched between us, thick with meaning. Then, in a soft whisper, Megan spoke. "Oh, George... I don't know what's happening, but I want this to stay with me forever."

I met her gaze, breathing in deeply. In the firelight, her eyes held something I hadn't noticed before—something that made my chest tighten with an emotion I couldn't quite name.

I reached for her hands, our fingers intertwining. "The spirit of goodness endures," I murmured. "And tonight, as we honor the resurrection of Christ, I can feel it—this sense of benevolence in the air. A compassion, a virtue we'll always share."

Silence returned, but this time it was different—richer, heavier with everything unspoken. Then, Megan's lips met mine, soft and sure. Deeper and deeper and deeper we went until we melted into each other, bound by more than just touch. The fire crackled, sending sparks into the air, its warmth echoing between us. In that moment, everything about us collided—our souls intertwined.

What Great Grandfather had passed down flowed into me, rushing like a river, and I could feel it—passing into Megan, touching her with a depth I hadn't expected.

As we lay wrapped in each other's arms, I looked at her—the woman who had stood by me through everything. But now, in this moment, I saw her with new eyes. And in that quiet, sacred space, a single word settled into my heart: ***Love***.

I closed my eyes, listening to the stillness of the night, the faint crackling of the fire as it dwindled. Then Megan pressed a soft kiss to my lips and whispered, "Happy Easter."

A slow smile spread across my face, warm and knowing. Because in that moment, I realized something simple and true: Life is... ***Good***. Really, really good.

Easter:

It's only when you've gone through the passages of time can one understand the meaning of Easter and what you believe to be true... there is a resurrection and therefore a heaven When you're an adult and with an adult, it's about the small sentimental things. When there's kids, it's all the excitement of the Easter Bunny. When the kids are older, the excitement wanes and with it some of the sensations of bliss. To come around to how it had been when it's just you and one other person sharing life, love and each other, is when Easter has its real meaning. And so it was this Easter Day Megan and me, alone, basking in the joy of each other.

After breakfast, we got in the truck and went into town and then to church. Eyes were upon us but I no longer cared. Time has a way of healing all wounds and my Theory of Acclimation meant that, through repetition, the glances would fade and we would blend in like all those who were there with us. The choir sounded magnificent as the Easter songs chosen included many of my favorites with "Amazing Grace" especially hitting home.

As church let out, we politely nodded at our fellow celebrants, got in the truck and headed back to Waldwick. We'd agreed to go into the forest and it was the one thing I really wanted to do that day.

We got home, changed out of our Sunday best, went to the barn and into our 'farm clothes' as Megan liked to call them. Like the days you see on spring calendars, the late March air was still cold and crisp, the sun shone brightly and there was a smile in the air.

"Are you sure you want to walk?" I asked Megan.

"Of course, silly. How many Easters have ever been like this?"

Needless to say, I knew the way as we traversed the frozen

fields now smoothed by a few inches of snow. As we passed the manhole cover, I thought of Simon and how he too was hibernating, not for the winter months but for a century.

We made our way to where Skunk Hollow School had existed and saw little mounds of snow capping the remaining boulders which reminded me of giant Hostess Snowballs covered in gooey white frosting, filled with coconut that had been the foundation of the school and life for so many of my ancestors.

We made our way to the obelisk and my favorite pensive spot. I slowly brushed the rows of snow from the bench's slats and then the remnants of winter's incursion from the sun dial such that the morning shadow indicated the time to be nearing noon.

"Come sit with me," I offered to Megan. "There's something we need to discuss."

A strange looked came across her face as if Megan didn't know whether to be excited or afraid as she simply replied, "OK."

We sat down on the cold bench and, instead of looking at Megan, I looked at the obelisk as I knew what I was about to say was coming from Great Grandfather's soul to me and my time had come to truly be 'Little Spirit'.

As I sat thinking of the man who'd reasoned and seasoned me from a boy I simply stated. "The spirit of the man who lies beneath the obelisk is the spirit who gave me life. While I'd been alive, I did not live. While the years have seen me try to help make the world a better place, there's been an effect to my cause simply because the net sum of the universe is always zero and for that, the goodness created has been compensated by the bad."

I glanced at Megan and continued in a very serious tone. "As you have stood by my side, you...through your patience and compassion have allowed me to heal, to bring me to this point in time where, for the first time since I can remember, I'm at peace, peace with the world and most of all, peace with myself."

I looked at the ground and then continued. "For Easter you gave me...'you', not just physically but emotionally and it's the best... Easter present... I've ever received."

"In the next few days, I'll become a very, very wealthy man again. With the money, I can literally have anything and everything. Fancy clothes, fancy cars, fancy houses and even a fancy jet. Yet, none of it matters as long as I have you."

"I've traveled the world and done it all. I've laughed and loved, cavorted and got silly. I've been happy and profoundly sad and yet there's always been this yearning... a hole within my heart that's never been filled until you came along."

"I've looked at you from both close and afar and marveled at the goodness that lies beneath. I've watched you and admired your passion and compassion. I've seen you and appreciated that when you too were down... and I mean really down, you picked yourself up, dusted yourself off and moved on. Because of this, you and only you, have made all the baubles and beads, all the perks and privileges and all the awards and recognition I once had simply insignificant."

"As I lived within the bowels of mother earth, the only thing that kept me going was you, for you were my guiding light as each day, my only prayer was simply to see you once again."

I paused for a moment and then continued. "As I 'came back' to reality, my first thought was to start where I left off until you and I ventured beyond here and now and I realized joy and satisfaction did not come from where I've been but where we dream to go."

I looked at Megan and saw the glisten of tears upon her cheeks. I took off my left glove and wiped the tears away with my index finger, taking the salty stream and placing it within my mouth as if it were some sort of elixir that would bond us even closer. I paused and then began again. "My only profound regret is that you and I cannot have children of our own."

"It's Ok," Megan assured me.

I knew that in her heart she'd chosen me over motherhood and that was profoundly humbling as I continued. "Assuming we can resolve the other issue and, even if we don't, my only goal is to make you happy."

Looking down at the ground and then back at Megan, I assured her. "No matter what, there's enough money that, if you want the perks of wealth they're yours. If you want to open a therapy clinic, we can do that. If you want me to re-start Terrill B&B so that we can travel the world, I will and yet I have another idea I want to share with you."

I paused to collect my thoughts and simply asked Megan. "What would you think if we built a different house on the other side of the valley?"

"You mean away from the farm?" Megan quietly, almost incredulously asked, not wanting to shatter the moment.

"Yes."

"But what about the farm?" Megan inquired.

I looked at her and smiled. "What if we made it into a place where children could come and play. We'd set aside days for those physically handicapped and make sure the facilities were there. We'd set aside days for those mentally challenged so they could enjoy a day away from their routine and reality. We'd set aside days for white, black, red and brown kids to all come together, out to the farm to learn the majesty of life and the goodness of simplicity, where cellphones and texts would not be allowed, social media would not exist and video games forbidden?"

"George, it sounds wonderful."

"If I can find Amy and get her to sign the papers, with the money I'm about to get, we could set up a program where there would be no cost to any child... rich, poor, black, white... all would be welcome. We would let our guests see the animals and work with social workers to ensure the curriculum was such that it created a positive bonding experience with food, fun and fascination. With cows and kittens, chickens and pigs, horses, goats and ponies for them to enjoy to celebrate life as it was meant to be."

Megan smiled and inquired. "Do you think we could take the lab and turn it into a veterinary hospital?

"Sure!" I said as I saw the excitement in Megan grow. "Perhaps a safe haven for abused farm animals?"

"Why not?" I inquired, now catching Megan's enthusiasm.

Megan continued. "You know, giving them a chance to live their lives with the dignity they deserve without the threat of ending up at a processing plant?"

"Of course!"

I'd never seen Megan this enthusiastic as she added. "What would you think of calling the farm 'Noah's Ark?' Loneliness isn't reserved for humans."

I looked again at Megan and added. "While we can't have our own kids, these children would become ours... at least for a day, where the magic of Christmas would fill their hearts with love and joy all year round."

I stopped and then added. "Depending on the season we could create events that would give the kids something special to look forward to and create memories they'd carry with them to their own reality. Bonfires with s'mores, a corn maze, Christmas tree farm, petting zoo, trick-or-treat, sleigh rides. All the things that are simple that would put joy in their hearts."

Now the tears of anticipation were collecting in both of our eyes as Megan looked at me and simply said, "This is the best present I could ever get."

We simply held each other and hugged. We sat and let the emotions that had been bound up within us, loosen as the majesty of love enveloped us in joy. Soon, the moment passed and we stood. I kissed Megan as a token of gratitude, took her by the hand and walked to the Springs. I brushed the snow from the top of the little wooden box, lifted the lid and took out the two tin cups.

As I knelt down to fill the receptacles, 'He' appeared. I looked up at Megan, slowly raised my hands to indicate to remain totally still as she nodded in affirmation.

Gradually I stood and handed a cup to Megan as 'He' did what he'd never done before. Instead of walking back into the bog, He came closer and then closer until I could see his warm breath escape from his nostrils. I looked deeply into his eyes and he in mine and there was peace, deep, deep peace. The peace I'd been looking for my entire life. The peace that only comes when there is love in your heart and knowledge you'd arrived at that point in time and place you'd only ever dreamt about.

The big buck nodded as if to tell me to take a drink as both Megan and I slowly put the old, battered tin cups to our lips and sipped the cold water that had changed so many lives. With that the mighty buck tilted his head and took a long drink that matched the sweet nectar that entered our hearts, minds and soul.

Slowly, our hands lowered as He looked at Megan and tilted his head to one side. It was then I noticed, which to this day I believe was a smile... a sentimental signal of approval that finally, peace had come.

Megan and I simply stood there as the spell was broken. I looked at Megan whose mouth was agape for she didn't understand what had transpired. I knew! I really knew! He'd come to tell me 'life is good' which flooded my mind with memories of mom for it was her favorite saying. He was telling me mom approved and I closed my eyes in profound gratitude.

Affirmation! Confirmation! Declaration of what I'd been seeking my entire life... the majesty that only comes from giving of oneself, not only to those whom you love but strangers in need, lonely people, sad people, challenged people to whom your heart acts as a bridge to a respite from the challenges they face on any other day.

The spell broke and our four-legged friend simply nodded, turned and walked from whence he came as satisfaction finally was within my reach and I knew it.

I turned as a profound smile erupted, looked at Megan and simply whispered, "Happy Easter," to which we silently headed hand-in-hand, home and back to reality.

Dreams:

The Easter weekend ended and I knew I needed to get a tentative plan in place and so Megan and I spent time laying out what all needed to be done to create the farm version of the Derrick Williams Foundation we decided to call 'The Terrill Farm Experience' and prioritizing the list... facilities, personnel, attractions, timetable...all the things we thought we needed until we came to the realization we couldn't do it all alone.

It had been nearly three years since I'd seen the man who could do it. It's amazing how time flies and also how guilt not only can motivate but impede you, especially when they live only seven miles away.

I finally knew I needed to break the ice and drove into Mineral Point and went down to Fountain Street and the orange brick house that had been filled with so many lives that made Mineral Point what it was.

I parked outside, went to the side door and knocked. No one in Mineral Point who knew anyone, ever went to the front door, that was for peddlers and company and not friends stopping by to say 'hello.'

I peered in through the window and saw the outline of a person that put a smile on my face. As the door opened, Indira was there. My dear friend Luke's wife as she smiled and offered. "George, what a pleasant surprise."

Indira had aged, but hadn't we all? Her jet-black hair had become quite gray and there seemed to be a bit of a stoop in her walk as if she was carrying the weight of the world on her shoulder as I replied. "Thank you, Indira. Is Luke home?"

"No, he's not. He had to go to Madison for some sort of Masonic thing. Is there anything I can do for you?"

I was uncomfortable as it had been a long time and knew I shouldn't have stayed away. I looked at Indira and finally said, "Could you please let Luke know I stopped by and simply tell him I said, 'I'm back.'"

Indira had a perplexed look on her face and so I added. "He'll understand and I'd like to explain what's all gone on and why I've stayed away so long."

"Do you want to come in and have some tea?" Indira inquired.

"No. Thanks anyway. I'm going up to the Red Rooster for lunch and just wanted to say 'Hi'. Do you think Luke could call me when he has time?"

"Sure. It was so nice to see you, George." "Thank you, Indira."

I turned and began the walk up to High Street and the Red Rooster. Along the way, I thought of how strange the conversation had been... so formal, so structured, so, well almost cold. I hoped we could break the ice as she and Luke were two on my favorite people.

I entered the restaurant took a whiff of the cooking pasty, made my way past the counter and sat in back behind the stairs and stares awaiting my Cornish Pasty fix. Betty was working and, after eating the whole thing, asked if I wanted a slice of apple pie. After all the Easter candy, I politely said 'no."

I walked down Chestnut hill and back to my car and saw Luke's truck in the driveway. I pondered whether I should make the move or simply wait to see if he'd call me. As I reached my car, the kitchen door opened and a smile met my face. "Are you going to come in or do I have to call you and invite you back again?"

For the next two hours Luke and I talked about anything and everything. Indira had been feeding him well and he had a little paunch with white temples to match. I explained why I'd left him out of the entire post-cave debacle to protect he and Indira and what I'd been going through. Luke asked me about Amy and I laid it all out about the 'And/Or' without going into the details.

Luke noted word had spread that I had a younger woman living with me and so I explained the whole situation regarding Megan and her work and how she'd been the one who literally brought me back to my sanity, whatever that meant.

As we got caught up, the comfort level friends have with each other finally reappeared and I told Luke about all that happened on the farm, about the CIA, about Peter and Bart, then about my premonition and, finally, about the Buck. Luke smiled as memories of his first experience with the 'Big Guy' as he called Him came rushing back to his present.

I apologized vociferously for not coming sooner but assured him it was out of care for he and Indira and their safety and not because I wanted to avoid them. As we were finishing our second cup of tea Luke finally looked at me and said, "So you need a foreman, don't you?"

I nodded 'yes' and added. "I need someone who understands what we want to do and why. Someone who can perceive all the challenges of trying to take a farm and turn it into a retreat that would be safe, attractive and appealing to all types of families including children ranging from those God has given the majesty of a normal life to those God has chosen to make special."

Luke looked at me, seemed to suck in his cheeks and then smiled as he inquired. "And the pay?"

"Same as mine." "Nothing?"

"Uh huh!"

"And no bad guys? No CIA? No computers?" Luke asked with a sarcastic grin.

"Just a bunch of animals and two old codgers."

"Who's going to take care of the animals? I've got an idea if she's still living in Baraboo." Luke noted.

"Who? I asked.

"Why not get Mary involved?" Luke queried.

Mary Magdaleno had been Sir Francis Bacon's trainer when we developed the chip for Amy's dad. She had a way with animals and spent the past fifteen years working at the Circus World Museum until she and her husband retired.

I expelled the air in my lungs and realized Luke was right. If one of the major attractions was going to be farm animals, I needed to make sure we had an expert of what I called public animals who wouldn't be spooked by humans who also had the right positive environment in which to live in... the animals that is.

I glanced at the kitchen clock and smiled. Here I was sitting with a woman who had a PHD in biology, whose husband had been a flight instructor and went into space a bazillion times, was a 32nd degree Mason and the two of them had one of those old-fashioned cat clocks whose big eyes and long tail moved back-and-forth, hanging above the kitchen stove. It read 4:30 and I knew I needed to get home.

We stood and Luke gave me a big hug and simply said, "welcome back."

I shyly smiled, looked down and then at the man who meant so much and replied. "I'm sorry it's been so long. I just didn't want to risk having you involved as you are too dear a friend and too decent for me to take you through the hell I've gone through."

We shook hands, got in my truck and headed home.

Mary Magdaleno? Why didn't I think of her? Of course! She and her husband could live in the farm house and Megan and I would build a new house where Melia's had been.

Fruition:

My New Year's resolution had been to clean up the Amy mess, one way or another, find Derrick and Tommie, resolve those issues and move ahead with the farm idea.

With no response from Amy and no way to get hold of her, half my assets were still frozen even though the government had lifted the sedition charges against both of us. It had been months and no word whatsoever. As for Tommie and Derrick, I just wanted to set the record straight. The last thing I needed was trouble from them. Next on my list was finding Melia. Finally, having 'V' and his Amelia meet Megan.

Time flew by and the farm plans were coming to fruition. We developed the agritourism destination profile where our goal was to provide a unique blend of agricultural experiences, family-friendly activities and educational opportunities as we learned about all the federal, state, county and township laws, regulations and limitations we had to abide by.

The more research I did, the more I began to realize how many people yearn for a connection to nature and simpler times where our entertainment farm could provide an opportunity to experience rural life, learn about farming practices and enjoy outdoor activities. While initially focusing on special needs children, I quickly began to see that we could reserve days for them and open the farm to the general market by incorporating educational elements such as farm tours, animal encounters and workshops.

One primary caveat was to incorporate family-friendly seasonal activities including art and craft fairs, hayrides, corn mazes, pumpkin patches, petting zoos and picnic areas, as well as, a Cornish village of bungalows that looked like Pendarvis House where families could stay with no TV, no cellphone coverage and no Wifi but plenty of puzzles and board games to create opportunities for families to spend quality time together and make lasting memories.

With so many area farms raising secondary crops, as well as all the art studios in Mineral Point, I thought why not turn the barn into some sort of 'store' that offered farm-fresh produce, homemade goods and artisan products to support local farmers and producers while enjoying delicious and unique food and gifts. I knew the key would be offering seasonal events and festivals such as fall festivals, holiday celebrations and summer concerts to attract visitors with live music, food vendors, and festive activities, then my mind went rampant and I added a farm restaurant that served food family style where you sat with other people instead of only your family to make new friends and create new memories.

I began to wake up at four in the morning and write things down until I had ten pages of ideas that I scanned and sent to Luke. He replied, "Welcome back my friend. The magic is still there."

What started out as a small acorn quickly grew into a mighty oak of an operation that was way beyond my initial thoughts. Even so, my requirement remained that we would incorporate programs and facilities that would allow all children, regardless of race, religion or physical or mental requirements, to have a day of innocence filled with love and laughter that would make the day special for them, as well as the parents, teachers or therapists who accompanied them.

Mary had been hired and was excited about the whole proposition and began Project Noah which was selecting the type and herd size for the animals. At the same time, Megan and I went to Spring Green and bought the blueprints Melia used on her original house plans. No word from Amy.

We were having an extremely cold spring, but the warmth of love and excitement of something new made it all seem worthwhile. For a break, we went to Madison and dined at Graze. It was nice to be able to afford all the trimmings and, boy, did we enjoy those as well as a night at the Edgewater. Whoopee!

Luke called and said he had the Terrill Farm initial plans completed and wanted to show them to Megan and me. We agreed on Thursday afternoon and he came out to the house. It was the first time he met Megan and I saw instant approval... attractive, intelligent, compassionate and polite.

Luke rolled the plans out on the kitchen table and my mouth dropped open. He'd literally taken the entire farm and cut it into quadrants and it made so much sense. First, as the Foundation had been, the entire farm would also be bio-inert. We would have our own solar field for electricity and there would be no gasoline powered equipment. The barn would be 'center stage' as he called it, where people would gain admission or register.

"Register?" I asked.

Luke looked up and smiled. "Well, I might be a little too optimistic but in addition to campgrounds, all with electrical outlets, I've also allocated an area for twenty-five cottages that look like Pendarvis on Shake Rag Street with swing sets and slides in the central commons."

"In addition, I've allocated twenty-five acres for the corn maze, five acres for a pumpkin patch and then ten acres for the apple orchard where you'd pick you own as well as strawberry, blackberry and raspberry patches."

"Closer to the barn I've included the petting zoo, as well as, keeping the milking parlor while adding both pony rides and a horse barn. Circling the entire farm would be a nature trail for walking in the warm weather that would become a cross-country ski path for winter," Luke added.

I'd never seen Luke so excited. I guess the Terrill farm was his way of creating the children he and Indira never had as he fashioned a Wisconsin version of Dollywood.

Luke continued. "Three nights a week, there'd be outdoor 'moovies' with live entertainment two other nights. I've also designed what looks like a pond for swimming which is actually a swimming pool in disguise to meet health and safety standards. I believe we can take Su's old lab and turn it into Mary's training area and clinic for both sick and injured animals. On the two nights when there isn't entertainment, we'd have an old-fashioned bonfire and roast wieners and make 'smores.'

Luke even created a proposed menu with traditional breakfast items while adding a full complement of sandwiches for lunch while dinner would focus on rotating meals of things like chicken and dumplings, pasty, macaroni with local cheese, hamburgers, fish and even a steak night which would all be included in the rental costs for both the campground and the houses.

"I really think it's important that we integrate Mineral Point into our plans. I don't want to be their competitor." I interjected.

"How about having local artwork on display in the dining hall that would be for sale with the name of the artist and where their studio is located. Also, how about a twice-daily bus into town that would drop the guests off on High Street, give them a discount card at the Red Rooster and the Ben Franklin where they could buy books on Mineral Point?" Luke inquired.

"Great idea," Megan added.

Mary and Luke had collaborated and she'd sent along a note of the types of animals she thought were appropriate and the list included the normal dairy cows, horses, pigs, sheep, goats, chicken and ducks along with bunnies, while also including badgers which most people have never seen, and ground hogs with the idea we could boost winter attendance on Groundhog Day.

"What about the Forest?" I asked.

Luke's enthusiastic nature turned a bit subdued as he said, "George, it's a place of religious significance. I would like to hold interdenominational services there on Sunday's if you wouldn't mind while also explaining the significance of the Ley Lines and how they have affected world history. I know any inclusion will be based on approval by the Hochunk and so I didn't incorporate it into the plans. I thought it over and asked, "What would you think if we had Native American information about the land and the truth of how it came to be? Perhaps, we could also include an outreach program so visitors would get a better idea of not only the history but challenges facing Native Americans today without making it a sob story?"

Luke simply smiled and nodded the gentle smile that indicated he thought it was a good idea and I was assigned to contact Rodney and see if it was OK with him.

"Can I make a suggestion?" I asked. "Of course."

"How about horse driven wagons that came by the camp ground and village every fifteen minutes?

"That would really be neat!" Megan commented as she got into the spirit of what was at hand.

"One last question," I offered. "What?"

"What about the winery caves?" There are seven of them, couldn't we convert them into housing units?"

"Sure, if you want to. Perhaps tell the story of how they were created and show photos of the buildings in Mineral Point created from the stone and when they were built."

Whew! In two hours, we set in motion a major plan that was going to change the function of Terrill Farms forever. My only hope was that mom and dad would have approved.

The following Monday, we finalized a modified version of Melia's house plans that included hydronic heating and poured concrete walls with precast, pre-stressed concrete beams for the floors. One thing that always bugged me at the farm house were the squeaky steps going upstairs and so concrete it was. The architect thought I was still wacko, but it was my money and I knew what I wanted and why.

With the walls, floors and house literally being built into the side of a hill, the structural integrity matched the Lighthouse design concepts used on Saint Martin after Hurricane Irma simply because I wasn't going to allow any tornado destroy my dreams like they did Melia's. I also detailed a vault like the one at the Lighthouse to be cut into the hill to serve the same purpose, hoping no hurricane would ever hit Wisconsin where the standard line was, is and remains...'we shovel our weather problems.'

With the plans completed, we signed the agreement and knew they were going to break ground as soon as the weather cleared. They said it would be Fall before we could move in which was all right as we still needed permits and money before we could do anything at the farm. No word from Amy!

April came and we started counting the days until our Lighthouse visitors would be gone. I contacted Mister Kincaid from the property management company and told him not to rent the property until after we met. I had no inclination of leasing a new jet and so I made one-way flight arrangements from Madison to Phillipsburg. No word from Amy!

With the early warmth and a dry spell, I got out dad's John Deere put the front loader on and went out to the quarry and found one great big rock and I mean one really, really big mother that weighed so much I was afraid the rear tractor wheels would come up off the ground. Slowly I made my way to the manhole and carefully placed the rock on top. No one, and I mean no one was going down in the silo to see if they could wake Simon. Megan and I then planted a couple dozen trees around the rock such that in a few years it would look quite natural. While the government knew where Simon was sleeping, no one else did and I wanted to keep it that way.

Mulligans:

Shazam! It was travel time, back to Saint Martin. I told Mister Kincaid to have the Lighthouse professionally cleaned and ready for our arrival on April fifth. The day came and we departed. I really didn't miss the private jet and, instead of flying first class, I "upgraded" to economy plus and selected 21D and 21F on the United flight that were the exit row seats. Five hours and twenty minutes later we set down at 'SXM', Princess Juliana Airport, and took a taxi to the Lighthouse. Along the way, I called Mister Kincaid and he said he'd meet us there.

We arrived at the Lighthouse and made our way up the stairs. The house was just as we left it and I thanked Mister Kincaid for the way it had been maintained.

Kincaid asked me if he should start renting it for the next season as the same family was interested in the property for three months. I told him to give me a few days and I'd let him know simply based on finding Amy and get the 'money matter', as Megan and I began calling it, resolved.

We said goodbye, activated the tram and opened the vault to find everything just as we'd left it. Megan got one of the salacious grins on her face and said she was going for a swim. Gee, I wonder what she was going to wear? Tee hee!

I knew the following morning would mean a trip to Carrefour and groceries and then the beach. Morning came and we did as planned, realizing yet another restaurant name had changed in the courtyard, where everything else was just as we left it except now we could afford to be there.

We settled in and set our routine. Megan visited Lucille's *Barely There Swimwear* where I really didn't think she could find anything more *Barely* than what she already had. She was having fun and that's what it was all about. Again, my Theory of Acclimation... been there, did that... saw that... got excited and then, well repetition, repetition, repetition until it was all so... normal.

Megan indicated she'd talked to Lucille and Lucille's seamstress could do the alterations to the jumpsuit and have it ready the following morning if I didn't mind.

I didn't mind, so we drove back to the Lighthouse, got the jumpsuit, drove back to Lucille's as Megan went in to get measured and I went next door to Chez Leandra for one, or make that three, dirty lemonades and then back home.

The next morning, it was back to Lucille's to pick up the alterations. That night, with Megan wearing her latest clothing acquisition, we made our way up and down Boulevard de Grand Case eating ourselves silly, promising to stop... well, maybe next week.

There's a fine line between inhibition and exhibition and I think the jumpsuit hit that juncture simply because everywhere we went, the eyes were on Megan and it was a cheap thrill knowing she was with me and no one else. Something about one's libido, I guess. What was really crazy was the fact that not only men were smiling but women were looking and, in some cases, hitting on Megan as well.

As we were walking back to the Rover, I asked Megan, "did it bother you to have women hitting on you?"

Megan did a gentle scoff and replied, "hardly! I considered it a compliment."

"You mean?"

"Sure, why not? Why do I need to only be attractive to men? Isn't the ultimate compliment, being attractive to everyone? What about you, George, what would happen if you got hit on by a man?"

"I'd have the creeps." "Why?"

"I don't know, it's just not something guys appreciate." "Even with today's expanded acceptance?"

"Yup!" I replied and then inquired, "So you'd...?"

"If the time, place and person were right? Sure, why not?" Megan responded in a somewhat cavalier way.

My mind wandered to Amy and all her guilt feelings and surmised 'times had certainly changed!' Or had they? Perhaps it was just that Megan was more comfortable with herself and certainly a lot more open about it.

As we drove back to the Lighthouse there was silence. My mind wandered as I asked myself 'why?' Why was I attracted to the same type of woman. What was it about me that pulled my heart strings in such a way that conservative me ended up with someone socially, physically and emotionally so liberal? I wasn't raised that way. I'm just a small-town farm boy who only wanted to be happy. Yet, I found myself in love AGAIN with a woman who challenged my own values.

I do admit I'm attracted to traits that I lack and find liberal, open- minded women exciting, refreshing, and inspiring because they represent qualities like freedom, exploration, and individuality I simply don't have. Is that a weakness on my part? A shortcoming?

As I've gone along for the 'ride', I've seen there's the appeal of contrast that creates a sense of balance. I'm the reserved one where, initially both Amy and Megan's openness and adaptability brought diversity and spontaneity to my more structured and traditional life creating a sense of intrigue and novelty.

On the outside, both Amy and Megan exude confidence, where their outer assuredness and self-comfort has been magnetic to the point, with both women, I was simply overwhelmed by their personal strength and tenacity.

Regarding Amy, I quickly began to realize the challenges she faced, but my love for her was, is and will always remain profound. As Megan and I lived together I've been able to see through her 'outer shield' that includes her 'liberal' persona to find a deep level of kindness, humor, intelligence and creativity such that our personal connection transcends our disparate personalities where, once again, I'm in love with a woman who makes me feel 'complete'.

If it was just the outer shield, I don't think I'd have fallen in love with Megan. Fortunately, we have so many other shared values that have generated levels mutual respect, ambition and personal goals, that outweigh our social differences, to the point,

I'm able to accept her idiosyncrasies and hopefully, she is mine.

I know attraction isn't always rational. People are often drawn to others based on unconscious psychological factors, and I shouldn't let it bother me that Megan personifies the 'good' Amy I fell in love with so long ago. My only prayer is that the 'bad' Amy doesn't show up as I really don't think I could handle it anymore.

I now wonder, would I have been happy with a 'Plain Jane' who simply walked through life with me constrained in so many ways? I really don't know and realize I'm simply getting too old to find out. Live with it, George! Live with it! There are no Mulligans in the game of life and be thankful for what you've got.

Surprise:

April twelfth meant it had been a week and we were tanning nicely, I might add. When the subject of Amy came up and going to Saint Barths, we agreed to take the ferry over, go to the clothing store and surprise her. If she wasn't there, we'd go out to the house. I had a duplicate set of 'And/Or', as well as, a copy of the no fault divorce papers with me knowing all she needed do was sign them and we'd be clear.

I went on line, checked the ferry schedule, drove to Phillipsburg, tried to find a parking place, found one, ran our butts off, made the ferry and headed across the strait, landing in Gustavia and going directly to the clothing store.

We walked in and Amy wasn't there. The clerk looked at Megan and me and decided we probably weren't worth her time of day. Somewhere in her early twenties, she had a look of indifference splashed across her face telling us the only reason she was there was because she needed the money and the ability to name drop when she went home. I figured, she was probably a contract worker from Paris who thought St. Barths would be glamorous. It was only when she got to St. Barths did she realize that, without money, the island really isn't that neat after all.

We walked up to the counter and I offered. "Excuse me, we're looking for Mrs. Amy Terrill who works here," which Megan translated into *" Excusez-moi, nous recherchons Mme Amy Terrill qui travaille ici."*

The clerk curled her upper lip and announced. *"Il n'y a personne qui travaille ici avec ce nom,"* which Megan reported to be "she said there's no one working here by that name."

"How long have you worked here?" I asked as Megan translated *"Depuis combien de temps travaillez-vous ici ?"*

"Since December," the girl offered in somewhat broken English letting us know it was our task to translate and she would decide what to say in return.

"Merci." Megan replied as we backed out of the store and realized we needed to go out to the house.

When we'd been there previously, Megan had typed the address into her phone, She gave it to the taxi driver who raised his eyebrows, shrugged his shoulders and took us to where the house should have been. The lot was empty!

"Où est la maison?" Megan inquired.

"Il a brûlé en décembre. Personne ne sait comment et personne n'a été blessé, donc il a brûlé." Megan offered, "It burned down in December. No one knows what happened. There was no one home and so it burned."

"Tell him to take us back to the dock. Shit!"

Instead, I took out my phone and used the translator app and played it for the taxi driver who laughed at *« Dis-lui de nous ramener au quai. Merde ! »* to the point I inquired "What did I say?"

Megan giggled and replied "Take us back to the shit!" "How do you say whoops in French?"

"Oops!" Megan replied, as we paid the man his fare and gave him twenty Euros for the entertainment, looked at the ferry schedule and noted we had two hours for the next one.

I told Megan we had one last chance to figure out where Amy was and that was by going to the Hotel Christopher where Amy would always go for lunch when she came over shopping and so we went out of the ferry terminal, got in the same taxi and went to the hotel.

We told the taxi driver to wait, entered the lobby and went to the front desk. With only 42 rooms and a clientele of very wealthy, very picky, very discreet guests, I knew our chances of getting information would be slim, narrow and none but it was worth the chance, especially with the wait for the next ferry or sixteen miles of swimming back to the ferry dock in Phillipsburg if we didn't make it.

I went up to the front desk and asked the desk clerk if he knew Mrs. Terrill. I described her and asked if he'd seen her. He simply shook his head 'no' but I could tell by his eyes he knew something.

"OK, let's do it this way. Here's one-hundred Euros. Maybe this will refresh your memory," as I slid the bill across the counter but kept my fingers tightly on the image of Princess Europa from Greek mythology.

Megan took over in French and said. *"C'est Monsieur Terrill et sa femme a disparu. Vous avez le choix : nous dire ce que vous savez ou le dire à la police et au directeur de l'hôtel. Préférez-vous cent euros ou la police et le directeur ?"*

The clerk looked at Megan and replied. "She was working at the clothing store when the house she was renting burned. She and her partner left Saint Barths in early December. No one knows where they went."

"But they're gone?" "Oui!"

I took my hand off the bill said *"Merce,"* and we walked out knowing that, like Elvis, Amy not only left the building but the island as well. Back into the waiting taxi and terminal and another twenty Euros. Toot! Toot! The ferry arrived and we boarded as Megan offered. "Wanna bet they reversed their tracks and headed back to Chile? Dime against a dollar, they're in Puerto Montt."

"Why not Peru?" I asked.

"Simply because Amy probably thinks Derrick and Tommie are in prison. The logic is, if Amy and Karen are in Peru, they could be held as accomplices and I don't think Peru's women's prisons have the quite same standards and accommodations as the Hotel Christopher. "

"Smart thinking, kid. You get your Junior Detective badge if you buy the right box of Cracker Jacks."

Megan had no idea what I was referring too, but then neither did I.

"Let's close up shop for now and see if we can find her."

We made it back to the Lighthouse and I went online to look

for flights and booked a quick hop-skip-and-a-jump, 16-hour flight from Phillipsburg back to Santiago with reservations for a suite at the Doubletree Hotel we stayed at near the airport.

The only problem was the fact our only clothes were our Saint Martin casuals. Now, I wouldn't have minded Megan in her short shorts, but she thought it best if we go into Phillipsburg and buy some clothes. There are a few things in life I really don't like doing and near the very top of the list is going clothes shopping with a woman.

"Do these pants make me look fat?" How do you answer that?

Megan went a little crazy on the clothes and then a suitcase and thought she was all set until we realized we were going to Southern Chile where April meant it was going to be Fall and the weather in Chile was also going to be chilly. All we needed to do was go out dinner and eat a hot dog covered in chili made with chili pepper, chili powder, on a bed of chili con carne covered with chili sauce, and you'd have a chili, chili, chili, chili dog in chili, chilly Chile. Tee Hee!

With 16 hours in an aluminum tube, I knew when we landed, we'd need some time to catch up and also buy some warmer clothes and so, I booked two nights with us leaving two days later for Puerto Montt.

Mission Almost Accomplished:

We made it to Santiago and I opened my phone to find a message from Peter. All it said was, "it's done."

I knew right then and there I was once again wealthy. I knew that all the financial worries were gone. I also knew that the US Government Treasury had the funds needed to make things right.

I looked at Megan and smiled.

"What?" Megan asked.

"Mission accomplished."

"You mean?"

"Uh huh!"

I contacted Tank and told him the news. In return I got a smiley face.

Megan and I went a little crazy buying fall clothes and then booked the same flight as when were there before on LATAM. After flying super discount, back-of-the-plane, nearly in the seat-in- front-of-you class, the last time, I wanted to splurge and buy business class. LATAM Airlines didn't offer a dedicated first-class cabin. However, their premium business class provided features like lie-flat seats, gourmet meals and priority service for our 90- minute flight to Temuco or the same amount of time it takes to fly from Madison to Atlanta. We booked coach!

Landing in Puerto Montt, we went to the same hotel, checked in and walked to the dock area looking for new restaurants, assuming that Amy and Karen would have opened the restaurant Pepe had mentioned.

Walking all the streets did us good in terms of exercise but we struck out in regards to finding Amy and Karen. This meant we needed to visit Pepe and see if he knew anything.

The next morning, we rented a car and made our way to Pepe's vineyard. As had been the case the first time, the scenery was breathtaking and was worth the drive even if we didn't find out anything. April in Southern Chile is the same as October in Wisconsin. Clear, crisp skies. fantastic sunsets and just enough chill to make you want to cuddle.

We pulled into the driveway and listened to the crunching sound of the gravel beneath the wheels of the car that reminded me of the farm as we pulled up, walked into the tasting area and found the same old lady who'd been there the first time.

Megan smiled, looked at the lady and said, *"Disculpa, no sé si te acuerdas de nosotros, pero estuvimos aquí hace unos meses y nos dirigiste a la amiga de Pepe. Me pregunto si Pepe está aquí?"* or, "Excuse me, I don't know if you remember us, but we were here a few months ago and you directed us to Pepe's friend. I'm wondering if Pepe is here."

The old lady replied, *"Sí, está en la viña, estamos recogiendo lo último de la cosecha de este año. ¿Prefieres esperar o salir a verlo?"* or, "Yes, he's out in the vineyard. We are harvesting the last of this year's crop. Would you like to wait or prefer going out to see him?"

I pulled out a photo of Amy and held it up so the lady could see as Megan inquired. *¿Has visto a esta señora recientemente?* "Have you seen this lady recently?"

The old lady said with a huge smile. *¡Ah, sí! Es Amelia. Trabaja aquí. Es una mujer maravillosa.* "That's Amelia. She works here. What a wonderful lady."

Megan replied. "*Creo que, si te parece bien, lo visitaremos en la viña. ¿Nos puedes dar indicaciones?*" or "I think, if it's all right, we'll visit the vineyard, can you give us directions?"

The old lady smiled, nodded, turned and pointed out the window where we could see the top of a tractor standing.

"Gracias!" I thanked, using my only Spanish except *Cinco de mayo*.

Megan being Megan in a way that touched my heart, realized that things might get a little dicey and noted she needed to use the restroom and she'd wait for me in the tasting room.

I nodded that I understood and made my way out the back door and headed for the tractor. Row-upon-row of grape vines informed me Pepe was doing all right for himself. As I made the last turn, my mouth dropped open as I stopped in disbelief. Standing in front of me, wearing a straw hat, a long-sleeve, gauze Gaucho blouse with black denim jeans and leather gloves was Amy, helping pick grapes.

"Amy!" I offered as she turned around, with her mouth dropping open in total surprise.

"George?"

"Amy, what are you doing here?" I asked.

"Picking grapes, what does it look like I'm doing?"

"But!"

"But what?"

"How? When?"

I pondered out loud.

"I've been here since December. Why are you here?"

"We need to, you know, we need to finalize everything."

"What are you talking about?"

"And/Or" for number one."

"George, I signed that and mailed it to you two days after you saw me at the Lighthouse."

"You did?" I responded incredulously.

"Yes. I signed it and K..." Megan stopped as a piece of the puzzle fell into place. She took a deep breath as I could see the anger beginning to take hold until she reluctantly added, "And Karen took it to the Saint Barths' post office."

Megan looked at the ground and shook her head in dismay before noting, "Bitch!"

"What?" I asked, still not connecting the dots.

"Karen said she mailed it. She never mailed it at all."

"Where is she? Let's ask her." I offered.

Amy looked at me and noted. "We're not together anymore."

"What?" I said as my mouth dropped open in total shock.

"She's gone." Amy replied as her teeth bit her lower lip.

"I'm sorry," I replied.

"It was early December. I was at the store and getting one of my 'attacks'. I knew if I didn't take my medication, it could get pretty ugly and so I excused myself and went back to the house. Letting myself in, I found Karen in bed doing 'it' with one of her male patrons. George, it broke my heart."

Amy looked down at the ground and then at me. "We were married and she cheated on me! I was angry. I was hurt! The whole thing escalated way beyond where it should have been. I was having one of my bad days and that's why I came home. I probably...make overreacted but then, so did Karen."

"The guy left and the argument literally turned into a verbal war. We were screaming at each other. Screaming! I took one of my pills and went back to the store. I needed to calm down and get away. The next thing I knew someone called the store and said the house was on fire. I went back and the whole place was burning and with it, everything I owned everything."

Amy continued. "I looked for Karen and didn't know if she was in the house or not. I panicked and went to where she worked and they said she'd left and told them she was leaving the island. I went to the airport and the agent said she'd boarded a plane for Guadeloupe."

"I realized I had nothing. I mean nothing! My wife cheated on me! I had no home and no clothes! Right then and there I decided to leave and caught a flight to San Juan. I was thinking about giving myself up but made it through customs and began to believe the government wasn't after me anymore or I was so far down the wanted list, they didn't care. Instead, I got a flight that brought me to Santiago and then I came to Puerto Montt."

"George, I've had a lot of time to think and the whole Karen ordeal made me begin to realize what I'd put you through. I never knew! I never realized the pain I'd caused you and I'm so, so sorry."

"It's OK," I replied.

"No, it's not. You, of all people. You're the one I hurt the most and I'll never forgive myself. You loved me more than I loved myself."

I thought back to the thumb drive and realized Amy was right, except I don't think she ever loved herself. How sad! How incredibly sad! To have so much and, yet, so little. If you can't love yourself, how can you ever love the one you're with?

Amy gazed at me with a somewhat forlorn expression and continued. "I've changed, George. I'm different. I no longer have the needs I once had. The needs that literally tore us apart. Here, I'm content and to remind me, I've gone back to using Amelia instead of Amy. It's just my way of signifying a rebirth while taking all the bad and hoping and praying that I can do good."

Drawing the Curtain:

If we were to put a pin in the timeline of life, it was right then and there in Pepe's vineyard when we both accepted it was over. Amy, because she finally realized the pain she caused. And me, because I knew, with all her issues and my slow journey back from the cave, I couldn't handle them anymore.

It's one thing to ride a roller coaster for the thrills. It's another to live every day not knowing if the roller coaster is going to be a thrill ride or simply scare you to death. Before 'the cave', I guess I could handle it. Now, I needed the consistency of a merry-go-round with someone who was totally committed to me and me to them.

I felt a forlorn sentiment make its way through my body and, in an attempt to soften the anguish, I noted. "I've got good news. The sedition charges against us have been dropped and you can come home."

Amy looked at me, frowned and incredulous asked. "Home? Home? Back to America? Why?" Why would I want to ever come back there? Back to the pressures? Back to the pain? Back to the anxiety of a stressed-out society where everyone hates each other? Back to a materialistic world where all that matters is what you've got and not what you can give? I don't need it, George! I don't want it. Life's too short to simply take all your effort to increase the speed of life."

"But it's where your family is," I countered.

"My family? Derrick disappeared. Melia's hiding. 'V's trying to save the world and, if she's still with you, you've found Megan and I can see you're finally happy."

"But America!" I countered.

"America? America where there's economic, racial and ethnic inequality, political polarization, barriers to good healthcare? America, where there's a mental health and drug crises led by a government run by those only interested in themselves and their own wellbeing, simply maintaining power because it's the narcotic they can't give up due to the perks and prestige?"

"America, where those we used to hobnob with have only one goal and that's to keep it all for themselves? George, the United States is no longer even ranked in the top twenty places to live in terms of quality of life."

I must have had a perplexed look on my face as Amy shook her head and continued. "America, where the civil war continues to rage... black against white against brown - hyper-ventilated by the media who's only goal is more viewers hooked on 'breaking news, breaking news' simply to boost the ratings so they can make more money."

"Here, George, I'm not a person whose half-black or mixed-race and not one that others immediately look down on. I'm not being judged by my 'blackness'... too dark to be white and to light to be black. I'm a blended woman who fits in without judgement because the color of my skin is like so many others. You see, George, the people here got over it a long time ago. Something I don't know if America ever will, simply because of money... rich versus poor, where the rich resent feeling like they're carrying the poor and the poor resent the fact they can't afford everything it takes to even lead a basic life."

Amy shook her head again as an exclamation of disdain and asked a rhetorical question. "What are the real issues in America? It's not just about money, it's also about race and the fact that it won't be long until white people will no longer be the majority and it scares them. It makes them afraid, but afraid of what? That people of color can have hopes and dreams like they do? That those who arrive can go through the same levels of acclimation the white folks' ancestors did when they arrived except that their skin is a different color?"

Amy paused, collected her thoughts lowered her voice and continued, "That's what's really wrong with America! Nothing has changed. It's just that it's out in the open more now due to social media and all the lies and crap that gets expulsed every day... lies that people believe because they want to, lies that make no sense but give them a sense of belonging where podcasts allow the ultra's in either direction to spew fabrications that those who are gullible consume as if it was some sort of social heroin to the point they believe it, while the podcasters get what they wanted...more money."

Amy looked at me with sorrowful eyes and inquired. "What has America become but a cauldron of public anger where it's not safe to go anywhere, be anywhere or do anything? Not to school! Not to church! Not even walking down the street. I know a lot of it has to do with drugs and, yet, the drug everyone really needs to take is love... simply love to the point they accept each other for what they are... people, people like them, to be judged for who they are and not what they are."

Staring at the ground and then at me Amy finally added. "This all leads up to the biggest difference of all, George. Here, people look out for each other, care for each other and support each other. In America, it's just the opposite, where competition wreaks its ugly head and everyone is out for themselves simply to be bigger and happier than the other, where putting someone down instead of lifting them up is the American way of life."

Amy was giving it to me with both barrels and yet I knew what she was saying was true so I asked. "So, you want to stay here?"

"Yes. Life is good here. The pace is slower and you know what, for the first time since I know when, I'm at peace... peace with myself. I've begun to even laugh. I've begun to appreciate the little things. Will I miss you and the kids? Yes! Hopefully someday you and they will come to visit and find the new me, the one I've been looking for my entire life."

"What about Karen?" I asked, not wanting to tip the boat but needing an answer.

Amy shook her head and pitifully said, "Karen was only after one thing... my money. She thought if she could keep us divided, she'd end up rich. When I caught her doing 'it' with the guy, I realized who she really was... a prostitute selling her body and soul for one thing... riches. When I finally woke up and we screamed at each other, I told her to get out. I told her to take what little she had and leave. Little did I ever think she'd burn the house down."

"Where is she now?"

"I don't know and I don't care. All I know is that I came here initially with one goal in mind and that's to have Karen and my marriage annulled.

"When will that be?" I asked, glancing at the workers who were moving further away from us.

Amy looked at me and went into her lawyer mode as she recited the factors that go into the Chilean speed of dissolution. "First, the grounds for annulment in Chile are limited and typically involve issues such as fraud, duress or lack of consent. I filed a brief based on all three... fraud, abandonment and duress."

"The second factor is court backlog. Because its Puerto Montt and not Santiago and Pepe knows everybody, he's greased the wheels from years to a few months. There are no disputes over property division because what we had in common burned in the house and, at that time, for all intents and purposes, the sedition act literally made me indigent. There's no child custody for obvious reasons and so it should be a simple procedural matter and not a technical situation because there are clear grounds and no significant disputes and I know she simply won't show up."

"Any idea?" I asked, trying to put her calendar in line with mine. "Three to six months," Amy replied.

"Then what?" I carefully asked.

Amy offered. "George, you're a good man. A man I will always love. A man who gave his heart and soul to me. The father of my children. Legally, I'm still your wife in America but I'm never coming back."

"So, in other words, this is the end?" I concluded. Amy nodded 'yes' as tears formed in her eyes.

It was the moment I wanted, yet, a moment I dreaded. I looked at Amy and realized no one should have to go through what we were enduring and offered. "Do you think we could go sit down somewhere for a few minutes?"

Amy looked at the workers who stopped picking and said. *"Amigos, necesito acompañar a esta pareja por unos minutos. Por favor, disculpen.* Friends, I need to go for a few minutes. Please excuse me."

The crew nodded and went back to work as the two of us began walking back to the tasting area.

We went inside and Amy saw Megan, politely nodded as if to tell Megan that Amy and I needed to be alone. Megan got the message and offered. "George, it's such a beautiful day, I think I'll sit outside, if you don't mind."

"Thank you," I replied as Amy and I progressed and sat at one of the tables as the old lady looked at us and realized it was an important meeting.

As we sat down and before we returned to the issues at hand I asked. "Where's Derrick?"

Amy shook her head and said. "No one knows. He found out someone drained the bank accounts and took away a big portion of his money and figured the US government did it and there was nothing Derrick could do about it."

I didn't say a word as Amy continued. "They thought they had it all, but Derrick always had an insurance policy and is still wealthy. I hope there's enough taken to pay off the Ponzi victims so the charges against him won't be so great."

"Do you know where he's at? I asked.

"No, not anymore. After the scare in Peru, he got out of there."

"What happened?" I inquired.

"Your brother had this scheme for enhanced protection for

he and Su while making money where people would show up at the house and then disappear."

"I know Devil's Mountain and drugs, right?"

"No drugs, which is what the Peruvian government thought until they raided the house and found none."

"That's why he and Derrick were released?" I asked.

Amy nodded and continued. "Among other reasons, yes. But, like America, money talks and a lot of money can get things deferred, diminished and even dismissed."

"What then?" I asked. "What about my brother?" "Tommie's an expediter."

"A what?" I asked.

"An expediter. All he's doing is making arrangements for people who want to sneak into America with the connections they need without the risk of being caught at the border."

"Let me guess. I'll bet Tommie was working with our beloved Senator?" I surmised.

Amy looked at me shrugged her shoulders while adding. "There are people in South America with a lot of money who think if they come to the States, they and their family will be safe. They're probably right. They just didn't have the connections needed to get there without the risks of the smugglers or getting caught."

"So, Tommie became their travel agent?" "Yes!" Amy concurred.

"Why all the stories about drugs, death and disappearance?"

"To protect Su."

"Su? I thought she was dead... got killed in a car accident." "Just like we thought you were killed, too."

"So Su's still alive?" I asked.

"Yes," Amy affirmed and continued, "with Simon out of commission and everyone thinking Su died, she and Tommie hope the threats will diminish and they can live in peace."

"I'll never forgive him for trying to kill me." I added.

Amy looked at me and shook her head and noted. "George, Tommie didn't try and kill you."

I shook my head and was getting irritated. "What? He used the laser pointer to freeze the lock so I couldn't get out."

Amy shook her head and clarified. "George, the bad guys knew you were in the cave. They thought if they got you, they'd be able to activate Simon. Tommie was being chased by them as was Melia and me. Tommie thought that if he burned the outside lenses, the door would still open from the inside. He burned the lens to save your life, not kill you."

"Oh, my God! I..." All of it was making sense and for all this time I was blaming my brother.

Amy continued. "Then when the car burned and the government reported you were with Agent Langdon, we all thought you were dead and so we left."

"And how did you get out of the country?" I asked, wanting to put the last piece of the puzzle in place.

"The opposite way people are getting in, which is how Tommie got the idea to start his travel business."

I leaned back in my chair, looked at Amy, shook my head and simply said, "Wow!"

"So, Derrick's gone and Tommie didn't try to kill me. All I need now is to find Melia."

Amy looked at me, leaned in and said, "Melia's living in Santa Fe, New Mexico"

"Really?"

"Yes, George. She and Jack changed their last name." "To what?"

"Melia's maiden name."

I thought for a moment and had to remember that Melia changed her name before she got married from Terrill to make tracking her that much more difficult and then I offered, "Amelia Marie Wilson?"

Amy nodded 'yes' as I shook my head in disbelief as Amy continued. "Jack Wilson is teaching at the Nambe Pueblo and San Ildefonso Pueblo reservations just north of Santa Fe."

"How did you find this out? I asked.

"Who do you know who's working with Native Americans?" "'V,'" I replied. "Then why didn't he tell me?" I added, now somewhat hurt.

Amy looked at me and noted. "George, you put everyone at risk. With 'V' even letting me know, things could have gone awry. You need to promise me you won't try to find her. Let her call you. If everything has cooled down, she'll contact you."

"She called you?" I asked.

"No! Right now, she's afraid and upset with me and I don't blame her."

"OK."

The Final Act:

Just then the door opened and Megan and Pepe walked in. In his mid-forties with salt and pepper hair Pepe had the build of a twenty- year-old with hands that were like vices. He approached and I stood. A broad smile crossed his face as he nodded towards me and offered, "Welcome amigo!"

We vigorously shook hands as he gave me the now-normal American bear hug as I replied. "Bet you didn't expect to see us here."

"I thought you'd come back. I just didn't think it would be so soon. How are you doing?"

"Things are starting to get resolved. Please, pull up a chair and let me tell you what's going on."

Pepe pulled up a chair for Megan and then his chair and sat beside Amy. The body language led me to surmise there was more going on between the two of them than I'd initially anticipated.

I began again. "As you might know, Amy and I had some issues with the US government."

"Yes."

"I'm here to let Amy know that the issue has been resolved and we'd just begun to go through all the details. With the resolution, our assets have become liquid."

"Yes," Pepe noted.

I looked at Amy, then Megan and, finally, Pepe as I said. "Pepe, over the past few years, as you know, Tommie and I developed the Terrill B&B brand and it has become a reference standard in beef, bourbon and wine throughout the world. Until I was here last time, I thought we had the best Pinot Noir there was. You changed that and I now realize our wine is second."

"OK."

"I don't think it's how its created nor cared for, I believe you have what we don't have, volcanic soil and just the right temperature variance to create an outstanding vintage."

"And?"

"When Megan and I visited the last time and had lunch with Edwardo Gonzalez I became aware that his health might not be as vibrant as it should be."

"You're right," Pepe replied.

"Normally, when I see what would be considered two competitors eating lunch it's because they're in the process of working together."

"You're very observant," Pepe replied as a serious look encroached his face and his always present smile simply evaporated.

"In looking at your vineyard and staff, it appears to me that Edwardo probably made you an offer you cannot refuse but can't afford...an opportunity that would reward you for your efforts and dedication."

Pepe nodded in agreement.

"What would happen if you had the money you needed to purchase Malleco del Magnifico instead of the other way around?" "What?" Pepe asked in an incredulous tone. "You have no idea what Malleco del Magnifico is worth."

"No, I don't. What I do know is that Amy and I have a lot of money. What I also know is that Amy has chosen to live here. Beyond that, I also know that you're an honest and diligent man. Finally, what I know is that I don't want to be in the wine business anymore travelling all over the world."

I paused, waited a brief moment and continued, "Edwardo's not in good health. I'm here and would like to have you and Edwardo consider that you and Amy purchase of Malleco del Magnifico where Amy would be your business partner. From me, I'd provide the connections with my Terrill B&B distributors, as well as the brand, mystique and structure you need to grow your business internationally."

"What about the beef and bourbon?" Pepe inquired. "What country's next door to Chile?" I asked. "Argentina," Pepe replied.

I continued. "And do you think, with your connections with the ranchers and my connections with the Japanese, we couldn't find an Argentinian partner who could raise Wagyu beef that you could market under the Terrill B&B label at the same time?"

Pepe shook his head and smiled and asked, "What about the bourbon?"

I looked at Pepe and then Amy and added. "Isn't Argentina a major producer of corn? The country has a suitable climate and fertile soil for corn cultivation and is one of the world's top corn exporters. All we need do is bring some of the University of Wisconsin kernels we used to fatten the cows, plant them, harvest them, make the mash and we literally could duplicate Terrill B&B here. "

"In other words, you would set up a distillery in Argentina?" "Not me! You and Amy."

"But, who would run it? Who knows the magic formula?" "I know just the person, don't you Amy?"

Amy shook her head, mentally agreeing Tommie could run it blindfolded as she then asked, "What about you George?"

I looked at Megan, smiled and asked Megan to lay out the plans for the farm. In the next five minutes Megan detailed our goals, what all we'd planned, where all the facilities would be located and the initial operating budget. Both Amy and Pepe's mouths dropped open.

I interjected. "I'm tired of traveling. The Derrick Williams Foundation was so great it became terrible and literally a risk to mankind. Simon's been put to sleep for at least a hundred years, I've got the farm and if Tommie will sell me his share, we can begin creating a place for American families to regain some of the innocence that's been worn away in the name of commerce."

Pepe looked at me and then at Amy. He looked down at the table and simply asked, "Did God send you?"

I shook my head and replied. "No, Pepe, it's just that, in the past few years, my life and therefore, my perspective on life has changed. I thought I had a way to do good and it didn't turn out."

With a smile on my face, I added. "Now, I sincerely want to do it on a face-to-face basis. I want to look in the eyes of children and see magic. I want to look in the faces of parents and see smiles. A long time ago, a great man named me 'Little Spirit' and told me I would someday do good. This is my opportunity to do just that while helping the community I love get better, stronger and more dynamic."

Having become a salesman, I knew it was time for the close and so I gave Pepe the either/or..."Do you want to move forward or should Megan and I depart?"

Pepe looked at Amy and asked, "What do you think?"

Amy looked at me and then at Megan and inquired. "Pepe, doesn't this answer a lot of the questions you had about tomorrow? Doesn't it solve a lot of the problems? Doesn't it make your dreams come true?"

Pepe smiled and nodded 'yes.'

I looked across the table and then next to me and asked, "Pepe, Megan if you don't mind, do you think Amy and I could have a few moments to go over some more details?"

Megan knew what was about to transpire. Pepe had an idea. They stood and went outside as I opened my satchel and removed the divorce papers, then the modified pre-nup I'd been calling 'And/Or' which had been rewritten to indicate all funds were to be split evenly such that Amy had the resources necessary to live comfortably the rest of her life with Tank was the executor. Finally, was the dissolution of our family trust which Tank indicated needed to be done where, he said, the easiest thing to do was called a 'revocation' and creation of new individual trusts.

I looked at Amy and she at me and the look was completely different. After three years of total B.S. we both knew it was over. The intense feelings were gone. I still loved Amy but in a different way where the passion had moved to the past tense. I was prepared for the worst where falling out of love, if you allowed it, could be a complex and emotionally challenging experience but simply wasn't the case.

As we sat there, a sense of sadness and grief that had been burying both of us was lifted. While one is the loneliest number, I was lucky I'd already fallen in love with Megan. Perhaps I should have felt guilty but for some reason, I didn't. Megan was the one who'd been with me during the darkest hours of my life. Not the good times, but the bad times. Not the happy times, but the sad. Yet, through it all, Megan was there, supporting me.

There was no anger and resentment on either Amy's or my side. I wasn't angry at Amy, myself, or the situation and there was no resentment towards Amy for her perceived shortcomings, peccadillos or hurting me. I was the one who told her it was all right to be herself and accepted all that transpired, 'that way.' On Amy's side, I think she felt the same way. Somewhere along the way, our relationship changed. Perhaps it was the kids. Perhaps her health. Perhaps...who knows. It just happened.

For three years I felt confused about my feelings, unsure about what to do, almost daily questioning myself and wondering what the right decision really was. It was the walk on Orient Beach that finally did it. For it was then what little emotion I had washed out to sea and I knew it was over. I could no longer try to fit the square peg in the round hole, no longer tolerate wondering what was going on, no longer accepting a position of being second in Amy's life.

I remember that, as we returned to the Lighthouse, I realized it had been so long since there had been any expression of love through spoken expressions or words of encouragement, appreciation and affection. Even before my 'demise' Amy and I had moved into a secular world, existing together while mentally and emotionally living apart. We'd lost the gift of union, that wonderful, wonderful gift of 'we' replaced by 'you and I' where spending quality time together, engaging in meaningful conversations and sharing experiences had simply faded until we were living like strangers. We'd changed and became unlocked from each other's hopes and dreams to the point it was just the two of us tolerating today and never dreaming about tomorrow. With it, we'd lost the expression of love through physical touch. My God, when and why did it happen? When and why didn't I see our lives together unravel the way it did?

I guess I knew I'd fallen out of love when I wasn't upset to see Amy with her mistress. And, quite honestly, it actually brought a sense of relief, especially after what I saw on the thumb drive. We'd both changed and were in an unhealthy and unhappy relationship, where I now realized ending it was actually liberating. I couldn't have gone on, even in a monogamous relationship. I guess, like a lot of men, I found someone else before it was over but, then, so did Amy. I found a woman I'd come to know, a woman I'd come to care for and a woman I now knew loved only

me as much as I loved her.

I know a lot of men do it because they think the grass is greener on the other side of the fence. Once they get there, they find out the grass is only greener because it's where they'd thrown all the bullshit. That wasn't my case. I did it reluctantly, simply because the other candle burned out. Perhaps it was Derrick. Perhaps it was the stress and strain put on us because of money. Perhaps, simply because Amy and I had both changed. Any marital post-mortem would never be able to weave all the threads together to determine the cause of our spousal demise.

I would always love Amy but in a different way and our 'change' wouldn't erase the deep feelings or connections I believed we still had. I would always remember the laughter and significant life experiences, the memories and, of course, our children that combined to create a lasting bond, even though our romantic relationship had ended. From my side, and hopefully Amy's, there would always be respect and friendship.

For three years we were separated and perhaps that's what caused the romantic candle to simply flicker and finally go out. I hoped we could always stay in touch. My heart would break if it were otherwise. This whole ordeal was so final and I knew beneath the formal facade there would always be unresolved love and attachment... the woulda's, coulda's, shoulda's of dreams from so long ago when only tomorrow stood before us and not yesterday as I began to only refer to Amy in the past tense even if we both recognized the romantic relationship was no longer viable.

During Megan and my hours flying from Saint Martin, I took out a pen and re-wrote the poem I'd written when Great Grandfather passed away. No longer referring to the death of a person, it became associated with the expiration of our marriage. I thought I'd give it to Amy but then thought otherwise.

Today will be yesterday, tomorrow.

And with it,

Will go another bit of our future,

Slowly slipping into the past.

I cannot remember each today,

And some I wish I could forget.

I only know that all today's must turn to yesterdays,

And slip slowly into the past.

Yesterdays ....

Once so near, slowly slip beneath our today's

That were once tomorrow's,

Before they too

Slipped slowly into the past.

Soon, all of our tomorrow's become yesterdays.

Making today's today and tomorrow's today's,

Nothing more than yesterday.

One's mind moves quickly. It had only been an instant as my attention came back to 'now'. With the return, I pulled out the divorce papers and handed them to Amy who read them, signed them and watched thirty years of marriage come amicably to an end. There were no tears. There was no angst. It was what it was.

Next, came the pre-nup and the issue of 'And/Or' where it was agreed that the assets were to be split evenly. The new wording had Tank as executor to divide accordingly. Amy looked at the document, picked up her pen and changed the 50/50 to 60/40 in my favor and said, "George, use the money for the farm. There's more than enough to do all you want and for me to live the life I want. In addition, I want the difference to be a reward to you for all I've put you through."

"The only thing left is the farm itself" I noted.

Amy looked at me and said, "I'm still in touch with Su, let me see what I can do."

I shook my head in disbelief. The woman who'd always measured everything in dollars and cents had come to realize there was more to life than money. I nodded and quietly said, "Thank you."

With that, it was over. We stood and hugged, not an amorous gesture but one of finality. Then Amy and I went outside into the bright Chilean fall sunlight to see Megan and Pepe standing by a trellis with Pepe deep in discourse about what he loved as if the grapes were his children to be nurtured and protected. As we approached, whatever it was they were discussing came to an end as they looked at Amy and me, wondering what all transpired.

Perhaps, it was mention of the farm and the cave, but for some reason, my thoughts went back to our research pig, Sir Francis Bacon, and then to Madison's Winkie, the elephant, who lived for sixteen years alone at the Vilas Park Zoo and the thrill I had as a little boy to visit her on a warm summer's day.

While Winkie was a beloved figure, she was also just like

humans with her own unique traits and behaviors - more outgoing and playful than many elephants, yet, beneath the façade was a darker side. Perhaps due to her confinement. Perhaps, due to her loneliness. Perhaps due to her lack of socialization, it was the dark side many people associate with Winkie when, in 1966 a three-year-old little girl, slipped beneath the security fence and attempted to feed Winkie a handful of popcorn by hand where Winkie possibly mistook the little girl's wrist for food and pulled her through the steel bars to her death.

It was tragic and, yet, beneath it all, there was probably the pain of isolation, lack of socialization and profound sense of frustration that Winkie endured no one really ever understood.

Scientists believe that, just like people, the combination of genetics and environmental factors shape not only an elephant's but all animal's personality. As the starting point in both human and elephant life, genetics play a role in determining both our temperament and general behavior. However, it's the environment in which we grow that plays a significant role regarding social interactions and challenges that influence our personality and development.

Now imagine taking a five-year-old societal being and literally placing Winkie in solitary confinement, away from those she'd learn from, while removing any form of socialization and sophisticated emotions and behaviors such as selflessness, grief and cooperation and you end up with a blank slate upon which other tendencies can be deeply etched into one's psyche.

Winkie was kept in a small concrete enclosure that did not meet her natural needs. In solitary confinement, there's no wonder why she had psychological stress and behavioral problems. Now, add in training methods that involved physical punishment and you have all the components to what we would consider animal cruelty today.

To be a singular captive is one thing, but constrained and limited and then terrorized is something else. Some of an elephant's greatest discomforts come from the presence of bees and lions. Winkie's winter housing was located in the same building as the lions!

No one back then realized that cohabiting with predators, especially one that hunted at night, could cause significant stress that may have impacted Winkie's overall well-being and possibly altered her nature.

No one could have predicted that Winkie's solitary confinement in a cage so small she could simply turn around, could lead to abnormal and potentially harmful behaviors.

No one could have imagined what's it's like to only have two days each year to look forward to... Spring when you went from the lion house cage to your outdoor cage and Fall when you returned. Just as no one realized that being alone in a completely inert environment with no change in light, sound or temperature for six months could do the same thing to a man as well.

When the tragedy happened, Winkie finally ended up at the Elephant Sanctuary in Tennessee where the first year found a lonely, confused Winkie shielding herself from the onslaught of friendship other Indian Elephants attempted to provide. Slowly, Winkie's social wounds began to heal. Gradually, all the anger, fear and mistrust that had accumulated began to wither until Winkie began to trust a fellow female Indian Elephant by the name of Sissy who became her companion, her friend, and most of all, someone with whom Winkie could spend the rest of her life with.

One certainly is the loneliest number and it's the majesty of friendship, the grandeur of trust and the splendor of having someone else to travel with through the speed of life that makes it all worthwhile. It was then I realized that Megan was my Sissy and I thanked God for sending her to me.

I don't know why I thought of Winkie as I simply blinked as she made her way back into the confines of my mind. Back where the coulda's, woulda's shoulda's of things I'd go back and change are neatly stored surrounded by the reality they are confined by the shackles of regret simply because there's no way one can go back and make things right.

It had only been a millisecond and then I was back to here-and now as I realized Newton was right, 'For every action there's an opposite and equal reaction' where in the end, the net sum of the universe is zero, good-and-bad, happy-and-sad.

Amy and I had reached the end. I smiled, then Amy smiled and then we all smiled as I caught Megan's eye and she knew 'mission accomplished' with no regrets.

The Waldwick Series: The ten-book series spans nearly 200 years and are independent yet intertwined in several ways including, characters, location and thematic objectives that examine current social issues from different perspectives. Regardless of the time period or the characters in question, the core component - judging people by who they are instead, of what they are, remains paramount.

Waldwick addresses the subject of physical, social, economic and political oppression in the 1800's. Set in Cornwall, England, Virginia and Southwestern Wisconsin, *Waldwick* frankly discusses what one family was willing to do to overcome oppression, as told through the eyes of the narrator, George Terrill. *Waldwick* then summarizes what happens when the oppression is removed and opportunity arises. Integrated into the story line are actual events and people and how the main characters are affected by their existence and their interaction with these people and events. Above all else, *Waldwick* is a love story … love of the land, love of one another and the love of freedom, woven in a tapestry of acceptance, tolerance and justice. *Award Winner*

War of My Brothers examines America of the early 20th century and how and why it changed as seen through the eyes of Hank Terrill, great grandson of George Terrill from the original Waldwick. Ride along as Hank witnesses World War I, the Spanish Flu, the 19th Amendment, that gave women the right to vote, the Great Depression, World War II, Korean War and Viet Nam and how life changed, people changed and those who govern changed, as well. Experience the traumas of life and the joys of the living as you thank God that it didn't happen to you.

The King of Hearts has been reviewed as *"ambitious, extensively researched and deeply engrossing"*…a story that traces the actual Terrill family through 60 generations as it learns the consequence of wealth, power and prestige over 700 years only to have it all collapse around them. Using a blend of magic realism, lyrical prose and imagery *The King of Hearts* weaves a complex tapestry of a family's history from 65 BCE through sixty generations. Beneath it all, the book is about friendship and the deep, mutual bond between people based on trust, support, and genuine connection that goes beyond just companionship—it's about understanding, loyalty, and being there for each other through life's ups and downs.

Little Spirit Based in contemporary Wisconsin, *Little Spirit* examines the concept of eminent domain and the taking of land and dignity, first from the Indian's perspective and then today, as seen through the eyes of George Terrill IV a descendant of the original George Terrill. Using flashbacks through a 94-year-old, blind, Ho-Chunk Indian elder, named Great Grandfather, George learns about the feelings and challenges of the Ho-Chunk nation and the taking of their land and also how contemporary America hasn't changed that much in terms of citizen rights.

Driftless revisits George and his wife fifteen years into their marriage. Reflecting on the challenges they face when their marriage becomes mundane while examining the profound question of which is worse… having nothing or everything. As the mystery of the Forest is revealed *Driftless* examines the consequence of technology and the power of special interest groups to control the status-quo for their financial gain, while addressing the issue of individual rights in time of personal need, where the one thing all people have in common is … time!

The Hayflick Limit addresses the challenges of parenthood, while discussing a person's rights to live and die. When affected by an incurable malady the question becomes *"Would you choose five-to-seven years of normal mental acuity, at which time you would abruptly expire, or risk everything and allow for the slow, gradual decline with hope that a different, longer-lasting cure might come along?"* The Hayflick Limit addresses the role of government in establishing the validity of the Hippocratic Oath?

Let Go examines the consequence of bullying as Melia Terrill is affected by the verbal onslaught and her commitment to the only friend who has shown her the beauty of acceptance for who she is. The books examines the perks and perils of extreme wealth, the solitude of loneliness and frustration of achieving one's goals only to realize that all dreams can become nightmares when one risks everything for perhaps nothing as it delves into thoughts, emotions, joys, sorrow and consequences of being a captive of one's own past and fleeting fame.

Survivor…How Death Saved My Life looks at the consequence of an altered set of priorities and how it can take a near-death experience to "right the ship". Totally immobilized for six days, George Terrill examines his life and it's mistakes and vows, if he survives, to make things right. *Survivor* addresses the psychology of fear, the challenges of being told you have less than a 5% chance of living three hours and what you think about when you sincerely believe you're going to die.

Greed is a thought-provoking literary tale of ambition gone awry, exposing how the pursuit of wealth can fracture family relationships. This intense novel, explores the intricacies of human nature and the pursuit of meaning. It serves as a critique of modern society's obsession with wealth and status that challenges readers to reconsider what success truly means, making this book not just an exhilarating journey but a profound reflection on the human condition.

And/Or Using Newton's Third Law as a lens to explore relationships where every action sets off a chain reaction, *And/Or* journeys in ways no one can predict or control while asking difficult questions about resilience, identity, and redemption. As such, it ponders deep philosophical reflections and existential questions by drawing sharp connections between science and human nature, asking such profound questions as…Is it possible for a person to truly recover from betrayal? Can love survive after it's been broken? And when one loses everything, what's left? *And/Or* is a gripping, thought-provoking read that will linger long after the final page.

Disclaimer: All books, including "And/Or" are pure fiction. Some of the events detailed herein may be true and have been faithfully rendered as researched by the author to the best of his abilities. The information contained is intended to provide helpful and informative material on the subjects and events addressed and written as an interpretation of his learning. It does not guarantee accuracy or social integrity and has been written for the purpose of education and entertainment.

There is a town called Mineral Point, Wisconsin where the author's childhood was filled with magical moments and marvelous memories and a village called Waldwick that remains nearby and is the birthplace of the author's grandmother and mother. There are many Terrill's and Harris's in the area who are the author's relatives and he hopes and prays he has done the family names justice by what he has written for they are the kindred spirit upon which our country was created. There is no reality to the names used as they are all of consequence.

There is a wonderful island, called St. Martin, that is filled with love and life where smiles come easy, the food is superb and the memories can last forever. The names of the restaurants are real and the food is GREAT and the author only hopes that he's done them all justice with his descriptions.